John Updike's
Rabbit Tetralogy

John Updike's Rabbit Tetralogy

Mastered Irony in Motion

Marshall Boswell

University of Missouri Press
Columbia and London

Copyright © 2001 by
The Curators of the University of Missouri
University of Missouri Press, Columbia, Missouri 65201
Printed and bound in the United States of America
All rights reserved
5 4 3 2 1   05 04 03 02 01

Library of Congress Cataloging-in-Publication Data

Boswell, Marshall, 1965–
  John Updike's Rabbit tetralogy : mastered irony in motion / Marshall Boswell.
    p   cm.
  Includes bibliographical references and index.
  ISBN 0-8262-1310-3 (alk. paper)
  1. Updike, John—Characters—Harry Angstrom.   2. National characteristics,
American, in literature.   3. Updike, John—Knowledge—United States.
  4. Angstrom, Harry (Fictitious character)   5. Irony in literature.   I. Title.

PS3571.P4 Z56   2001
813′.54—dc21   00-046684

♾ This paper meets the requirements of the
American National Standard for Permanence of Paper
for Printed Library Materials, Z39.48, 1984.

Text design: Stephanie Foley
Jacket design: Susan Ferber
Typesetter: The Composing Room of Michigan, Inc.
Printer and binder: Edwards Brothers, Inc.
Typeface: Adobe Garamond

Quotations from the following books written by John Updike are reprinted by permission
of Alfred A. Knopf, a Division of Random House Inc., and Penguin UK: *Rabbit, Run,* ©
1960, renewed 1988 by John Updike; *Rabbit Redux,* © 1971; *A Month of Sundays,* © 1975;
Rabbit Is Rich, © 1981; *Roger's Version,* © 1986; *Rabbit at Rest,* © 1990.

For my family, both the original text
—Jim, June, Christian, and Rob—
and the sequel—
Rebecca and Graham

Contents

Acknowledgments

For his invaluable guidance during every stage of this book's creation, I wish first and foremost to thank Mark Bauerlein. Additionally, I wish to thank Peter Dowell and Barbara Ladd for their helpful advice and encouragement during the book's earliest stages. Much warmth and gratitude go to James Yerkes, Ralph Wood, and Avis Hewitt for their enthusiasm and their clear-eyed editorial suggestions later on in the writing process. And for their much-appreciated support and patience, I wish to thank Clair Willcox and Jane Lago.

To complete the final revision of this book, I was aided by a Rhodes College Faculty Development Endowment Grant, for which I wish to thank the 1997–1998 members of the Faculty Development Committee. For allowing me to use previously published material, I wish to thank the editors at *Contemporary Literature* and the people at Eerdmans Publishing. A substantially revised section of chapter 2 originally appeared as "The Black Jesus: Racism and Redemption in John Updike's *Rabbit Redux,*" *Contemporary Literature* 39 (spring 1998): 99–132. Portions of chapter 3 originally appeared as "The World and the Void: *Creatio ex Nihilo* and Homoeroticism in Updike's *Rabbit Is Rich,*" in *John Updike and Religion: The Sense of the Sacred and the Motions of Grace,* edited by James O. Yerkes, 162–79 (Grand Rapids, Mich.: Eerdmans Publishing Co., 1999).

For their support and their friendship, I wish to thank the members of the Rhodes College English Department, with special recognition going to Bob Entzminger, mentor and friend.

Finally, a warm bear hug to Tod Marshall, kindred soul.

A Note on the Texts

All citations to the "Rabbit novels" contain two page references. The first page reference corresponds to the original Knopf cloth edition of that specific novel. The second reference corresponds to the Everyman's Library single-volume edition of the complete tetralogy, *Rabbit Angstrom* (1995). Recently, Fawcett Ballentine has reissued the four individual Rabbit novels in trade paperback. These new editions consist of the newest galleyproofs from the Everyman's Library volume, with individuated page references for each novel. To locate citations in the new Fawcett Ballentine trade paperbacks, simply perform the following subtractions from the *Rabbit Angstrom* citations:

Rabbit, Run:	No subtractions necessary
Rabbit Redux:	subtract 267
Rabbit Is Rich:	subtract 623
Rabbit at Rest:	subtract 1051

All other references to Updike's work correspond to the original Knopf cloth editions.

John Updike's
Rabbit Tetralogy

Introduction

Rabbit Rebound
Mastered Irony and the Mega-Novel

John Updike published *Rabbit, Run,* the first of his four novels about Harry "Rabbit" Angstrom, in 1960. *Rabbit Redux,* the second installment in the series, came out in the fall of 1971. The third and fourth installments, *Rabbit Is Rich* and *Rabbit at Rest,* followed in 1981 and 1990, respectively. All totaled, the four-part series—or tetralogy—took John Updike nearly thirty years to complete. This is not to suggest that Updike spent thirty years working *only* on the Rabbit tetralogy. In fact, between each installment he continued to produce a prolific stream of novels, essays, short stories, and poems. What's more, each Rabbit novel is cast in the present tense and is set in the year or so just prior to its publication date: *Rabbit, Run* takes place in 1959, *Rabbit Redux* in 1969, and so on. Updike could only have written each Rabbit novel in the final year of whatever decade that particular installment explores. Indeed, this tidy, decade-by-decade structure has served as one of the tetralogy's most popular features: fans of the series can check their own experiences against that of Updike's gruff, hard-hearted Toyota salesman. In this regard, the Rabbit novels serve as a fictionalized time line of the postwar American experience.

All of which is no less than what Updike always intended. In his Introduction to *Rabbit Angstrom,* the 1995 Everyman's Library omnibus edition of the completed tetralogy, he describes the novels as "a kind of running commentary on the state of my hero and his nation" whose "ideal reader" is "a fellow-American who had read and remembered the previous novels about Rabbit Angstrom" (ix). As a "fellow-American," this "ideal reader" is equipped to recognize the actual consumer products Harry purchases and uses, the pop songs he listens to on his car stereo, and the national events he encounters in the newspaper and thinks about on his twilight jogs through his neighborhood. To read a Rabbit novel in the year of its publication is to watch the world get transformed into art. With their up-to-the-minute present-tense narratives, their seamless blend of the "actual" and the imaginary, and their sociologically exact references to pop culture and brand-name products, the Rabbit novels document contemporary American life so precisely that they function as the fictional equivalent of "real television" or cinema verité.

In view of this liberal use of contemporary American history, coupled with the remarkable fact that Updike apparently composed each novel during the year in which it is set, one might conclude that the Rabbit tetralogy gains in historical accuracy what it sacrifices in aesthetic integrity. Updike has kept the novels so close chronologically to the experience they depict that he seems to have given himself no time to revise, let alone organize and structure, the completed manuscripts. Astonishingly, however, this seems not to be the case. On the contrary, each individual Rabbit novel compares in structural elegance with any of Updike's other books, including such intricate, Nabokovian creations as *The Coup* and *A Month of Sundays*. Upon close inspection, moreover, and despite its interrupted, thirty-year composition history, the completed tetralogy proves in the end to be a unified, coherent work of the highest formal achievement. At the same time that the Rabbit novels are "open to accident," they are also fiercely determined in their formalistic design. Each novel follows a carefully laid-out plan even as it fits into the overarching structural logic of the complete four-part work. As each decade spiraled to a close, Updike searched the contemporary landscape for "real life" material to incorporate into the pre-set structure he apparently had laid out in advance, a structure that was presumably malleable enough both to absorb and to withstand ongoing alteration. In short, the Rabbit novels represent rigid formalism in existential action.

This, too, is no less than what Updike has always intended—if not from the beginning, then at least as early as *Rabbit Redux*. Again, the place to turn for illumination is his Introduction to *Rabbit Angstrom*.

"At some point between the second and third of the series," he declares, "I began to visualize four completed novels that together make a coherent volume, a mega-novel" (x).[1] Herein lies the thesis of this book. Taking Updike at his word, I shall "bind" together the four Rabbit novels and read them as the "mega-novel" that Updike has been working toward since the second installment. As such, I shall argue that this "rebound" Rabbit novel—referred to hereafter by its Everyman's Library title, *Rabbit Angstrom*—provides a sustained, linear, and ultimately cumulative articulation of Updike's unique dialectical vision. Primarily existential in nature, this vision—an interdependent matrix of ethical precepts, theological beliefs, and aesthetic principles—is less a creed than a versatile formal device; it is, in effect, the scaffold on which Updike has built the entire tetralogy. In its broadest terms, this vision is dialectical: Updike has organized his "mega-novel" around dialectical relationships that remain unresolved. In each individual installment, all the various thematic threads coalesce neatly into a series of linked dialectical units; likewise, the four novels in the series also relate to one another dialectically, so that *Rabbit Redux* deliberately reverses the tone and thematic emphasis of *Rabbit, Run,* its immediate predecessor, while *Rabbit at Rest* similarly contrasts with its prequel, *Rabbit Is Rich.* In the same vein, the first two novels in the series compose a cohesive unit that in turn relates dialectically to the tetralogy's last two novels, thereby establishing the formal structure of the finished "mega-novel" as a direct echo of the work's thematic organization, and vice versa. Ultimately, I shall demonstrate that the full scope of Updike's formal achievement emerges only after all four novels are read in succession, one after the other.

I shall organize my discussion of this dialectical vision under the

1. Although Updike dates this "mega-novel" vision as occurring "between the second and third of the series," the idea seems to have been with him sometime earlier. See especially "Bech Meets Me," a "self-interview" with his own fictional character Harry Bech, which appeared in the November 1971 issue of the *New York Times Book Review* as part of Knopf's promotion of *Rabbit Redux,* published that same month. There, Updike outlines for Bech his plans for two more Rabbit volumes, the third of which, scheduled for 1981, to be called *Rural Rabbit* and the fourth, "to come out in 1991 if we all live," to be called *Rabbit Is Rich* (Updike, "Bech Meets Me," 13). *Rural Rabbit* never happened, of course, while *Rabbit Is Rich* got moved back a decade.

rubric of "mastered irony." Søren Kierkegaard, the great Danish existentialist philosopher, coined this term to describe his own method of presenting two sides of an issue and then leaving this paradox unresolved. Kierkegaard modeled his method on that of Socrates, who, in Kierkegaard's interpretation, employed an irony of deferral. Through his questioning style and his tendency to leave contradictory ideas unresolved, Socrates concealed his own views on the issues he raised and thereby shifted the burden of interpretation onto his auditors. The final aim of this strategy was to undermine any abstract truth that could not be privately translated into the auditor's personal life. In a sense, by resolving the contradictions left in place by Socrates, the auditor effectively resolved the issues for himself, in accordance with his own desires and needs. For all its potential power to unsettle and inspire, however, the Socratic method was not without its risks, and that is why Kierkegaard insisted that an ironic author must "master" his irony, which is to say he must deliberately organize all this contradictory material so that the intended meaning emerges as a product of the differential play of that contradictory material. Hence the successfully ironic work both contains and maintains a species of controlled dialectical tension between its contradictory, constitutive ideas. The work's message is not represented by one or the other of these dialectical units, nor is it produced by a facile blending of the two; rather, the ironic author's vision emerges indirectly via the unresolved tension produced by the interplay of that thematic dialectic. And because the tension remains unresolved, the vision that emerges cannot be easily paraphrased. It remains in motion, in action, in play. Or, to employ Kierkegaard's characteristic term, it becomes "infinite." That dynamic energy constitutes the "freedom" Kierkegaard has in mind when he writes, "[I]rony renders both the poem and the poet free. For this to occur, however, the poet must himself be master over irony." The work's governing vision, complex and unstable, does not reside in the text so much as it emerges from the tension produced by the contradictory thematic material. Yet if that tension-filled vision exists "outside" the text, where does it in fact reside? In the readers, who must contend privately and personally with the text's unresolved tensions. By thus forcing itself upon the text's readers, who "exist" outside the text, mastered irony in Kierkegaard's conception returns that text to reality, or to what he calls "actuality": "Irony as a mastered moment exhibits itself in its truth precisely by the fact that it teaches us to actualize actuality, by the fact that it places due emphasis on actuality."[2] Mastered irony is truth made active.

Perhaps the most schematic example of Kierkegaard's ironic method can be found in his massive, two-volume work, *Either/Or.* The completed text consists of two contrasting volumes, each alleged to be written by someone other than Kierkegaard and the whole allegedly "edited" by yet another fictional persona, one Victor Eremita. The first part of *Either/Or* describes what Kierkegaard calls "aesthetic" existence, a life of sophisticated alienation and ennui in which the fear of death is neutralized by the nontemporal consolations of aesthetic appreciation and sensuality; the second section, written in direct response to the former, explores what Kierkegaard terms "ethical" existence, a life characterized by intense inwardness and deep-rooted moral commitment. In Kierkegaard's scheme, part two of the work does not simply "refute" part one; rather, he sets the two sections against one another in an act of sustained irresolution. As for Kierkegaard himself, he hides invisibly behind his pseudonymous spokesmen, each of whom is allowed freely to articulate his own representative worldview. The two sections taken together, as well as the worldview expressed in each, contradict one another in such a way that the reader is forced to choose between them, and this final movement represents the heart of Kierkegaard's whole method. Several years after publishing *Either/Or,* he offered this explanation of his technique: "That there is no conclusion and no final decision is an indirect expression for truth as inwardness and in this way perhaps a polemic against truth as knowledge." That "perhaps" is crucial: Kierkegaard is not refuting knowledge per se but rather the notion that abstract precepts, philosophical or otherwise, ever really apply to an individual *in existence.* The truth he cares about most is inward truth, that species of private subjective awareness that can apply only to the individual reader. Kierkegaard generates this brand of private truth by forcing upon his reader the process of self-questioning. As his pseudo-

2. Søren Kierkegaard, *The Concept of Irony, with Constant Reference to Socrates,* 336; 340.

nymous narrator declares at the close of *Either/Or II:* "only the truth that edifies is truth for you."[3]

Here, as elsewhere, Kierkegaard sets his ideas in direct opposition to those of his great bête noire, Friedrich Hegel, whose famous dialectical method attempted to secure a means by which antithetical ideas could be made consistent with the demands of higher truth. In many ways Kierkegaard's thinking recalls that of Hegel; certainly Kierkegaard was deeply influenced by the great German metaphysician. Yet although both thinkers foreground the dialectic as the path to truth, they differ on several key points, and these points of difference make, to coin a phrase, all the difference in the world. Hegel insisted that every positive concept (thesis) implies implicitly its own negation (antithesis); in his dialectical system, however, these two concepts, the thesis and its antithesis, do not cancel one another out but are rather resolved by a *synthesis* of the two concepts, a synthesis that both preserves and supersedes the antecedent categories while in turn producing new concepts for contemplation, since that synthesis will unavoidably suggest its own negation and so on. Kierkegaard countered that authentic dialectical truth is that which *does not* synthesize, does not resolve. Truth does not consist, as Hegel would argue, in an abstract synthesis of opposites, of a both/and; rather, it lies in the private contemplation of irreducible contradiction, in individual confrontation with an unresolved either/or. In this way, Kierkegaard argued for a living, existential notion of truth founded on fluctuating tension, for since life is unfinished as long as it lasts, so must truth remain unfinished, unresolved, insofar as it is deemed to be a *living* truth.

In *Rabbit Angstrom,* Updike employs a similar strategy of "mastered irony" whose inspiration can be traced directly to Kierkegaard. Indeed, so interested is he in Kierkegaardian dialectics that, in his long poem, *Midpoint,* he launches an encomium to his "heroes" with this concise couplet: "Praise *Kierkegaard,* who splintered Hegel's creed / Upon the rock of existential need." More than this: In a private letter to George Hunt, author of *John Updike and the Three Great Secret Things,* Updike confirms that his reading of Kierkegaard encompasses the *Philosophical*

---

3. Kierkegaard, *The Concluding Unscientific Postscript to the "Philosophical Fragments,"* 252; Kierkegaard, *Either/Or,* 356.

Fragments, The Sickness Unto Death, The Concept of Dread, and parts of the *Concluding Unscientific Postscript.* And in a recent essay entitled "A Book That Changed Me," Updike lists *Fear and Trembling* as the single text that most altered him, both as a person and as a writer. Dating his reading of the book in "1955 or early 1956," he describes himself at the time as "a nervous newcomer to New York City, husbandhood, and paternity." His encounter with Kierkegaard, he continues, came as a watershed: "After *Fear and Trembling,* I had a secret twist inside, a precarious tender core of cosmic defiance; for a time, I thought of all my fiction as illustrations of Kierkegaard." His own work, meanwhile, is ever energized by a sustained play of thematic tension that he calls the "yes-but" quality of his writing "that evades entirely pleasing everybody." This "yes-but" quality describes not so much the critical reception of the work as its thematic core: his novels affirm even as they question. "I meant my *work* says 'yes-but,'" he once clarified. "Yes, in *Rabbit, Run,* to our inner urgent whispers, but—the social fabric collapses murderously." In still another instance, he has made overt the connections between his own conception of the "yes-but" and Kierkegaard's "either/ or": "Both the 'yes-but' and the 'either/or' imply there are two sides to things, don't they? So to that extent it is Kierkegaardian, and no sooner do you look at one side than you see the other again." Similarly, he has repeatedly expressed his Kierkegaardian faith in the essentially unresolved and dialectical quality of human existence: "Un-fallen Adam is an ape. . . . I find that to be a person is to be in a situation of tension, to be in a dialectical situation. A truly adjusted person is not a person at all—just an animal with clothes on or a statistic."[4] The unresolved quality of this dialectic constitutes for Updike its human quality, for a human being free of tension ceases somehow to be human.

Taken all together, these elements form the basis of Updike's own conception of "mastered irony," a device whose chief purpose, for Updike and Kierkegaard both, is to inspire in the reader the process of existential self-questioning. As with Kierkegaard, Updike conveys his mes-

---

4. John Updike, "Midpoint," canto V, lines 11–12; George Hunt, *John Updike and the Three Great Secret Things: Sex, Religion, and Art,* 216n; Updike, "Can a Nice Novelist Finish First?" 16; Updike, "The Art of Fiction XLIII: John Updike," 33, 34; Jeff Campbell, *Updike's Novels: Thorns Spell a Word,* 295.

sage(s) in *Rabbit Angstrom* indirectly, ironically, without attributable grounds: the only place for the dialectical tensions to resolve themselves (if at all) is within the reader, and the only way for the reader to accomplish this resolution—however partial—is through self-reflection. Updike has remarked that he conceives all his books as "moral debates with the reader" in which the primary question is "usually 'What is a good man?' or 'What is goodness?'"[5] He is able to spark this debate by affirming, through the "mastered irony" of his dialectical method, paradox and ambiguity. Forced into resolving those paradoxes and ambiguities for themselves, Updike's readers are indirectly cast into a mode of self-evaluation in the first person.

Mastered irony also finds physical embodiment in the character of Rabbit Angstrom, a literary creation who seems to have an uncanny knack of producing a powerful "yes-but" response in just about anyone.[6] In the dust jacket copy to *Rabbit, Run,* one of the most "Kierkegaardian" of Updike's novels, we learn Rabbit is "caught in the potentially tragic clash between instinct and law, between biology and society." The novel is then said to trace Rabbit's "zig-zag of evasion" only to affirm in the end Rabbit's "faith that his inner life—an unstable compound of lust and nostalgia, affection and fear—has an intrinsic, final importance." For "fear" above, read "angst" in its strictest, most Kierkegaardian sense: Rabbit's last name, after all, is Angstrom, which might be glossed as "stream of angst." The aforementioned "potentially tragic clash" seems initially to involve a conflict between sensual freedom and societal restriction: Rabbit's selfish pursuit of pleasure runs up against his duties as a family man. Yet this is only a surface reading at best, for Updike also seems to have in mind here Kierkegaard's aesthetic and ethical spheres. As will be shown in chapter 1 of this study, the world of objective, earthbound wisdom—represented in *Rabbit, Run* by the minister Eccles, but also present in one form or another in each of the subsequent novels—corresponds not to the ethical but rather to the aesthetic sphere: it is the world of extrinsic control whose inhabitants try to hide from their own anxiety and despair. Conversely, Rabbit's faith

---

5. Updike, "Interview with John Updike," 80.
6. Rabbit's status as a Kierkegaardian existential hero has been touched upon by several previous readers, David Galloway and George Hunt chief among them.

in his inner life emerges as the novel's, as well as the tetralogy's, Kierke-gaardian ethical center.

Still, like Kierkegaard, Updike offers neither synthesis nor resolution to this dialectical situation. Rabbit does not seek a mediating position but rather fluctuates between the two spheres in perpetual unrest. Sim-ilarly, Rabbit's belief in his inner life, which is posited as the book's over-arching affirmation, does not serve as the solution to this battle of op-posites but is itself an irresolvable paradox—that is, the paradox of faith. Again Updike directly invokes Kierkegaard's work here, particu-larly *Fear and Trembling,* the Dane's most impassioned exhortation on the paradox of "inwardness." In what does this paradox lie? In the way that Harry's inwardness supersedes both his own sensual urges and the ethical precepts of his culture. In Kierkegaardian terms, Harry, as a sin-gle individual, "is higher than the universal" primarily because, like the biblical Abraham to whom most of *Fear and Trembling* is devoted, he acts out of faith. And faith itself is the paradox by which God's will and the will of the individual become one and the same.[7] As we shall see, it is on this paradox, on this unstable third possibility *beyond* the dialectic yes-and-no, that Updike bases the entire four-volume work.

Secure though he is in the faith of his most famous fictional protag-onist, however, Updike is quite un-Kierkegaardian in his blithe disre-gard for the faith of his readers. Kierkegaard knew very well what he hoped to achieve with his ironically constructed two-part book. As Up-dike himself recently revealed in a *New York Review of Books* essay on "The Seducer's Diary," the concluding chapter to volume one of *Either/ Or,* Kierkegaard briefly considered including a startling disclaimer to the book's second edition. In this short passage, Kierkegaard explains, in un-characteristically direct terms, what he hoped to achieve through the book's pseudonymous authorship and its two unresolved sections: "It was a necessary deception in order, if possible, to deceive men into the religious, which has continually been my task all along."[8] This is an im-portant distinction to make, for Kierkegaard regarded the competing vi-sions represented in *Either/Or's* twin sections not as equals but as two "stages," the first being the aesthetic, the second being the ethical. In his

---

7. Kierkegaard, *Fear and Trembling/Repetition,* 55–59.
8. Updike, "Introduction to 'The Seducer's Diary,'" 140.

famous formulation, the third and highest stage was the religious, which he viewed as essentially inward and personal. Therefore *Either/Or,* while not didactic in the proper sense, does establish a hierarchy of values, if only because the second volume is allowed to refute the first without having to contend with a contrasting third volume which would move the dialectic along even further. That third "volume" is in fact the personal religious choice made by Kierkegaard's unsettled reader; it is the volume Kierkegaard did not have to write because it was produced by the differential play of the first two.

Updike establishes no such hierarchy, nor does his strategy hope to "deceive" his reader into embracing a personally relevant spiritual resolution to his works' various unresolved dialectics. A realistic novelist rather than a religious thinker, Updike eschews edification in favor of empirical precision and thematic ambiguity. The true artist, he feels, stares unflinchingly at both the good and the bad; the writer of integrity depicts both the positive attributes of creaturely reality as well as its shadow side. Whereas in Kierkegaard the movement of the dialectic is always progressive, inching the reader closer and closer to religious inwardness, in Updike the corresponding movement is always back and forth. The "either" of *Rabbit, Run* is matched with the "or" of *Rabbit Redux,* the latter of which is then reversed by *Rabbit Is Rich,* only to be answered once again by *Rabbit at Rest.* For each thesis, its antithesis, and vice versa. For each yes, its no, and back again.

This back-and-forth approach, this incessant move toward formal equilibrium, explains why Updike employs irony but rarely resorts to satire, the latter of which always assumes a grounded judgment on one side or the other. As he remarked in 1968, "I'm not conscious of any piece of fiction of mine which has even the slightest taint of satirical attempt. You can't be satirical at the expense of fictional characters, because they're your creations. You must only love them."[9] Conversely, irony preserves what Updike sees as the essential moral ambiguity of existential reality. It allows for contradiction and disagreement between the author's vision and that of the characters. It also demands that all utterances within the novel be regarded as part of a complex pattern of

---

9. Updike, "Art of Fiction," 38.

interconnected and unresolved meaning, in which disagreement is part of the novel's overarching order, and the *interaction* of competing ideas, rather than the ideas themselves, is the novel's primary subject. Milan Kundera, in his recent book-length essay *Testaments Betrayed*, provides a definition of novelistic irony that is of use here: "Irony means: none of the assertions found in a novel can be taken by itself, each of them stands in a complex and contradictory juxtaposition with other assertions, other situations, other gestures, other ideas, other events. Only a slow reading, twice and many times over, can bring out all the *ironic connections* inside a novel, without which the novel remains uncomprehended."[10] Notwithstanding Harold Bloom's imperious assessment that the Rabbit novels "scarcely sustain rereading,"[11] I submit that only a "slow reading" such as Kundera describes will reveal the full scope of Updike's remarkable formal achievement. *Rabbit Angstrom* is best read ironically, whereby each assertion, and even each section of the four-part work, is regarded as an incomplete and contingent component of the tetralogy's ongoing orchestration of "complex and contradictory" ideas. This sort of reading—in truth, a form of rereading—will show that this chaotic and self-contradictory material is actually the stuff of a profoundly organic and coherent literary vision.

From Kierkegaard Updike also derives Rabbit's peculiarly existential *presence*, what Martin Heidegger later terms *Dasein*, or being-there in-the-world, a feature Updike manifests through his use of the present tense narrative mode.[12] Throughout the tetralogy, Rabbit remains passionately and immeasurably astonished at the mere fact that he exists, that he is alive in the world. His *being-there* is a subject of vast wonderment which he expresses through his profound interest in and curiosity about the phenomenal world about him. Updike emphasizes this sense of wonder by casting the entire four-volume work in the present tense, albeit a present tense that advances ten years with each new installment. Although the present tense has lately become something of a

10. Milan Kundera, *Testaments Betrayed*, 203.
11. Harold Bloom, "Introduction," 1.
12. Incidentally, Walker Percy's *The Moviegoer*, which was published a year after *Rabbit, Run*, shares with Updike's novel not only its use of Kierkegaardian existential philosophy but also the present tense narrative mode.

literary cliché, regarded at best as a mere staple of the *New Yorker* short story and the twentysomething *Bildungsroman,* it has not always been so commonplace. Long before the writing workshops institutionalized the present tense mode, with its staccato bursts of surface observations and its placid, mechanical "subtlety," John Updike created a mini-revolution in literary sensibility when he elected to cast his second novel in the existential "here and now." For in both *Rabbit, Run* and *Rabbit Angstrom* as a whole, the present tense proclaims a very precise thematic idea: Rabbit's fictional identity is existential in the sense that it is predicated on pure tendency, on pure becoming, as existence in the Rabbit books is founded upon the fleeting claims of freedom and flux. In fact, the present tense is nearly as crucial to the basic structure of the completed work as its employment of dialectical irresolution.

Updike has repeatedly made this self-same argument. Although most of his readers have done little more than point out how effectively the present tense mode "brings the reader immediately into the stream of events," Updike has always had something much more suggestive and resonant in mind. In his "Special Message" to purchasers of the Franklin Library edition of *Rabbit, Run* (1977), for instance, he points out that his use of the present tense mode in *Rabbit, Run* constituted "a piece of technical daring in 1959, though commonplace now"; he then explains that this mode helped him "emphasize how thoroughly the zigzagging character live[s] in the present."[13] In both the "Special Message" and his new introduction to *Rabbit Angstrom,* moreover, he goes on to cite Joyce Cary's *Mr. Johnson* (1939) as his only present tense precedent, then adds an excerpt from Cary's own introduction to the novel that bears repeating here: "[The present tense] can give to the reader that sudden feeling of insecurity (as if the very ground were made only of a deeper kind of darkness) which comes to a traveller who is bushed in unmapped country, when he feels all at once that not only has he utterly lost his way, but also his own identity" (xxi). One can readily see why this passage might appeal to the Kierkegaardian-minded Updike. One is even compelled to wonder if Updike encountered this passage before or after writing *Rabbit, Run.* What better way to depict a being in ontological doubt

13. Campbell, *Thorns Spell a Word,* 279; Updike, "A 'Special Message' to Purchasers of the Franklin Library Limited Edition, in 1977, of *Rabbit, Run,*" 850.

than to employ a narrative technique that gives the *reader* "that sudden feeling of insecurity" (once again, for "insecurity" here, read "angst"), a feeling so disorienting that the reader feels he has not only "lost his way, but also his own identity"? The present tense both depicts the existential individual concerned with his/her own life as it is played out in immediacy *and* manages to inspire in the reader a sense of displacement and uncertainty—angst, in other words—that can eventually lead to the kind of first-person self-examination that is the hallmark of *Rabbit Angstrom*'s literary methodology. How does it do this? By stripping narrated events of their completeness in time, of their promise of a happy, or at least a coherent, resolution. While the reader of the preterite narrative hovers above the events secure in the knowledge that everything being related has already happened, the reader of *Rabbit Angstrom* hunkers down with Harry in the messiness of immediacy, where events unfold at the edge of randomness, at the cusp of the unknown future. "In the present tense," Updike explains in his new introduction, "thought and act exist on one shimmering plane; the writer and the reader move in a purged space" (xiii). Of what has this space been purged? Of the "grammatical bonds of the traditional past tense and of the subtly dead, muffling hand it lays upon every action" (xii). Without recourse to a providential "map" governing the movement of the narrated events, the reader of *Rabbit Angstrom* is asked to share in Harry's own anxiety at the unknown that lies beyond.

But there is more. As Dilvo I. Ristoff demonstrates convincingly in his early full-length study of the Rabbit novels, *Updike's America: The Presence of Contemporary History in John Updike's Rabbit Trilogy* (as the title indicates, Ristoff's study, published two years before the appearance in 1990 of *Rabbit at Rest,* is necessarily incomplete), every scene in the Rabbit novels is situated within a very specific historical present. In his introduction, Ristoff writes, "Not only do we know, for example, the exact year these novels start and end, but we also know the exact month, the exact day, and almost the exact hour in which the actions start unfolding and, in due course, end." During a trip to Harvard's Houghton Library to examine Updike's working papers, Ristoff encountered "blanks in the original manuscripts . . . where news broadcasts were meant to be added later," newspaper clippings for events that later figure in the novels themselves (clippings Rabbit is even shown to be reading in the finished work), and calendars with dates, all of which was used "to accompany the characters' journey in time, through a very specific year, month, day, and hour."[14] Updike confirms Ristoff's researches in the concluding paragraph of his new introduction, where he designates not only Rabbit's exact birthday but also the range of "real world" dates encompassed in the four principal sections of *Rabbit Angstrom*. In short, he places his characters in what Kierkegaard would call "immediacy" or "world-historical actuality," that is, in the world itself—*our* world— with all its contingencies and present tense urgencies. Instead of presenting his material as a rendering of events that have been completed and thus removed from the existential now, Updike embraces a radical temporality that opens out into the contemporary world. Moreover, this world is also the *reader's* world, obviously rendered as a fiction and yet, paradoxically, dated and calibrated so as to correspond to the phenomenal immediacy possibly experienced by each reader.

To appreciate fully just how innovative this approach to novelistic temporality can be, one need only look across the Atlantic to the continental semioticians. According to the French critic Roland Barthes, postmodernity and the present tense are inseparable. In *Writing Degree Zero,* he distinguishes the mode of most contemporary French novels— present or present-perfect—from the outmoded (for him) preterite mode, which he claims serves "to reduce reality to a point of time, and to abstract, from the depth of a multiplicity of experiences a pure verbal act, freed from the existential roots of knowledge, and directed towards a logical link with other acts, other processes, a general movement of the world: it aims at maintaining a hierarchy in the realm of facts." He further regards the pervasive use of the past tense in almost all nineteenth-century fiction as a way to tame the world, which, for the preterite-minded artist, is "neither mysterious nor absurd" since, through hindsight, it has been ordered into making sense. The present tense, on the other hand, frees writers from the tyranny of the "closed, well-defined, substantive act." Rather, it produces a "full-blooded" literature that in turn becomes "the receptacle of existence in all its density and no longer of its meaning alone. The acts it recounts are still separated

14. Dilvo I. Ristoff, *Updike's America: The Presence of Contemporary History in John Updike's Rabbit Trilogy,* 1, xiii, viv.

from history, but no longer from people."[15] What Barthes is proposing here has little if anything to do with the convention-strangled, workshop-approved present tense minimalism of the 1970s and 1980s and everything to do with the kind of "full-blooded" writing that characterizes the Rabbit tetralogy. Rather than use the present tense to convey Rabbit's ennui and alienation (neither of which he seems to suffer from all that much), Updike rejects the preterite mode (which he amply employs elsewhere in his corpus) in order to convey Rabbit's individual existence in "all its density" of feeling and communion both with the world around him and with the reader.[16]

Updike's thinking, what I am characterizing here as his "vision," has also been profoundly influenced by many of Kierkegaard's numerous twentieth-century heirs, chief among them Paul Tillich, Karl Barth, and the Martin Heidegger of *Being and Time*. During the 1960s and 1970s, Updike reviewed their works for the *New Yorker,* an endeavor he wryly characterizes, in the Foreword to *Picked-Up Pieces,* as a task bestowed upon him by editorial necessity: "Those slim, worthy-looking volumes by Tillich and Heidegger that keep cluttering a book editor's desk—what better disposal than to send them off to Updike for a 'note'?"[17] While Tillich and Heidegger exert an oblique influence on Updike's overall Kierkegaardian mode, Karl Barth makes the strongest claim on our attention, for his neo-orthodox theology has proven down the years to be every bit as central to Updike's thinking as Kierkegaard's existentialist dialectic. Updike first began reading Barth in Ipswich, Massachusetts, while drafting *Rabbit, Run,* and, according to his own account, the experience was nearly as mind-altering as his first encounter, several years before, with Kierkegaard. Whereas New York belonged to Kierkegaard, "Ipswich," he says, "belonged to Barth." In fact, Barth's influence is so strong, and so formative, that it is incumbent that we outline here at the outset the specifically Barthian elements of Updike's vision. The various connections between Updike's thinking and that of Tillich or Heidegger will be taken up in due

15. Roland Barthes, *Writing Degree Zero and Elements of Semiology,* 26–27, 28.
16. See also James A. Schiff, *John Updike Revisited,* 32–33 for an excellent discussion of the relationship between the Rabbit novels and their readers.
17. Updike, *Picked-Up Pieces,* xv.

course, as such connections manifest themselves in the individual readings of the Rabbit novels.

Updike's borrowings from Barth are largely confined to those ideas and concepts associated with Barth's middle phase, the period of his dialectical theology. Notwithstanding a number of smaller texts he reviewed in the late sixties and early seventies, Updike seems to have gleaned the bulk of his Barth from two or three primary texts, the principle one being a collection of addresses gathered under the title *The Word of God and the Word of Man,* originally issued in 1929 and translated and reissued in America in 1957. From this work and others, Updike seized upon three central ideas from Barth's theology: the dialectic of evil, the concept of "something and nothingness," and the argument for a serenely unprovable God. Although Barth in various ways would later revise many of these ideas, particularly in his massive *Church Dogmatics,* they nevertheless form the core of Updike's Barthian borrowings. In all three instances, Updike's Barth shares not only Kierkegaard's downgrading of universal theology in favor of subjective grace but also his dialectical method. The theology here balances atop an unresolved Yes and No—"Yes" to the possibility of God's grace, "No" to the merely naturalistic, humanistic, and theological; "Yes" to God's creation in all its imperfection, "No" to all those who, in the words of Ralph C. Wood, would make God into a "well-tempered university deity who must abide by the noblest dictates of human consciousness."[18] Even more important, Barth views creation itself as founded on a similarly unresolved dialectic that balances "something" with "nothing." The "something" represents all of God's willed creation; the "nothing" represents all that which God has not willed, including, for instance, evil itself. An unsettling Manichaean vision, Barth's dialectical theology appeals to Updike for its worldliness and its intellectually elegant explanation for the presence of evil. In the end, Updike's own thematizing of "nothingness" and redemption draw their inspiration directly from Barth.

In his introduction to Frank Sheed's *Soundings in Satanism,* Updike not only outlines his own vision of "nothingness" but also links this vi-

---

18. Ralph C. Wood, *The Comedy of Redemption: Christian Faith and the Comic Vision of Four American Novelists,* 36.

sion directly to Barth, its primary inspiration.[19] Updike argues that evil, properly understood, is really a manifestation of the "nothingness" necessarily posited by God's "something"—that is, God's creation: "A potent 'nothingness' was unavoidably conjured up by God's creating *something.* The existence of something demands the existence of *something else."* The "nothing" *is* that something else: it is a "metaphysical possibility, if not necessity."[20] The presence of a something necessarily implies the possibility of a corresponding nothing. Where there is order, there must also be a rejected but still latent and potent disorder. God's light has a shadow, just as his positive will implies all that he did not will.

Perhaps not surprisingly, a great portion of the introduction is occupied by a lengthy quotation from Barth's *Church Dogmatics.* In *Dogmatics in Outline,* Barth succinctly affirms that "creaturely reality" is always a *"creatio ex nihilo,* a creation out of nothing." Why? Because the world is not a pantheistic manifestation of God, but rather a distinct creation summoned into existence *by* God. If God "alone is real and essential and free," then heaven and earth, man and the universe "are something else, and this something else is not God, though it exists through God." In other words, when God creates "something," there must originally have been a "nothing" beforehand. The problem of evil gets dealt with in the same teasing, paradoxical way. In a metaphor Updike calls "frightening," Barth describes evil as "the reality behind God's back." It is a "repudiated and excluded thing" that nevertheless exists by the necessity of God's will. Barth's argument runs as follows: If God's will represents all that God has made—the whole of which, as Genesis insists, is "good"—then evil represents all that God "did not will." In the act of creation, God made choices, and in willing a good creation he necessarily willed against the bad, yet these rejected possibilities were thereby granted a real albeit negative existence in creaturely reality. Or to quote Barth directly: "The whole realm that we term evil—death, sin, the Devil and hell—is *not* God's creation, but rather what was ex-

19. This discussion of Updike's *Soundings* introduction and its connection to Barth's theology is indebted to George Hunt. See Hunt, *Three Great Secret Things,* 30–37.

20. Updike, "Introduction to *Soundings in Satanism,"* 89.

cluded by God's creation, that to which God said 'No.'" The "being" of evil—that is, of nothingness—has definite ontological validity, but only insofar as it is "the power of the being which arises out of the weight of the divine 'No.'"[21] Thus does Barth allow evil to exist as part of God's creation without making it a *positive* part of God's will. It is not "nothing" but rather "something else."

By thus positing a creatio ex nihilo, Updike and Barth also argue for what Barth resoundingly calls a "Wholly Other" God. For Barth, God is and must remain *totaliter aliter*, or Wholly Other: a Creation that contained him would be perfect as is and hence in no need of a Savior. But in the "unhappy separation" that characterizes our earthbound condition, we can hold out hope of deliverance from above. In *The Word of God and the Word of Man*, the emphatic Barth thunders, "There is no way from us to God—not even a *via negativa*—not even a *via dialectica*, nor *paradoxa*. The god who stood at the end of some human way—even of his way—would not be God." The God of the modern liberal church, the God of earthbound ethical precepts, and the God of Good Works are all, for Barth *and* Updike, figures for the "Patron Saint of our human righteousness, morality, state, civilization or religion."[22] Whatever they are, they are *not* God. God, rather, is the creator who made the world from nothing and yet who must remain entirely separate from that creation. The world follows its own course, and God does not intervene.

Updike has taken great solace in this dogmatic theology. What's more, it serves as the bedrock for Rabbit's own theological vision. Early in *Rabbit Angstrom*, Rabbit remarks, "Well I don't know all this about theology, but I'll tell you, I do feel, I guess, that somewhere behind all this . . . there's something that wants me to find it" (127/110). Yes, *but* there is also a "nothing" that wants Rabbit to find it—and if he

21. Karl Barth, *Dogmatics in Outline*, 55, 57. In the *Soundings* introduction, Updike cites the phrase "the reality behind God's back," though he admits he was unable to locate its actual source.

22. Barth, *The Word of God and the Word of Man*, 177, 22. Updike quotes the earlier passage on two prominent occasions: at the beginning of his review of Barth's *Anselm: Fides Quaerens Intellectum*, the first of Updike's numerous essays on Barth (Updike, "Faith in Search of Understanding," 273–82), and early in *Roger's Version* (p. 41).

doesn't find it on his own, it will certainly find him. For although the "something" aspect of God's creation is everywhere in this massive, densely written, richly detailed "mega-novel"—all those internal monologues, all that Joycean attention to the trivial objects of bourgeois life—it is with the "nothing" aspect of creation that Rabbit is constantly having to come to terms. "Harry," we are told early in the Rabbit tetralogy, "has no taste for the dark, tangled, visceral aspect of Christianity, the *going through* quality of it, the passage *into* death and suffering that redeems and inverts these things, like an umbrella blowing inside out. He lacks the mindful will to walk the straight line of a paradox" (237/203). Herein lies the core of Rabbit's primary task in *Rabbit Angstrom:* to walk the straight line of the Barthian paradox, to *go through* the something and into "death and suffering," to confront that "dark, tangled" aspect of God's creation. Only by embracing this dialectical Other can Rabbit understand how death and suffering are redeemed and made good.

If there is a single thematic thread running through the whole of the Rabbit tetralogy, then this is it. When read as one coherent work, *Rabbit Angstrom* proves to be the story of an education, specifically of Rabbit's gradual confrontation with the nothing aspect of Creation, with the God of Chaos and Death, the God who resides in the void from which He launched creation. This God is the God with whom Updike is primarily concerned, for this is the God he raises to primary importance in his great work. "I've never really understood theologies which would absolve God of earthquakes and typhoons, of starving children," he has remarked. "So that, yes, it certainly *is* God who throws the lightning bolt, and this God is above the nice god, the god we can worship and empathize with." The message could not be any clearer: *This God is above the nice god.*[23]

In this respect more than any other, Updike marks a decisive break

---

23. Updike, "Art of Fiction," 33. This fierce God is also the God that has attained mounting importance in Updike's increasingly negative corpus. Since publishing, at the beginning of the 1990s, the dour, death-obsessed conclusion to the Rabbit tetralogy, *Rabbit at Rest,* Updike has launched a series of subsequent novels, each one darker and more pessimistic than the last. These works include the makeshift historical novel, *Memories of the Ford Administration* (1992), the ambitious but archly indifferent generational saga *In the Beauty of the Lilies* (1996), and the unremittingly bleak science-fiction fantasy *Toward the End of the Time* (1997).

with his Barthian source text. For example, Barth does not stop with his insistence on a Wholly Other God, for that God has been made manifest in creation through the concrete event of Christ's birth, death, and resurrection. This event, moreover, ensures that the divine "Yes" has defeated the "No." Updike, by way of contrast, is rather ambivalent about the importance of the Christ event. Rabbit's religious sensibility certainly does not address the centrality of Christ's intervention into creaturely reality. His spiritual convictions barely rise above a sense of himself as a "God-made one-of-a-kind with an immortal soul breathed in" and a "vehicle of grace" (*Rabbit at Rest* 237/1265). In fact, Updike once explained, "Rabbit is not a formal Christian, really. He's been exposed to it, but he proceeds by more basic notions: an instinctiveness that somehow life must be important, even though there's no eternal confirmation of this— only the belief that the reality within must matter and must be served."[24] With the Christ event, the "Yes" triumphs; without the Christ event, the "Yes" and "No" remain balanced. A few minor exceptions notwithstanding, *Rabbit Angstrom* largely supports the latter vision. Much like his leveling out of Kierkegaard's stages of existence, Updike seems to have adapted a complex writer's dialectic without adapting *all* of it.

Similarly, Updike seems to be misreading, or perhaps revising, Barthian theology in the way that he reduces all evil to a necessary "nothing" that resides on the underside of creaturely reality. For, as John Hick has cogently demonstrated, Barth is very careful to distinguish between the merely dialectical shadowside of creation and genuine, metaphysical evil, what Barth calls *das Nichtige*. The shadowside merely marks the limit of creation, whereas *das Nichtige* designates a very powerful metaphysical entity that might best be regarded as the potent enemy of God, albeit an enemy defeated by Christ. In and of themselves, death and chaos are mere parts of creation's shadow, yet they become associated with *das Nichtige* through their manifestation in our sinful existence.[25] Evil is very real in Barth's universe, so real that it needs a real adversary, which it finds in Christ. Updike's dialectical vision seems to conflate these two concepts, the shadow and *das Nichtige*, to the extent that evil is eventually shown to be a manifestation of the shadowside of creation,

24. Updike, "Thoughts of Faith Infused Updike's Novels," 254.
25. John Hick, *Evil and the God of Love*, 128, 132.

rather than vice versa. For instance, throughout *Rabbit Angstrom,* the shadowside of creation is generally referred to as the nothing, or nothingness *(das Nichtige),* and at several very key moments in the tetralogy it is associated with evil. For Rabbit to acquire a full understanding of creaturely reality, then, he must give both the Yes and the No equal weight. As regards the cosmic battle beyond this dialectic, the one where the Yes triumphs, Updike has little, really, to say.

Updike is apparently quite aware of what's missing in his use of Barth. In his wide-ranging 1976 interview with Jeff Campbell, perhaps the best place to go for information on his own conception of the Barthian elements in his work, he declares, "I'm not a good Barthian— I'm not a good Christian, really, when you come right down to it. I don't find that [Barth's emphasis on the centrality of Christology] gets in the way, though, somehow. I'm willing to believe that Christ was real, *to him."* And earlier in the same interview, he defends his own use of mythical archetypes in his novel *The Centaur* against what Campbell cites as Barth's dismissal of mythic understanding in favor of the concrete historical reality of Christ. Updike says, "Lacking, I think, this kind of concrete experience, I'm not so willing to dismiss myth as Barth is. But basically I'm with him, not so much religiously as a way of viewing reality; you have to take a thing seriously as itself." In a sense, Updike's dialectical understanding of evil boils down to Barth minus the Christology. As he explained in 1993, "I only really took out of Barth what I wanted and what I needed. There's a lot left over that I didn't use."[26]

Updike all but corroborates this latter assessment in his 1975 novel, *A Month of Sundays,* the narrator of which, Tom Marshfield, is a defrocked Barthian minister on retreat from his parish. A precursor to his 1986 work *Roger's Version* (and the second novel in his trilogy of books based on Nathaniel Hawthorne's *Scarlet Letter,* the final installment of which is the flippantly lightweight *S.),* *A Month of Sundays* is rich in Updikean theological dialogues, most of which involve Marshfield and his young assistant minister, Ned Bork. In one episode, after Marshfield has used Barth to justify his own moral passivity as well as his political indifference, Bork shoots back,

---

26. Campbell, *Thorns Spell a Word,* 301 (emphasis mine), 295; Updike, "Thoughts of Faith," 255.

> You know, this thing with you and Barth. . . . They had us read
> him in seminary. It was impressive, in that he doesn't crawl like
> most of the mod-rens [*sic*]. . . . But after a while I began to figure
> out why. . . . It's atheism. Barth beheads all the liberal, synthesiz-
> ing theologians with it, and then at the last minute whips away
> the "a" and says, "Presto! *Theism!*" It's sleight of hand, Tom. It sets
> up a diastasis with nothing over against man except this exultant
> emptiness. This terrible absolute unknowable other. It panders to
> despair. I came off it with more respect for Tillich and Bultmann;
> it's true they sell everything short, but after they've had the bar-
> gain sale there's something left; they say there's *something*, don't
> you see?

While Bork's reading of Barth would easily be refuted by a qualified
Barthian, it operates ironically within *A Month of Sundays* as a covert
confirmation of Updike's own reading of Barth. According to Bork,
Marshfield uses Barth to turn heaven into little more than an unknow-
able limit to what is otherwise a vast nothingness. In his response to this
outburst, Marshfield, rather than refute Bork, merely says, "Reading
Barth gives me air I can breathe." Fourteen years later, in *Self-Consciousness,* Updike would resoundingly support both Bork's reading of Barth
and Marshfield's noncommittal reply. After describing his first years in
Ipswich (circa 1957 to 1960) as a period of deep spiritual crisis in which
he felt his "spirit could scarcely breathe," he explains, "[T]o give myself
brightness and air I read Karl Barth and fell in love with other men's
wives." With Barth's Wholly Other God perched precariously atop the
vast overarching nothingness above us, Updike feels emboldened to
confront the world as it is, secure in the belief that the surrounding void
is capped by an elusive divine limit. Or, as he puts it, "Religion enables
us to ignore nothingness and get on with the jobs of life."[27]

To be sure, this is a maddening, and also very slippery, reading of Karl
Barth, and it has occasioned no small amount of criticism. At the very
least it compels one to wonder, Does such a radical theology absolve
God of responsibility for evil, or at any rate for natural disasters, if not
for Hitler as well? Similarly, does Updike's Barthian insistence upon a
Wholly Other God prevent him from interpreting human actions with-

27. Updike, *A Month of Sundays,* 89–90; Updike, *Self-Consciousness,* 98, 228.

in a transcendent, God-centered ethical frame? Many of Updike's critics have answered these questions in the affirmative. One of the most famous attacks in this regard comes from Frederick Crews, who in a blistering pan of *Roger's Version* argues that Updike has long since taken "comfort" in Barth's downgrading of ethics, which in turn has justified the reprehensible behavior of the novelist's "libertines," if not, Crews implies, also that of the novelist as well. "In Barth," Crews opines, "Updike has found a means of talking back to a prickly conscience and a set of reasons for believing that, regardless of his conduct, he may yet be counted among the saved." Along similar lines, Ralph C. Wood interprets this aspect of Updike's vision as "moral passivity," as his "reluctance to find fault and assess blame, his conviction that our lives are shaped by forces too vast for mere mortals to master."[28]

Forceful though these arguments are, they overlook the strange ethical component of Updike's dialectical method. At the end of the day, Updike *does* "find fault and assess blame"—just not in the way most people might expect. *Roger's Version* itself provides a lucid articulation of Updike's approach. Much as he did in *A Month of Sundays,* here Updike conducts a series of Socratic dialogues, this time between a Barthian divinity professor and a young computer programmer who thinks he can prove the existence of God on a computer. Dale, the computer programmer, argues for a divine plan through the sheer improbability of the mathematical conditions necessary for creation to have occurred at all. Roger, the professor, counters that God must remain grandly aloof from, and eternally unseen by, his creation so as to guarantee free will. In Roger's view, the only real God is God the creator, yet such a God is also God the destroyer since, in remaining implacably separate from the creation he has willed into existence, he allows death to occur without so much as lifting a finger. In other words, the Lord giveth and the Lord taketh away. Hence Roger affirms that "majesty resides in our continuing to love and honor God even as He inflicts blows upon us—as much as resides in the silence He maintains so that we may enjoy and explore our human free will." "This," he forcefully adds, "was *my* proof of His existence." Roger also points out that matter is implacable, and that "all

---

28. Frederick Crews, "Mr. Updike's Planet," 174; Wood, *Comedy,* 190.

the prayers and ardent wishing in the world can't budge a blob of cancer, or the AIDS virus, or the bars of a prison, or the latch of a refrigerator a child accidentally locked himself into."[29] Even so, God has created this matter from nothing, and so it belongs to him, however separate from him it must remain. As with most things in Updike's universe, then, a Wholly Other God is a mixed blessing, for although such a god guarantees our freedom, it also leaves us at the mercy of the fallen world. The only way for Updike to honor the complexity and seeming randomness of reality while at the same time holding to his faith in a Wholly Other God is to hold God both culpable *and* absolved. God becomes responsible by his inaction, for only in this way can that God be allowed freely to exist. The angel of light and life, Updike's God is also, dialectically, the angel of death.

One thing more: the criticisms of Updike's libertine use of Barth and Kierkegaard, while indispensable to a full understanding of what is actually going on in his unsettling fiction, fail to account for one very essential fact. In short: Updike is not a theologian. He is an artist, specifically a novelist, whose first responsibility is an aesthetic one. Kierkegaard and Barth provided Updike with ideas, with ways of seeing the world and with methods of artistic expression—but that is all. Not only has Updike freely adapted these ideas to his own use, but he has also freely indulged in his artistic prerogative to do so. What has emerged through the years is his own aesthetic vision and not a novelistic illustration of someone else's philosophy or theology. Hence it would be a grave mistake to look to Updike's work for an accurate description of Barthian Christianity or of Kierkegaardian inwardness, and Updike has been careful to warn readers against just such a mistake. In a 1993 interview published in *Episcopal Life,* Updike's interviewer, Jan Nunley, asked, "How does it feel to know that people will probably learn more about Barth, Tillich, and Kierkegaard from your writing than from reading them?" Clearly bristling, Updike replied, "I'm afraid if they depend entirely on my writing they won't learn enough," forcefully adding, "I can't believe, in short, what you say is true. It's always better to go to the source." Warnings such as this litter his incidental prose and his inter-

29. Updike, *Roger's Version,* 281, 170.

views, and the message in these warnings is always the same: do not equate me with the theologians I might have read, and do not confuse the presence of religious themes in my work with evangelical intent. As recently as 1996, for example, in an essay entitled "Religion and Literature," he says of the religious element in Shakespeare, "God is invoked, ghosts appear, and curses are laid, but the events in Shakespeare seem purely human, in all the contradictory richness of which human nature is capable—a torrential spillage of self-importance beneath an enigmatic heaven." Updike could almost be describing his own work, and perhaps is obliquely doing so. Tellingly, he caps off this section of the essay with the following sternly worded caveat: "A writer's professed religious convictions do not necessarily control the religious content of his writing."[30] In other words, although Updike has declared himself a Christian, one should not look to his work for a straight confirmation of those Christian principles. Similarly, to look to Updike for a consistent reading of Barth and Kierkegaard is tantamount to treating Walt Whitman's "Song of Myself" as a primer on Emersonianism, or reading Henry David Thoreau's *Walden* as a substitute for the *Bhagavad-Gita*. One should go to Updike to learn about Updike. And that is what this book will endeavor to do.

30. Updike, "Thoughts of Faith," 254; Updike, "Religion and Literature," 60, 61. Perhaps equally telling is the brief mention this essay receives in the introduction to *More Matter,* the massive new collection of essays and criticism in which "Religion and Literature" has been reprinted. Updike explains that, in this essay, "I took it upon myself, perhaps wickedly, to remind the presumed students of divinity that a once-healthy religion existed outside the Judaeo-Christian belief system and died, as it were, in literature's embrace" (xxii).

One

Rabbit, Run
Kierkegaard, Updike, and the Zigzag of Angst

For a time, I thought of all my fiction as illustrations
of Kierkegaard.—John Updike

"I like middles," Updike has remarked. "It is in middles that extremes
clash, where ambiguity restlessly rules." In *Rabbit, Run*, Updike's character, Harry "Rabbit" Angstrom, is a man in the middle, a middle-class
father sandwiched between the competing demands of sensuality and
society, the sacred and the profane. But Rabbit's middle position is also
the source of his vitality. For Joyce Markle, this vitality marks Rabbit as
one of Updike's characteristic "life-giving" heroes, and certainly the
novel provides ample evidence to support this reading.[1] As Mrs. Smith,
an elderly character from *Rabbit, Run*, remarks, "That's what you have,
Harry: Life. It's a strange gift and I don't know how we're supposed to
use it but I know it's the only gift we got and it's a good one" (224/192).
Because this life-gift, this vitality, arises from the tension of his middle
position, Rabbit can only maintain it by moving, as in a game of fast-
break, back and forth from one goal to the other, never resting on one
side lest his vitality wane and his gift for life atrophy.

This back-and-forth movement lies at the center of Updike's odd in-

1. Updike, "Nice Novelist," 11; Joyce B. Markle, *Fighters and Lovers: Theme in
the Novels of John Updike*, 3.

sistence that the novel is a "zig-zag." He has often explained that each of his books has "some kind of solid, coherent image": *The Poorhouse Fair* is a "sort of Y shape," *The Centaur* is a "sandwich," and *Rabbit, Run* is "a kind of zig-zag." Indeed, as was shown in the previous chapter, even the original dust-jacket copy, with its description of Rabbit's "zig-zag of evasion," evoked the image. But the zigzag governs not just the book's thematic purpose but its formal structure as well. In his interview with Jeff Campbell, Updike goes so far as to describe the whole novel as "darting, fragmentary, zigzaggy," with a structure that "settles at no fixed point."[2] So although Rabbit resides in the middle, this space is not static: rather, like the lane underneath the basket on a basketball court, it is a "hot" ground he can only pass through on his way to the other side.

Throughout *Rabbit, Run,* Updike reinforces this trope of the zigzag and the nonstatic middle via his use of metaphoric leitmotifs. The two towns that make up the novel's primary locale, Mt. Judge and Brewer (fictionalized renderings of Updike's hometown of Shillington, Pennsylvania, and its accompanying commercial hub, Reading), meet but "never merge, for between them [a] mountain lifts a broad green spine" (17/17)—a mountain up which Rabbit will run at the novel's close. Later, when Rabbit charts his course for the south, he decides he wants to go "right down the middle" of the country rather than along the coast, "right into the broad soft belly of the land" (32/29). One of the most telling of these leitmotifs appears early in the novel, just before Rabbit makes his foray into West Virginia. Slipping by his parents' house to pick up his son, Nelson, he recollects an incident from his childhood involving a strip of grass between his home and that of the people next door, "strict Methodists," according to Rabbit. Operating from a rigid moral code, the Methodist neighbors refused to cut the strip of grass marking the property boundary between their house and the Angstroms'. Similarly, Rabbit's mother refused to let her husband cut the strip, despite the fact that it was "not much more than a foot across." Left unattended amid this battle of wills, the grass "grew knee-high in that little sunless space." In other words, the tension between the families produced, ironically, vitality and growth. Recalling this episode

2. Updike, "John Updike Talks about the Shapes and Subjects of His Fiction," 48; Campbell, *Thorns Spell a Word,* 279.

years later, Rabbit tries to walk along this strip, which to him feels "slightly precarious . . . like treading the top of a wall" (21/20). To maintain his balance he must keep treading, swaying back and forth in perpetual motion. In a sense, he walks precariously along the top of this wall throughout the rest of the novel.

What lies on either side of that wall? Numerous things, all of which can be divided up into two discrete groups, a right and a left side, an either and an or, a yes and a no. On the yes side, Updike has placed such issues as instinct, sensuality, biology, subjective faith, inwardness, and freedom. On the no side he has gathered the law, marriage, social custom, secular reason, outwardness, and captivity. This dialectic can be read according to Kierkegaard's aesthetic and ethical spheres. Although a brief glance at the above division might lead one to assume that the yes side refers to the aesthetic sphere—the sensual, the immediate, the feral—whereas the no side suggests the ethical—the restrictive, the rule-obsessed—in fact, both Kierkegaard and Updike are determined to overturn this surface dichotomy. Like Kierkegaard, Updike says yes to inwardness and freedom and no to so-called objectivity and the secular social order.

Kierkegaard explores these spheres of existence most extensively in his earlier, pseudonymous works, chiefly *Either/Or*, *Stages on Life's Way*, and *Concluding Unscientific Postscript to "Philosophical Fragments."* As indicated by the title of the second of these works, these spheres represent progressive stages through which individuals must pass on their way to spiritual wholeness. The aesthetic sphere comes first. Much like Martin Heidegger's "inauthenticity," aesthetic existence refers to the alienated life most people live most of the time. It is, in one of Kierkegaard's more famous formulations, a mere "existence-possibility," a life of self-delusion and intellectual overconfidence. Rather than face up to the terrifying responsibility of one's own free existence, the aesthete, Kierkegaard explains, "holds existence at bay by the most subtle of all deceptions, by thinking. He has thought everything possible, and yet he has not existed at all."[3] Objective precepts and universal abstractions, while useful in deepening our understanding of the world around us, can never obliterate the fact that we exist individually in time, and that

3. Kierkegaard, *Concluding Unscientific Postscript*, 253.

we are doomed to die. By avoiding the fact of experiential time and existential actuality, aesthetes live lives of *despair* resulting from their failed attempt to hide the essential fact of their temporal existence.

Conversely, *ethical* individuals embrace both their existence-in-time and the despair that accompanies this embrace. Once individuals despair of escaping their temporal condition, they are left with no choice but to assert themselves as existing, temporal beings, and in so choosing, they assume what Kierkegaard terms "passionate self-interest" in their private, individual, and unavoidably temporal conditions. This gesture in turn leaves them open both to the world around them and to their *own* full potential. Regarded as such, "ethical" existence immediately calls to mind Heidegger's notion of "authenticity," just as "passionate self-interest" bears affinities with his concept of "resoluteness," which he describes as the subjective ("reticent") decision to assert, and hence take full responsibility for, one's own free existence as it unfolds in the world of others. For Heidegger, inauthentic existence, like Kierkegaardian aestheticism, begins with an anonymous self-forgetting, a surrendering of one's individual freedom and responsibility to the "loud idle talk" and "common sense" of the masses, the "they"; authentic existence, on the other hand, parallels Kierkegaard's ethical sphere in the way it begins with a concentrated owning up to one's essential existential freedom, as well to one's existence in time. In short, self-interest and resoluteness contrast directly with the so-called "disinterestedness" of aesthetic/inauthentic existence, a stance of anxious objectivity that for both Kierkegaard and Heidegger represents willful self-deception, however tempting and consoling a form of self-deception it may be. Indeed, Kierkegaard and Heidegger both freely grant the seductiveness, if not the necessity, of such objectivity. Heidegger regards inauthenticity not only as "a positive possibility" of human existence but also as the "essential" mode of being "absorbed in a world."[4] Similarly, Kierkegaard, in a crucial passage from the *Concluding Unscientific Postscript,* defends the laudable practicality of aesthetic existence: "Ethically, the highest pathos is the pathos of interestedness (which is expressed in this way, that I, acting, transform my whole existence in relation to the object of interest); aesthetically the highest pathos is the pathos of disin-

4. Martin Heidegger, *Being and Time,* 343–48, 242, 220.

terestedness. If an individual throws himself away in order to grasp something great, he is aesthetically inspired; if he gives up everything in order to save himself, he is ethically inspired." Despite his insistence that, for each existing individual, the ethical is the higher of the two spheres, Kierkegaard affirms that each sphere inspires in the individual ethically laudable behavior. Whereas the aesthete moves the world at the expense of him/herself, the ethical individual saves himself in possible opposition to the world around him or her. "Action in the external," he argues, "does transform the individual's existence . . . but it does not transform the individual's inner existence."[5] A difficult choice, to be sure, but an unavoidable one nevertheless—an either/or, a combined yes and no.

As if to announce his Kierkegaardian intentions at the outset, Updike uses the novel's opening episode—a sustained, unbroken sequence of forty-seven pages—to explore fictionally a number of Kierkegaard's most prominent concepts. This sequence operates as a sort of overture not only for the rest of the novel but also for the entire tetralogy, for here Updike establishes the essential components of Rabbit's condition—a condition which does not change significantly over the course of the subsequent three novels. First, Updike establishes the primacy of Rabbit's *angst*. Second, he introduces the mastered irony that will serve as the prevailing methodology of all that follows. Third, he dramatizes the Kierkegaardian movement from anxiety to ontological sin and guilt and offers up a mini-allegory demonstrating both the centrality and the nature of Rabbit's peculiar faith, a faith which is grounded in subjective experience and which *Rabbit Angstrom's* internal monologue form validates and thematizes in equal measure. So crucial are angst, guilt, and faith to the series as a whole that they—as well as the opening sequence that first outlines them—will all be treated at some length in the next section.

I. Anxiety, Irony, and the Primacy of Subjective Experience

The overture to the Rabbit tetralogy begins, rather famously, on a basketball court.[6] Dressed in a business suit and smoking a cigarette, Rab-

5. Kierkegaard, *Concluding Unscientific Postscript*, 390–91, 431–32.
6. Updike has several times explained that he originally intended *Rabbit, Run* to be subtitled "A Movie." Accordingly, this opening scene was supposed to suggest a sequence suitable for the displaying of titles and credits. See Updike, *Hugging the Shore*, 850.

bit represents in this introductory sequence the solid citizen of 1950s America—a twenty-six-year-old father and husband locked into a meaningless, white-collar job he can neither embrace nor dismiss, at least not without unraveling the intricate social net into which he has been trapped. Conversely, the basketball game he watches represents everything his current social situation denies, for here Rabbit gets to witness both freedom and excellence, both of which are evoked by an activity that, for him, has intense, inward meaning.

This inward significance is in part a product of nostalgia, as the reader is quickly informed that Rabbit was once a high-school basketball star. Yet basketball also affirms an intrinsic uniqueness that his job as a demonstrator of kitchen gadgets would dispel. "I once did something right," he later explains. "I played first-rate basketball . . . and after you're first-rate at something, no matter what, it kind of takes the kick out of being second-rate" (107/192). Witnessing this pick-up game of basketball, Rabbit remembers his own excellence. The mere feel of the basketball "makes his whole body go taut, gives his arms wings," so much so that they "lift of their own accord" (5/6). His own skill, which he regards as a "natural" part of him, he sees reflected in one of the boys on the court. "He's a natural," Rabbit thinks. "The way he moves sideways without taking any steps, gliding on a blessing: you can tell" (5/6). The gift he and the boy share is a blessing that Rabbit, in his current life, does not honor. Still in his suit—an outward manifestation of the depersonalized middle-class world—Rabbit leaves the game, "feels the sour aftertaste of chance in the air," and starts running in exuberant affirmation of what he all at once recognizes as his special inner blessedness. He even decides to quit smoking, to which his wife Janice sardonically responds, "What are you doing, becoming a saint?" (9/10). Perhaps not a saint but at least an ethical individual in the Kierkegaardian mode, a person passionately and infinitely interested in his own existence. Dressed in his suit demonstrating the MagiPeeler, Rabbit was an aesthete hiding from himself. Now, after touching the basketball and "reaching down through the years to touch . . . tautness," he chooses himself in his temporal condition.

This choice should not be confused with the Socratic dictum to "know thyself," which Updike ironically deflates by placing in the unctuous mouth of Jimmy, the "big Mousketeer" from the famous Walt Disney program of the 1950s. According to Jimmy, Socrates' dictum simply means "be what you are," an interpretation with which Rabbit seems to be in agreement, for he calls Jimmy's advice "good." One may even imagine the excellence-minded Rabbit advocating Jimmy's idea that God "gives to each of us special talents" which we must "work to develop." However, what Rabbit most admires about Jimmy's performance is its phoniness, for, as he is quick to notice, Jimmy concludes the lesson with a wink, representing for Rabbit Jimmy's free admission that "it's all a fraud, but what the hell," a fraud behind which lies the "enemy"—"Walt Disney or the MagiPeel Peeler Company" (10/10). In other words, he recognizes—or imagines—that Jimmy is being ironic.

For Kierkegaard, "irony" and Socrates are never very far apart. In *The Concept of Anxiety*, he directly cites Socrates as the first person who "introduced irony into the world and gave a name to the child." Socratic irony for Kierkegaard is a "dialectic in constant movement," which represents not a "negative" rhetorical strategy but rather an instance of "inclosing reserve," that is, a means by which Socrates could keep his inner self hidden as he communed with the outside world: "he began by closing himself off from men, by closing himself in with himself in order to be expanded in the divine, who also began by closing his door and making a jest to those outside in order to talk in secret." In the latter part of this passage, where he alludes to Matthew 6:6 and Jesus' advice that one should "enter thy door [and] pray to thy father in secret," Kierkegaard conflates Socratic irony with his own notions of inward, subjective faith. Similarly, Updike, perhaps drawing directly from these same pages of *The Concept of Anxiety*, combines Socrates, irony, and inner faith. According to this reading, Jimmy's Socratic advice to "be what you are" is in fact an admonition to practice ironic inclosing reserve, whereby one attempts to "be" something outwardly while "closing oneself in" so as to be "expanded in the divine." For although the God whom Jimmy invokes—a God who "wants some of us to become scientists, some of us to become artists," etc.—is an aesthetic God, a God of atemporal being and despair, the mere mention of this God nevertheless causes Rabbit and Janice to "become unnaturally still; both are Christians. God's name makes them feel guilty" (9/10). Hence Jimmy invokes this God ironically, in "jest to those outside in order to talk in secret" to those who, like Rabbit, can ascertain the real meaning behind the "wink." Hermann Diem, in his introduction to Kierkegaard's work, describes the "ironic method" as a "dialectical dialogue": behind his ironic stance the speaker "conceals his own positivity" so that the listener is "free to work out his own answers and the ideality of his existence is awakened."[7] Similarly, Rabbit works out his own answers to Jimmy's ironic lesson, awakening, in the process, the ideality of his own existence.

What are some of the answers Rabbit works out? First he learns that his social identity as a MagiPeel demonstrator is a fraudulent mask that merely serves to conceal his inward, existential identity. This mask is a social role, a *way to be,* that distorts the way he views himself. Behind this mask, Rabbit cannot properly access his authentic self. On the other hand, being made aware through Jimmy's dialectical irony of the obfuscating nature of that mask, Rabbit begins to disclose the authentic self that lies below. That is the second outcome of Rabbit's "dialogue" with Jimmy: he recognizes his MagiPeel identity as a fraud and so finds himself face-to-face with his authentic identity, the disclosure of which produces in him the sensation that gives him his name—namely, "angst."

Unlike fear, which always has an object, anxiety has no target and no observable cause. Nothing causes it because its cause is, in fact, "nothing." To experience angst or dread is merely to apprehend the always already latent possibility of nonbeing, of nothingness itself. Or, to employ Heidegger's famous formulation, "Anxiety reveals the nothing." Paul Tillich, building on Kierkegaard and Heidegger, further argues that anxiety also reveals the *opposite* of the nothing. First, he points out that *angst* always accompanies the moment of ontological self-awareness because the individual in effect *transcends* him/herself and regards that self as something that exists, and this insight thus implies the possibility of its *not* existing. At the same time, this moment of awareness and its attendant recognition of finitude also presupposes an awareness of infinity, the realm beyond the finitude just imagined and from which the individual seems to be viewing his/her finite self. As Tillich explains, "In order to be aware of moving toward death man must look out over his finite being as a whole; he must in some way be beyond it."[8] Trapped

7. Kierkegaard, *Concept of Irony,* 134, 151; Hermann Diem, *Kierkegaard: An Introduction,* 19–20.

8. Heidegger, "What Is Metaphysics?" 101; Paul Tillich, *Systematic Theology,* 190.

between the simultaneous and dual awareness of its own finitude *and* infinity, the being in ontological self-awareness experiences a nameless feeling of *angst* at the irreconcilable fact of this paradox, a paradox that has "nothing" as its source.

Just so, Updike depicts Rabbit's own anxiety as a feeling of entrapment between the irreconcilable possibilities of finitude and infinity, confinement and freedom, decision and potentiality. As these possibilities bear down on him on either side, he experiences the sensation that, derived from the Latin *angustiae*, quite literally translates as "narrows."[9] In a sense, the nagging claims of his daily life—however innocuous—become during his period of self-evaluation a surrogate for the objectless anxiety he feels welling within him. Since anxiety has "nothing" as its cause, the thing that threatens comes, as Heidegger puts it, from "nowhere." "It is already 'there' and yet nowhere; it is so close that it is oppressive and stifles one's breath, and yet it is nowhere."[10] Likewise, everything around Rabbit suddenly seems stifling and oppressive. The small apartment he shares with his wife and baby is suddenly said to "cling to his back like a tightening net" (14/14). His wife Janice's simple request for him to pick up a pack of cigarettes makes him feel that "he is in a trap. It seems certain" (15/15), while the complex traffic arrangement of the city as he flees "threatens him" and "begins to feel like a part of the same trap." Even the question of which to pick up first, his car or his son, "knits in front of him and he feels sickened by the intricacy" (15/15). Yet all these apparent causes for Rabbit's anxiety are really just surrogates, for in fact the source of his dread lies "nowhere."

Meanwhile, the various objects that clutter the apartment carry for Rabbit the stink of formlessness, finitude, and death: "the Old-fashioned glass with its corrupt dregs, the choked ashtray balanced on the easy-chair arm . . . the kid's toys here and there broken and stuck and jammed" and so on (14/14). In a similar vein, Janice's emotional confusion "frightens" Rabbit in its threat of chaos (10/11). This disorder and disarray open up a hole within him under which yawns the void, and at this moment he recognizes both the finitude of his everyday existence and the infinity of *other* possibilities evoked in its stead. These other possibilities in turn represent manifestations of his authentic self.

9. Ibid.
10. Heidegger, *Being and Time,* 231.

As Heidegger argues, accessing our authentic self causes us simultaneously to appreciate our full potential, to understand all the *other* things that we could be doing were we not so caught up in everyday life.[11] Once we make contact with these other possibilities, we begin to feel estranged from our own day-to-day existence. We acquire, in Heidegger's famous formulation, the *unheimlich* sense that we are not at home here. And when Rabbit experiences this *unheimlich* sensation, he quite literally *runs from home.*

Rabbit's spur-of-the-moment excursion to West Virginia has often been interpreted as an affirmation of freedom. Updike would certainly not dispute this reading. Still, despite the novel's relative contemporaneity with Jack Kerouac's *On the Road,* one should not conflate Rabbit's impulsive leap into his '55 Ford with the beatnik journeying of Sal Paradise and Dean Moriarty, for even though Updike might evoke Kerouac in *Rabbit, Run,* his chief intention in this regard seems to be parodic. Rabbit's act of abandonment is no simple celebration of Dionysian energy, nor is it strictly an act of cowardice that Updike hopes to critique, though he does do exactly that. Rather, Rabbit exercises his freedom primarily because its *possibility* has been disclosed to him during his moment of anxiety. Here, finally, we arrive at Kierkegaard's germinal definition of *angst,* the definition that launched those of Tillich and Heidegger. "Anxiety," Kierkegaard argues, "is defined as freedom's disclosure to itself as possibility." Again, this awareness of pure freedom has no object, for the individual in anxiety senses only a nonspecific possibility, a feeling of what one might be in contradistinction to the finite, obdurate reality of what one, at that moment, is. Anxiety does not lead to freedom, but rather to a recognition of freedom's possibility. Building on this ground-breaking insight, Heidegger later argues that angst, in making us aware of the nothing upon which we stand, also makes us aware of our boundless freedom: "Anxiety makes manifest in Dasein . . . its *Being-free for* the freedom of choosing itself and taking hold of itself."[12] So Rabbit gets in his car and leaves his family not so much

11. Ibid.

12. As recently as 1990, Updike has explained that he read *On the Road* around the time of writing *Rabbit, Run,* but did so "with some antagonism" because, to him, the book seemed to be "so very unreal, so very evasive." See Updike, "Forty Years of Middle America with John Updike," 224. It is also interesting to note that in the February 21, 1959, issue of the *New Yorker,* Updike published a parody of Kerouac entitled "On the Sidewalk" and subtitled, "After Reading, At Long Last,

because he wants freedom as because his anxiety has simply raised the possibility of other ways of living, or, as Heidegger would say, ways of Being.

More important, the moment Rabbit *does* act upon his freedom, he turns his angst into guilt. His decision to leave is a leap from anxiety, the recognition of freedom's possibility, to guilt, the attainment of freedom itself. Like angst, this guilt is not directed at some specific act for which one might accept responsibility. Rather, the guilt disclosed through angst is ontological and therefore intrinsic to our makeup. In other words, this guilt refers to our acceptance of the total freedom made manifest through the disclosure of angst. Angst, meanwhile, is "the pivot upon which everything turns." Kierkegaard illustrates his theory through a curious, idiosyncratic reading of Adam's fall. When God tells Adam of the prohibition guarding the tree of knowledge of good and evil, Adam experiences the anxiety of freedom's possibility: he feels anxious at the realization that he can disobey. Adam does not know what he is going to do, let alone what he should or should not do. He only knows "the anxious possibility of *being able.*" We begin to see what Kierkegaard means by the following teasing passage: "Anxiety is *a sympathetic antipathy* and *an antipathetic sympathy.*" Upon hearing of the prohibition, Adam immediately desires to do what he fears to do, that is, disobey. This is the "sympathetic antipathy." At the same time, he fears what he desires: hence "antipathetic sympathy." He is also anxious about this fearful desire because he realizes that, as a free being, he is the only agent who can stop himself from claiming that desire. In recognizing his solitary, fearful responsibility, he becomes guilty of, that is to say, culpable for, that boundless freedom. Not tied to a specific act, guilt is an ontological condition that calls attention to the primordial fact that we are responsible for our own freedom. "Hence," Kierkegaard writes, "anxiety is the dizziness of freedom, which emerges when . . . freedom

---

On the Road." The publishing date of this piece perfectly corresponds to the composition period of *Rabbit, Run.* See Updike, *Assorted Prose,* 24–27. In the same interview in 1990, Updike distinguishes his narrative purpose from that of Kerouac: "I was trying to make the good Protestant point that we're all involved with our fellow man, and we're all members of families, and so the basic image of [*Rabbit, Run*] is of a man running or leaving or going on the road and disrupting his own family." Kierkegaard, *The Concept of Anxiety,* 111; Heidegger, *Being and Time,* 232.

looks down into its own possibility, laying hold of finiteness to support itself. Freedom succumbs in this dizziness. Further than this, psychology cannot and will not go. In that very moment everything is changed, and freedom, when it rises, sees that it is guilty. Between these two moments lies the leap, which no science has explained and which no science can explain."[13] The leap is neither gradual nor progressive, nor is guilt attributable to some source action for which one can atone. Rather, it is a "debt" to ourselves that we can never fully repay.

Updike renders Rabbit's decision to abandon his wife and family as a similar leap from anxious innocence to guilt-laden sinfulness. He signals this leap not by any sort of transition or gradual movement. Rabbit simply feels trapped, decides to act, and enters into a state of guilt and sinfulness. Starting his own car out in front of his in-laws', he fears being "caught" by his mother-in-law, even though he is doing nothing more criminal than retrieving his automobile, which he should be doing anyway. "Nevertheless," the narrator writes, "he doesn't want to be put to the inconvenience of lying, however plausibly." Later, as he tries to get out of Mt. Judge, he finds himself unable to recall the feeling of "tautness" recovered during his basketball game, or the nostalgic image of Nelson being fed happily in his old childhood home: "He imagines himself about to shoot a long one-hander, but he feels he's on a cliff, there's an abyss he will fall into when the ball leaves his hands. He tries to repicture his mother and sister feeding his son, but the boy is crying in backward vision, his forehead red and his mouth stretched wide and his helpless breath hot" (24/23). The "abyss" here suggests the cliff from which, in Kierkegaard's striking figure, "freedom looks into its own possibility" and returns as "guilty." Indeed, every pleasant thing Rabbit tries to think of turns back upon him and announces his guilt. Recollections from childhood yield to images of his wife's deflowering and his unconscionable abandonment of her. "Poor Janice would probably have the wind up now," he thinks, "on the phone to her mother or his mother, somebody, wondering why her supper was getting cold. So dumb. *Forgive me*" (25/23, emphasis added). Later at a gas station, with no

13. Kierkegaard, *Concept of Anxiety,* 43, 44, 43, 61. Note the similarities here between Kierkegaard's language and that of Heidegger in this passage from *Being and Time:* "Therefore, with that which it is anxious about, anxiety discloses Dasein as *Being-possible*" (232).

prompting whatsoever, he "realizes he is a criminal" as "[s]enseless fear cakes over [his] body" (27/25). In sum, Rabbit's guilt is nonspecific and ontological. It is not determined "by analogy to judgments of the police court."[14] That is why it is depicted as disproportionate to any specific thing he has done.

In their nonspecificity, the two ontological conditions of anxiety and guilt would be insurmountable but for the "way out" offered by both Kierkegaard and Updike—that is, the way of faith, "the inner certainty that anticipates infinity." When accompanied by faith, anxiety becomes "a serving spirit that against its will leads [the individual] where he wishes to go." Without faith, anxiety leads to a despair from which one can escape only provisionally through the temporary sedative of objective thought. In *Rabbit, Run*, one among numerous agents of despair is the old man at the gas station who tells a very lost Rabbit, "The only way to get somewhere, you know, is to figure out where you're going before you go there" (28/26). The old man's advice might at first seem to be Updike's advice as well, yet clearly the man's admonition is meant to be refuted. For instance, the glasses he wears, and which prompt Rabbit to label him "a scholar," assign him to one of Updike's "antagonist figures" as outlined by Markle—the "well-intentioned but emotionally sterile man who fails to recognize or augment people's sense of their own specialness." His complicity with despair is further signaled by the whiskey Rabbit smells on his breath. "Everyone who tells you how to act," Rabbit thinks, "has whisky on their breath" (29/26). The old man's advice is "aesthetic" because it is nominally objective and therefore applicable to all—the kind of advice, in other words, which is always, in Updike and in Kierkegaard, associated with despair. Within the scope of Updike's narrative, the advice corresponds to the aesthetic component of Jimmy's homiletic admonition to "be what you are." Later Rabbit will find he cannot "think past [the old man], his smugness, his *solidity*, somehow," for in offering such practical, self-sufficient advice the old man mocks "the furtive wordless hopes that at moments make the ground firm for Harry" (37/34).[15]

14. Ibid., 161.
15. Ibid., 157, 159. See also Campbell, *Thorns Spell a Word*, 114; and Edward Vargo, *Rainstorms and Fire: Ritual in the Novels of John Updike*, 69–70. Markle, *Fighters and Lovers*, 2–3. In the most recent editions of *Rabbit, Run*, Updike revises this line to read, "the furtive wordless hopes that give Harry the sensation of arrival."

Instead, Updike, through Rabbit, affirms the ethical and subjective truth of inner certainty, what Rabbit calls his "instinct" (37/34).

The dynamics of Kierkegaardian faith get played out in the concentrated allegorical episode that follows Rabbit's encounter with the old man. Throughout his journey he tries to avoid cities, which he feels want to trap him in a net similar to the one back home. He imagines he "is being drawn into Philadelphia" and so turns south and then west, back toward Mt. Judge, from whence he came. He continues to zigzag as he enters Lancaster and then changes his course due southeast, only to veer west again so as to avoid Baltimore and Washington, "which like a two-headed dog guards the coastal route to the south" (32/29). However, outside his head and its current objective correlative, the car—"his only haven" (34/31)—the trap he wants to escape is in fact everywhere. Even the map he consults becomes "a net he is somewhere caught in" (36/33). Because the map holds out the promise of self-sufficiency, it causes despair, so much so that eventually Rabbit tears it up "with a gasp of exasperation" and tosses out the window the remaining scraps, which "like disembodied wings flicker back over the top of the car"—an image suggestive of angels being grounded.

Against the despair-producing information provided by the map, he pits his "instincts," his inner certainty. The novel clearly affirms these instincts as superior to practical advice, for they constitute the site of the divine voice within. Nowhere in *Rabbit Angstrom* is this idea more overtly championed than in the scene in which Rabbit, at the turning point of his first run, turns down a dark country road. "[T]hough his instincts cry against it," he follows this road anyway, deciding that there "is a quality, in things, of the right way seeming wrong at first. To test our faith" (35/32). That faith is instantly tested when the chosen road "climbs and narrows. Narrows not so much by plan as naturally" (35/32). *Angustiae*, it will be recalled, is the Latin word for "narrows." The deeper he goes the more he feels that the natural world, the opposite of the cities that would entrap him, is becoming yet another trap. In fact, he views the surrounding growth as a "web of wilderness" that leads to "a black core where he fears his probe of light will stir some beast or ghost." It is here that Rabbit reaches the nadir of his anxiety, that he experiences his most direct encounter with the nothing. Panicked, he "supports speed with prayer, praying that the road not stop" (35/32).

This prayer for continuity and infinity amounts to a request for "repetition," Kierkegaard's term for "recollecting forward." An article of faith, repetition affirms the belief that what has been in the past will continue to be in the future, whether one refers to one's life after death or to a lifelong love for one's spouse. (Marriage represents for Kierkegaard the most concrete, earthbound manifestation of repetition in action.) More than this, repetition also contains the absurd hope that all that has been lost will be returned *double*. He designates this last dynamic the double movement of resignation and faith, his most resonant emblem for which is the biblical figure of Job, who lost all his earthly possessions and had them all returned to him twofold because he held steadfastly to his idea that "every human interpretation [of God] is only a misconception." His worldly goods were returned to him when "every *thinkable* human certainty and probability were impossible. Bit by bit he loses everything, and hope thereby vanishes, inasmuch as actuality, far from being placated, rather lodges stronger and stronger allegations against him. From that point of view of immediacy, everything is lost. . . . With that the knot and the entanglement are tightened and can be untied only by a thunderstorm."[16] Kierkegaard's "knot and entanglement" become, in *Rabbit, Run,* the "web of wilderness" that has rendered Rabbit helpless in his fear, while the heavenly thunderstorm of Job gets transformed into a pair of oncoming headlights on high beam—God's light—which Updike calls the "blinding" answer to Rabbit's "prayer for speed." Though the car that passes is as "faceless as death," it still arrives for Rabbit as a piece of "good news," for the car also symbolizes death overcome—or, as Rabbit puts it, "the news that this road goes two ways" (35/32).

After this exhilarating experience, there is nothing for him to do but rip up his map, turn around and head back home to the finite death-evoking place he renounced and which now, in the Kierkegaardian "double movement of faith," is returned to him by an infinite and absurd God. Later, when Rev. Eccles asks him why he came back to Mt. Judge, he says, "Oh I don't know. A combination of things. It seemed safer to be in a place I know" (106/92). Safe from what? From

16. Kierkegaard, *Fear and Trembling/Repetition,* 212–13.

the vision of nothing he encountered on that dark unlit road, and from the sense of metaphysical helplessness that he has managed to overcome through prayer and for which he has been rewarded through repetition. In his Introduction to *Rabbit Angstrom,* Updike requotes the Joyce Cary passage cited earlier—in which Cary speaks of an "unmapped country" wherein one feels he has not only "utterly lost his way but also his identity"—and then obliquely glosses it by referring to the moment in *Rabbit, Run* when Harry "is literally lost, and tears up a map he cannot read" (xii). With this "reading map," Updike directs his reader to the first, and perhaps most important, turning point in *Rabbit, Run,* if not in all of *Rabbit Angstrom.* Harry returns home not out of cowardice but out of faith: his world has been returned to him, the finite and the everyday have been imbued with a celestial gleam. Indeed, as he reenters Brewer, he notes that there is "a lavender touch of light in the air," while a "cool pink pallor tinges the buildings" (39/35–36). In "Lifeguard," a lovely lyrical story from this same period (1961), Updike has his divinity-student narrator observe, "Swimming offers a parable. We struggle and thrash, and drown; we succumb, even in despair, and float, and are saved."[17] From this moment on Rabbit too floats above what Updike calls in *Rabbit Is Rich* "that old remembered world" (69/682).

II. Safe Inside His Skin

The Rabbit who returns to Mt. Judge endowed with the faith of repetition is essentially the same complex character who prevails throughout the rest of *Rabbit Angstrom*—both a good thing and a bad thing. The various and competing strains that constitute his character have long since elicited strong responses from many readers. By the time Updike published *Rabbit at Rest,* the issue of Rabbit's likability had become something of a literary hothouse argument. On the one hand, Gary Wills used the Rabbit novels to level a direct indictment of what he construed as Updike's selfish, solipsistic middle-class values, which he as-

17. Updike, "Lifeguard," 214.

sumed Updike had transmitted directly into Rabbit. The *Wall Street Journal* went so far as to call Rabbit "an almost entirely unsympathetic character." On the other hand, Louis Menand argued in *Esquire* that Rabbit's selfishness has "an attractive side . . . something about the simple act of running, its loneliness and vulnerability to chance, is eternally appealing," while Hermione Lee, in the *New Republic,* insisted that Rabbit's unsympathetic qualities are redeemed by the fact that "inside his brutish exterior, he is tender, feminine, and empathetic, like Leopold Bloom."[18] The debate even made it onto the editorial page of the *New York Times* in a piece by Brent Staples entitled, "Why So Hard on Rabbit?" This argument dates back to the novel's initial reception, during which *Time* called Rabbit a "hollow hero" and a "desperate weakling," while the *Saturday Review* argued that, despite his irresponsibility, "there is something in this man—call it 'the motions of Grace' if you choose—that demands our respect."[19] Clearly, Rabbit is not entirely unsympathetic—as the *Wall Street Journal* would insist—and yet at the same time he stands as no public role model either. What is it about Rabbit that is so unlikable? And what qualities does he possess that redeem him?

His two main shortcomings are his selfishness and what Updike calls his "hardness of heart," a phrase he borrows from Blaise Pascal in a passage that serves as *Rabbit, Run*'s epigraph: "The motions of Grace, the hardness of heart; external circumstances." Throughout *Rabbit, Run* his selfishness is not only well documented but also repeatedly commented upon. At one point Rev. Eccles tells him, "The truth is, you're monstrously selfish . . . you worship nothing but your own worst instincts" (134/115). His lover Ruth echoes this sentiment when she observes, "He just lived in his skin and didn't give a thought to the consequences about anything" (149/128). Janice's mother calls him "spoiled" while his own father thinks he is "the worst kind of Brewer bum" (163/141). Rabbit's hardness of heart is equally well documented. To take one example: upon returning to Janice after his abandonment, he learns from

---

18. Gary Wills, "Long-Distance Runner," 11–12; Brent Staples, "Why So Hard on Rabbit?"; Hermione Lee, "The Trouble with Harry," 35. For more on the connections between Rabbit and Bloom, see the end of this section.
19. "Desperate Weakling," 108; Granville Hicks, "A Little Good in Evil," 28.

her that she had not done anything about paying the rent on their old apartment—his old responsibility. Hearing this news he tells her, "The trouble with you, kid, is you just don't give a damn" (216/186). Finally, nowhere in *Rabbit, Run*—or perhaps in all of *Rabbit Angstrom*—is this "hardness" better demonstrated than in the scene devoted to Becky's funeral, in which Rabbit turns to the gathering and, apropos of nothing, snaps, "Don't look at *me* . . . I didn't kill her" (295/253). At moments such as this, it becomes rather difficult to like Rabbit. In fact, Updike seems at times to *demand* that we not like him.

Yet many readers do like him—much like the characters within the books themselves. Eccles, despite his reservations about Rabbit's selfishness, still declares, "Harry is in some respects a special case" (154/133). He also explains, "There's a great deal of goodness in [him]. When I'm with him—it's rather unfortunate, really—I feel so cheerful I quite forget what the point of my seeing him is" (164/141). Rabbit repeatedly insists, "I'm lovable," and he is not often contradicted. "Oh all the *world* loves you," Ruth tells him, then adds, "What I wonder is why?" (144/124). Rabbit's answer is not nearly so glib as it might sound on the surface: "I'm a mystic," he proclaims. "I give people faith." Indeed, that *is* Rabbit's power, the source of his magnetism. His energy—what Mrs. Smith calls his "gift of life"—touches those around him in such a way that he gives people faith in their *own* specialness—a gift which, as we have seen, operates as Markle's defining trait of the Updike hero. Rabbit accomplishes this faith-giving task primarily by example—specifically, by the example of his own selfish, hard-hearted insistence upon his own specialness. "If you have the guts to be yourself," he tells Ruth at one point, "other people will pay your price" (149/129). In *Rabbit, Run,* other people do just that. As in the Pascal passage quoted above, "hardness of heart" and "the motions of grace" stand opposite one another as balanced equals. So balanced are they in Rabbit that they become intimately dependent on one another. As Updike tells Jeff Campbell: "[T]here's a way in which hardness of heart and the motions of grace are intertwined. I was struck as a child, and continue to be struck, by the hardness of heart that Jesus shows now and then in the New Testament, advising people to leave their families, driving the money-lenders out of the temple in quite a fierce way. And I think there seems to be an extent to which hardness of heart is tied in with being alive at all."[20] The "grace" that earned the respect of the critic from the *Saturday Review* is inextricably tied to the unsympathetic selfishness that prompted *Time* to label Rabbit a "desperate weakling." Like all things in this zigzagging novel, every "yes" has its "no," every "either" its "or." The judgments of Rabbit as a "desperate weakling" must be taken alongside the assessments of Rabbit as an appealing character of vitality and charm. To isolate one quality over the other—as numerous readers have done—is to miss an essential component of Updike's dialectical vision.[21]

The evocation of Jesus in the above passage is no accident, for Rabbit's role as mystic does make a tidy parallel with this curious reading of Christ's earthly mission. Which is not to say that Rabbit is a "Christ-figure." Rather, he operates as an ironic Christ-like "saint," just as Janice rightly surmises early in the novel. Likewise, Ruth calls him a "Christian gentleman" and Eccles calls him both "a good man" and "a mystic." When Rabbit at one point goes so far as to compare himself to Jesus, Eccles does not contradict him, pointing out instead that Christ *"did* say . . . that saints shouldn't marry" (128/110). Updike reinforces this trope via numerous incidental details, such as the episode in which Rabbit looks at a painting of Joseph and the child Jesus: "the glass this print is protected by gives back to Rabbit the shadow of his own head" (124/107). Rabbit also identifies with the Dalai Lama, who, on the evening of Rabbit's flight to West Virginia (March 20, 1959), has escaped the invading Communist Chinese: "[Rabbit] adjusts his necktie with infinite attention, as if the little lines of this juncture of the Windsor knot, the collar of Tothero's shirt, and the base of his own throat were the atoms of a star that will, when he is finished, extend outward to the rim of the universe. *He* is the Dalai Lama" (50–51/45). To be sure, Rabbit's saintliness, his godliness, is solipsistic—in the passage above he becomes, in a sense, the center of the universe—but such self-absorption is, for Updike, a necessary component of individuality. In his autobiographical memoir, "The Dogwood Tree: A Boyhood," he asserts that his own "subjective geography" is, for him, "still the center of the world."[22] We are all, in this sense, the Dalai Lama.

20. Campbell, *Thorns Spell a Word*, 278–79.

21. See Hunt, *Three Great Secret Things*, 42.

22. Updike, "The Dogwood Tree: A Boyhood," 186. In a related autobiographical passage from *Self-Consciousness*, Updike seems deliberately to invoke

Solipsism and saintliness: although the two concepts seem entirely alien, Updike conflates them. He does so, in fact, with guidance from Kierkegaard. In *Fear and Trembling*—the one book, it will be recalled, that most changed Updike—Kierkegaard outlines the "paradox of faith" by which "inwardness" takes precedence over "outwardness" and subjective existence surpasses in importance the dictates of human-constructed ethics. It is this version of faith that Updike draws upon to develop his portrait of Rabbit, the saintly rake. Kierkegaard's emblematic figure for the "faith built on a paradox" is Abraham, who, in setting forth to sacrifice his son Isaac, introduced into the world the whole concept of faith. By the standards of any earthly ethical system, Kierkegaard reminds us, Abraham's proposed act of filicide is an abomination. God's intervention does not at all change this unavoidable fact, since Abraham undertook the act with no knowledge of, nor hope for, such an intervention. He went through with the act anyway, for which he earned the distinction as the Father of Faith. Herein lies the "paradox of faith" that, as Kierkegaard argues, "makes a murder into a holy and God-pleasing act, a paradox that gives Isaac back to Abraham again, which no thought can grasp, because faith begins precisely where thought stops."[23] Abraham's faith represents a "teleological suspension of the ethical" whereby "the single individual is higher than the universal"—the "universal" being Kierkegaard's term for objective man-made ethical precepts. Two "absurd" movements govern Abraham's faith: first, he agrees to commit what in human terms is the most atrocious act imaginable, all in obedience to God; second, he undertakes this act in the absurd belief—the "preposterous" belief, Kierkegaard insists—that God, for whom "all things are possible," will return Isaac to him—not in heaven, but here on earth. In other words, faith is the subjective, perhaps even solipsistic, belief in the impossible.

Updike writes of this reading of faith, "Eagerly I took from Kierke-

---

both this passage from "The Dogwood Tree" and Rabbit's moment of identification with the Dalai Lama: "I loved Shillington not as one loves Capri or New York, because they are special, but as one loves one's own body and consciousness, because they are synonymous with being. It was exciting for me to be in Shillington, as if my life, like the expanding universe, when projected backwards gained heat and intensity" (30). Obviously, Shillington is the most primordial site on John Updike's "subjective geography."

23. Kierkegaard, *Fear and Trembling/Repetition*, 53.

gaard the idea that subjectivity too has its rightful claims, amid all the desolating objective evidence of our insignificance and futility and final nonexistence; faith is not a deduction but an act of will, a heroism." Subjectivity is heroic, Rabbit is a saint. But Updike also takes another key component from *Fear and Trembling,* namely Kierkegaard's concept of the Knight of Faith, the ordinary man of subjectivity who, in renouncing the finite in exchange for the infinite, believes wholly in the return, here on earth, of that renounced finitude. John Neary, who also discusses at some length *Fear and Trembling's* relation to *Rabbit, Run,* writes that Kierkegaardian faith, like the repetition with which it is associated, is "founded in the world of the ordinary: after being negated by the transcendent, the ordinary is returned by an infinitely, absurdly gracious God." Similarly, the Knight of Faith is grounded in the ordinary: he is a man who, on the outside, seems to belong wholly to the world—"no bourgeois philistine could belong to it more"—while inwardly he carries intimate knowledge of infinitude.[24]

As Neary points out, "Kierkegaard . . . could almost be describing Harry Angstrom here."[25] Or perhaps Updike, in developing the character of Harry Angstrom, set out to create a Knight of Faith—or at least a Knight of Faith in training. For Rabbit, too, is something of an earthy bourgeois philistine who nevertheless claims to have access to the infinite. "His feeling that there is an unseen world is instinctive," the narrator asserts, "and more of his actions than anyone suspects constitute transactions with it" (235/201). The light behind a circular rose window on the front of a church seems to him "a hole punched in reality to show the abstract brilliance burning underneath" (80/90), while the mere sight of children dressed for church strikes him as "visual proof of the unseen world" (91/99). God's existence is as obvious to Rabbit as his nonexistence is to Ruth. And on his way to play golf—that most bourgeois of all activities—he says to Rev. Eccles: "Well, I don't know all this about theology, but I'll tell you, I *do* feel, I guess, that somewhere behind all this"—he gestures outward at the scenery; they are passing

24. Updike, "A Book That Changed Me," 844; John Neary, *Something and Nothingness: The Fiction of John Updike and John Fowles,* 72; Kierkegaard, *Fear and Trembling/Repetition,* 39.
25. Neary, *Something and Nothingness,* 72.

the housing development this side of the golf course, half-wood half-brick one-and-a-half-stories in little flat bulldozed yards holding tricycles and spindly three-year-old trees, the un-grandest landscape in the world—"there's something that wants me to find it" (127/110). Amid the "un-glamorous" world of Mt. Judge, amid his middle-class pursuits and worldly activities, Rabbit clings to his faith that behind the visible world lies an unseen world that not only redeems all but also includes him. As Nelson sardonically observes about his father in *Rabbit Is Rich:* "such a fool he really believes there is a God he is the apple of the eye of" (325/915). It is a foolish belief, as Updike freely admits, and for that very reason also represents "an act of will, a heroism."

Such heroism would be empty and insignificant if it did not resonate beyond the cave of Rabbit's subjective experience. But resonate it does, if not so much for the novel's other characters then for the novel's readers. In belonging wholly to the world, the Knight of Faith affirms the world, if only insofar as that world has been "returned" to him through the graciousness of God. "He finds pleasure in everything," Kierkegaard writes, "takes part in everything, and every time one sees him participating in something particular, he does it with an assiduousness that marks the worldly man who is attached to such things."[26] Rabbit also performs this act of affirmation; it is, in fact, one of the chief components of his claim as a "good man." In the same way that he reminds those around him of their own specialness by the paradox of his selfish example, so, too, does Updike's careful and meticulous rendering of Rabbit's inner life remind readers of the essential specialness of all things. Despite Rabbit's active selfishness, his subjective life is remarkably self*less* and other-directed. Possessed of one of the keenest senses of wonder this side of Leopold Bloom, Rabbit absorbs the world and returns it to the reader bathed in the shimmering light of Updike's incandescent prose.

Both here and in his insistence upon despair, Updike breaks with the existentialists and remains true to his Lutheran roots. The Continental existentialists—Sartre, for example—would argue that Rabbit's "morality" must be judged according to what he does, to the ways in which he asserts his freedom in action. And of course several critics have tried to

26. Kierkegaard, *Fear and Trembling/Repetition*, 39.

analyze Rabbit in precisely this manner, David Galloway chief among them.[27] As a Lutheran, however, Updike distrusts a morality based on "works." For him, salvation is based wholly on faith. And as a Kierke-gaardian, he is less interested in concrete universals and human ethical precepts than in the absurdity of faith and the primacy of subjective experience. Philosophy does not know what to do with subjectivity because it cannot observe it, which is why Updike is not a philosopher but a novelist: in the novel subjectivity can be rendered and so observed. And it is in subjective experience that he places the highest value—the highest *moral* value, teleologically suspended above the humanly ethical. The Rabbit tetralogy is, among other things, a sustained demonstration of the supreme moral value of subjective experience.

In this respect, Updike affirms the moral philosophy set forth by Iris Murdoch in *The Sovereignty of Good.* Long an admirer of Murdoch's work, he seems to agree with her insistence that the internal, nonobservable motions of the *cogitatio* constitute genuine moral action. He would also agree with her accompanying maxim, "Where virtue is concerned we often apprehend more than we clearly understand and *grow by looking.*" Her treatise argues against the idea that morality must be action and that salvation is dependent upon works. Instead, she insists on the ethical sovereignty of subjective experience, on the moral significance of mental concepts, even those concepts that have no external, public correspondence. A decision made but not acted upon, for instance, still carries for Murdoch moral weight. These thoughts, these decisions, are functions of vision, of one's perception of the world, and the moral criterion evoked by these perceptions is precisely this: does one try to view the world "justly and lovingly"? Borrowing the term from Simone Weil, Murdoch places enormous value on "attention," which she uses "to express the idea of a just and loving gaze upon individual reality." This gaze, she believes, stands as the "characteristic and proper mark of the active moral agent." Seeing the world "as it is," and seeing it benevolently, becomes the task of that agent. Before "accurate vision" can be obtained, however, there must be a suppression of self, a freedom from self, or—what for Murdoch is the same thing—a "freedom from fantasy." Fantasy becomes in her system "the proliferation of blind-

27. See David Galloway, *The Absurd Hero in American Fiction,* 30–40.

ing self-centered aims and images," while "reality" becomes the external world viewed with compassion and a selfless attention to individuality.[28]

Though Rabbit is "self-centered," his gaze is not. The moment he tears up that map and surrenders, he is, in a sense, released from the bindings of self-centered aims, from fantasy, paradoxically because he has embraced the most absurd fantasy of all. Speaking of his own spiritual crisis—which, by his own account, corresponds chronologically to the composition of *Rabbit, Run*—Updike asserts, "After one has conquered this sort of existential terror . . . then one is able to open to the world again."[29] His hero Karl Barth, for instance, was "very open to the world. Wonderfully alive and relaxed." This seeming contradiction between subjectivity and external openness has confused many of Updike's more strident critics, particularly critics of his prose style. Often described as "self-indulgent," the style is in fact anything but. From *Self-Consciousness:* "My own style seemed to me a groping and elemental attempt to approximate the complexity of envisioned phenomena . . . self-indulgent, surely, is exactly what it wasn't—*other*-indulgent, rather." Self-consciousness, moreover, is really, in the hands of a writer, "a mode of interestedness, that inevitably turns outward." By turning outward and honoring the "complexity" of phenomena, Updike insists he is performing a moral, even holy, duty—that of giving praise. This task he designates, in a brief answer to the question "Why Are We Here?" as, more or less, The Meaning of Life: "We are here to give praise. Or, to slightly tip the expression, to pay attention." Meanwhile, in the *Rabbit Angstrom* introduction, he declares, "A non-judgmental immersion was my aesthetic and moral aim. . . . The religious faith that a useful truth will be imprinted by a perfect artistic submission underlies these Rabbit novels" (xiii). Attention expresses gratitude, curiosity about the

---

28. Iris Murdoch in *The Sovereignty of Good,* 31, 34, 66–67. Updike has written extensively on Murdoch. See the extended sections devoted to her work in *Hugging the Shore* (345–55) and *Odd Jobs* (413–41).

29. See *Self-Consciousness,* 97–98. "In my memory," he begins, "there is a grayness to that period of my life in Ipswich." In this account, "grayness" represents a nihilistic obliteration of all distinctions between good and evil, life and death. Not accidentally, this period of "grayness" began for Updike on a basketball court: "I was playing basketball . . . and I looked up at the naked, netless hoop: gray sky outside it, gray sky inside it" (97). From this moment of insight emerged *Rabbit, Run,* Updike's dialectical response to that grayness.

world is an act of worship, and the writing life constitutes a genuine contribution to this moral endeavor. In a passage that combines subjective faith and Murdoch's "just and loving" gaze, Updike describes his artistic credo: "Imitation is praise. Description expresses love. I early arrived at these self-justifying inklings. Having accepted that old Shillington blessing, I have felt free to describe life as accurately as I could, with especial attention to human erosions and betrayals. What small faith I have has given me what artistic courage I have. My theory was that God already knows everything and cannot be shocked. And only truth is useful. Only truth can be built upon. From a higher, inhuman point of view, only truth, however harsh, is holy." In sum, religious faith, though subjective, is for Updike also contingent upon the outside world, the material world. Things at rest, he has often asserted, radiate a "quiet but tireless goodness," for (as he affirms in "Midpoint") "the beaded curtain / of Matter hid an understanding Eye."[30] Subjective faith and selfless outward attention: another inextricable either/or.

"There's a touch of the old artist about old Bloom," remarks Lenehan, a minor character in James Joyce's *Ulysses,* an assessment that applies equally to Bloom's postwar American counterpart, Harry "Rabbit" Angstrom. Quite a large portion of *Rabbit, Run*—and of *Rabbit Angstrom*—takes place inside Rabbit's head in the form of lingering, Joycean internal monologues. And like Joyce, Updike values the internal monologue for its affirmation of subjectivity. Yet this vast exploration of the workings of Rabbit's internal life also demonstrates how rich and just can be the interaction between the interior psyche and external world. Because Rabbit seems to be interested in everything, his perceptions animate all that he sees. His conviction that an "understanding Eye lurks" behind all phenomena further gives everything and everyone he encounters a redemptive sheen.

A few choice examples illustrate this point. While gardening for Mr. Smith, Rabbit observes of the seeds he plants, "Sealed, they cease to be his. The simplicity. Getting rid of something by giving it to itself. God Himself folded into the tiny adamant structure, Self-destined to a succession of explosions, the great slow gathering out of water and air and

30. Campbell, *Thorns Spell a Word,* 302; Updike, *Self-Consciousness,* 103, 24, 231; Updike, *Odd Jobs,* 864; Updike, "Midpoint," I., 47–48.

silicon: this is felt without words in the turn of the round hoe-handle in his palms" (136/117). Rabbit must feel rather than articulate these lyrical observations, cast as they are in Updike's most self-consciously poetic diction, yet feel them he does, in accordance with Murdoch's conviction that "where virtue is concerned we often apprehend more than we clearly understand."[31] Note how Rabbit takes solace in "giving" the plants to themselves, in his sense of their own individual complexity and self-justified importance.

His first vision of his baby daughter, Becky, elicits similar observations: "The folds around the nostril, worked out on such small scale, seem miraculously precise; the tiny stitchless seam of the closed eyelid runs diagonally a great length, as if the eye, when it is opened, will be huge and see everything. In the suggestion of pressure behind the tranquil lid and in the tilt of the protruding upper lip he reads a delightful hint of disdain. She knows she's good" (218/187). Like the previous passage—though without the urge for parable—this description carries beneath it an insistent spiritual throb. By taking in with such attention these visual details, Rabbit discloses the "miracle" of all phenomena and its uncanny sense of being "worked out" by some Transcendent Craftsman. In the process, he is able to "read" the message ("She knows she's good") left behind by that Craftsman, in the same way that David Kern, the spiritually anguished young protagonist of Updike's short story "Pigeon Feathers," "reads" in the intricate detail of a dead pigeon's wings God's infinite concern for all things.

Yet inasmuch as such an approach to perception enlivens Rabbit's dealings with the world and physical phenomena, it does not cloud that approach. If the "truth" is holy for Updike, and if faith gives one the courage to tell the truth, then hardness of heart—inexorably linked with "the motions of Grace"—must also accompany one's comportment through the world. Rabbit best demonstrates both qualities—that is, hardness and Grace—in his observations of people. With regard to the elderly Mrs. Smith, he takes in not only the "tiny brown sockets afflicted by creases like so many drawstrings" that surround her eyes, but also the "cracked blue eyes" themselves which "bulge frantically with captive life." Ruth he also appraises with an unsentimental, fascinated

---

31. Murdoch, *Sovereignty of Good,* 31.

gaze. A large woman—"Chunky, more"—Ruth wobbles a bit in her shoes, a detail Rabbit acknowledges and, in the same breath, redeems by his outwardly directed attention: "Rabbit sees from behind that her heels, yellow with strain, tend to slip sideways in the net of lavender straps that pin her feet to the spikes of her shoes. But under the shiny green stretch of her dress her broad bottom packs the cloth with a certain composure" (56/50). Of Rev. Eccles, Rabbit observes immediately that "there is something friendly and silly about him" (102/88). On the one hand, Eccles has a charming, seductive quality—"this knack," Rabbit calls it—while on the other hand the minister is petty, quick to anger: "Eccles really does have a mean streak. . . . Without the collar around his throat, he kind of lets go" (129/111). Still, Rabbit remains open to Eccles, open to Ruth, open to everyone. Everybody is wild about Harry, and Harry is wild about everyone.

Although the numerous features of Rabbit's character laid out in this section remain consistent throughout the rest of *Rabbit Angstrom,* perhaps no feature takes greater precedence than Rabbit's open, observant response to the world around him. As the completed work rolls on, Harry's role as Updike's Bloomian eye becomes more pronounced, its moral significance increasingly more profound. That Updike had Bloom in mind while writing *Rabbit, Run* seems clear and uncontested enough. Updike says as much in his new Introduction to *Rabbit Angstrom,* wherein he admits that the Joycean influence resounds "perhaps all too audibly," particularly in the novel's "female soliloquies." There are other connections as well. Conceived as a novella, *Rabbit, Run* was originally to be paired with what turned out to be Updike's third and most clearly Joycean novel, *The Centaur:* one novella would borrow the internal monologue device and the other Joyce's "mythic method." Joyce's epiphanic technique from *Dubliners* is clearly invoked in *Pigeon Feathers*—for example, "A&P," the title story, the brief episode "You'll Never Know, Dear, How Much I Love You," which overtly rewrites "Araby"—stories written and published contemporaneously with *Rabbit, Run.* Rev. Eccles has a daughter named Joyce, while Leopold Bloom lives at 7 *Eccles* Street. And so on. As a result of these affinities, many, if not most, of the things said about Joyce's Bloom apply equally to Updike's Angstrom. Craig Raines, in his introduction to the Everyman's edition of *Ulysses,* makes precisely this same Bloom-Rabbit connection.

He calls Updike's creation a "fictional character conceived by an admirer of Joyce's average sensual man," yet adds (as praise, I should think), that Rabbit is, "if anything, even more basic a challenge to the novelist's redemptive imagination."[32] Updike's imagination *is* redemptive, and in Rabbit, he meets the extraordinary challenge he set himself at the age of twenty-seven—if not entirely here in *Rabbit, Run,* then surely in *Rabbit Angstrom* as a whole.

III. Karl Barth and the *Creatio ex Nihilo*

Against Rabbit's positive, redemptive openness to the world around him and to his own specialness—against, in other words, Rabbit's insistent "yes" to life—Updike pits a series of "negative" characters whose role, in part, is to say "no." The two most prominent of these are Ruth and Rev. Eccles. Both characters not only confront Rabbit with his selfishness but also level critiques of Rabbit that the book largely does not contradict. One is a prostitute and one a minister, yet Updike endows both characters with depth and multi-dimensionality. Antagonists they are, but villains they are not. Ambiguous as always, the novelist hedges his bets even here with a pair of characters who provide the novel's "no-but" equilibrium.

Ruth, Rabbit's lover, is consistently associated with the nothing. Even at their first meeting, Rabbit notices that at her feet "four sidewalk squares meet in an x" (55/49), suggesting she is, as in an algebra problem, an empty variable. When Rabbit asks her what she does for a living, she answers, "Nothing. . . . Nothing." When he asks her to describe her orgasm, she replies, "Oh. It's like falling through [to] . . . Nowhere" (86/95). On his way back to Ruth's one morning, Rabbit is caught by Eccles, who asks where he is going. Rabbit replies, "Nowhere" (102/88). Her last line in the novel is "No" (307/263). In short, Rabbit's angst, his fear of nothing, has now found something to attach itself to, and that something turns out to be a woman who somehow *personifies* the nothing. And unlike Rabbit, who instinctively feels that there is "something that wants [him] to find it," Ruth believes, quite literally, in noth-

32. Craig Raines, "Introduction," xxi.

ing. Whereas God's existence seems "obvious" to Rabbit, to Ruth "It seems obvious just the other way. All the time." For her, things do not affirm reclining goodness, nor do they reveal God's "text": "Things just are" (91/79). Yet Ruth is no blank slate. Her "nothing," like Heidegger's, is a necessary and unavoidable entity that possesses genuine power. Rabbit realizes as much. The net that, in the novel's opening pages, threatens to trap him in finite everydayness dissolves in Ruth's presence, dissolves into a blank, godless sky that strikes Rabbit as worthy of his attention, if not his worship: "Yesterday . . . he was exhausted, heading into the center of the net, where alone there seemed a chance of rest. Now . . . he feels nothing ahead of him, Ruth's blue-eyed nothing, the nothing she told him she did, the nothing she believes in. Your heart lifts forever through that blank sky" (97/84). In the same way that Tillich's finitude suggests infinity, Ruth's godless emptiness suggests an endlessness through which the heart "lifts forever." Ruth provides Rabbit with a vision of finitude that does not suggest nets and traps and death, but rather a blank, wide-open emptiness that he finds, for awhile at least, comforting.

Ruth also serves to put a necessary check on Rabbit's rampant, reckless search for the "something that wants [him] to find it," for often Rabbit goes searching for "it" in places where "it" is not lurking. As in sex, for instance. For Ruth, sex has "no mystery" (146/126), and she instructs Rabbit in learning this basic lesson. It is a lesson he resists as much as he resists letting go of the triumph he once felt as a high school basketball star. In fact, he resists the lesson precisely because he has confused the two activities—sports and sex—in his inner theology of grace. Throughout *Rabbit, Run,* Updike draws overt connections between Rabbit's love of sports and his valorization of sex as a path to transcendence, connections which many other critics have already pointed out.[33] Early in the novel, for instance, Rabbit recalls "the high perfect hole" of the basketball rim with its "pretty skirt of net" (38/34). Later, while playing golf with Eccles, he first thinks of his intractable clubs as different women and then imagines himself as the ball, with the bushes figured as his mother (131–32/113–14). But perhaps the most

33. See Markle, *Fighters and Lovers,* 42–45; and Edward P. Vargo, *Rainstorms and Fire: Ritual in the Novels of John Updike,* 58–62.

telling connection between sports and sex comes two-thirds of the way through the novel, during a reverie in which Rabbit remembers both his old basketball glory and an old lover named Mary Ann. Having seduced her on the same evening as his first real triumph on the basketball court, he finds that "the two kinds of triumph"—sexual and athletic—"were united in his mind" (198/170). Both triumphs provided Rabbit with the conviction that he was special, so much so that sex and sports become his means of attaining that feeling all over again: "He came to her as a winner and that's the feeling he's missed ever since" (198/170). Like that circular rose church window with its suggestion of divine light, the empty space of the basketball net—with its "pretty skirt of net"—and the female sexual organ become for him sites of transcendence, places where he can locate the "something" that has its eye specifically on him.

Rabbit's faith in sex as a path to grace inspires him to ritualize his first sexual encounter with Ruth—to turn it into a quasi-wedding ceremony or, as Edward Vargo persuasively argues, a "rite of preparation."[34] He cleans her, removes her rings, forbids her to use contraceptives, and so on. Vargo feels that Rabbit uses this act to pursue some sort of transcendental "communion." At one point, for instance, Harry "feels impatience that through all their twists they remain separate flesh" (84/73). Yet Rabbit is also searching for that "something" that wants him to find it, the same something whose presence makes him feel so sure he is special. By ritualizing the act, he hopes to turn it into another arena in which he can recover that sense of triumph he feels he has lost. And at first his efforts seem to work. Ruth's shyness, he thinks, "praises him," while her use of his name makes him think "she sees him as special." He even imagines that she has become "his friend in this search" (84/73). But sex turns out *not* to be a path to that something, for "everywhere they meet a wall" that obstructs their search, a search which ends, for Rabbit anyway, not in triumph but in despair: "He looks at her face and seems to read in its shadows a sad expression of forgiveness, as if she knows that at the moment of release, the root of love, he betrayed her by feeling despair. Nature leads you up like a mother and as soon as she gets her little price leaves you with nothing" (86/75). Forgiveness is Ruth's to give because she knows in advance that "nothing" awaits them

34. Vargo, *Rainstorms and Fire,* 61.

at the end of the act. Rabbit's despair, she seems implicitly to understand, is not directed at her but at the blind, obdurate fact of sexuality itself. Whereas in the climactic moments of sports Rabbit is able to find some semblance of grace, here he only finds a ruse, a trick—not of God's handiwork, however, but of Nature's. There is also no possibility here for the "transcendental communion" which Vargo proposes, precisely because the "wall" that separates them is, in effect, the "wall of flesh" behind which each resides in his and her own subjective individuality: As Rabbit affirms elsewhere, "All I know is what's inside *me*," later adding, "It's just, well, it's all there is" (107/93, 125/108). Outside that subjectivity there is, quite possibly, nothing.

So Updike does not present Ruth's version of the nothing merely as an antagonistic formulation that Rabbit's vitality must blithely overcome. He explores this nothing as a viable and integral part of the book's overall dialectical vision: beneath the basic goodness of God's creation —life—lies the nothingness of death. If Harry, with his "gift of life," is the exemplar of the "something" aspect of creation, then Ruth is the prophetess of the necessary nothing, for it is she more than anyone else in the novel who forces Rabbit to confront this inescapable dark underside—a side, it is important to add, he himself possesses as well. When, late in the novel, she calls him "Mr. Death" and "worse than nothing" (304/260), she is right, no matter how many Mrs. Smiths there are to praise Rabbit otherwise. Rabbit is *both* Mr. Life *and* Mr. Death, a something and, by extension, a nothing, a yes and a no.

Rabbit's dream of "lovely life eclipsed by lovely death" articulates this important dialectic. In the dream, Rabbit sees "two perfect disks, identical in size but the one a dense white and the other slightly transparent, move toward one another slowly" (283/242). The bright disk symbolizes the sun and life, while the transparent disk symbolizes the moon and death. Though the sun is "stronger," the moon manages to cover the sun so that "just one circle is before his eyes, pale and pure" (283/242). Life, the dream suggests, is an eclipsing of death—and vice versa. For every something, a nothing. Both life *and* death, however, are characterized by Rabbit as "lovely," just as Updike insists, in the *Soundings* introduction, that the nothing "thrives in proportion" with God's something: "The world always topples. A century of progressivism bears the fruit of Hitler; our own supertechnology breeds witches and warlocks from the loins of engineers."[35] This dialectical vision represents what Updike elsewhere in *Rabbit, Run* calls "the dark, tangled, visceral aspect of Christianity, the *going through* quality of it, the passage *into* death and suffering that redeems and inverts these things, like an umbrella blowing inside out" (237/203). The nothing is there, to be sure, but it is redeemed by the something that lies at its back. Thus redeemed, it becomes part of God's creation, though not of His will. And although, as the narrator observes, Rabbit "has no taste" for this aspect of Christianity, he nevertheless has to confront it head on. Ruth represents one part of this lesson, and the dream outlined above represents another. As will be shown, the lesson concludes—for the time being, at least—with the death of Becky.

As we saw in the introduction, this yes-and-no dialectic of divine order owes its genealogy to Karl Barth. In keeping with his Barthian model, Updike also links his dialectic to two of Barth's other characteristic ideas, the *creatio ex nihilo* and the "Wholly Other" God. Barth's most emphatic announcement of this credo, as formulated in his essay, "The Problem of Ethics Today" from *The Word of God and the Word of Man*, has already been quoted, yet he makes similar pronouncements again and again throughout his work. In *Dogmatics in Outline* he insists, "God is not only unprovable and unsearchable, but is also *inconceivable.*" He also argues that "He who is called God in Holy Scripture is unsearchable—that is, He has not been discovered by any man"; rather, all knowledge of God in Barth's terms is the result not of human investigation but of revelation: "He who has hidden from us has disclosed Himself." Updike has said that such bold and uncompromising assertions "would seem to discourage all theology," and yet they clearly did not discourage Barth. They do discourage, however, ethical systems that seek for God's sanction. The world is distinct from God, lest it would not be God's creation. Likewise, we must remain equally distinct from God, lest we lose what Updike calls "our precious creaturely freedom, which finds self-assertion in defiance and existence in sin and dreads beyond hell a heaven of automatons 'freed from the possibility of falling away.'" What keeps us from falling away? God's grace. How do we receive this grace? When God wills it. "We count on God's *grace,*" Barth

35. Updike, "Soundings in Satanism," 90.

states, "[b]ut it is not our own! *Everything* depends upon that grace! But we do not bring it into being by any magic turn of our dialectic. He *is* and *remains free:* else he were not God." Or, as Updike's Barth-obsessed divinity professor Roger Lambert proclaims in *Roger's Version,* "Free him, even though He die." Theology then is not about ethical arguments, nor is it concerned with proving God's existence which, Barth would sardonically declaim, needs no proving from *us.* According to this theory, theology only has relevance to the faithful, but this, both Barth and Updike would agree, is how it must be, since a theology of a Wholly Other God can only be concerned with providing believers with a "demonstration of the *ratio* of their faith."[36]

By failing to appreciate this stridently Barthian conception of the ministry, Rev. Eccles secures his role as the novel's second negative character. A liberal Episcopalian minister, Eccles is a man without faith, a believer in human solutions and conventional ethics. His name not only evokes Ecclesiasticus, the author of the eponymously titled Old Testament book of stoic, earthbound wisdom,[37] but also hints at Updike's ironic strategy: Rabbit's outwardly animalistic and sensuous demeanor conceals an intensely spiritual man, while the minister's ecclesiastical surface conceals an almost pagan unbeliever. Whereas Rabbit is a Knight of Faith, Eccles is a pastoral shepherd. Updike reinforces these symbolic associations by connecting Eccles with the earthly color green. Eccles drives a green car, his wife Lucy—a sardonic, atheistic Freudian—has green eyes, and so on. Only on the golf course does he truly come alive, for there, "Down in the pagan groves and green alleys," he "is transformed" (130/112). Similarly, he feels "most at home in public places" (172/148), for there he can concern himself with "external circumstances," with the immediate and the temporal. Otherwise—as he himself frankly admits (via a third-person transcription of his internal voice)—"He doesn't, he doesn't believe anything" (155/133). In fact, the only father he looks to is his own earthly father, the "real father he has been trying to please all his life" (154/133). His gaze extends no fur-

36. Barth, *Dogmatics,* 38; Updike, "Soundings in Satanism," 90; Barth, *Word of God,* 178; Updike, *Roger's Version,* 80; Barth, quoted in Updike, "Faith in Search of an Understanding," 277.
37. Hunt, *Three Great Secret Things,* 40.

ther, penetrates no deeper, than that. In place of the frank supernaturalism and intense subjectivity that Updike posits as the two prerequisites of faith, Eccles substitutes an approach to world events that—as Updike says of the teaching of Paul Tillich and the rest of the liberal theologians of the postwar period—"is not so different from that of an agnostic."[38] Such a worldview, when presented as a function of faith, in fact "murders faith in the minds of any who really listen" (154/133), because it treats each individual—each God-created vessel of faith—as an abstract entity answerable to objective ethical precepts.

According to Kierkegaard, such faithless piety, agnostic or otherwise, is "simply comical." And, to be sure, there is something comical about Eccles, as he seeks succor amid teenagers in a soda shop and achieves "brainless gaiety" on a golf course. Primarily, however, Eccles is misguided: he simply does not understand his job, at least insofar as Updike, via Barth, would define it. Rev. Kruppenbach, the character whom Updike has described as "Barth in action," apprises Eccles of this job description. The affinities between Kruppenbach's harangue of Eccles and Barth's similar harangue of his ecclesiastical brethren, "The Word of God and the Task of the Ministry," are striking and illustrative. To Eccles's psychological/sociological assessment of Rabbit's predicament, Kruppenbach declares, "You think now your job is to be an unpaid doctor, to run around and plug up holes and make everything smooth. I don't think that. I don't think that's your job" (170/146). Neither does Barth, who declares, "Obviously, the people have *no* real need of *our* observations upon morality and culture, or even our disquisitions upon religion, worship and the possible existence of other worlds." Both Kruppenbach and Barth also agree as to what Eccles's role *should* be. Kruppenbach thunders, "*There* is your role: to make yourself an exemplar of faith. . . . so when the call comes you can tell them, 'Yes, he is dead, but you will see him again in heaven. Yes, you suffer, but you must *love* your pain, for it is *Christ's* pain'" (170–71/146–47). Similarly, Barth states, "Churchgoers have a passionate longing to hear the *word* which promises life in death beyond the here and now," a "word" which it is a minister's primary task to spread. Any other "social function" the

---

38. Campbell, *Thorns Spell a Word,* 301. Updike adds as an aside, "[Y]ou scratch most ministers, at least in the East, and you find a liberal."

minister might see fit to fill is, in Barth's terms, wholly "superfluous": "When they come to us for help they do not really want to learn more about *living:* they want to learn more about what is on the farther side of living—*God.* We cut a ridiculous figure as village sages—or city sages. As such we are socially superfluous." As a "village sage," Eccles *is* ridiculous—or, as Kierkegaard says, simply comical—yet he is nevertheless an apt figure for a church that, in Updike's terms, has abdicated its primary role as witness to another world. As he writes his introduction to *Soundings in Satanism,* "[W]herever a church spire is raised . . . Hell is opposed by a rumor of good news, by an irrational confirmation of the plenitude we feel is our birthright."[39] In trying to police Rabbit's behavior, Eccles says nothing to Rabbit that Rabbit does not already know. Kruppenbach himself points this out when he says to Eccles, "Anything else we can do or say anyone can do and say. They have doctors and lawyers for that" (171/147). The one thing that Eccles has it in his power to supply—confirmation of that other world—Rabbit does not need, nor is Eccles capable of supplying it. Indeed, the first time he meets Eccles Rabbit observes, "he doesn't seem to know his job" (103/89), while Mrs. Springer, Janice's mother, rightly asks, "Well if the world is going to be full of Harry Angstroms how much longer do you think they'll need your church?" (154/133). Not much longer, the answer seems to be, insofar as that church persists in its socially superfluous task of playing "doctor."

At the same time, Kruppenbach's words invoke Kierkegaard as well. When Kruppenbach says, "It seems to you our role is to be cops, cops without handcuffs, without guns, without anything but our human good nature" (170/146), he directly invokes Kierkegaard who, in the *Concluding Unscientific Postscript,* writes, "If the intent of the religious address is to help the police by being able to thunder against people who evade the power of the police, . . . then His Reverence mistakes himself for a kind of police sergeant, and he more suitably ought to walk around with a policeman's club and be paid by the municipality. In everyday life, in the marketplace, in social life, one person is guilty of this, another of that, and there is nothing more to be said; but the religious ad-

---

39. Kierkegaard, *Concept of Anxiety,* 141; Barth, *Word of God,* 188, 109, 189; Updike, "Soundings in Satanism," 91.

dress deals with inwardness . . . "[40] This Kierkegaardian gloss successfully directs Kruppenbach's indictment away from Rabbit and toward
Eccles. For although George Hunt must be credited with foreground-
ing Kruppenbach as one of the novel's chief moral voices, he limits his
reading by insisting too narrowly for a strictly Barthian subtext. Hunt
argues that "Kruppenbach's criticism of Eccles is effectively a criticism
of Rabbit as well," and yet Hunt never supports this argument.[41] Even
Hunt notes that of all the novel's characters, Kruppenbach is the only
one whom Rabbit never meets. How, then, is Kruppenbach's "sermon"
supposed to be "addressed" to him? In fact, Kruppenbach is serenely *un-*
concerned with Rabbit and strictly concerned with Eccles, for he says,
"I've listened to your story but I wasn't listening to what it said about
the people, I was listening to what it said about you" (170/146). Fur-
thermore, one of the hallmarks of Rabbit's claim as an Updikean hero
is the way in which he demonstrates, by his own example, the specialness of each person: in this respect, *he* becomes the preacher Kruppenbach evokes in his peroration. Ultimately, Hunt wants to make Kruppenbach the novel's "main beam" because doing so allows him to usher
into his reading Barth's argument for the centrality of Christ to human
salvation, an issue which Updike otherwise does not address in *Rabbit,
Run.*

So although Kruppenbach's sermon has a Barthian source, it does not
serve as a plea for Christian salvation. Rather, it serves as a clue to how
we might respond to Eccles as a minister. To be sure, Updike has borrowed Barth's concept of the *creatio ex nihilo* and his Wholly Other God,
but he has adapted them to his own ends. He is not, as a result, Barth's
mouthpiece. Even so, the novel might be read as a "religious address"
along the lines laid out in the Kierkegaard passage quoted above—insofar as a "religious address" is understood to invoke Socratic irony and
to address inwardness. We have seen how, via the episode with Jimmy
the Mousketeer, Updike invokes the "ironic method," and we have also
addressed the centrality of subjectivity to the novel's narrative voice.
Now, as we turn to the final section of *Rabbit, Run*—which deals with
the death of the Angstroms' baby and its shattering aftermath—we will

40. Kierkgaard, *Concluding Unscientific Postscript*, 538.
41. See Hunt, *Three Great Secret Things*, 42–44.

see how these two ideas, irony and inwardness, merge with one last Kierkegaardian concept already touched upon, ontological guilt, to produce a conclusion that disturbs both in its narrative content and its unsettling ambiguity.

IV. Infant Death and the Wholly Other God

As we have seen, guilt for both Kierkegaard and Updike is, like anxiety, an ontological category, an essential part of our being that has no specific referent outside itself—or us. Kierkegaard later calls guilt a "totality-category," as well as "the expression for the strongest self-assertion of existence." These ideas make sense if we remember that ontological guilt in Kierkegaard's conception is tantamount to "self-responsibility." Self-responsibility therefore inspires willful self-assertion. Updike seems to have something similar in mind when he champions Harry's hardness of heart. Rather than indicate moral passivity, Updike's serene tolerance of cruelty represents a crucial component of his ethical vision. He actively affirms his characters' right to act unethically—their *need* to act unethically. There is nothing passive or callously self-justifying about it at all. Such acts affirm for Updike not only the necessary "contempt for the world" posited by faith in the first place but also contempt for, as he puts it, "attempts to locate salvation and perfection here. The world is fallen, and in a fallen world animals and men and nations make space for themselves through a willingness to fight." Via sin, his characters disclose their "creaturely reality," their freedom. In fact, the two concepts, guilt and freedom, function as contingent ideas that constitute one more inextricable yes/no. Kierkegaard maps out the relationship between these two concepts most succinctly in Volume II of *Either/Or:* "The greater the freedom the greater the guilt, and this is one of the secrets of blessedness, and if it be not cowardice, it is at least faint-heartedness not to be willing to repent the guilt of the forefathers; if not paltriness, it is at least pettiness and lack of magnanimity."[42] By "guilt of the forefathers" Kierkegaard means hereditary guilt, or what we have

---

42. Kierkegaard, *Concluding Unscientific Postscript,* 528; Updike, *Self-Consciousness,* 130; Kierkegaard, *Either/Or,* 222.

been calling ontological guilt. In the episodes relating to the death of the baby Becky—perhaps the most shocking and heartbreaking incident in his entire oeuvre—Updike explores the ramifications this hereditary guilt has on the two-part process of assigning blame and receiving forgiveness.

He foreshadows Becky's death some seventy pages before the death itself. Significantly, this foreshadowing occurs during the scene in which Rabbit sexually humiliates Ruth. His demand that she fellate him arises from his sense, late in their affair, that "a wall" has come between him: "this" he says, "is the one way through it" (187/160). Ever the pragmatist, Ruth sneers back, "That's pretty cute. You just want it, really." He is still learning that sex only promises a passage through the wall of flesh and into the subjectivity of the other. He has yet to accept the cold truth that it actually leads to nothing, to the nothing that Ruth believes in and the nothing from whence the Barthian creaturely reality emerges. Ruth's and Rabbit's first sexual encounter directly evokes Barth's *creatio ex nihilo,* for Ruth gets pregnant. Their final tryst, however, undertaken in desperation and conflict, flips the coin of that nothing to reveal its other side—that is, the nothing to which creaturely reality tends. *"I've killed her,"* Rabbit thinks afterward, looking down at Ruth as he tries to process the news that his wife has just had his baby. "It's ridiculous," he thinks to himself, "such a thing wouldn't kill her, it has nothing to do with death; but the thought paralyzes him" (192/165). Later, while in the hospital waiting room, he observes that his lust has been little more than a "sequence of grotesque poses assumed to no purpose, a magic dance draining him of belief. *There is no God; Janice can die:* the two thoughts come at once, in a slow wave. He feels underwater, caught in the chains of transparent slime, ghosts of the urgent ejaculations he has spat into the mild bodies of women" (198/170). Throughout *Rabbit Angstrom* Updike employs water as the figurative element of death, an association made specific by baby Becky's drowning. By the same token, it is also a figure for the *nihil* from which creation emerges. It is the element of the womb, so to speak, and hence an intimate component of Updike's complex symbolic network of sex and death. Accordingly, Ruth's morning sickness comes to her as "the taste of seawater in her mouth" (192/165).

From sex and death Updike moves immediately to sex and death and guilt. As Rabbit rushes to the hospital to see his new daughter, he feels "certain that as a consequence of his sin Janice or the baby will die" (196/169). What sin, precisely? Apparently all of them, all at once: "His sin a conglomerate of flight, cruelty, obscenity, and conceit; a black clot embodied in the entrails of the birth" (197/169). The image is a striking one, literalizing as it does the Pelagian doctrine that original sin is transmitted through the generations via the reproductive process. For Updike, this explanation for original, or hereditary, sin, monstrous though it seems, is an inescapable fact of existence. Otherwise, as his character Roger Lambert explains, "the world isn't truly fallen, and there's no need for Redemption, there's no Christian story." Yet we have already seen that Rabbit, upon first viewing his daughter, reads in her closed eyelids a solemn conviction that "she knows she is good." How can Updike unite these two opposing doctrines? Dialectically. According to the image above, original sin, a "black clot" attached to the "entrails of birth," is intimately bound up with sexuality and carnality, both of which serve as paths to the nothing. Because the body dies, the body must carry the burden of corruption and guilt. It must fight for its survival amid the fallen outer world that has emerged from nothing. The subjective self, on the other hand, particularly the subjective self in repose, is blithely innocent. Describing the pleasures of being sheltered from an outside rainstorm, Updike writes:

> Early in his life the child I once was sensed the guilt in all things, inseparable from the pain, the competition: the sparrow dead on the lawn, the flies swatting on the porch, the impervious leer of the bully on the school playground. The burden of activity must be shouldered, and has its pleasures. But they are cruel pleasures. There was nothing cruel about crouching in a shelter and letting phenomena slide by: it was ecstasy. The essential self is innocent, and when it tastes its own innocence knows that it lives forever. If we keep utterly still, we can suffer no wear and tear, and will never die.[43]

Updike marks an irreconcilable split between the fallenness of the outer world and its ceaseless activity—a world whose actions are best controlled by policemen, lawyers, and doctors—and the essential inno-

43. Updike, *Roger's Version*, 187–88; Updike, *Self-Consciousness*, 35.

cence of inwardness, the seat of faith and the site of Rabbit's own claim to goodness, an innocence which both objects and people at rest affirm.

So Rabbit's conviction that the baby will die "as a consequence of his sin" is both accurate and elusive. His own original sin, passed down to Becky via the reproductive process, is, metaphorically at least, the "cause" of her death. Does it also follow, however, that Becky will die as a consequence of some specific sin of Rabbit's? The actions leading up to her drowning seem to suggest as much. First, after a service at Rev. Eccles's church, Rabbit makes the arrogant assumption that Lucy Eccles has made him a proposition. Although he is forcefully spurned, he nevertheless "reaches his apartment clever and *cold* with lust" (243/208, emphasis added). Back at home his lust, which he transfers to Janice, becomes "a small angel to which all afternoon lead weights are attached" (243/208). This angel of lust, cold and clever, hovers over the apartment with such persistence that even the baby comprehends its presence: "The baby squawks tirelessly. It lies in its crib all afternoon and makes an infuriating noise of strain, *hnnnnnnah ah ah nnnnh*, a persistent feeble scratching at some interior door" (243/208). Meanwhile Rabbit, himself no stranger to instinctive knowledge, imagines the baby is trying to warn him and Janice of a "threat," of a "shadow invisible to their better-formed senses." In bed with Janice, Rabbit persists with his confused sexual impulse, yet with a change, for after three months with Ruth he has finally begun to appreciate the basic earthbound carnality of sex. It is a trick of Nature with nothing at the end. But in his single-minded effort to get *past* the act, to get past the grip his lust seems to have on him, he offends Janice, whom he makes feel cheap. Aware of this, he tries to rationalize his selfish pursuit, the same way he tried to rationalize his lust for Ruth by framing it as some sort of quasi-religious experience: "[Janice] exaggerates its importance, has imagined it into something rare and precious she's entitled to half of when all he wants is to get rid of it so he can move on, on into sleep, down the straight path, for her sake. It's for her sake" (248/213). Although later he admits that "she was in the right for once and he was wrong and stupid," he clings to his original interpretation and persists. Rightly spurned by Janice—his second rejection that day—he runs again.

At this point, the perspective shifts to Janice. In the second of the novel's two "female soliloquies"—both of which at times read like parodies of the "Penelope" episode from *Ulysses,* as Updike himself admits with a kind of squeamish embarrassment—we follow Janice through the harrowing, drunken evening and morning during which she accidentally drowns her own infant daughter. Here the narrative's causal chain begins to unravel. Certainly Rabbit's abrupt, childish exit inspires Janice's drinking, yet is it the *cause?* Or is the cause Janice's own drunkenness—which, of course, also precipitated Rabbit's first childish exit? Or are both to blame? Her own mother hints at this latter possibility. When Janice accidentally reveals to her that Rabbit has left again, Mrs. Springer snaps, "The first time I thought it was all his fault but I'm not so sure any more. Do you hear? I'm not so sure" (262/224). Moreover, although Rabbit seems to have brought home from church the threat that keeps Becky crying all day, the threat does not leave with him. It stays behind in the apartment, terrifying Janice: "But something whose presence she feels on the wrinkled bed frightens her so that she draws back and goes into the other room to be with the children" (257/220). What's more, she feels convinced that this threat, this "other person," is distinct from her husband: "There *is* another person in the apartment she knows but it's not Harry and the person has no business here anyway" (261/223). This "other person" clearly refers to the "small angel" of lust whose presence so disturbed Becky and Nelson. And it is this same "small angel" who reaches up through the bath water and takes Becky away, an angel summoned by both of them in their reckless disregard.

But who, exactly, *is* this "other person"? Janice provides a confusing hint as she clutches the water-logged corpse of her infant daughter: "she seems to be clasping the knees of a vast third person whose name, Father, Father, beats against her head like physical blows" (265/226). Is it God, then? Yes, if we keep in mind that Updike's creator God is also, dialectically, the God of death. But if we also heed the argument of the novel, we see that nearly everyone else in the novel is to blame, as well. The book's final thirty pages read like a litany of blame. Lucy Eccles is the first character to point the finger at Harry when she tells her husband, "Well, he as good as did [it]. Runs off and sends his idiot wife on a bender. You never should have brought them back together" (267/228). Interpreting this as an accusation leveled at him, Eccles asks her: "So you're saying I really killed the baby?" Though she denies implying any such thing, he nevertheless concedes, "No. I think you're probably right." Indeed, when Rabbit calls him moments later, Eccles breaks the news of Becky's death by saying, "A terrible thing has happened to *us*" (269/230, emphasis added). Even Mr. Springer, while talking to Harry at the hospital, admits that he, too, must shoulder some of the responsibility: "I won't say I don't blame you because of course I do. But you're not the only one to blame. Her mother and I somehow never made her feel secure" (274/234). Finally, in one of the book's most chilling moments, Rabbit returns to his apartment to find that the water in which Becky had drowned is still in the tub. Reaching down to pull the plug he "thinks how easy it was, yet in all His strength God did nothing. Just that little rubber stopper to lift" (277/237). So even God, that majestic, implacable Other, is to blame.

Here we see revealed that tendency in Updike that Ralph Wood characterized as the novelist's "reluctance to find fault and assess blame, his conviction that our lives are shaped by forces too vast for mere mortals to master." Regarding this feature of Updike's vision theologically, Wood ruefully concludes that Updike's work evinces a "tragic pessimism" that makes him "ambivalent about every moral reality."[44] In place of Updike's Wholly Other God Wood seems to ask for an active, incarnate deity who would give divine sanction to the world's "necessary social restraints." To be sure, a God like Updike's—one who, in remaining aloof from the human world, will not, and indeed cannot, even so much as lift his divine finger to unplug a bathtub stopper in order to save a drowning baby—is quite nearly tantamount to no God at all. Most of Updike's theologically minded critics—Hunt among them— arrive at this same conclusion, for which they find Updike wanting as a member of their party. Having caught wind that Updike is a self-proclaimed Christian, priests and other fellow believers have gone to his work expecting confirmation of their positivistic, God-ordered moral vision, only to encounter a dialectical anti-theology that borders on existential atheism. Yet this same rumor of faith has kept at bay readings that would connect Updike with those contemporary novelists whose vision is grounded—or is perhaps ungrounded—in an abiding sense of the world's godless absurdity. The best assessment of this strange

44. Wood, *Comedy,* 190.

predicament with the critics still belongs to Updike himself, who says, "There's a . . . quality about my writing that evades entirely pleasing anybody." It is precisely in such sections as this final movement of *Rabbit, Run* that Updike resoundingly fails to please the theologians on his side. It is also here that he most overtly connects with the novelists of his generation from whom his Christian faith would seem to alienate him.

As an inevitable product of the reconstructing imagination, the Judeo-Christian reading of history corresponds to the vision of reality presented in most preterit novels of the Western canon. William Spanos describes this vision as the "monolithic certainty that immediate psychic or historical experience is part of a comforting, even exciting and suspenseful well-made cosmic drama or novel, more particularly, a detective story." Like the Christian view of history, the detective novel presupposes that "an acute and all-encompassing 'eye,' private or otherwise, can solve the crime with resounding finality by inferring causal relationships between clues that point to it." On the other hand, the ostensibly "postmodern" novelists that Spanos champions—writers working in the wake of the various aporias in Newton's Universe enacted by everyone from Einstein to Derrida—refuse, in his words, "to fulfill causal expectations, to provide 'solutions' for the 'crime' of existence." Although freely admitting that such disruptive narrative strategies date back, at least, to Euripides' *Orestes,* Spanos nevertheless insists that only the postmodern novelists of the current era fully recognize the futility of Western man's "obsessive perception of the universe as a well-made fiction." By equating the standard linear plot of Western fiction with, on one hand, the Judeo-Christian reading of history and, on the other hand, the conventions of the detective story, Spanos offers a useful model for understanding the epistemological assumptions behind what he would term the "traditional literature of closure."[45] Perhaps unwittingly, he also offers an equally useful model for understanding John Updike's own distrust of these same epistemological assumptions. What Updike's theologically preoccupied readers have called his "moral passivity," his "ethical quietism," and his "deep tragic pessimism" turns out to be the product of a fierce distrust of the positivistic assumptions of

45. William Spanos, *Repetitions,* 18, 19, 21.

not only the Judeo-Christian historical narrative but also the traditional literary plot as well. Here more than in any other single aspect of his
work, Updike splits with the "traditional" novelists of whom he is supposed to serve as an exemplar.

In fact, what few—if any—of Updike's critics have seemed to notice
is that *Rabbit, Run* quite deliberately becomes, in its final fifty pages, a
sort of anti–murder mystery. In structuring his narrative in such a way
as to disrupt the identifiable causal chain of events leading to the baby's
death, Updike does more than demonstrate a mere "reluctance to assess
blame"—if indeed he does that at all. The narrative also questions those
received methods of assessing blame, all of them, Updike wants us to
realize, products of hindsight. The novel's present tense mode is one aspect of this questioning process. God's interaction with human affairs—
the whole Christian machinery of providence and fate—is, as Updike
clearly realizes, a narrative, a fiction imposed in retrospect upon events
that, as they occur, seem to unravel utterly at random. As a nameless fear
of the unknown, anxiety is the living condition of the now, for at any
given moment we *do not know what is coming next.* That in part explains
what Cary means when he speaks of the present tense as giving to a
reader "that sudden feeling of insecurity . . . which comes to a traveler
who is bushed in unmapped country." By his use of the present tense,
Updike is able to suggest the absence of a Guiding Hand—which is
markedly different from the Understanding Eye which views, blesses,
but does not act. In fact, in his introduction to *Rabbit Angstrom,* he
speaks not only of the "muffling hand" the traditional past tense "lays
on every action," but also of the "purged space" opened up by the present tense. Within this purged space actions seem to occur as they do in
"life," at the cusp of chaos, without rhyme or reason. Rabbit leaves, Janice gets drunk: these two factors precipitate the death, yet are they the
cause of it? Not overtly. Rather, the accident just "happens." But Updike does not stop there. To his unblinking eye, if such accidents are allowed to occur then God is either responsible or absolved. If responsible, then such a God is hardly worthy of worship; if absolved, then there
is no way to accept the Judeo-Christian view of history which posits a
God who directs events toward a final, eschatological denouement. The
only way for Updike to honor the complexity and seeming randomness
of reality while at the same time holding to his faith in a creator God is

to displace that God entirely. God becomes responsible by his inaction, for only in this way, in Updike's view, can that God be allowed freely to exist.

But the novel does not end with this paradoxical blaming-and-absolution of God. Left alone in this God-created yet curiously God-abandoned universe, Updike's characters must face the ramifications of the mess they have both inherited and made. Harry's old coach, Marty Tothero—whose name Hunt has helpfully glossed as "dead (*Tod*) hero"—provides perhaps the novel's final word on the inescapable construct-edness of earthbound ethics. Though something of a buffoon—Uphaus calls him "an old man trying to recapture his youth"[46]—Tothero nev-ertheless counts as one of Updike' s lovers and life-givers, even though his capacity in this regard has been considerably vitiated. Rabbit likes him because, next to his own mother, "Tothero had the most *force*"(17/17), while Tothero himself thinks that he and Harry are "two of a kind" (49/44). Tothero's coaching strategy, moreover, aligns him more with a Kruppenbach than an Eccles, for as Tothero puts it, a good coach has his most "solemn opportunity" in developing the hearts of his players: "Give the boys the will to achieve. I've always liked that better than the will to win, for there can be achievement even in defeat. Make them feel the, yes, I think the word is good, the *sacredness* of achievement, in the form of giving our best" (62/54–55). So Tothero's is a reliable voice, and never more so than when, late in the novel, he warns Rabbit, "Right and wrong aren't dropped from the sky. We. We make them. Against misery. Invariably, Harry, invariably . . . misery follows their disobedi-ence. Not our own, often at first not our own. Now you've had an ex-ample of that in your own life" (280/240). Although Rabbit resists this truth at first—he "wants to believe in the sky as the source of all dic-tates" (281/241)[47]—Tothero undoubtedly speaks for Updike here, of-fering perhaps one of the most succinct formulations of Updike's own feelings about ethics. In his view, we make our way as best we can in a fallen world where even the checks we develop against chaos are in

46. Suzanne Uphaus, *John Updike*, 20.
47. The original 1960 edition reads "he wants to believe in the sky as the source of all *things*"(emphasis added). With this new revision, Updike makes overt his se-vere distinction between the essential goodness of created "things" and the inher-ently human and therefore fallible nature of moral precepts ("dictates").

themselves as fallible as the people who created them. Roger Lambert, another of Updike's Barthian mouthpieces, frames the issue similarly: "[T]he world is mired in sin. In this mire we try to determine the lesser of available evil. We try to choose, and take the consequences." Only faith can save us from that "pit of horror" that is the natural order. As Updike admitted early in his career, "I believe that all problems are basically insoluble and that faith is a leap out of total despair."[48]

The novel's disturbing ending, then, emerges from this irritating unwillingness to offer any simple resolution, be it Christian or nihilist. Despite the numerous assignations of blame sprinkled throughout the final pages of the novel, Rabbit alone understands that his own guilt is, to quote Updike, "insoluble." When he asks Eccles how he can ever receive forgiveness, the minister typically misinterprets Rabbit's question, thinking Rabbit is referring simply to the incident at hand. Eccles's answer reveals his characteristic earthly perspective: "Do what you are doing. . . . Be a good husband. Love what you have left" (281/241). Though Rabbit "clings" to this advice, he nevertheless recognizes that it bears "no relation to the colors and sounds of the big sorrowing house" (282/241). It is not, in other words, enough. Such forgiveness can only come from above. Rabbit begins to realize this inevitable fact just before the funeral when, viewing his reflection, he thinks of himself as "a smudge on the glass. He wonders why the universe doesn't just erase a thing so dirty and small" (288/247). With this realization, Rabbit accepts not only the inevitability of his guilt but also his helplessness in the face of the divine. Later, at the funeral home, he has a related moment of metaphysical terror in which he finally confronts the finality of his daughter's death. Diving "deeper and deeper into the limitless volume of his loss," Rabbit realizes that he will "never see her marbled skin again, never cup her faint weight in his arms again," and so on. He realizes that "the word never stops, there is never a gap in its thickness" (293/251).

As we have already seen, in Updike's universe such a realization of cosmic helplessness marks the moment when grace can arrive, for only in the face of despair can the absurd possibility of repetition seem palpable. At the funeral home, Rabbit alone is able to feel the possibility of

---

48. Updike, *Roger's Version*, 187; Updike, "Nice Novelist," 14.

the eternal life promised in Eccles's eulogy. Only he has properly reached the bottom from which he can be pulled only with help from above. Though Eccles does not believe the words he utters, he speaks directly to Rabbit when, at the funeral itself, he asks God to "[g]ive us the Grace . . . to entrust the soul of this child to thy never-failing care and love," to which Rabbit thinks, "Yes. That's how it is" (295/252). As the scene around him becomes in his ecstatic vision of divine forgiveness one vast vale of death—the "heads as still . . . as tombstones" amid the company of the "undertaker's men"—he recalls Eccles's line, "Casting every care on thee," and looks up: "The sky greets him. A strange strength sinks down into him. It is as if he has been crawling in a cave and now at last beyond the dark recession of crowding rocks he has seen a patch of light" (295/253). Like those headlights that appear on the dark road earlier in the novel, light appears to Rabbit again with the promise of repetition. His ontological guilt is expiated.

What Rabbit does with this knowledge is undoubtedly shocking and unnerving. Having been forgiven, he imagines himself free of the delicate causal chain that has tied him to the death of his daughter. The death now takes shape in his mind in all its simplicity, and he sees it finally for what it is. Becky's drowning is a horrifying accident that, like most such horrors, cannot be mitigated by human atonement, but it is also a product of all that guilt-laden activity that Updike, in his memoir, associates with pain and competition, and which encompasses both "the sparrow dead on the lawn" and "the impervious leer of the bully." When Rabbit turns to Janice, he realizes that she has not arrived at this same realization, and so, in exasperation, he abruptly snaps, "I didn't kill her" (295/253). To compound the apparent callousness of this scene, Updike has Rabbit add, "You all keep acting as if *I* did it. I wasn't anywhere near. *She's* the one" (296/253). Here Rabbit wants the members of this congregation to know that their earthbound interpretation of the event's complex causal chain—a chain which, as we have seen, links Rabbit himself—does not necessarily square with his spiritual interpretation of the same. According to the latter, Rabbit *is* guilty, but only obliquely through the agency of Original Sin, that "black clot" attached to the "entrails of birth." At the same time, such guilt implicates everyone gathered at the funeral. In dialectical opposition to this version of the tragedy stand the hard, nominal facts: Janice dropped the baby in the water, which, by the implacable laws of physical reality, resulted in death. Rabbit's ecstatic vision of the sky's "greeting" makes manifest to him this hard distinction between spiritual and physical law. By realizing his helplessness in the face of his own Original Sin, he has been forgiven for his spiritual part in the death. Once he has separated the metaphysical dimension of the accident from the concrete facts, Rabbit understands clearly his part in the physical act itself. He was nowhere near that bathtub. Astonishingly, this same spiritual truth Rabbit hopes to impart to Janice when he announces to all assembled, *"She's* the one." Although Janice *was* in fact "there," her part in the death does not necessarily constitute her "guilt." Rather, she was merely one element in a string of physical events that God, in his Wholly Other indifference, let unwind. That is what Rabbit tries to explain when he takes Janice's hand and adds, "Hey it's O.K. . . . You didn't mean to" (296/253). He tells Janice, in effect, "Yes, you were the one who dropped her in that tub, but that's not why you're guilty. You're guilty for other reasons, and I now know how you can find forgiveness."

But this final consoling gesture fails, as it must. Unable to make clear to those around him this inward, ethical truth, he finds himself the still center of a shocked gathering. Although "forgiveness had been big in his heart," he now knows he has mis-stepped (296/253). Properly humiliated, Rabbit takes off again, this time, in a parody of Christ's forty-day fast in the wilderness, up the mountain that separates Mt. Judge and Brewer. Finally, Rabbit has moved into the middle across which he has been zigzagging for the duration of the whole novel. But this middle is no comfort either, for here he is struck by the terrifying fact of his dialectical situation: "he obscurely feels lit by a great spark, the spark whereby the blind tumble of matter recognized itself, a spark struck in the collision of two opposed realms, an encounter a terrible God willed" (299/256). The two realms are the realm of life and its dark underside, death. His own existence is little more than a "spark," albeit a "great" one, created by the friction of these two realms and willed into existence by Updike's "terrible" creator God. Armed with this insight, Rabbit, true to form, retreats, another zigzag.

Back on solid ground, he finds he has no new answers—except perhaps one. Because the dialectic he confronted at the top of the mountain has no resolution, he is left once again with his fluctuating inner certainty. "Goodness lies inside," he reasons, "there is nothing outside, those things he was trying to balance have no weight" (308/264). Yet even that inner goodness, that inner certainty, might not be enough in a world where most problems are insoluble. Only now does Rabbit begin to realize this. After Ruth informs him that she is pregnant, for instance, he tries to convince her to keep the baby, though he cannot explain why she should. "All I know is what feels right. You feel right to me sometimes, Sometimes Janice used to. Sometimes nothing does" (306/262). As Ruth has understood all along, nothingness is also a possibility. What's more, even his precious subjectivity, the only thing Rabbit truly *knows*, is itself subject to the something-versus-nothing dialectic he encountered on that mountain. Evoking yet another basketball analogy, Rabbit experiences this final, perplexing realization:

> He feels his inside as very real suddenly, a pure blank space in the middle of a dense net. *I don't know,* he kept telling Ruth; he doesn't know, what to do, where to go, what will happen, the thought that he doesn't know seems to make him infinitely small and impossible to capture. Its smallness fills him like a vastness. It's like when they heard you were great and put two men on you and no matter which way you turned you bumped into one of them and the only thing to do was pass. So you passed and the ball belonged to the others and your hands were empty and the men on you looked foolish because in effect *there was nobody there.* (308/264, emphasis added)

Passing the ball, like "casting every care" on God, is a gesture of faith, a recognition of despair in the face of irreconcilable conflict. Yet whereas at the funeral Rabbit feels that such a gesture can save him, here he recognizes that it also erases him. Between these two poles—the yes and the no, the either and the or—the self is both something and nothing.

Here Updike spectacularly brings to a culmination his strategy of mastered irony. Like the Socratic irony of Kierkegaard's early work, *Rabbit, Run* does not end in "the immediate unity of what was said" but rather in a "constant ebb." Yet this constant ebb, in both Socrates and Updike, possesses forward movement, heads somewhere, much like the image of the zigzag that controls the novel. And that forward movement finally reaches its end right here—in nothing, with nobody. The promise of resolution has been shown to lead to nothing. Similarly, Kierkegaard writes of Socrates, "The more Socrates undermined existence, the deeper and more necessarily must each particular utterance gravitate towards that ironical totality which, as a spiritual state, is bottomless, invisible, and indivisible." Kierkegaard explains what he means by describing an engraving of Napoleon's grave. In the engraving, Napoleon is absent. He is evoked, rather, by the negative space created by two overshadowing trees. Only the contour of Napoleon's image is discernible. "Napoleon himself appears out of the nothingness, and now it is impossible to make him disappear." Socratic irony operates the same way, Kierkegaard argues: "As one sees the trees, so one hears his discourse; as the trees are trees, so his words mean exactly what they sound like. There is not a single syllable to give hint of another interpretation, just as there is not a single brush stroke to suggest Napoleon. Yet it is this empty space, this nothingness, that is most important."[49] Socrates, practicing "inclosing reserve," resides in that empty space, while the discourse that ironically represents his genuine thinking can only lead to the absence that is in fact "the most important" part of the discourse as a whole. Confronted with that nothingness, that absence, the reader is left with little recourse but to turn back and, to requote Diem, "to work out the ideality of his own existence."

Rabbit, Run ends in just such an empty space. Readers who come to this ending hoping to nail down Rabbit, to find out, finally, who he is and what his story is supposed to reveal, find themselves in the same position as those players on the basketball court who are left foolishly to guard the star player who not only does not have the ball anymore but who also, in effect, is not there at all. Lest readers miss this point, Updike ends the novel by having Rabbit run away once again—this time, however, from the reader. The conflicts raised in the book are deliberately left unresolved so that Rabbit can maintain the spark that lies within and which, to the outside observer, is as elusive as physical proof of God's existence. Any more resolution than this must take place within the individual reader.

49. All quotations from Kierkegaard, *Concept of Irony,* 56.

Two

Rabbit Redux
The Doorway into Utter Confusion

> Civilization only produces a greater variety of sensations
> in man—and absolutely nothing more. And through
> the development of this variety, man may even come to
> find enjoyment in bloodshed.
> —Fyodor Dostoevsky, *Notes from Underground*

If the central thematic conflict of *Rabbit, Run* is freedom versus domesticity, then the corresponding conflict of *Rabbit Redux* is its more
sociopolitical counterpart, revolution versus preservation. What was
private in the first volume becomes public in its sequel, as Rabbit's quest
for freedom's possibility gets taken up by the 1960s mass culture. "You
know," Rabbit tells Charlie Stavros, Janice's lover and one of the novel's
numerous swingers, "you're just like me, the way I used to be. Everybody now is like the way I used to be" (182/422). *Used to be* is the key,
for in the intervening ten years Rabbit has radically changed, not so
much with the times as in stubborn opposition to them. The restless
proto-beatnik who, in *Rabbit, Run*, tries to rid himself of the death-
evoking chains of middle-class Eisenhower-era husbandhood becomes,
in *Rabbit Redux*, a staunchly conservative "family man" and "responsible citizen" of the lurid air-conditioned suburban landscape of the late
1960s. The world that Rabbit once knew has been turned upside down
so completely that Updike, in order to maintain the dialectical equilib-

rium that is the hallmark of his vision, must turn his hero upside down as well, just to right the balance. In this and in many other ways, *Rabbit Redux* serves as *Rabbit, Run*'s thematic negative, as the "No" to *Run*'s "Yes," the diffident "or" to *Run*'s ambiguous "either." "[I]n a way they look at each other," Updike has remarked of the two novels, "they seem to me to make almost a set."[1]

Extraordinarily, changed though he seems to be, Harry remains absolutely consistent over the course of these two yin-and-yang novels. Updike has imagined Rabbit so deeply and thoroughly that he can transform his character from restless seeker to sedentary reactionary without altering Rabbit's basic character. In fact, by making the Rabbit of the sixties the polar opposite of the Rabbit of the fifties, Updike does more than maintain the tidy dialectical strategy that governed *Rabbit, Run* and, beginning with *Redux*, will govern the development of the rest of tetralogy. He also endows Rabbit with the one unchanging personality trait that will keep his hero both spiritually vital and artistically useful for the next two decades—incorrigibility. Speaking with great passionate bravado in his introduction to *Rabbit Angstrom*, Updike employs this latter term in its most Dostoevskyan sense: "Rabbit is, like the Underground Man, *incorrigible;* from first to last he bridles at good advice, taking direction only from his personal, also incorrigible God" (xxii). In the Eisenhower world of *Rabbit, Run*, the prevailing good advice demanded that Rabbit return to his family and shoulder the burden of domesticity. He bridled. By 1969, the year depicted in *Rabbit Redux*, the prevailing good advice has taken a 180-degree turn. Yet rather than treat the battle-cry *Tune in! Drop out! Turn on!* as a sign of victory, Rabbit treats it as pretty much more of the same old song, only in a different key. The problem lies less with the message of these overriding cultural attitudes than with their mere condition *as* overriding cultural attitudes. In Rabbit's world, both good and bad advice suffer from their being advice period. Good advice is the hobgoblin retreat of the self-alienated aesthete. Rabbit, the self-interested ethicist, listens only to the dictates of his "personal, incorrigible God." That is why Rabbit's sixties' conservatism represents such a happy discovery on Updike's part, for it provided him with a simple rule of thumb that would guide him through

---

1. Campbell, *Thorns Spell A Word*, 285.

two more novels: whatever everyone else is for, Rabbit must be against, and whatever everyone is against, Rabbit must be for. In the fifties it is domesticity (Rabbit runs), in the sixties it is freedom (Rabbit resists), in the seventies it is entropy and decadence (Rabbit gets rich), and in the eighties it is greed (Rabbit gives up). As early as *Rabbit, Run* Harry determines, "Everybody who tells you how to act has whisky on their breath" (29/26), while thirty years and more than a thousand pages later, he finds occasion to remark to his granddaughter, "Whenever somebody tells me to do something my instinct's always to do the opposite. It's got me into a lot of trouble, but I've had a lot of fun" (*Rest* 22/1068). In each case Rabbit asserts his independence of prevailing norms, his serene immunity to good advice, and his irrational right to demand, like Dostoevsky's spiteful hero, that two times two equals five, if that is what his will so desires.

The connections between Rabbit and Dostoevsky's Underground Man deserve further exploration, for nowhere in *Rabbit Angstrom* are these connections more overt than in *Rabbit Redux*, the tetralogy's darkest, most lurid—and hence, most Dostoevskyan—section. Dostoevsky wrote *Notes from Underground* partly as a response to *What Is to Be Done?*, Nikolai Chernyshevsky's famous (and famously bad) polemical novel of those other turbulent sixties, the *1860s*. Intoxicated by the utilitarian ideals of New Enlightenment thinkers as diverse as Charles Fourier and John Stuart Mill, Chernyshevsky used the novel to promote his vision of a perfectly rational society in which human desire corresponds directly with sound, practical, and enlightened self-interest. Near the end of the novel the heroine, Víera Pavlona, has a Utopian vision of a great Crystal Palace overlooking a field harvested entirely by machines: "The men have scarcely more to do than look on, drive and manage the machines, and how well everything is arranged for themselves! . . . How can they help working quickly and gayly? How can they help singing?"[2] All the principal characters in *What Is to Be Done?* cannot help singing, so happy and sustained are they in Chernyshevsky's perfect, utilitarian society.

With great enthusiasm and aplomb, Dostoevsky attacks this guileless, sentimental trust in scientific progress. What seems most to infu-

2. Nikolai Chernyshevsky, *What Is to Be Done?* 379–80.

riate Dostoevsky is Chernyshevsky's naive utilitarian faith in "enlight-ened self-interest," that cherished nineteenth-century belief that "not a single man can knowingly act to his own disadvantage." In response to this dogmatic assumption, the Underground Man asks, *"What is to be done* with the millions of facts that bear witness that men, *knowingly,* that is, fully understanding their real advantages, have left them in the background and have rushed headlong on another path, to risk, to chance, compelled to this course by nobody and nothing, but, as it were, precisely because they did not want the beaten track, and stubbornly, willfully, went off on another difficult, absurd way seeking it almost in darkness. After all, it means that this stubbornness and willfulness were more pleasant to them than any advantages" (first emphasis added). In a sense, *Notes from Underground* reads like an extended paean to "stubbornness and willfulness," to humankind's urge, capacity, and even need to do exactly as it pleases, against all better judgment. Such stubbornness is necessary for Dostoevsky primarily because the alternative, presented by the likes of Chernyshevsky as the long-awaited fruits of progress, is even more terrifying: namely, the loss of individuality. The Underground Man affirms a man's right to "desire what is injurious to himself" in order to preserve "what is most precious and most important—that is, our personality, our individuality." And this individuality takes precedence over any abstraction that would limit it. Hence the Underground Man lavishes scorn upon every conclusion about human nature set forth by rationalism and scientific determinism, abstract ideas that would reduce humankind to a mere component in a vast natural system—or, in his terms, would try to transform a human being into "something like a piano key or an organ stop." So urgent is this need to resist being made into an "organ stop" that the Underground Man is moved at one point to declare, "Why, one may choose what is contrary to one's interests, and sometimes one *positively ought to* (that is my idea)." In 1945, amid the horrors of Hitler's Europe, Thomas Mann remarked that the Underground Man's theories seemed like "hazardous talk," suggesting as they do that man "really does not want the crystal palace . . . and that he will never renounce his predilection for destruction and chaos." And yet, Mann is forced to add, "those heresies are the truth: the dark side of truth, away from the sun, which no one dares to neglect who is interested in the truth, the whole truth, truth about man."[3] Whereas Chernyshevsky presumes that man's predilection for destruction and chaos can be eradicated through progress, Dostoevsky insists that this predilection, however distasteful, must be embraced. That, essentially, is the dark, the whole dark truth, about man.

It is also the dark truth that activates *Rabbit Redux,* a novel that, in its thematizing of the NASA moon shot and the Civil Rights movement of the 1960s, explores darkness in all its ramifications. As a novel of the sixties, it stands almost alone as the sole attempt to depict the tumult of the era as it happened in contemporary American culture. While Norman Mailer took on Vietnam via oblique Faulknerian allegory (*Why Are We in Vietnam?*) and Philip Roth parodied the sexual revolution in the form of extended Lenny Bruce gags (*Portnoy's Complaint),* the other famed writers of the era—John Barth, Thomas Pynchon, John Hawkes, and others—busied themselves with self-referential fabulations. Although Saul Bellow, Joyce Carol Oates, and Bernard Malamud joined Updike in chronicling the decade's turmoil, even these writers did not match Updike's immersion in, and his engagement with, the era's spectacular disarray. Unfashionable at the time of its publication by virtue of its up-to-the-minute timeliness, *Rabbit Redux* must now be regarded as one of the most important documents we have of that overdocumented time, a brilliant and focused portrait unmarred by sentimentalism or shortsightedness. Updike looked out the window and called it as he saw it, and history has largely borne him out. To be sure, the novel does not paint a very rosy picture, but then again, the sixties could not have been a rosy time for such a hard-hearted realist as John Updike, with his fallen world and his implacable Barthian God. To Updike's way of thinking, the great liberatory dreams of the decade were fatally undermined by Chernyshevskyan naïveté—with a difference, of course. Instead of asking, as Chernyshevsky did, *what is to be done?,* Updike's social determinists of the American 1960s ask, "Why not?" The question is, Rabbit decides, the "[c]hief question facing these troubled times" (163/406). And *Rabbit Redux* is Updike's dark answer to that question.

Updike's refusal to join many of his colleagues in embracing the ideals

---

3. Fyodor Dostoevsky, *Notes from Underground and The Grand Inquisitor,* 18, 19, 26, 23; Thomas Mann, "Preface: Dostoevsky—In Moderation," xix.

of the 1960s counterculture has dogged him ever since, unfairly branding him as a conservative. *Rabbit Redux,* his first and most thorough attempt to explain his position, seems on first reading like a confused fugue that, in place of a clear statement, mixes ambiguity with cranky disapproval. His subsequent attempts to explain his position have not clarified matters all that much. The *Rabbit Angstrom* introduction contains perhaps his most succinct statement on the matter. With what seems like slightly irritated exhaustion, Updike writes, "The calls for civil rights, racial equality, sexual equality, freer sex, and peace in Vietnam were in themselves commendable and nonthreatening; it was the savagery, between 1965 and 1973, of the domestic attack upon the good faith and common sense of our government, especially of that would-be Roosevelt Lyndon B. Johnson, that astonished me" (xiv). In other words, it was not the ideas that bothered him, it was the arrogance. Again and again, Updike has explained that his beef lay not with the disenfranchised demanding more power and representation but with the "intellectual elite and their draft-vulnerable children" (xiv) who, in a way, took credit for the emergence of these laudable demands. At one point Rabbit reflects, "Rich kids make all the trouble" (129/376), a view that is echoed by Skeeter, the black revolutionary whom Rabbit shelters: "It's not the poor blacks setting the bombs, it's the offspring of the white rich" (245/479). What most infuriated Updike was the Chernyshevskyan conviction on the part of the intellectual establishment that *they had all the answers,* that they had finally seen the truth about everything—about racial injustice, about the horrors of war, about the liberatory innocence of sex, whatever. By taking this precarious middle position—*for* the social advancements, *against* the social protesters—Updike once again "evaded entirely pleasing anybody."

The press response to his 1989 essay, "On Not Being a Dove," is a good case in point. One of the six pieces composing his memoir, *Self-Consciousness,* "On Not Being a Dove" explores in considerable detail exactly why he refused to join the decade's anti-Vietnam protest. Richard Vigilante, writing in the conservative *National Review,* praised the piece as "the best of the six autobiographical essays," then proceeded to trash the rest of the book and, while he was at it, the rest of Updike's work as well. Conversely, David Denby, writing in the then liberal *New Republic,* praised *Self-Consciousness* yet singled out the Vietnam essay as "disastrous," claiming that it presented readers with what he called "an amazing spectacle: John Updike writing stupidly about something."[4] The conservatives liked the politics but not the writer, while the liberals liked the writer but not the politics.

But are the two things really so incongruous? Can one accept—or, for that matter, reject—both? The answer, obviously, is yes, and *Rabbit Redux* is Updike's audacious attempt at just such an integration. Often misread as Updike's full-scale attack on the counterculture, the novel in fact remains diffident, hedging all its criticisms in the author's characteristic ambiguity. It gives full and uncontradicted space to views Updike would otherwise refute, and it ushers onto its stage an array of characters who, on the one hand, represent the decade's various protest factions and, on the other hand, undermine through their complexity the often too discrete divisions among these factions. The novel's lengthy middle section even serves as an extended debate on the ideas of the sixties, constituting a sort of Socratic dialogue, or perhaps even a mini *Magic Mountain,* with Rabbit in role of Hans Castorp. In the first part of this middle section, "Jill," Updike confronts and at the same time questions his disapproval of the "intellectual elite and their draft-vulnerable children." In the second part, "Skeeter," he expresses his impatience with the failure on the part of most of the counterculture fully to recognize Dostoevsky's dark human truth. Most important of all, *Rab-*

---

4. Richard Vigilante, "The Observer Observed," 51. Although Updike spends much of the essay accounting for both his fierce adherence to the Democratic party and his "delusional filial attachment to Lyndon Baines Johnson," Vigilante (inevitably! inevitably!) reads "On Not Being a Dove" as a vindication, on the part of a northern liberal, of *Nixon's* Vietnam policy, which Updike's essay quite overtly is *not.* Updike tells us, for instance, that in 1968 he voted, "of course, for the Democrat, the shrill and embattled Hubert Humphrey." He also reveals that he had "no trouble voting in 1972 . . . [for] the implausible rabbit-mouthed McGovern" *(Self-Consciousness,* 146). David Denby, "A Life of Sundays," 32. As if responding to a personal insult, Denby declares, "That the privileged kids, despite their awful manners, might have been correct, or at least have had something of a point, doesn't strike [Updike] as a possibility." But that possibility is everywhere in "On Not Being a Dove." "Was it possible," he asks near the end, " . . . that, in being 'for' or at least not unconflictedly 'against' the war, I was less caring, less sensitive to suffering than others?" And he concludes, "Perhaps there *was* something too smooth in my rise and style, something unthinkingly egocentric in my sopping up love and attention . . . something that drained my immediate vicinity" (149).

bit Redux represents Updike's first attempt to—as the fictional Henry
Bech puts it in a contemporaneous "interview" with his creator—"as it
were, sing America." It is in this volume that Harry first assumes his place
as both an Everyman and a representative of "Middle America." And it
is in the novel's splendid first chapter that Harry first accepts his Uncle
Sam mantle. Ultimately, what happens to Harry after chapter 1 is, in
John Updike's diffident but prescient view, more or less what happened
to America—a formula that will hold true for the rest of the tetralogy.

I. America on the Moon

In *Rabbit Redux,* Updike transforms America itself into a direct analogue for his Wholly Other God. He also establishes Rabbit as an exemplar of an America that the sixties have begun to eradicate—that is,
a white, middle-class America built on such values as hard work, manifest destiny, and trust in the liberal working-class policies of Roosevelt's
Democratic party. Eleven pages into the novel, Updike calls this world
a "garden," suggesting, obviously, an Eden of sorts, or at least a place fit
for a rabbit. For the garden, Updike tells us, is "[h]is garden. Rabbit
knows it's his garden and that's why he's put a flag decal on the back window of the Falcon" (13/277). Likewise, during a Vietnam argument
with Charlie Stavros, Janice's lover, Rabbit takes Stavros's anti-American
criticisms quite personally: "it makes him frantic, the thoughts of the
treachery and ingratitude befouling the flag, befouling him" (45/305).[5]
So personal for Rabbit is this vision of old America that, in *Rabbit Redux,* it becomes a stand-in for Rabbit's subjective God. In fact, God and
America become conflated in Rabbit's inner theology. For instance, we
are told that the phrase "the American dream" evokes for him an image
of "God lying sleeping, the quilt-colored map of the U.S. coming out
of his head like a cloud" (114/364). And America's actions on the world

---

5. The original 1971 edition reads, "it makes him *rigid"* (emphasis added). In
his 1989 memoir *Self-Consciousness,* while describing his own demeanor during his
frequent Vietnam arguments of the sixties, Updike writes, "My face would become
hot, my voice high and tense and wildly stuttery; I could feel my heart race in a
kind of panic whenever the subject [of Vietnam] came up, and my excitement
threatened to suffocate me" (124).

stage have for Rabbit the same lofty, Barthian otherness and infallibility as the actions of Updike's own remote, Wholly Other God. "America is beyond power," Rabbit thinks at one point, "it acts as in a dream, as a face of God. Wherever America is, there is freedom, and wherever America is not, madness rules with chains" (47/307). Whereas in *Rabbit, Run* Harry becomes, via his faith, a Christ figure, in *Rabbit Redux* he becomes America's own begotten son, the tiller of the garden and the defender of the faith. For in defending America, Rabbit feels that he is "defending something infinitely tender, the star lit with his birth" (47/307).[6]

As the sixties come to a close, however, Rabbit begins to sense that "his" garden is beginning to rot. Most distressing of all is his conviction that behind all the plastic and wiring of the new America lies a vast nothing, that an emptiness has opened up where once there was—for him, at any rate—ripeness. In the novel's opening scene, as Rabbit and his father share a drink at the Phoenix bar, Mr. Angstrom clutches two quarters in such a way that he "betrays that they are real silver to him instead of just cut copper sandwich coins that ring flat on the bar top. Old values. The Depression when money was money. Never be sacred again, not even dimes are silver now" (10/275). The money of the sixties is little more than a symbol for money, an artificial version of the once obdurate real thing. Whereas the coins of the Depression were backed by silver, the artificial money of the sixties is backed by nothing more than a promise. His home is also a site of the new technological emptiness. He eats TV dinners made from man-made materials (21–22/284–85), he drinks orange juice that "is not even frozen orange juice but some chemical mix tinted orange" (72/328), and he lives amid furniture that gives back to him a "slippery disposable gloss" (25/288). Even his own front lawn strikes him as "artificial, lifeless, dry, no-color: a snapshot of grass" (298/525). In this world he is a stranger, a visitant. His natural earthy sensuality renders him a foreigner in a land built from synthetic materials that have no direct relation to the garden that he imagines as his very own.

6. Again in *Self-Consciousness*, Updike offers the following account of his own feelings about Vietnam: "I did not have a few cool reservations about the anti-war movement; I felt hot. I was emotionally involved. 'Defending Vietnam'—the vernacular opposite of being 'anti-war'—I was defending myself" (127).

To highlight this bitter assessment of contemporary America, Updike draws a direct parallel between the barren landscape of the sixties and the new frontier of the moon. Beginning the novel on Wednesday, July 16, 1969, the day of the Apollo 11 launch, he immediately associates this event with the new America that has made it possible. We are told, for instance, that on the newscasts which Rabbit repeatedly watches, the anchors "keep mentioning Columbus." The NASA project has become the new Columbus, the moon the new America. And the baseball team he watches—a team which, in its listlessness, in its surrendering of the "gallant pretense," is associated with this new America—is called the "Blasts." Updike even reminds us that the silver which once backed those Depression-era dollars is now, thanks to Kennedy's budgetary policies, more or less "on the moon" (10/275). "Uncle Sam is on the moon!" shouts Mr. Angstrom at the moment of Eagle's landing. "That's just. The place for him," replies Rabbit's mother (93/347). But Rabbit detects a crucial difference in the two Columbuses: "as far as [he] can see it's the exact opposite: Columbus flew blind and hit something, these guys see exactly what they're aiming for and it's a big round nothing" (22/284). Indeed, for Rabbit, all the news about space is really just news about "emptiness" (22/284). And the dramatic lift-off, with its volcanic rocket engines and its heroic power, strikes him as a leap toward the void, with "the numbers pouring backwards in tenths of seconds faster than the eye until zero is reached" (7/272). The countdown merely marks the progression to nothing.

Yet the rise of technology is not the only thing stripping Rabbit of his belief in America's pastoral blessedness. America's own moral soundness, its God-like perfection, is also being called into question—on television, in the newspaper, even in his own home. And Updike enthusiastically participates in this questioning process. He first reveals his criticism of old American values via an ostensibly trivial episode in which Rabbit and Nelson watch *The Carol Burnett Show* on television. From the vantage point of the novel's almost one-to-one rewriting of *Rabbit, Run,* this episode recalls the *Mickey Mouse Club* scene from the previous novel. In that scene, Updike evokes the *Mickey Mouse Club* in order to announce what turns out to be that novel's exploration of Kierkegaardian irony. Similarly, Updike uses *The Carol Burnett Show* to pave the way for this novel's extended exploration of the exploitative history of white America—that is, Rabbit's America. Andrew Horton, in "Ken Kesey, John Updike and the Lone Ranger," has argued that the Lone Ranger is not only the most American but also the most bourgeois of any hero of contemporary pop culture. Not only does he exist in the fictional West of Hollywood's middle-class imagination, but he also defends such bourgeois institutions as the home, marriage, and womanhood.[7] In short, he is the perfect hero for a middle-class conservative like Harry Angstrom. Briefly, the *Carol Burnett* program he and Nelson watch features a "pretty funny" skit about the domestic life of the Lone Ranger. The Lone Ranger's wife, played by Burnett, complains that she does all the housework while her husband gets all the glory. With the Lone Ranger is Tonto, who, Rabbit observes, is played "not [by] Sammy Davis Jr. but [by] another TV Negro." As the skit winds to its conclusion, the Lone Ranger and Tonto leave the wife to her housework. Once she sees that her husband is gone, she changes the music from her husband's traditional *William Tell* Overture to a song called "Indian Love Call." By way of a final punch line, Tonto returns—summoned by the music—and takes Burnett in his arms, after which she turns to the audience and quips, "I've always been interested . . . in Indian affairs" (24/285).

For all its banality, the skit cleverly encapsulates several of the novel's main motifs. Rabbit assumes the role of the Lone Ranger, while his adulterous wife Janice serves as the correlative to Burnett's feminist frontier woman. Skeeter and Stavros, both of them outsiders from different minorities (the first a black Vietnam vet, the second a Greek immigrant), vie for Tonto's role. The skit also provides a compressed means for Updike to convey the changes that have occurred in the American cultural imagination since the Eisenhower world of *Rabbit, Run.* For example, Burnett's restless Ranger wife reflects the sexual independence made possible for women by the feminist movement, just as Janice's affair with Stavros in *Rabbit Redux* rewrites along feminist lines Rabbit's 1959 affair with Ruth. Finally, in its humorous deflating of the Lone Ranger myth, the skit participates in the process of historical revision

7. Andrew Horton, "Ken Kesey, John Updike and the Lone Ranger," 571.

inaugurated by the gradual acknowledgment in the 1960s of the white power structure's exploitation of groups such as women, blacks, and Native Americans. Watching the skit, Rabbit himself engages in this same process of historical revision, of questioning the prevailing narratives. Unable to tell Nelson what *que más sabe* really means, Rabbit realizes "he understands nothing about Tonto. The Lone Ranger is a white man, so law and order on the range will work to his benefit, but what about Tonto? A Judas to his race, the more disinterested and lonely and heroic figure of virtue. When did he get his payoff? Why was he faithful to the masked stranger? In the days of the war one never asked, Tonto was simply on 'the side of right.' It seemed a correct dream then, red and white together, red loving white as naturally as stripes in the flag. Where has 'the side of right' gone?" (24–25/285). The image of "red and white together" here calls to mind not only the plight of Native Americans in the western, Anglo-Saxon United States, but also the plight of blacks in predominantly white America. Moreover, the flag stripes mentioned here anticipate the novel's original 1971 dust-jacket art, which featured a black-and-white photograph of the moon set against red, blue, and *gray* stripes: the new America will be a place where white and black must mix. Significantly, Rabbit experiences this insight only in the late sixties, a time when, as Updike writes in *Self-Consciousness,* the protest movement tried "to gouge us all out of our corners, to force us into the open and make us stare at our bloody hands and confront the rapacious motive underneath the tricolor slogans and question our favored-nation status under God."[8] Accordingly, Rabbit's old America—the America from "the days of the war"—is here revealed to be an imperfect paradise after all, one in which the established order of things worked primarily, if not exclusively, for the benefit of white males. This was "the side of right," and now this side is under attack. Ultimately what Rabbit both recognizes and begins to question is what Skeeter will later call his "white gentleman's concept of the police and their exemplary works" (207/446). As Skeeter explains, "There is nothing, let me repeat no thing, that gives them more pleasurable sensation than pulling the wings off of witless poor black men. . . . Truly, they are constituted for that

8. Updike, *Self-Consciousness,* 143.

very sacred purpose" (207/446).[9] In fact, as will be shown, Rabbit's questioning of the Lone Ranger myth inaugurates the "education in exploitation" that Rabbit will undergo during the novel's "Jill" and "Skeeter" sections, for the questions he raises here about Tonto's cultural position directly anticipate many of the issues he will explore later with Skeeter, an ironic, combative Tonto to Rabbit's diffident Lone Ranger.

In addition to being identified with the masked avenger of American justice, Harry is also associated in *Rabbit Redux* with the wayward son of America's political "first family." Once again, Updike cleverly rewrites *Rabbit, Run,* for whereas in that metaphysically minded work Rabbit becomes the newsworthy Dalai Lama, in the more political *Rabbit Redux* he becomes scandal-ridden Senator Edward Kennedy. On June 18, 1969, the Friday after the moonshot—and two days into the novel's narrative—Kennedy infamously drove his car off an unmarked bridge on Chappaquidick Island, Mass., leaving his companion, Mary Jo Kopechne—a native Philadelphian—to drown. Rabbit identifies with the scandal-ridden Kennedy in his complicity—however partial—in the murder of young girls. First, the Chappaquidick scandal recalls baby Becky's death by drowning in *Rabbit, Run.* Second, it foreshadows Rabbit's partial guilt in the death of his own teenage lover, Jill, who will die by fire. That Rabbit is meant to identify himself with Kennedy is made clear ten years later, in *Rabbit Is Rich.* During a dinner conversation, Rabbit says, "I never understood what was so bad about Chappaquidick. He *tried* to get her out"; then, perhaps with his own dead daughters on his mind, he thinks, "Water, flames, the tongues of God: a man is helpless" (*Rich* 104/714).

Yet Chappaquidick also connects Rabbit to the general plight of Vietnam-torn America in general. Rabbit's father-in-law, Mr. Springer, brings up the incident while he, Rabbit, and Nelson drive to the Blasts baseball game. An encrusted and bitter Republican, Springer sees Chappaquidick as evidence that America is less a democracy than a "police state run by the Kennedys." In addition to hating the Kennedys and

9. "It was an audacious thing for me to attempt," Updike has said in reference to his creation of Skeeter. "For a white small-town boy to try to write about a militant black *is* audacious." See Updike, "Forty Years of Middle America," 225.

Lyndon Baines Johnson, Springer despises FDR who, in his view, tried "to turn the economy upside down for the benefit of the black and white trash" (81/335). Rabbit, however, clearly sides with FDR, Lyndon Johnson, Harry S. Truman, and the Kennedys as a whole. When his father blurts out, "They called LBJ every name in the book but believe me he did a lot of good for the little man" (11/275), he means to include himself and Rabbit in the category of "little men." And Rabbit agrees, saying "Right" in response to his father's outburst. By associating the Chappaquidick incident with the general liberal tradition with which Rabbit identifies, Updike makes a characteristically unsentimental and pragmatic assertion about American politics—namely, that even in its best intentions, America will find blood on its hands. In other words, Rabbit's identification with the Roosevelt liberal tradition embraces not only the well-meaning policies directed at the working poor but also the excesses and imperfections to which that tradition must own up. In Updike's, and Rabbit's, view, the liberalism of Johnson and Kennedy—Jack, Bobby, *and* Teddy—is little more than a makeshift effort to assuage the brutality of earthly life. Skeeter will put the case this way: "What is lib-er-alism? Bringin' joy to the world, right? Puttin' enough sugar on dog-eat-dog so it tastes good, right?" (263/495). Necessary and laudable liberalism is, but perfect it is not.

Similarly, both Chappaquidick and, later in the novel, Vietnam become for Updike reminders that—as he explains in "On Not Being a Dove"—there is no way to pretend "that our great nation hadn't had bloody hands from the start . . . that bloody hands didn't go with having hands at all." Rather, both events serve as a "plea . . . for the doctrine of Original Sin and its obscure consolations."[10] The chain of connections Updike has established here is dazzling in its resourcefulness and audacity. In the same way that baby Becky's death declared the infinite guilt residing in every principal character of *Rabbit, Run,* Chappaquidick declares the infinite guilt lying at the heart of both new and old America, symbolized here by the suggestive, transitional figure of the young Ted Kennedy. And because Kennedy's Chappaquidick inci-

---

10. Updike, *Self-Consciousness,* 136. Actually, in this passage Updike is referring exclusively to the Vietnam War. I have simply applied this sentiment to *Rabbit Redux,* where Vietnam and Chappaquidick become intertwined.

dent evokes Harry's two brushes with murder, Harry and Kennedy become conflated. Harry, too, embodies America in all its infinite guilt and good intentions. Finally, Vietnam, liberalism's emblematic war, and Updike's own symbol for the doctrine of Original Sin, joins this chain of connections in such a way that it will be possible for Skeeter to declare, midway through the novel, "Man don't like Vietnam, he don't like America" (264/496). "Right," Rabbit once again replies. *"Right."*

II. The Adulterous Lover and the Claims of Freedom

Like the Lone Ranger skit, Chappaquidick also calls into play the other main thread of *Rabbit Redux's* lurid plot: Janice's adultery. If Rabbit is a Kennedy, then Janice is a *Jackie* Kennedy, for, like the wife of the slain president, Janice also takes up with a Greek—in her case, Charlie Stavros. Updike clearly intends for us to regard the newly confident Janice as a direct product of the new decade. As a woman, she is on the receiving end of the new liberatory programs, and in assuming this role as one of the decade's "freedom seekers," she joins ranks with the novel's other "new Tontos," a group which, Updike insists, also includes women. For whereas the sixties make Rabbit feel cumbersome and out of place, they make her feel absolutely alive.

Joyce Markle notes that the white characters in the book are "always coupled with a sense of their dissipation and lack of vigor," and this is especially true for the white *male* characters, the Kennedys and the Lone Rangers and the Rabbits, whose garden is becoming obsolete in the new technological super-society.[11] When Janice looks at Rabbit, for instance, she "sees a large white man a knife would slice like lard" (34/296). Later she calls him a "beautiful brainless guy" whom she has had to watch "die day by day" (74/329). Meanwhile, around his black coworker Buchanan, Rabbit feels "tall and pale . . . and feminine, a tingling target of fun and tenderness and avarice mixed" (103/354). "You're just turnin' old, the way you're goin' now," Buchanan tells him, and Rabbit agrees: "Something in what Buchanan said. He was laying

11. Markle, *Fighters and Lovers,* 152. See also pages 150–55 for her splendid examination of the novel's motif of "whiteness."

down to die, had been for years. . . . has to fight sleep before supper and then can't get under at night, can't even get it up to jerk off to relax himself" (103–4/355). In the ten years since Becky's death, he has all but ceased to have sexual relations with Janice, his anarchic sensuality checked and tamed: "It had all seemed like a pit to him then, her womb and the grave, sex and death, he had fled her cunt as a tiger's mouth" (27/289).

Janice, on the other hand, is full of vigor, sexual and otherwise. Armed with her father's inheritance and her own paycheck, she has acquired enough self-sufficiency to make Rabbit wonder, "Does she need [me] at all?" This new self-sufficiency has in turn made her increasingly more resentful of Rabbit's neglect. The tables have turned, for now it is she who does not receive from her spouse needed confirmation of her "specialness." In its domestic absence, she goes in search of this confirmation elsewhere. In other words, she has become one more character in *Rabbit Redux* who is now "the way [Rabbit] used to be." Her affair, meanwhile, is Updike's attempt to open up his own angst-ridden vision along gender lines, the same way he will open it up along race lines via Skeeter.

That Janice is meant to take over Rabbit's old role is made clear in the novel's opening pages. After receiving what seems to be corroboration of the rumors about Janice's affair, Rabbit "has a vision: sees her wings hover, her song suspended: imagines himself soaring, rootless, free" (20/284). Man and wife change places. Her angel wings, earned through blamelessness, get transferred to his back; she drops to earth as he rises heavenward. Yet as we have seen, Updike has no patience for such piety, for temporal and conventional conceptions of innocence and blame. Assuming our guilt, rather, is tantamount to earning our freedom. In *Rabbit Redux,* Janice earns her freedom by sinning, for which Updike largely applauds her. Astonishingly, Rabbit applauds Janice, too. "Is she happy?" he wonders at one point. "He hopes so. Poor mutt, he somehow squelched her potential. Let things bloom" (147/392). Adultery in Updike *is* a way of blooming, as sin is a barometer of our sensual vitality and "precious creaturely freedom." In betraying Harry, she embraces her sensuality, her decay-ridden, nature-bred temporality—in short, all those features of earthly existence that Harry fears are being ignored in the face of the cold, lifeless artificiality of the current era. Janice's adulterous adventure refutes the despair-producing evasions of 1960s technology the same way Rabbit's affair with Ruth refuted the aesthetic despair of Rev. Eccles's faithless piety. Both affairs represent Updikean "yes-but" gestures—both of them more "yes" than "but."

Whether by accident or design, Updike has long since established adultery as one of his chief thematic concerns. By his own admission, he has perhaps written about the subject to the point of exhaustion.[12] Yet adultery is more than a preoccupation for Updike: it is, rather, an integral part of the same Barthian, dialectical vision of earthly guilt-and-innocence. According to Reverend Thomas Marshfield, the Barthian narrator of Updike's 1974 novel *A Month of Sundays,* adultery is an unavoidable offshoot of our earthly condition, "not a choice to be avoided" but a "circumstance to be embraced." "Verily," he exhorts, "the sacrament of marriage, as instituted in its adamant impossibility by our Savior, exists as a precondition for the sacrament of adultery." Although it is true that the Commandments forbid us to commit adultery, it is also true that Christ observed, "Whosoever looketh on a woman to lust after hath committed adultery already in his heart." And, Marshfield asks, "who that has eyes to see cannot so lust?" Having made this logical leap, he assigns adulterous love to the physical realm and conjugal love to the heavenly. The two kinds of love are as necessary and inextricable as body and soul, black and white, the aesthetic and the ethical, freedom and necessity, earth and heaven. Adultery is to the body as marriage is to the spirit. "For what is the body," Marshfield asks, "but a swamp in which the spirit drowns? And what is marriage . . . but a deep well up out of which the man and woman stare at the impossible sun, the bright disc, of freedom?"[13] Consequently, whereas marriage partakes of that part of us sanctioned and hallowed by Updike's Wholly Other God, adultery affirms our earthly *thrownness,* our physical and temporal uniqueness, and our necessary independence from both the Creator and the aesthetic moral constructions of human society.

In Updike's universe, to embrace adultery—real, genuine adultery, that is, the kind of adultery that occurs within marriage and stays

12. See Updike, *Hugging the Shore,* 855. Also see Donald Greiner, *Adultery in the American Novel: Updike, James, and Hawthorne.*
13. Updike, *A Month of Sundays,* 44, 46.

there—is to embrace the dual nature of truth, the polychromatic and indivisibly twofold quality of earthly existence. It is to wallow in ambiguity and contradiction, Updike's characteristic mode. It is, finally, to assert one's creaturely freedom within the God-created, but largely God-forgotten, world-as-given, a place where each life demands a death and each step requires the trampling of the grass underfoot. From the belly of blasphemy, Updike conceives theology.

It is on these same Barthian grounds that Rabbit affirms Janice's adultery. First, he recognizes that the affair has allowed Janice to grow in a way that their marriage will not permit. It has also given her an opportunity to recover her dignity and even the score. Most important, the affair testifies to moxie, to drive, which Harry has lost. Unable to locate such energy in himself, he steps aside to let Janice discover what he went searching for ten years prior. Second, he regards the affair as an inevitable product of an inevitably imperfect world. Although she has betrayed him, he concedes that such betrayal is necessary in a universe in which, as he observes, all "growth is betrayal. There is no other route. There is no arriving somewhere without leaving somewhere" (78/333). His own affair was justified on the same grounds, as Janice herself admits. His leaving she regards as evidence of "angelic cold strength," for which she has forgiven him. What she cannot forgive is his "coming back and clinging," which undermined that strength and, in its own peculiar betrayal, "justifies her" (34–35/296). What also justifies her is the purity of her love for Stavros, a purity lost in her dutiful, freedom-confining love for Harry. "How sad it was with Harry now," she reflects at one point, "they had become locked rooms to each other, they could hear each other cry but could not get in" (54/313). With Stavros, on the other hand, she feels alive and "holy," his love sanctified by the same God who stood by and let her baby drown. "[T]here had been some man in the room with her," she remembers, and "he was here with her now, not Charlie but containing Charlie, everything you do is done in front of this man and how good it is to have him made flesh" (54/313). The adulterous lover is the messiah of the physical, God's Wholly Other creation made flesh. As such, Charlie Stavros becomes, astonishingly enough, the redeemer of Janice's earthly existence. "It feels holy," she insists, thinking of her and Charlie's illicit lovemaking, "she doesn't care, you have to live" (56/315).

In passages such as these, Janice is not the only character who sounds a bit like the Rabbit of *Rabbit, Run.* Stavros does as well. Her description of him as the embodiment of God's Wholly Other creation recalls Rabbit's Dalai Lama role, as does his free and open sexuality. Most important, Stavros is one of the novel's chief lovers and life-givers, one of those Updikean characters whose job it is to remind others of their intrinsic specialness and worth. In her first soliloquy, Janice thinks lovingly of the way Stavros, a car salesman, "sells her herself, murmuring about her parts, giving them the names Harry uses only in anger" (52/ 311). Later, while confessing her affair to Rabbit, she says, "He has a gift, Charlie does, of making everything exciting . . . He loves life. He really does, Harry. He loves life" (73/329). Her language directly parallels Mrs. Smith's assessment, in *Rabbit, Run,* of Rabbit's similar "gift." And Rabbit appreciates Charlie's allure, his power to inspire, for he tells Janice, "Sure I can [understand it]. I've known some good people. They make you feel good" (75/331). Therein resides one of the chief components of Updike's concept of "goodness": a good person makes others feel good.

Whereas in the earlier novel Rabbit fairly embodied this idea, by 1969 he seems entirely to have lost his gift for goodness. Once a salesman himself—of kitchen gadgets, of other peoples' specialness—he is now a stodgy linotypist who "squelches" people's potential. What has happened? In a word: the sixties. The new life-givers are what Horton calls "the new Tontos, black and foreign," a group which, as we have seen, includes even Janice, whom Rabbit describes at one point as "dark and tense: an Indian squaw" (50/310).[14] As the embodiment of white America—home of the Lone Ranger, the Kennedy family, baseball, and all the rest—Rabbit has become both Stavros's dialectical opposite and a stable check on the freedom-oriented excesses of the sixties. In *Rabbit, Run,* Janice's stoic fidelity, Eccles's faithless piety, and Ruth's frank atheism, though critiqued by Updike, were necessary to offset Rabbit's destructive search for freedom, which was itself critiqued and affirmed in more or less equal measure. If freedom is necessary, then a check on freedom is necessary, too. Likewise, Rabbit's role as the embodiment of white America provides Updike with an opportunity both to defend and

14. See Horton, "Lone Ranger," 575–76.

to critique that vanishing order, while Janice and Stavros, in their life-affirming attempts to overturn the social order that has "squelched their potential," serve as objects of affirmation and denunciation in Updike's either/or world.

III. Ego-less Free Love and Other Hippie Dreams

Although Ruth does not literally reappear in *Rabbit Redux,* her presence is keenly felt throughout. As Rabbit's high priestess of the *nihil,* she persists in his memory as both nostalgic object and teacher. Thanks to her challenging example, Rabbit has fully incorporated into his own world-view her vision of the nothing. He now appreciates sex's lack of mystery, its window into the void, and his own expectations about the workaday world and his own role therein have become correspondingly more modest, more realistic. Be that as it may, Rabbit's lesson in Nothingness is not over yet. In *Rabbit Redux,* his education is taken up by two new characters, both of whom assume Ruth's former role as lover/teacher. One is white, the other is black. One is female, the other is male. One is rich, the other is poor. One embraces the void out of negation, the other confronts it in order to enact a brave and forceful gesture of affirmation. From these two characters, Rabbit receives an education in nothingness that far outstrips the lesson he received from Ruth and sits at the core of *Rabbit Redux*'s eschatological critique of the sixties counterculture. Whereas *Rabbit, Run* affirmed, in the end, the "something" whose presence Rabbit felt so keenly, *Rabbit Redux* affirms that something's "nothing" with equal force and clarity.

Jill, the first of this pair, serves as the most obvious stand-in for Ruth. As with Ruth, Rabbit is introduced to her by a surrogate father figure, in this case his black coworker Buchanan, whose solicitude makes Rabbit think "he's found another father" (127/374). Also, as with Ruth, Rabbit meets her in what is for him an exotic public place—not a Chinese restaurant but a bar-and-lounge called Jimbo's, which is frequented primarily by the blacks of Brewer. Both women are down on their luck when they meet Rabbit, both stick with him despite his callousness, and both get more than they bargained for in the end. Walking home with Jill, Rabbit even notices on the sidewalks the same series of

X-patterns he had noticed with Ruth—X being that empty variable signifying something in nothing (*Run* 55/49, *Redux* 137/383). Updike's
prose directly asks us to make these connections. In fact, he employs vir-
tually the same language to describe Rabbit's leaving each exotic place
with each new lover. "With this Ruth," he writes in *Rabbit, Run*, "Rabbit enters the street. On his right, away from the mountain, the heart of
the city shines" (73/64). *Rabbit Redux* contains almost the exact same
passage—with a crucial difference: "With this Jill, then, Rabbit enters
the street. On his right, toward the mountain, Weiser stretches sallow
under blue street lights" (135/381). The "shine" from *Rabbit, Run* has
turned "sallow." Whereas in the earlier text Rabbit begins his affair with
his mistress-of-the-void in the light of an "enormous sunflower" adver-
tising Sunflower Beer, in the sequel he views "the *back* of the Sunflower
Beer clock . . . ; otherwise the great street is dim" (135/381, emphasis
added). Accordingly, his new lover is the "other side" of the earlier one.
Although she shares Ruth's deep affinity with the nothing, her example
is hardly one Rabbit is meant ultimately to take to heart: that capacity
is fulfilled by the other member of this pair of educators, Skeeter. Jill
becomes Rabbit's lover, yet her association with the void serves as a
warning. She is Ruth's stand-in only in the form of a mirror opposite.

The distinctions between the two women line up so directly that they
demand to be taken as intentional. Whereas Ruth is a plump brunette,
Jill is a razor-thin blonde. And whereas Ruth is working class, Jill is from
a wealthy family in Connecticut. Rabbit's initial impression of each
woman sets up a similar point of comparison. Ruth's laughter causes
"the space between the muscles of his chest to feel padded with warm
air," his conviction early on is that she is "good-natured," and their
shared age puts him on solid ground: "Like the touch of her hand on
his arm, her being his age pleases him. . . . The Class of '51 view" (55/
49). Conversely, eighteen-year-old Jill is half Rabbit's age, while her initial aura strikes him as anything but warm and comforting. Before he
even meets her, and entirely on the strength of what he has heard about
her from the other people at the table at Jimbo's, he pictures her as "this
approaching cloud, this Jill, who will be pale like the Stinger [a drink
he has been given], and poisonous" (122/371). When he finally does
meet her, she is dressed "in a white dress casual and dirty as smoke," and
her hair "hangs dull, without fire, almost flesh color" (128/375). Con-

trast this with Ruth's hair, which is "many colors, red and yellow and brown and black, each hair passing in the light through a series of tints, like the hair of a dog" (58/51). For all her atheism, Ruth is still a vital dynamic presence, a life-giver in more ways than one: remember, she is pregnant at the conclusion of *Rabbit, Run.* Jill, on the other hand, is a "pale" and "poisonous" cloud of negation.

These latter associations she earns not so much through her affinity —both positive and negative—with Ruth as through her function as this novel's stand-in for *Rabbit Angstrom's* primary angel of death, the infant Rebecca June, whose name, of course, Jill's own name allitera-tively evokes. One of the principal themes of *Rabbit Angstrom* is Rab-bit's search for Becky's replacement, and each novel after *Rabbit, Run* accordingly introduces a new candidate. Jill is the first of this triumvi-rate.[15] Almost immediately, Rabbit makes this connection, not so much by remembering Becky specifically as by regarding Jill as somehow Nel-son's "sister." Back in Jimbo's, her vulnerability and her pale wan youth make him feel "protective, timidly. In her tension of small bones she re-minds him of Nelson" (128/375). And when she and Nelson meet, he is struck by the fact they "are nearly the same height" (151/395). To Jan-ice, he even goes so far as to characterize Jill as "like a sister to" Nelson (156/400). In making these connections between Jill and Becky, Up-dike seeks to reveal the underlying significance of Jill's variation on Ruth's "Nothing." Whereas Ruth represented a Heideggerian Nothing that was paradoxically a "something," Jill represents a Nothing that is just that—a void, a vast blankness without substance, an emptiness symbolized in *Rabbit Redux* by outer space. Indeed, during one of their stoned lovemaking sessions, Rabbit characterizes the two of them as "moonchild and earthman" (202/443). Becky is the perfect correlative for Jill's nothing, for she is, in effect, the void personified. Killed in her first week of earthly existence, she exists in the tetralogy less as a char-acter than as an occasion for guilt. She is an ache attached to an absence. Her parents and her brother can remember nothing specific about her,

15. The daughter figure in *Rabbit Is Rich* is a woman whom Rabbit feels cer-tain *is* in fact his daughter—by Ruth. In *Rabbit at Rest,* Becky June is reincarnat-ed in the person of his granddaughter, Judy—another "J" name. Significantly, Judy "saves" Rabbit from drowning, thereby redeeming, finally, June's death by the same means. See chapters 3 and 4 respectively.

nothing, that is, that might allow them to think of her as a subject, and so they register her existence only through their own shame. As such, she is not present at all, not even in the memories of those around her. Jill, too, invokes the possibility of pure absence, the difference being that, in Jill's case, such pure absence is the product of deliberate choice rather than tragic accident. For Jill has chosen to suppress her ego, her subjectivity, in the cause of enlightened selflessness, a commendable goal that Updike nevertheless regards as fatal, as the associations with Becky suggest.

Sociologically, Updike connects Jill's selflessness to her affluent, white, and northeastern background, for it is her wealth, rather than any specific moral conviction, that inspires her to become a hippie. A wealthy white runaway thumbing her nose at the values of her parents, she fits the bill perfectly. As she explains, she left her wealthy home in Connecticut because "it was all ego. Sick ego" (136/383). She also paints her parents as typically self-absorbed and cold. As for Rabbit, he certainly has no great regard for the rich at this stage in his life. He resents them as fervently as Jill repudiates them. At one point, Skeeter gets Rabbit to admit, "I hate those Penn Park motherfuckers" (249/483), Penn Park being the high-rent district that skirts Rabbit's own Penn Villas.

Although Updike grants that her repudiation of material goods represents an ethical gesture, it is still an empty one in his assessment, a far too easy protest for someone of Jill's background to make, if only because the values she rejects were also instrumental in guaranteeing the kind of prosperity and leisure that made such a rebellion possible in the first place. As he sees it, material goods might logically mean little to someone who has never had to work for them. Similarly, Rabbit cannot bring himself to embrace entirely Jill's hippie ideals. His most glib swipe at her involves her supposed rejection of "ego." "Something pretty egotistical about running away," he tells her, speaking, of course, from experience. "What'd that do to your mother?" (136/383). But his critique goes even further, touching upon his own values and convictions. In a sense, he takes her rebellion personally. First, he resents her wealth as much as he resents the wealth of those "Penn Park motherfuckers." Second, he resents the fact that she does not appreciate this wealth. He associates her with the other "rich kids" who are, in his view anyway, destroying America. Her white Porsche, which her parents gave her and which she treats with cavalier disregard, best symbolizes for Rabbit this aspect of Jill's hippie protest. "[T]hat's the way young people are these days," he tells another working-class stiff late in the novel, "ruin one car and on to the next. Material things don't mean a thing to 'em" (271/ 501–2). It is not simply the condition of the Porsche itself that angers him. It is the Porsche as a symbol of the fruits of diligence and hard work, those old-America values that have given Rabbit whatever structure his life has had since his own rebellion ten years ago.

Yet Jill is not merely the object of Updike's facile, polemical attack on hippies. Endowed by her creator with the same degree of depth and complexity with which he endows all of his characters, Jill is a formidably vital figure in her own right, a lost soul who demands our sympathy and respect. She certainly receives both from Rabbit. One way Updike rises above his reflexive dismissal of her hippie ideals is to transform her trendy protest against materialism and "ego" into a spiritual cry for help. This cry in turn sparks Updike's searching inquiry into his own doctrine of pragmatic self-preservation and divinely sanctioned subjectivity. As Rabbit's lover and dialectical antagonist, she forces him to confront and even question his Updikean ideals, just as Rabbit's forceful example directs her away from the path of self-destruction she had lately been following.

Superficially, her self-destructive behavior—involving drugs, mostly —ties into her hippie lifestyle. On a deeper level, it corresponds to her repudiation of ego. "I'm not interested in holding anything for myself," she admits at one point (214/453). All self-preserving functions of the human body have become for her emblems of the flawed human world that she would denounce. Whereas "the light of common day, and the sights and streets . . . [have] been the food of Rabbit's life," they seem to "nauseate" Jill (158/402).[16] In a typical exchange between these two unlikely lovers, she announces,

> "Usually I try to rise above eating."
> "Why?"
> "It's so ugly. Don't you think, it's one of the uglier things we do?"

16. The original edition of *Rabbit Redux* reads: " . . . the light of common day, and the sights and streets that have been the food of Rabbit's life, seem to strike her as poisonous and too powerful" (158).

"It has to be done."
"That's your philosophy, isn't it?" (140/386)

It is also, roughly, Updike's philosophy, which might be formulated as follows: the world, ugly or not, must be embraced and praised as God made it. The flesh, moreover, is for Updike God's grand theater, the seat of the soul and the site of the Incarnation, all in accordance with Tertullian's *De resurrectione carnis*, a text he seems to hold in high esteem.[17] Jill, on the other hand, would reject this spiritual gloss. She is positively repulsed by the flesh, regarding it primarily as the site of what she terms "the world's shit," its refuse and decay, its manifest ugliness. Eating, copulating, dying—all of it repulses her, so much so that her self-negation becomes an effort to rise above these necessary evils. At one point, she even tells Rabbit, "I want you to fuck all the shit out of me, all the shit and dreariness of the shit-dreary world" (201/442). Such a grim view of sex makes Ruth's unsentimental pragmatism look like purple passion. Indeed, sex for Jill is neither a spiritual union of the flesh nor a natural bodily function bereft of mystery. It is an act of surrender—to the world's ugliness, to another person. Its purpose is not self-validation but renunciation.

The first sexual encounter between Jill and Rabbit articulates all of these themes. As with the passages detailing their initial meeting in Jimbo's, this scene contrasts with its counterpart, with Ruth, in *Rabbit, Run*. Gone are the Lawrencean metaphysics, of which Rabbit has been thoroughly cured, by none other than Ruth herself. Gone also are Rabbit's gestures toward gallantry and ritualization. Yet even Rabbit's matter-of-fact attitude toward sex can hardly compare to Jill's clear-eyed coldness. She not only initiates the act, but insists on regarding it as little more than a transaction. Ruth's past experience as a prostitute, which Rabbit had imagined was his to redeem, becomes in Jill a present reality, about which Rabbit can do little. "Don't you want to sleep with me?" she asks with bland directness. "That's not your idea of bliss, is it? " he asks, as if stalling. "Sleeping with a creep?" "You are a creep," she assures him,

---

17. See *Roger's Version,* 149–52, for Updike's impassioned and enthusiastic explication of this text, an explication cast, of course, in the voice of his fictional divinity professor, Roger Lambert.

"but you just fed me" (141/387). In the scene with Ruth, Rabbit tried
to control the mounting drama by directing the undressing and so forth.
Here, Jill obeys his commands with blithe, trusting indifference. None
of her actions seems to him genuine, nothing she does strikes him as
arising from genuine desire. She simply "stays cool, a prep-school kid
applying what she knows" (146/392). As a result, her body, in its cold
disregard for either of them, offers no welcome, and when he touches
her, her skin "stings his fingertips like glass we don't expect is there"
(143/389). In a sense, her body *is* glass, an opaque vessel holding a soul
that seems deliberately not to be there at all. And it is this absence of
soul that ultimately dulls his desire. Just when the two of them, in their
disconnected and groping way, seem finally ready to consummate the
act, "her lack of self-consciousness again strikes him as sad, and puts
him off" (147/392). She falls asleep. He goes downstairs and eats a plate
of cracker-and-peanut-butter sandwiches. Contrast this conclusion with
that of the "wedding night" scene in *Rabbit, Run,* in which both partners reach orgasm, Joycean internal monologues abound,[18] and Rabbit,
not Ruth, falls asleep first, content in his postcoital languor. Point for
point, the *Rabbit Redux* scene rewrites, in the negative, its partner scene
in *Rabbit, Run.*

Another way Jill contrasts with Ruth is in the spiritual dimensions of
her conception of the *nihil.* Whereas for Ruth the nothing was simply
an outgrowth of her atheism, for Jill it is part and parcel of a coherent
religious vision—much as it is for Updike. It is here, in fact, that Jill's
status in the novel acquires full ironic ambiguity. So far, we have discussed Jill's status as an antagonist figure, as a mere contesting voice in
Updike's overall vision. But Jill is a seat of contradictions and ambiguities as well, since her beliefs do not constitute a set of doctrines that the
novel's final argument will dispel. As with Ruth, Rabbit discusses God
with Jill, yet once again the roles have been reversed. Rabbit, not Jill,
plays the skeptic. Jill's conception of God's universe ties into her repudiation of ego, of matter and natural decay. Recalling the glasslike skin

18. From *Rabbit, Run:* "His thigh slides over hers, weight on warmth. Wonderful, women, from such hungry wombs to such amiable fat; *he wants the heat his
groin gave given back in gentle ebb.* Best bedfriend, fucked woman. Bowl bellies.
Oh, how! when she got up on him like the bell of a big blue lily slipped down on
his slow head" (87/75). (Italicized passage cut from the *Rabbit Angstrom* text.)

Rabbit imagined when he touched her on their first night together, she calls matter the "mirror of spirit." That mirror can only reflect onto other mirrors, so that the world of matter is "like an enormous room, a ballroom. And inside it are these tiny *other* mirrors tilted this way and that and throwing the light back the wrong way" (159/402). The mirrors serve as Jill's metaphor for our egos, which "make us blind." Without them, she asserts, "the universe would be absolutely clean, all the animals and spiders and moon-rocks and stars and grains of sand absolutely doing their things, unself-consciously" (159/402). In contrast to these self-reflecting mirrors stands God's consciousness, which should be, in her view, the only consciousness in this universe of unself-conscious matter. Instead, our self-reflections, our egos, becloud in the form of "dark spots" the otherwise clean universe. We *could* become blameless participants in creation were it not for our egos, which displace rather than reflect God. When Rabbit asks why God does not merely obliterate these blotches on his pristine creation, she suggests that God might not even have noticed us yet. "The cosmos is so large and our portion of it so small," she says. "So small and recent" (160/403). She even entertains the possibility—suggested to her, sardonically, by Rabbit—that we might obliterate ourselves before God has a chance to do it Himself. "There is that death-wish," she admits (160/403).

Interestingly enough, this metaphysical take on Jill's repudiation of ego does not significantly contradict Updike's own Barthian conception of the Wholly Other God. We have already seen how Updike perceives "a quiet but tireless goodness that things at rest, a brick wall or a small stone, seem to affirm," and we have also seen how, in *Self-Consciousness,* he contrasts this goodness with the guilt inherent in living things, in the competitive, self-preserving activity of life itself. His admonition, moreover, that if we "keep utterly still" we can "taste" the innocence of the "essential self" corresponds, in part, to Jill's own repudiation of ego: by keeping still, by "crouching in a shelter and letting phenomena slide by," we can, however momentarily, submerge our self-preserving egos and hence participate in the "goodness" of "things at rest." The key word here, however, is "momentarily." Although Jill's conception of the ego's relation to the physical universe more or less jibes with Updike's, it disconnects in its corrective element. Jill wants to clean herself by erasing the dark spot of her ego, while Updike would insist that there can be no such absolute cleansing. Only God, through the free granting of His grace, can do that. And although Jill speaks for Updike in her depiction of God's immense indifference to human activity, she crosses Updike in her argument that this same God has created the world "by the way." One of the main tenets of Updike's Barthian/Kierkegaardian conception of faith is its acceptance of what Kierkegaard terms the absurd: it is absurd, for instance, to think that the Creator of this immense waste would concern Himself with our well-being, and yet the absurdity of it guarantees its truth as an article of faith. In a passage from *Dogmatics in Outline* that seems to lie behind Jill's discussion of God's clean creation, Karl Barth declares that "the world with its sorrow and its happiness will always be a dark mirror to us, about which we may have optimistic or pessimistic thoughts; but it gives no information about God the Creator." Like Jill, Barth affirms that our view of creation is always filtered through our egos, through a dark mirror that tells us more about ourselves than about God, who remains separate from his creation. He does not, however, interpret this situation as evidence of God's failure to recognize us as the star actors in his immense theater. Glossing the article in the Apostles' Creed that speaks of God as the creator of heaven and earth, he is moved to ask Jill's own question:

> Whence can we be told authoritatively that [creation] is not a perversion and that life is not a dream but reality, that I myself am, and that the world around me is? From the standpoint of the Christian Confession there can only be one answer: this Confession tells us in its centre, in the second article, that it pleased God to become man, that in Jesus Christ we have to do with God Himself, with God the Creator, who became a creature, who existed in time and space, here, there, at that time, just as we all exist. If this is true, and this is the presupposition everything starts with, that God was in Christ, then we have a place where creation stands before us in reality and becomes recognizable.

This is the presupposition with which Updike starts. God is not, therefore, "in the tiger as well as in the lamb," as Jill argues later on. God is distinct from his creation, for otherwise he could not have become a creature within it. He does not "reside" in all things. Rather, as Updike asserts in *Mid-point,* he lurks behind matter in the form of "an understanding Eye" which watches but, except for the Christian revelation of Jesus Christ, does not interfere.[19]

In addition to these complex and hair-splitting theological issues, Rabbit has one final, and perhaps overarching, objection to Jill's hippie ideals. In his view, her dreamy-eyed optimism about the possibility of pure selflessness is flawed in its unthinking disavowal of that primordial condition that drives all human passion and desire and which, ten years ago, made him run so desperately and so destructively: angst. Her failure to incorporate this fundamental condition into her utopian program of egoless free love marks for Rabbit that program's final invalidity. What Jill proposes simply will not come to pass for the very simple reason that human beings are not capable of the behavior she would demand of them. The way Rabbit sees it, she is able to propose these sweeping societal correctives only because she has been spared the need to rely on that Darwinian drive. Her life, up until then, has been too sheltered for her to put her ideas to the test. "You rich kids playing at life make me sick," he tells her, "throwing rocks at the poor dumb cops protecting your daddy's loot. You're just playing, baby" (170/411). He continues: "You have no juice, baby. You're all sucked out and you're just eighteen. You've tried everything and you're not scared of nothing and you wonder why it's all so dead. You've had it handed to you, that's why it's so dead. Fucking Christ, you think you're going to make the world over you don't have a clue what makes people run. Fear. That's what makes people run. You don't know what fear is, do you, poor baby? That's why you're so dead" (170/412). This attack, the most virulent denunciation Rabbit will make of Jill, sits at the heart of the novel's critique of sixties thinking. In leveling this charge against her, he also levels an indirect yet forceful charge against the trendy ethos of free love that has overtaken America. For it is not just Jill who is "all sucked out," who has "tried everything" so that everything is dead. The whole culture, in Rabbit's view, is suffering from this same malaise. Thanks to the new labor-saving technologies and the steady accumulation of wealth, the entire nation has had it "handed to them" in such a way that everyone, Jill included, has forgotten "what makes people run." (The echo

19. Updike, "Dogwood," 186; Updike, *Self-Consciousness*, 35; Barth, *Dogmatics*, 52–53.

from *Rabbit, Run* here is obviously intentional.) Rabbit's objections are also Updike's: a great deal of the new thinking, laudable though much of it is, fails to address the fear, the angst, that drives the world in the first place. And make no mistake about it: Rabbit is not talking of the kind of fear that is distinguishable from angst. He is talking about angst itself—that is, the fear of nothing. Jill and her compatriots of the era, he specifically says, are "not scared of nothing." Rabbit's ungrammatical construction is deliberate, for the nothing is precisely what Jill does not properly fear. Her attempt to erase her ego is finally a sham, in Rabbit's view, for if she genuinely confronted the nothing in all its blank terror, she too would recognize the difficulty of accepting it for what it is. "People've run on fear long enough," she argues back. "Let's try love for a change." He responds, "Then you better find yourself another universe" (170/412).

As well as invoking angst, this scene also invokes the theme of Original Sin. When, early in the argument, Rabbit strikes her, Updike employs the language of the Vietnam War, that national signifier of America's inherent guilt, as Rabbit likens her frightened green eyes to a "microscopic forest he wants to bomb" (169/411). "You know why you did that," she snaps back, "you just wanted to hurt me, that's why. You just wanted to have that kick. You don't give a shit about me and Nelson hustling" (169/411). Jill's assessment of Rabbit's cowardly, unforgivable act is more or less accurate. He *does* strike her for the "kick" of it, for the mere assertion of power. But that assertion is part of the angst whose existence he insists cannot be avoided, for it is angst that drives us to acts of disobedience, to gestures of destruction, and it is this same rage for disobedience that will guarantee the failure of any system based on egoless free love. What's more, in asserting one's power, one also owns up to one's guilt, one's freedom to disobey, whether that disobedience involves the Ten Commandments or the precepts of Jill's Chernyshevskyan utopia. And with disobedience comes the need for forgiveness. Immediately after clutching her wrists, for instance, Rabbit also realizes "he wants to hold her absolutely quiet in his arms for the months while it will heal" (170/411). Like most acts of outrage in Updike, this slap is both an assertion of freedom and an announcement of guilt, yet such a gloss does not exonerate Rabbit from the act itself, any more than this same doctrine of ontological guilt exonerated Rabbit from complicity in baby Becky's death. What Updike demands of his characters is not spotless behavior but recognition of imperfection, of the need for forgiveness. Indeed, later that evening, Rabbit does ask for forgiveness, to which Jill demands that he kiss her feet. When his ready compliance suggests to her that he is taking pleasure in this abasement—this is, after all, what he wanted—she kicks him in the cheek (176/416–17). The whole scene is sordid, and remains that way.

And it gets even more sordid after this. *Rabbit Redux* is in fact the most sordid novel of Updike's relatively sordid oeuvre. Unfortunately, Updike explains in the introduction to *Rabbit Angstrom,* the times demanded it. "[*Rabbit Redux*] is the most violent and bizarre of [the Rabbit novels]," he writes, "but then the sixties were the most violent and bizarre of these decades" (xv–xvi). But Updike does more than simply reflect the violence of the era. He tries quite deliberately to rub the reader's nose in it. One of the central paradoxes of the era—of which *Rabbit Redux* is aggressively aware—is the concomitant rise of love-based social philosophies *and* violent national protest. Even more perplexing is the fact that both phenomena grew out of the same basic soil. How and why this contradictory set of occurrences came to pass becomes the main burden of *Rabbit Redux*'s electrifying third chapter, which Updike has likened to another "Sixties invention, a 'teach in'" (xv–xvi). It is here that all the novel's competing voices finally converge in ironic counterpoise, and it is here also that the novel's self-contradictory, yet ultimately organic, order begins to emerge in full.

IV. The Black Jesus

Skeeter's appearance in the novel functions almost as a direct response to Rabbit's outburst at Jill, for Skeeter is, in more ways than one, Rabbit's darkest fear personified. Ever the unsentimental realist, Updike does not blink in demonstrating the full scope of Rabbit's racism, which is offered not only in the name of verisimilitude but also in the service of dialectical truth-seeking. Updike introduces Rabbit's racism as early as the second scene of the novel, the first sentence of which reads, "The bus has too many Negroes. Rabbit notices them more and more. They've been here all along . . . but now they're noisier" (12/276). He "notices them more and more" for the same reason he notices the latent political message conveyed by Tonto in the Lone Ranger myth: the times have forced him to take this notice. Before then, he had never considered blacks in any other light than the one offered to him by the popular culture of his own era, wherein the "side of right" was indelibly associated with "whiteness" and middle-class achievement. Now, he notes, blacks are on *Let's Make A Deal!*, on *Laugh-In,* and in the NBA. His racist reaction to this new visibility, meanwhile, is shown to be the product of ignorance, plain and simple. Jill is the first character in the novel to make this case to Rabbit. Jill observes, "[T]he reason Skeeter annoys and frightens you is he's opaque, you don't know a thing about his history, I don't mean his personal history so much as the history of his race, how he got here. Things that threaten you like riots and welfare have jumped into the newspapers out of nowhere for you" (229/445–46). Although Skeeter does successfully educate Rabbit about the "history of his race," and in the process brings Rabbit around to a more enlightened view of blacks and their complex social situation, he conducts this education on a man who harbors all the fears and prejudices endemic to white racism —prejudices rooted, as all prejudices are, in ignorance. Unschooled in the historical forces that have shaped the marginalized role forced on blacks, Rabbit treats the African Americans around him as foreign and threatening others who fascinate and repel him in equal measure.

He meets Skeeter on the same night he meets Jill, and at the same place, Jimbo's. The scene in Jimbo's, a tour de force of compressed drama and atmosphere, is central to the novel's complex black-white symbolic structure. At the head of the chapter containing the Jimbo's episode, Updike has included one of the novel's four epigraphs, all of which are drawn from the actual transcripts of the Apollo mission. In this epigraph, Neil Armstrong, gazing into outer space, is quoted as saying, "It's different but it's very pretty out here" (101/353). Updike provides a nice correlative to this quotation via a brief episode preceding Rabbit's actual entrance into Jimbo's, wherein he stops for a bite to eat at a fast-food restaurant called Burger Bliss. After knocking back a Lunar Special—"a double cheeseburger with an American flag stuck into the bun"—he steps from the restaurant's incandescent brightness, its "lake of light," and into the "unfriendly darkness" outside. According to the novel's metaphoric pattern, the restaurant suggests the new, technology-obsessed America, where the light is man-made and even the milkshakes "taste toward the bottom of chemical sludge" (113/363). Conversely, the outside, the natural world that was once Rabbit's "garden," is now an "unfriendly darkness." Updike even asserts that, on this night, "Mt. Judge is one with the night." But it is only "unfriendly" to Rabbit, unfriendly because it is unfamiliar. The darkness imagery continues when Rabbit enters Jimbo's itself and notes that everyone but himself is black. Though the entrance of this "large soft white man in a sticky gray suit" causes a brief "snag," the activity inside Jimbo's continues on in living, fluid vitality: "the liquid of laughter and ticked muttering resumes flowing" (114/364). Here lies the organic unity that white America has lost, the real America that Rabbit feels has been exchanged for empty artificiality.

One of the people present at the table with Rabbit is a torch singer named Babe, and during her performance Updike makes overt this association between the black community and the real America. She plays songs—Gershwin, Rodgers & Hart—from a vanished era, "when Americans moved within the American dream, laughing at it, starving on it, but living it, humming it, the national anthem everywhere" (124/372). The performance calls to Rabbit's mind a time just before "the world shrank like an apple going bad and America was no longer the wisest hick town within a boat ride of Europe" (124/372), the apple here suggesting the fruit of the tree of knowledge, which America, in the sixties, is no longer allowed to pretend it never ate. Babe then moves through the years, incorporating more recent tunes into the mix and concluding with what appears to be the Byrds' "Turn Turn Turn," a contemporary hit whose lyrics are lifted from the third chapter of the book of Ecclesiastes. "For everything there is a season, and a time for every matter under the sun," reads the opening verse of the chapter, a line which also serves as the chorus to the Byrds' record. Whereas this biblical text was associated in *Rabbit, Run* with Rev. Eccles's hollow faith, here it becomes Updike's book of existential wisdom, the "Lord's last word." Singing the paraphrased lyrics, Babe's voice becomes "no woman's voice at all and no man's," but "merely human." Stoned for the first time in his life, Rabbit feels himself crossing, also for the first time in his life, the racial barrier: "Her singing opens up, grows enormous, frightens Rabbit with its enormous black maw of truth yet makes him overjoyed that he is here; he brims with joy, to be here with these black others, he wants to shout love through the darkness of Babe's noise to the sullen brother in goatee and glasses. He brims with this itch but does not spill" (125/ 373). Although they are still "black others," they are not so foreign to Rabbit now. Thanks to the humbling truth of Ecclesiastes, its stoic pragmatic wisdom, Rabbit is able, for once, to set aside his differences and feel the possibility of, as well as the need for, community. Babe's performance, ending as it does with this lesson in transience, is at the same time a message to Rabbit to let go of that old America and to embrace the new America he now sees all around him.

The "sullen brother in goatee and glasses" is, of course, Skeeter. At first, Rabbit can only perceive him as a black space broken by the silver disks of his lenses, which "tilt" and "glint" in the murky light of Jimbo's. But Skeeter emerges from this "nowhere" soon enough. Immediately, he unleashes on Rabbit the full rage of his rhetoric, a compound of sociology, politics, history, and theology. He has Rabbit's number from the get go, seeing right through Rabbit's Protestant convictions, all of which Skeeter reinterprets along racial lines. "The reason they so mean," he begins—"they" being Rabbit and his "cracker" brethren—"they has so much religion, right?" (117/366). Observing Rabbit refuse the joint offered him, Skeeter bitterly remarks, "They're going to live forever, right?" adding, "God's on their side, right? God's white, right? He doesn't want no more Charlies up there to cut into his take, he has it just fine the way it is, him and all those black angels out in the cotton" (119–20/368). And he can't let it go. When Babe, upbraiding him for the hate in his heart, tells him "he needs to wash," Skeeter goes on the attack: "Wash is what they said to Jesus, right? . . . Wash is what Pilate said he thought he might do, right? Don't go saying clean to me, Babe, that's one darkie bag they had us in too long" (121/370). Everywhere Skeeter looks he sees the subtle, dividing language of race, a tendency Rabbit's brooding white presence in this black sanctum has only exacerbated.

His mentioning of Jesus here is no accident, either, for Skeeter claims to be "the real Jesus . . . *the* black Jesus" (210/449). The specific Christ reference above seems to recall Luke 11:38, in which a Pharisee, overhearing Christ's exhortations, is said to have "marveled that [Christ] had not washed before dinner." Christ replies, "Now do ye Pharisees make clean the outside of the cup and the platter; but the inward part is full of ravening and wickedness. Ye fools, did not he that made that which is without make that which is within also?" (Luke 11: 39–40). Skeeter's appropriation of this passage turns precisely on this play of inner and outer cleanliness. His supposed "uncleanness" is, he insists, a racist label forced on him by whites, a literalization of possible symbolic meanings provided by surface qualities such as, say, skin color. Like Christ, he shifts the emphasis to inner cleanliness and thereby turns the tables 180 degrees. In this scenario, Skeeter assumes the role of the unclean Lord, while the outwardly clean but inwardly corrupt whites become stand-ins for Pharisees, law-givers, hypocrites, and unclean arbiters of superficial cleanliness. Later he asks, "[W]hat's clean? White is clean, right? Cunt is clean, right? Shit is clean, right? There's nothin' not clean the law don't go pointing its finger at, right?" (121/370). The confusing double negatives in the final line reflect Skeeter's general reversal of conventional values. The white law—legal, biblical, social—that assigns cleanliness to whiteness and dirtiness to shit is the same law that makes a parallel distinction between whites and blacks, and Skeeter rejects these distinctions. In this complex narrative of reversal, Pilate becomes another emblem of white uncleanness, of the ramifications of washing, for to wash in this sense is to attempt to absolve oneself of culpability—in Pilate's case, culpability for the death of Jesus. And in this novel, Jesus is none other than Skeeter himself. Responding later to Babe's assessment of Jill as clean—of drugs, apparently—he makes overt this identification of himself as the sacrificial martyr of white racist hatred: "We're the blood to wash away her sins, right?" (122/371). Although early on Rabbit dismisses Skeeter as a hothead, when he hears this last statement he pauses long enough to reflect, "There seems to be not only a history but a theology behind his anger" (122/371).

Few critics have taken Updike up on his challenge to view Skeeter in the light that Skeeter asks to be viewed, that is, as the "black Jesus." Indeed, Updike has expressed "surprise" that "no one's given serious consideration to the idea that Skeeter, the angry black, might *be* Jesus. He *says* he is. I think probably he might be. And if that's so, then people *ought* to be very nice to him." Rabbit echoes this same sentiment to Jill: "Well, . . . if he is the next Jesus, we got to keep on His good side" (215/453). Richard Locke, in his hosanna-filled review of *Rabbit Redux* for the *New York Times Book Review,* simply ignored Skeeter's assessment of

himself and called him an anti-Christ, while George Hunt unhesitant-
ly dismisses Skeeter as a "despicable character" and the biblical imagery
surrounding him as "arbitrary and jarring, given the discrepancy between the dramatic character and the symbol." Robert Detweiler dodges
the issue entirely by granting Skeeter mere "plausibility": Skeeter's wide-
ranging political and theological theories Detweiler simply sees as evidence of schizophrenia and paranoia, both of which have been imposed
on Skeeter by the culture's need for a "scapegoat." Like Locke, Edward
Vargo defends Skeeter as "the most vibrant and credible black in literature written by a white man," yet also, like Locke, he insists on viewing
Skeeter as an *anti*-Christ. Only Joyce Markle takes Skeeter at his word
by granting him Christ-like status.[20]

Markle's reading is the most convincing, and not only because it co-
incides with Updike's own statements on the matter. It also corresponds
to the novel's overarching order and to its thematic position within the
tetralogy. If *Rabbit, Run* affirms the "something" aspect of God, then
Rabbit Redux affirms that aspect's opposite. Accordingly, Skeeter is not
an anti-Christ at all, but rather the messiah of the novel's God of Nothingness. In Updike's Barthian world, the God of life is also the God of
death, while the "yes" and the "no" must always be held in dialectical
tension. Whereas the Christ of light is the messiah of order, the Christ
of darkness—that is, Skeeter—is the messiah of chaos, that is, the
Christ of the new religion Rabbit discovered in his dream of "lovely life"
and "lovely death." He is the harbinger of God's hardness of heart, of
God's culpability in the manufacture of death. And yet he is still Christ
for all of that. That is what Updike means when he says "people *ought*
to be very nice to him." Just as our goodness evokes in us its opposite,
so, too, does God's creation and its divine order have its shadow side,
and that shadow side is embodied by Skeeter. As Updike has remarked,
"Revolt, rebellion, violence, disgust are themselves there for a reason,
they too are organically evolved out of a distinct reality, and must be
considered respectfully."[21]

20. Updike, "One Big Interview," 510; Richard Locke, "*Rabbit Redux*," 22;
Hunt, *The Three Great Secret Things,* 179; Robert Detweiler, *John Updike,* 136; Vargo, *Rainstorms and Fire,* 210–11; Markle, *Fighters and Lovers,* 151.
    21. Updike, "Updike Redux," 62.

In addition to being the figurative "black Jesus," Skeeter is a literal one as well, the incarnation of the shadow cast by God's light *and* the messiah of America's oppressed race. By conjoining blackness and death in this way, Updike seems openly to be courting the charge of racism. Like Skeeter, he provokes in order to turn that provocation on its head. Without the Barthian subtext, Updike's symbolism might seem to the casual reader to make careless connections between blackness, darkness, and evil. Indeed, Rabbit makes these very connections when Skeeter first enters his home: "So Skeeter is evil. Rabbit in his childhood used to lift, out of the same curiosity that made him put his finger into his belly-button and then sniff it, the metal waffle-patterned lid on the back yard cesspool, around the corner of the garage from the basketball hoop. Now this black man opens under him in the same way: a pit of scummed stench impossible to see the bottom of" (208/447). Everything is here to suggest a conventionally racist linking of blackness and the satanic, even down to the "stench impossible to see the bottom of." Roger Lambert, in *Roger's Version,* has a similarly racist revelation the morning after he sleeps with his step-niece, Verna, who lives in an inner-city housing project and whose illegitimate child is half black: "Messy depths had opened under me, where poverty and government merge." Earlier in the novel, moreover, while viewing Verna's living conditions for the first time, he characterizes this mess in very "Skeeter-like" terms: "One received an impression . . . of random energy too fierce to contain in any structure." Perhaps not surprisingly, Frederick Crews, in his review of *Roger's Version,* cites these two passages as proof of Updike's "class-based misanthropy" and "general ill will toward the marginal." Although Crews spends much of his review patiently tracing the novel's theological material to its various Barthian sources, here, when he makes this racist charge, he drops Barth completely. And yet the omission could not be more vital—nor more unfair to Updike—for, in the end, it is Barth's dialectical vision that turns Roger's racism on its head. As Roger himself tells Verna, "[A]ccording to the Bible, what looks like a mess may be just right, really, and people that look very fine and smooth and shiny from the outside are really the lost ones." In precisely the same fashion, Harry's vile observations about Skeeter serve primarily as a set-up for a very elaborate game of topsy-turvy in which Updike deliberately employs racist sentiments in order to construct a larger, more encompassing metaphysical theory that undermines those same sentiments. Those critics who can only view Skeeter as an *Anti*-Christ fail to appreciate not only Updike's dialectical strategy but also the novel's complex theological context. These same critics also never advance beyond Rabbit's early, conditioned response. At the very least, it is important to remember that, in the scene quoted above, Rabbit has only just begun dealing with Skeeter. His—and our—education is still some ways off.[22]

Skeeter's teachings have both a historical and a theological component. The former, in fact, serves as the bedrock for the latter. During the first of the novel's several "seminars" in "Afro-American history" (229/ 466), Skeeter traces the events following the emancipation of the slaves. Mindful of his audience, he begins his lesson quietly, benevolently. "Let's forget about slavery, Chuck," he tells Rabbit. "It was forever ago, everybody used to do it, it was a country kind of thing, right?" (229/ 466). Rabbit is thus stripped of the luxury of apologizing for slavery and thereby absolving himself. Skeeter is more interested in tracing what white America did *after* the end of slavery. "[H]ere I begin to get mad," he says, and his rhetoric consequently heats up. Sometime around 1876, following the first wave of emancipation—during which black senators and legislators established, among other things, the first public school system in Dixie—the United States, Skeeter proclaims, waded into "the biggest happiest muck of greed and graft and exploitation and pollution and slum-building and Indian-killing this poor old whore of a planet has ever been saddled with" (232/468). To carry out this program of exploitation, he continues, the "Southern assholes" and the "Northern assholes" cut a "deal," in which the Southerners agreed to "screw [its] black labor" and the Northerners agreed to "screw [its] immigrant honky and Mongolian idiot labor" (232/468). Here Skeeter, a black man, allies himself with the novel's other "new Tontos," Charlie Stavros and the

22. Updike, *Roger's Version,* 286, 59; Crews, "Mr. Updike's Planet," 186; Updike, *Roger's Version,* 278. The similarities between *Rabbit Redux* and *Roger's Version* hardly end here. Judy Newman notes the novels' shared interest in technology—plastics, space travel, television, and linotyping in *Rabbit Redux,* computers in *Roger's Version*—while elsewhere she notes that "Updike structures the novel in a fashion to call attention to the computational and the mechanical, just as, in *Rabbit Redux,* McLuhanite messages were inscribed within the fictional medium" (148). Even Crews connects Verna with "the demonic Skeeter and the spaced-out Jill in *Rabbit Redux*" (186).

South Vietnamese among them. "Far as the black man goes," he adds, "that's the '76 that hurt, the one a hundred years before was just a bunch of English gents dodging taxes." Just relating this sordid tale makes Skeeter so angry that he is moved to tell Rabbit, "[I]f I had a knife right now I'd poke it in your throat and watch that milk-white blood come out and would love it, oh, would I love it" (233/469). Stunned into silence, Rabbit can only step back and say, "O.K., O.K."

But Skeeter's lesson is not over. He is angry not just because white America had its chance to do right by its freed slaves, but because, in the process, white America sold itself out as well. It sold out the whole country, in fact: "To keep that capitalist thing rolling you let those ass-hole crackers have their way and now you're all asshole crackers, North and South however you look there's assholes, you lapped up the poison and now it shows, Chuck, you say America to you and you still get bugles and stars but say it to any black man or yellow man and you get hate, right? Man the world does hate you, you're the big pig keeping it down" (234/470). Rabbit has no answer to this but to accuse Skeeter of self-pity. Rather than lash out at Rabbit for his obtuseness, however, Skeeter tries to make Rabbit understand why he, a white man, cannot accept his complicity in this history of exploitation. According to Skeeter, Rabbit clings to his conviction that blacks have only themselves to blame for the very simple reason that he cannot stand to surrender the symbolic function African Americans perform for him. "White man sees a black man," Skeeter says later, "he sees a symbol, right?" (242/476). But a symbol of what? In short, a symbol of all the pain and suffering produced by white America's capitalist greed, suffering of which this same white America would like to absolve itself. And African Americans remain the scapegoats of that sordid legacy. As Skeeter puts it: "We fascinate you, white man. We are in your dreams. We are technology's nightmare. We are all the good satisfied nature you put down in yourselves when you took that mucky greedy turn. We are what has been left *out* of the industrial revolution, so we are the *next* revolution" (235/470). We can now hear Updike speaking directly through Skeeter. Indeed, Skeeter employs here the exact same metaphors Updike used in his examination of Barth's *nihil.*

And like Updike, Skeeter delights in literalizing this metaphoric language. In another one of these seminars, this one devoted to slavery,

Skeeter describes the mind-set that allowed white slave-owners to deny the humanity of their slaves. After listing the economic and legal issues surrounding these acts of degradation, he delves deeper into the psychology of the slave-owner, trying, in the process, to understand what else was at stake. "Now how could the law get that way?" he asks. "Because they did believe a nigger was a piece of shit. And they was scared of their own shit" (241/476). Rather than accept their "shit" as their own, the slave-owners transformed their slaves into "pieces of shit" and heaped abuse upon abuse in the form of transferred self-hatred. During this same discussion, Skeeter also takes on Rabbit's conception of the American dream as "God lying sleeping, the quilt-colored map of the U.S. coming out of his head like a cloud." Whereas for Rabbit this image places America above human blame, much like Updike's God, for Skeeter the image of the American dream is direct evidence of the country's culpability for its action—also, paradoxically, like Updike's God. Both Skeeter's America and Updike's God are aloof from the human misery they have set in motion and, at the same time, culpable by that very refusal to intervene. America, he says, was never a place where "this happens because that happens." Rather, it is the way it is because it has willed to be so: "no sir, this place was never such a place it was a *dream*, it was a state of mind from those poor fool pilgrims on, right?" (242/ 476). There is no escaping our guilt, Skeeter insists. Although we are a free nation, we have nevertheless freely chosen to exploit blacks and Indians and other "immigrant honkies." This is the oddly Calvinistic message of this black Jesus, a brilliant political and historical spin on Updike's own doctrine of Original Sin.

And how does Rabbit respond to all of this? The question of whether or not Rabbit does in fact learn anything from Skeeter has been the subject of considerable debate in Updike scholarship. Usually, the question boils down to, "Does or does not Rabbit change his racist thinking?" Ignoring ample textual evidence to the contrary—and, on more than one occasion, misquoting the text—Edward Jackson states bluntly, "No matter what Skeeter says or does, Rabbit remains annoyed and angry, but he does not act." Although Detweiler argues that Rabbit does move away from "his defense of America's moral superiority and toward a negative-critical view of his country's history and present state," he insists that this "conversion" does not represent a genuine "change of heart" but rather a "personal response" to Jill and Skeeter. Vargo, reading the whole Skeeter section as a ritual of redemption performed for Rabbit's benefit, concludes that the atonement never fully comes off. Only Markle argues for a genuine positive change in Rabbit's attitude. Her reading convinces because it places the race issue in context not only with the novel's other teeming issues but also with many of the issues raised in *Rabbit, Run*. She regards the race issue as continuous with Updike's overarching exploration of guilt and Original Sin. As a result, she is able to treat Rabbit's change of heart from within the novel's ambiguous, self-contradictory, and ironic fictional space.[23] In the end, it would constitute novelistic bad faith for Updike to have turned Rabbit into an unblemished paragon of sound, nonracist thinking. Such a strategy would not only be untrue to Rabbit's basic character but would also serve to transform *Rabbit Redux* into a bland polemic about the evils of racism, which it quite simply is not. It is rather a novel, that is, a work of art whose higher truth is the sloppy, unmanageable stuff of existential reality.

This caveat aside, it seems clear that Rabbit responds, on the whole, positively to Skeeter's lessons. "Chuck," Skeeter says at one point, "this gives you pretty much a pain in the ass, right?" "No," Rabbit replies, "I like it. I like learning stuff. I have an open mind" (242/477). And learn he does. When Skeeter asks him, "You believe any of this?" Rabbit replies, without hesitation, "I believe all of it" (469/233). Rabbit's change of heart is nowhere made more apparent than in the confrontation between him and his two neighbors, Mahlon Showalter and Eddie Brumbach. Showalter is in computers, Brumbach works on an assembly line: two more solid white citizens it is hard to imagine. Instinctively, Rabbit takes to both men. Brumbach, the more aggressive of the two, particularly appeals to Rabbit because of his tour of duty in Vietnam. Though they come to threaten Rabbit about Skeeter and Jill living together in his house, he humors them, even helps them along as they try to raise this charged issue. Nevertheless, Rabbit stands up to their threats. He even offers to move out of the neighborhood himself (290/518). But when the two neighbors insist on his kicking out Skeeter,

23. Edward M. Jackson, "Rabbit is Racist," 448; Detweiler, *John Updike*, 133; Vargo, *Rainstorms and Fire*, 166; Markle, *Fighters and Lovers*, 159–60.

Rabbit serenely replies, "He goes when he stops being my guest. Have a nice supper" (290/518). It is a bold stance, hardly the stuff of moral passivity, as many readers have interpreted Rabbit's involvement with Skeeter. He even tells Nelson, who has lately been receiving taunts for living with Skeeter, "Hey. I'm sorry. I'm sorry you have to live in the mess we all make" (293/521).

Instances such as these only begin to tap into the depth of Rabbit's change of heart. He does more than simply defend his black houseguest. As Updike himself argues in his introduction to *Rabbit Angstrom*, Rabbit symbolically "becomes black, and in a fashion seeks solidarity with Skeeter" (xvi). Skeeter himself pursues this solidarity. When he first appears in Rabbit's house, he remarks, "I like your hostility, Chuck. As we used to say in Nam, it is my meat" (206/445). He then goes on to provoke Rabbit to lash out. "Throw me out," he insists. "I want you to touch me" (209/448). Rabbit does touch him: he punches him, in fact. Yet this is precisely the reaction Skeeter wants. Only by getting Rabbit's racist hostility out in the open can the two of them genuinely begin reaching out toward one another. Sure enough, within days after Skeeter moves in, Rabbit finds himself sleeping soundly (235/471). And after spending the long moon-shot summer learning from this angry man of bitter, ugly truth, Rabbit even starts "[t]rying to be Skeeter," talking tough and uttering the unutterable (295/523). He is enthralled by Skeeter's energetic vitality, by the palpable heat of his anger and the finely chiseled economy of his body. He gazes in fascination at Skeeter's "curious greased grace of gestures, rapid and watchful as a lizard's motion, free of mammalian fat" (251/484). Yet despite this urge for connection, Rabbit cannot make the final step over the racial barrier. "Skeeter in his house feels like a finely made electric toy," the narrator tells us, then adds, "Harry wants to touch him but is afraid he will get a shock" (251/484).

Still, the novel provides two moments of clear solidarity. The first occurs when Rabbit, on Skeeter's insistence, reads from *The Life of Frederick Douglass*. Before handing him the text, Skeeter remarks, "As a white man, Chuck, you don't amount to much, but niggerwise you groove" (277/507). As Rabbit reads—"With feeling," Jill remarks—he assumes Douglass's voice, which is what Skeeter wanted in the first place. It is Rabbit, the soft bloated white man, who announces, through Douglass's

emphatic prose, "The poor slave, on his hard pine plank, scantily cov-
ered with his thin blanket, slept more soundly than the feverish volup-
tuary who reclined upon his downy pillow. Food to the indolent is poison, not sustenance" (280/510).[24] And it is Rabbit, until now afraid of
the "noisy" blacks around him, who retells the story of Douglass standing up to his slave-owner, a tale whose blinding moral is, "A man without force is without the essential dignity of humanity." "Oh, you do
make one lovely nigger," Skeeter remarks (283/512).

   The second moment occurs several nights later, during which Skeeter
reverses roles once again, forcing Rabbit to play the part of the "nigger."
In this scene, Rabbit becomes "a big black man . . . chained to [a] chair,"
Skeeter assumes the role of the white slave-owner, and Jill becomes a
black slave woman on the market scaffold (296/524). Getting into his
role, Skeeter asks Jill to turn around, to show her teeth, and so on. Then
he transforms the scenario into a sexual rite. He declares, "[W]e will
have a demon-stray-shun of o-bee-deeyance, from this coal-black lady
. . . who is guaranteed by them ab-so-lutily to give no trouble in the
kitchen, hallway, stable, or bedroom!" (297/524). In this "demon-stray-
shun," Jill drops to her knees to fellate the "white" slave-owner, as her
lover, the "big black man . . . chained to [a] chair," looks on, helpless.
Turning on the light, Rabbit sees that "Skeeter is not black, he is a gentle brown" (297/525). Skeeter and Jill seem to him not like a black man
and a white woman, nor even their play-acting reverse, but like
"smooth-skinned children being gently punished, one being made to
stand and the other kneel" (297/525). Rather than being threatened by
this tableau, Rabbit finds it "beautiful." By joining in, Rabbit can
achieve communion with his antagonist, blurring the distinctions between white and black through this redeeming act of sensual contact.
But Rabbit cannot make this final move. When Skeeter asks him to
"strip and get into it," he declines. "I'm scared to," he tells Skeeter.

   Vargo reads this scene as Skeeter's attempt to create an atonement
"ritual" whereby the white characters, Jill and Harry, can experience the
humiliation forced on black slaves and hence atone for their complicity in white racism.[25] As a result, he regards Rabbit's refusal to partici-

24. The latter line will later serve as one of the epigraphs of *Rabbit at Rest.*
25. Vargo, *Rainstorms and Fire,* 166.

pate as a failure in his education, for since the fellatio rite goes uncon-
summated, Rabbit is unable to receive the atonement Skeeter promises. This seems partially correct, but not entirely. Vargo writes that Harry holds back because he is "fearful of being forced into the darkness,"
yet there is no textual evidence to support that claim. The narrator states
quite explicitly that Rabbit is frightened because Jill and Skeeter seem
to him "an interlocked machine that might pull him apart" (298/525).
In other words, what Rabbit fears most is not so much the lure of darkness as the loss of his own Kierkegaardian singularity. Always the man
in the middle, Rabbit clings to the need to identify himself against a dialectical play of opposites. The "machine" he watches, and finds beautiful, is an interlocked mechanism of white and black, male and female,
in which the defining lines between all four have been blurred. The
tableau itself is an emblem of the future Skeeter prophecies, that is, the
next revolution, in which white and black, male and female interlock
and blend. Though Rabbit finds the vision beautiful, he does not see
how he can fit into it without "pulling himself apart." He feels he must
stay stable, to keep both him and the machine together. When he loses
his job, for instance, his boss, Pasajek, tells him, "Everything moves
faster nowadays," to which Harry ruefully replies, "Except me" (563/
342). Elsewhere he characterizes himself as an "old lump whose only use
is to stay in place to keep the lumps on top of him from tumbling" (198/
436). In refusing to join in, Rabbit is not refusing Skeeter's invitation
to cross the racial barrier. He has already accepted that invitation, and
then some. Rather, he is holding himself rigid against the entropic chaos
that Skeeter wants to usher in, a chaos Rabbit acknowledges as entirely
necessary—with checks, of course. He is Skeeter's "check." And Skeeter
is his.

V. Chaos and the Devil's Chains

This scene—the last one involving Skeeter's lessons in racial history—
marks the culmination of Rabbit's attempt to seek solidarity with black
America. Typically, Updike concludes on an ambiguous note. But the
ambiguity does not necessarily hinge on the race issue. For Skeeter's
teachings transcend race, taking on as well a whole host of larger meta-

physical issues. And it is because of those metaphysical aspects of Skeeter's message that Harry holds back. Ironically, Rabbit overwhelmingly agrees with most of what Skeeter teaches in this latter regard.

As touched upon already, Skeeter does not only bring a message of racial deliverance. He also proclaims a gospel of chaos. To convey the full weight and charge of what he means, he appeals to his recent experience in the jungles of Vietnam, which place he regards as "the doorway into utter confusion" (405/618). In the only extended section of the novel narrated from his point of view, Skeeter speaks of the war as a window into "another world," a "world of hurt" and death and pure chaos, a manifestation on this earth of the "nothing" behind the "something." As such, it has a "holy quality" that he has difficulty nailing down (259/492). The chaos is in part social. "Nam," he tells them, "must be the only place in Uncle Sam's world where black-white doesn't matter. Truly. . . . The Army treats a black man truly swell, black body can stop a bullet as well as any other" (259/492). Indeed, it is the overwhelming, unavoidable presence of death that erases all these human, social distinctions.

And the death is formless, without direction or intent. "It was very complicated," he explains, "there isn't a net . . . to grab it all in" (258/490). Again employing Updike's Barthian language, he tries to "get it all in" by outlining for Rabbit, Nelson, and Jill two theories of creation. The first, the Big Bang, he describes in terms of Barth's *creatio ex nihilo:* "it all came out of nothing all at once, like the Good Book say, right?" The second theory, which he prefers, posits a continuum whereby the universe expands infinitely outwards. Yet not entirely, he adds. "[I]t does not thin out to next to nothingness on account of the reason that through strange holes in this nothingness new somethingness comes pouring in from exactly nowhere" (261/494). This image comes to him in the form of a drug-inspired vision of holes forming in Harry's ceiling, white holes through which something is pouring through (261/493). Later, Skeeter will identify this "something" as God "pouring through the white holes of their faces" (264/496). God is not a "white man," then, but the "something" that penetrates through the holes in their white "nothingness."

Similarly, Vietnam is another of these holes, and through this hole a new something, a new God, is pouring through. Invoking metaphors that recall Rabbit's first assessment of him as evil, Skeeter provides the following description of war-torn Vietnam: "It is where the world is redoing itself. It is the tail of ourselves we are eating. It is the bottom you have to have. It is the well you look into and are frightened by your own face in the dark waters down there. It is as they say Number One and Number Ten. It is the end. It is the beginning. It is beautiful, men do beautiful things in that mud. It is where God is pushing through. He's coming, Chuck, and Babychuck, and Ladychuck, let Him in. Pull down, shoot to kill, Chaos is His holy face" (261/493). With this passage, Updike hoists the crowded bag of Skeeter's metaphoric significance and draws tight the drawstring. Here, *Rabbit Redux*'s relentless piling up of either/ors reaches its culmination, and it does so, significantly, in the voice of Skeeter, Rabbit's most powerful dialectical partner. Taken out of context, the passage can convincingly read like Skeeter's final word on white racism. What Rabbit first saw in Skeeter and which he termed "evil" was nothing more and nothing less than the sight of his own face in dark waters. In fact, Updike invokes this very same image earlier in the novel, during a scene in which Rabbit and Skeeter watch an episode of *Laugh In!* In the opening bit, Arte Johnson and Sammy Davis, Jr., share a park bench and stare at one another "like one man looking into a crazy mirror" (247/481). Returned to its context, the passage restores the "it" to its proper antecedent—Vietnam—and Skeeter's bag therefore bulges even wider. As the black Jesus, he has come to let that chaos in. First he wants whites to confront their own "bottoms" and accept their own "shit," rather than displace that "shit" onto their black neighbors. Second, he wants to unleash the chaos that resides in that bottom, to force everyone, white or black, to accept death and suffering as unavoidable components of existence, as parts of an unbreakable equation linking life-and-death, black-and-white, yes-and-no. In short, Skeeter's gospel is the culmination of Rabbit's dream of the two spheres.

Rabbit is not the only target of Skeeter's unsettling gospel of race and chaos, for Jill, too, becomes directly implicated. Earlier we saw that, when Rabbit first meets Jill at Jimbo's, she is diagnosed as clean of heroin. Immediately afterwards, Skeeter associates heroin with his own black blood, which white America symbolically uses to "wash away [its] sins" (122/371). This brief exchange foreshadows one of the novel's most disturbing plot developments, Skeeter's deliberate attempt to rehook Jill on heroin. Perhaps Hunt has these episodes in mind when he dismisses Skeeter as a "despicable" character. Nevertheless, Skeeter's actions, despicable though they are, also serve to illuminate further the novel's theopolitical vision. When Skeeter shoots the drugs into Jill's veins, for instance, he insists that she call him her "Lord Jesus" and her "Savior" (299–300 /526–527). She agrees. Meanwhile, the drugs Skeeter pumps into her veins he characterizes as "Bad, bad, bad" (527). Here, Skeeter's role as black America's savior dovetails seamlessly with his related role as the messiah of the God of death. If the heroin represents the "blood to wash away" the sins of white America, then Skeeter is merely returning white America's sin to its original source. He thereby absolves himself of "carrying" the burden of white America's racial hatred. At the same time, Updike associates the drug scenes with Vietnam, Skeeter's explosive metaphor for "God's holy face." Watching Skeeter administer the heroin to Jill, Rabbit imagines that he and Skeeter are two warriors in the Pacific jungle who "have taken a hostage. Everywhere out there, there are unfriendlies" (300/527). The war has come home, and the heroin, which Skeeter describes as "bad," is the conduit through which the war has traveled. As a result of Skeeter's complex rhetorical orchestrations, the heroin he pumps into Jill's veins ends up symbolizing not only the "blood" of white sin but also the stuff of God's death-dealing nature. Hence, although Skeeter preaches the gospel of death, he is not that gospel's martyr. Rather, he transfers the task of martyrdom onto Jill, the same way he transfers to her the burden of white sin. This gentle white girl, with her naive hippie faith in free love and universal oneness, ends up carrying within her veins both the sin of white America and the blood of "badness," as well.

But Skeeter is not all theory and theological table-turning, for his prophecies in fact come to pass in *Rabbit Redux*. Perhaps blinded by the lofty metaphysical reach of Skeeter's theories, Updike's readers have by and large failed to note that the burning of Rabbit's house is the fulfillment of Skeeter's direst warnings. Through this compact piece of plotting, Updike finds a way to dramatize both the racial and the theological components of Skeeter's gospel. As most critics have already noted, the disaster in which Jill perishes replays the drowning of baby Becky from *Rabbit, Run*. From water we come to fire. Similarly, the fire is foreshadowed exactly as was Becky's drowning. During the scene involving

Rabbit and his angry neighbors, Showalter and Brumbach reveal that some of the neighborhood kids have been looking through Rabbit's window. The scene ends with Brumbach making the following unambiguous threat: "You better do fucking more than pull the fucking curtains, you better fucking barricade the whole place" (289/518). Then, on the night of the fellatio rite, Jill and Rabbit both see, during the brief moment when Rabbit has the light on, a set of eyes looking through the window. When he steps outside to see who it is, however, no one is there. Back inside he tells Skeeter and Jill it was "Nobody" (299/526). This "nobody" is the same "nobody" who, in *Rabbit, Run*, hovers over Janice during the terrifying drunken night before she drowns her baby (261–65/223–26). That is, it is God. This play on "nobody/God" suggests an allusion to Blake's Nobodaddy—with a difference, of course. Blake's Nobodaddy stands for the god of sterile human reason; elsewhere in Blake's vision, this same figure is called Urizen ("your reason"). Updike's "Nobodaddy," on the other hand, is the God of Nothingness, that is, Skeeter's God of death and chaos. Indeed, the next morning Rabbit imagines that this "'nobody' has become an evil presence" (305/532). With Skeeter's brief phone call from out of the mysterious night, Rabbit has been made aware that this Nobodaddy, once again, has struck.

One can only admire Updike's narrative economy, for he informs every aspect of this incident with provocative metaphoric significance without once losing his grip on the quotidian reality being presented. The "nobody/Nobodaddy" Updike posits as the progenitor of this disaster corresponds exactly to Skeeter's own complex system of correlations between white racism and the dark avenging God of death and chaos. In other words, both the white child at the window, armed with racist fear and hatred, and Skeeter's God are the proper antecedents to "nobody." Another clue is the car Harry drives to the scene—Peggy Fosnacht's "Fury," which, in the original 1971 edition, was a less suggestive Mustang. Also, the fire is so "magisterial" that it "makes it hard to see the sun," that symbol in *Rabbit, Run* of the God of life (319/543). Even Skeeter's Vietnam metaphor finds its way into this beautifully controlled piece of narrative. Describing how the fire got started, he tells Rabbit that he heard "this *whoosh* and soft *woomp*," presumably Brumbach and Showalter setting the fire. The noise reminded him of "an APM hitting the bush" and he is moved to think, *"The war is coming home"* (334/

556). According to Skeeter's reading of the war as a local hole through which the face of the God of chaos is shining, that is exactly what has happened.

Yet just as he did in southeast Asia, Skeeter also escapes this "suburban Vietnam." The fire's lone victim is not the novel's "black Jesus" but rather its sacrificial lamb, Jill. In his "Special Message" to purchasers of the Franklin Library edition of *Rabbit Redux* (1981), Updike directly argues for a sacrificial reading of Jill's death: "The cost of the disruption of the social fabric [is] paid, as in the earlier novel, by a girl. Iphigenia is sacrificed and the fleet sails on, with its quarreling crew."[26] According to this Iphigenia metaphor, the fleet with its "quarreling crew" is America itself, while the Trojan War of the myth finds an analogue in the Vietnam War. Hence Jill functions as the debt America pays for war. Yet her death by fire pays another debt as well, for through her heroin addiction she also carries within her the blood of white America's racial sins. When Skeeter's God of chaos strikes Rabbit's house, Jill is there to serve as the white race's crucified martyr. With her death, she assumes the burden of white sin, represented here by heroin-contaminated blood. No wonder Updike is careful to characterize the fleet of America as carrying a "quarreling crew": the "quarrel" here involves race, and although Jill has paid a "price" for America's past sins, the sin has not been washed away entirely, and so the "quarrel" continues. Like Updike's aloof, Barthian God, white America remains paradoxically responsible for and absolved of evil, racial or otherwise.

Even Rabbit acknowledges this paradox when, in the wake of the fire, he finds that he feels both to blame and not to blame, all at the same time. Throughout the novel he has silently asserted his innocence about the world's unavoidable harshness. Around his lonely, frightened father, for instance, he reminds himself that "it's not his fault, he didn't invent old age" (305/531). When Peggy Fosnacht, a friend of Janice's with whom Rabbit makes love, accuses him of using her ex-husband as an emotional escape hatch, he tells her, "Well, that's not my fault,"—that is, it is not his fault that she is already married. "No," she replies dryly, "nothing's your fault" (314–15/539). Similarly, although Nelson

---

26. Updike, "A 'Special Message' to Purchasers of the Franklin Library Edition, in 1981, of *Rabbit Redux*," 858–59.

blames his father for Jill's death, Harry points the finger much higher. For Harry, "luck and God are both up there," whereas Nelson "has not been raised to believe in anything higher than his father's head. Blame stops for him in the human world, it has nowhere else to go" (325/548). Mim, Rabbit's sister, and Charlie Stavros offer a more damning interpretation of Rabbit's blithe claim of innocence. They theorize that he "likes any disaster that might spring [him] free." "You liked it when Janice left," Mim explains, "[and] you liked it when your house burned down" (366/584). Indeed, when he finally walks away from the charred remains of his Penn Villas home, he feels relief as his "house slips from him. He is free" (332/555). Updike himself has remarked, "People are basically very anarchistic. Harry's search for infinite freedom—that's anarchy too. He loves destruction. Who doesn't?"[27]

Yet whereas actual guilt, detectable on human terms through a workmanlike cause-and-effect analysis of the pertinent events, is always in Updike's work ambiguous, ontological guilt is an essential condition we can only accept. In the end, Harry does come to accept his metaphysical complicity in Jill's death, even if he exonerates himself in quotidian terms. In the novel's concluding exchange, he tells Janice,

> "I feel so guilty."
> "About what?"
> "About everything."
> "Relax. Not everything is your fault."
> "I can't accept that." (406/618–19)

In his conflating of Original Sin and white supremacy, Updike makes a similar distinction: Rabbit is free to make fussy distinctions concerning his complicity in Skeeter's specific fate, yet he cannot fully exonerate himself from complicity in producing his cultural position as a black man in America. Significantly, between the 1971 publication of *Rabbit Redux* and its revised republication in last year's *Rabbit Angstrom*, Updike seems to have changed his mind about how he wants finally to equate these two forms of guilt within the concentrated disaster of the Penn Villas fire. In both editions, Rabbit leaves the destroyed house, gets

27. Updike, "One Big Interview," 510.

into Peggy's car, and finds Skeeter waiting in the back seat. In both texts, he fingers the blame on Skeeter, who was, after all, in the house when the fire started. He could have helped her out, Rabbit reasons, and instead he saved his own skin. Then Updike makes some significant changes. The 1971 text contains the following exchange:

> "How could you let her die?" [Rabbit] asks.
> "Man, you want to talk guilt, we got to go back hundreds of years."
> "I don't *feel* guilty," Rabbit says.
> "Goddam green pickles, Chuck, then just don't. But don't pull that long face on me neither. Everybody's stuck inside his own skin, might as well make himself at home there, right?" (335)

Rabbit's plea of innocence is typically ambiguous. He does not feel guilty about *what*, exactly? Jill's death? White racism? Skeeter's response answers this question even as it sustains the ambiguity of Rabbit's position. Through ethical subjectivity, Skeeter suggests, Rabbit can both shoulder his ontological guilt and recognize his relative helplessness and innocence in the face of the world's madness and rage for destruction. Fair enough. Yet the edited version in *Rabbit Angstrom* reads:

> "How could you let her die?" he asks.
> "Man, you want to talk guilt, we got to go back hundreds of years."
> "I wasn't there then. But you were there last night."
> "I was severely disadvantaged." (557)

The new version seems to shift the focus entirely, yet does not—not really. Here Rabbit cuts right through Skeeter's evasive answer in order to make an unambiguous distinction between the two versions of guilt. On one hand, Skeeter is right: to talk about guilt, you have to go back— hundreds of years for racial guilt, back to Eden for ontological guilt. On the other hand, he has failed to answer Rabbit's question, which is pointed directly at the other kind of guilt, that is, guilt about Jill's death. Still, Skeeter's final comeback—"I was severely disadvantaged"—is a humorously indirect dodge. In a sense, he *still* could be talking about racial guilt.

Nevertheless, despite these subtle differences, Updike is careful to sustain the scene's concluding ambiguity, for in neither version is it possible to determine conclusively who bears final responsibility for Jill's death. The criterion for complicity shifts with the focus. On one hand, Skeeter is directly guilty for not helping Jill out of the house. On the other hand, he is exonerated ("severely disadvantaged") by virtue of the fact that the fire was set in response to white racist anger, of which he himself is a victim. Yet this white racism in turn taps into the novel's larger thematization of ontological guilt, whereby the failure to recognize both is shown to breed dire consequences. The dialectical possibilities of the scene itself—guilty/not-guilty—are only resolved through an additional third turning in which the dialectic doubles back on the reader. In this way Updike manages to implicate his readers into this complex chain of guilt. Because the specific circumstances of the scene are impossible to separate from the theological and political themes the scene brings to an unnerving, ambiguous close, any assessment of Harry's guilt necessarily entails these self-same theopolitical issues. These issues in turn apply to Updike's readers—particularly, let it be said, to his *white* readers. To say Harry is guilty of Jill's death is to accept not only his ontological guilt but also his shared complicity in the political "sin" she dies for—all at the expense of narrative evidence, moreover, which is very clear about the fact that Harry simply *was not there*. At the same time, to cite the narrative chain of events as proof of his innocence is to ignore his *symbolic* complicity, spiritually, politically, or otherwise. All of which is to say that, in order to decide this knotty either/or, readers must first examine their own feelings about racism, complicity, and Original Sin. The key thing to keep in mind is that *readers must decide for themselves*.

VI. Back Here on Earth

The long coda that follows the burning of Rabbit's house represents Updike's attempt to find a way to affirm, however diffidently, the 1960s world he spent the first part of the novel attacking so vociferously. To bring about this hesitant affirmation, he brings back a minor character from *Rabbit, Run*, Harry's sister Mim. More so than any other figure in the novel, Mim has made her peace with the world around her. The technological emptiness of the new culture has become her element, while the artificiality of modern existence has become her own best weapon. Yet Mim is no *deus ex machina,* for she has been on the horizon throughout the entire book. She appears as a healing figure in the book, reconciling Rabbit not only with Janice but with his beloved America as well.

Mim has been living in Las Vegas, trying to make it as an actress or entertainer yet actually making it as an expensive call-girl for gangsters and other high-stakes gamblers. She makes no apologies for her life, using it instead as a means for self-improvement. In treating herself as a commodity, she has, in a sense, surrendered to the spirit of the age. She is lean, utterly without excess fat, and everything about her is as efficient as a machine. Watching her react to others, Harry "imagines [that] a coded tape is being fed into her head and producing, rapid as electronic images, this alphabet of expression" (352/572). Similarly, one afternoon she regales Nelson and the other Angstroms with her imitation of a Disney "animitron," those robotic presidents and pirates that punctuate the omnipresent amusement park's more tepid attractions (362–63/580–81). The men she "dates" in Las Vegas all demand this kind of robotic efficiency—flat stomachs, health food—while most of her time is spent indoors, in artificial light. Outside, the world is a moonlike desert, which Mim prophecies is the way of the future—the future of America, the Land on the Moon. "That's what it is, a desert," she says. "Look out for it, Harry. It's coming East" (359/578).

As a fully integrated citizen of the new technological culture, Mim is able to see the positive features of the world around her. Whereas Harry saw Jill's hippie belief in selfless love as a betrayal of force and will, Mim sees it as a brave attempt to prepare for the desertlike conditions of the future. What she likes about the younger generation is the way it is trying to "kill" the softness that people of Harry's generation carry around like excess baggage. "They're going to make themselves hard clean through. Like, oh, cockroaches. That's the way to live in the desert. . . . [O]nce these kids get it together, they'll be no killing them. They'll live on poison" (361/579). As we have seen, America is already living on poison—artificial TV dinners, milkshakes laced with chemical sludge—while people like Harry—whom Janice once described as a "large white man a knife would slice like lard"—lag behind.

It is also Mim, lean and hard and ready for the future, who effects the novel's tidy resolution and thereby gives Janice and Harry a future. By sleeping with Stavros—part of her "job," in a sense, which she describes to Harry as "perform[ing] a service" (359/578)—she gives Janice a way to come back to Rabbit while saving face. And Rabbit takes her back, just as she took him back ten years before. Both now have blood on their hands, both have accidentally killed a daughter. In the final scene, Janice and Rabbit take a room in a hotel called the "Safe Haven," and though they do not make love, they do stumble toward something resembling tenderness. Updike points out in his introduction that their final reunion "is managed with the care and gingerly vocabulary of a spacecraft docking" (xv), and indeed it is. While in bed, for instance, Rabbit feels he and Janice "are still adjusting in space, slowly twirling in some gorgeous ink that filters through his lids as red" (405/17). Again, Updike's metaphoric language clues the reader into larger thematic concerns. In the same introduction, he reveals, "The novel is itself a moon shot: Janice's affair launches her husband, as he and his father witness the takeoff of Apollo 11 in the Phoenix bar, into the extraterrestrial world of Jill and Skeeter" (xv). Even the epigraph from the Apollo mission that precedes Rabbit's entrance into Jimbo's contributes to this metaphoric framework. Hence Rabbit and Janice's reconciliation in the Safe Haven suggests Updike's own reconciliation with moon-obsessed America, which for all its violence and guilt, is still a "Safe Haven." As Harry puts it, "I think . . . about America, it's still the only place" (83/337).

Three

Rabbit Is Rich
More Stately Mansions

[T]he religious speaker, if I may say so, should have his fun in making his heroes just as fortunate as they want to be, turn them into kings and emperors and millionaires and happy lovers who win the girl and so on—but he must also see to procuring suffering for them in their inner beings
—Søren Kierkegaard, *Concluding Unscientific Postscript*

Because most work on the Rabbit novels has up until now dealt with a "trilogy," few of Updike's readers have been able to identify the complex structure of the finished tetralogy, a structure Updike seems to have had in mind as early as *Rabbit Redux.* Generally, *Rabbit Is Rich,* the third novel in the series, has been regarded as a conclusion, a summing up of the unresolved issues raised in the first two novels. In other words, it has been seen as the synthesis of the "thesis-antithesis" dialectic of its predecessors. But Updike is rarely, if ever, interested in such "summing up"; his dialectical vision remains always unresolved and in tension. Likewise, *Rabbit Angstrom* as a whole is structured around the unresolved antinomial tensions produced by the work's four discrete units. With *Rabbit Is Rich,* Updike's Rabbit tetralogy does not begin summing up but rather inaugurates its second half. Just as *Rabbit, Run* and *Rabbit Redux* constitute a single dialectical unit, so, too, do *Rabbit Is Rich* and

Rabbit at Rest. Moreover, each pair of novels forms yet another unit to which the other pair/unit responds in the same tension-filled way. Even the individual novel titles support this overarching two-part structure, whereby the concise two-word titles of the first unit contrast with the three-word titles of novels in the second unit.

Formally, *Rabbit Is Rich* presented Updike with an interesting artistic challenge. Ever the fussy craftsman, he had to devise some way to structure this third installment of his tetralogy in such a way that it built on the themes and formal devices introduced in the earlier two novels, even though those two novels were as inseparable as a right and a left hand. At the same time, this new structure had to serve as the floorplan for one final installment. He met this challenge by dividing the novel into two primary components, one that looks backwards and another that looks forward. The backward component concerns the plight of twenty-three-year-old Nelson Angstrom, who returns home from college to reenact a telescoped version of the basic plot of *Rabbit, Run.* This is only fitting since, as the first novel of *Rabbit Angstrom's* second movement, *Rabbit Is Rich* aligns itself with the first novel of the tetralogy's *first* movement, *Rabbit, Run.* Indeed, the first word of the novel is "Running." Conversely, the forward component concerns the continuing fortunes of Rabbit himself who, in his mid-forties, is happy and wealthy at last. Ultimately, this structural design accomplishes three things. First, it incorporates in the form of narrative repetition the first of the previous two novels. Second, it allows the overall work to move forward in a new direction even as it recapitulates what has come before. Third, it lays out a blueprint for its sequel, much as *Rabbit, Run,* inadvertently or not, establishes the groundplan for *Rabbit Redux.* Not only will Nelson replay *Rabbit Redux* in *Rabbit at Rest,* but that novel will bear much the same structural relationship to *Rabbit Is Rich* that *Rabbit Redux* did to *Rabbit, Run.* Four novels, two halves, the second half larger than the first due to the burden of recapitulation: such is the full floorplan of Updike's massive edifice.

Such a four-part plan does not allow for a third or fifth part that might resolve what has come before, as would be the case in a trilogy or a five-act drama. Neither does the plan correspond to the development of, say, a four-movement symphony in the Classical mode, with its conventional arrangement of a self-contained allegro followed by three additional movements in mounting tempos, usually minuet, scherzo, and rondo. It is closer, rather, to the four-part structure of a late Beethoven symphony, with its attention to overall organic unity and its tendency to employ full-scale recapitulation in the prominent final movement. In this musical metaphor, the first two movements of Updike's novelistic symphony are sonata-like in structure—exposition, development, recapitulation—while the third movement is a sprightly, comic scherzo in which a secondary theme, drawn from the first movement, alternates with a main theme that both grows out of what has come before and anticipates what is to come. The secondary theme, which we might term theme "B," corresponds to Nelson's narrative. Although it is present throughout the novel, it appears most prominently in the three instances in which Nelson takes over as the controlling consciousness. Surrounding these three sections are four larger narrative blocks focusing on Rabbit. These passages constitute theme "A." The final arrangement, then, follows a simple pattern of ABABABA, similar to the pattern of the third movement of Beethoven's Seventh Symphony, which consists of a framing scherzo arrangement with full orchestra alternating with a trio in D major.

This structure makes *Rabbit Is Rich* the odd book in the series, the contrasting, bright third movement of the overall work. Even down to its book jacket artwork—the only Rabbit cover not to feature those glaring tri-color stripes—the novel demonstrates a relative freedom and originality of composition that breathes new life into the tetralogy as a whole. Gone are the twin antagonist figures that occupy the development sections of the previous novels. Gone also are the Socratic discussions that make the first half of the series so information-laden. Rabbit is now a blend of the rebelling mystic of his twenties and the political conservative of his thirties. He is content and satisfied, his past, he thinks, now solidly behind him. He is no longer even called Rabbit. Everyone, including the narrator, refers to him as Harry. As the narrator observes early in the novel, "Rabbit basks above that old remembered world, rich, at rest" (69/682), a line which will later function as the epigraph to *Rabbit at Rest.*

Nevertheless, that past will not leave him entirely alone, any more than this third addition to the structure of *Rabbit Angstrom* ignores the groundwork laid by the two previous works. First, the past haunts him in the form of ghosts of the dead, who hover over this novel as poignantly as the Apollo astronauts brooded over *Rabbit Redux*. Second, it returns to him in the form of his own son, who forces Rabbit to watch his own mistakes being played out once again, an exercise in heredity as repetition. Indeed, Nelson, all by himself, assumes the role as this novel's primary antagonist figure. At one point, Harry says to Janice, "I like having Nelson in the house . . . It's great to have an enemy. Sharpens your senses" (125/733). Rather than challenge Rabbit to explore his faith or his assumptions about American history, however, Nelson simply forces Rabbit to realize that wisdom, experience, and, especially, money cannot insulate him from his past. This past in turn serves as the chief symbol in *Rabbit Is Rich* of what Kierkegaard calls hereditary guilt, that ontological component of human existence from which Updike admits no escape. *Rabbit, Run*, a private, psychological exploration of one character's grappling with *angst*, depicts such guilt as an outgrowth of the dialectic tension produced by the competing demands of sensuality and society. *Rabbit Redux*, a "public" novel in the form of contemporary pop sociohistory, transfers this diagnosis of ontological guilt to the fate of an entire nation. *Rabbit Is Rich*, a domestic drama about familial repetition and paternity, resumes the personal focus of *Rabbit, Run* but shifts the direction of the diagnosis vertically, demonstrating how such private guilt is passed on from father to son. One might even say that Nelson literalizes Kierkegaard's term in such a way that heredity is guilt.

As he did in the previous novels, Updike organizes this clustering of themes—money, houses, heredity, and the persistence of the past—under a few significant image motifs. The characteristic shape of *Run* was the zigzag, while the most resonant image was the sphere, suggestive as it was of moons and basketballs and holes through which God's "something" could break through. *Redux* was modeled on the parabolic arc of the moon shot, an event which also provided the novel with a well-stocked storehouse of images and tropes. The governing shape of *Rabbit Is Rich* is that of a chute or a tunnel. Updike manages to compress the novel's numerous competing themes into this image by establishing an elaborate chain of references that links seashells to new houses, new houses to new money, money to feces ("filthy lucre"), feces to the anal cavity, and the anal cavity back to the "tunnel," which in turn leads to the void. A seashell, for instance, is a spiraling tunnel of sorts that is both a house and a visible symbol of the accreted past. At the same time, it is a natural jewel suggestive of wealth.

These various associations all converge in an Oliver Wendell Holmes poem that Harry, early in the novel, obliquely quotes. The poem is "The Chambered Nautilus" from 1858, a misremembered line of which Harry recalls one afternoon while viewing the comfortable homes in his neighborhood. "How did that poem used to go?" he thinks to himself. *"Build thee more stately something O my soul"* (159/765). The missing word here is "mansions," and it appears in the first line of the poem's final stanza. In the piece, Holmes's speaker meditates on the metaphoric significance of the "pearl"-like shell of a "nautilus" mollusk from the Indian Ocean. The shell is a "lustrous coil" built up "year after year," each section representing a "dwelling" which the mollusk leaves in favor of the new. This reading of the shell is for the speaker a "heavenly message," the import of which he reveals in the celebratory final stanza which Rabbit vaguely remembers.

> Build thee more stately mansions, O my soul,
> As the swift seasons roll!
> Leave thy low-vaulted past!
> Let each new temple, nobler than the last,
> Shut thee from heaven with a dome more vast,
> Till thou at length art free,
> Leaving thine outgrown shell by life's unresting sea![1]

This brief stanza nicely encapsulates much of the novel's thematic material. Rabbit, too, spends much of the novel trying to leave his "low-vaulted past," both literally and figuratively. Literally, he moves out of his mother-in-law's dark and confining house and into a new house of his own, in Penn Park, no less. Figuratively, he tries to put the past behind him, "running" over the buried dead who, Rabbit feels, "reach up, they catch at his heels" (225/824). One of those dead, the drowned infant Becky, was indeed left by "life's unresting sea," yet her presence returns in *Rabbit Is Rich* with more force than in any other Rabbit novel save *Rabbit, Run*. Rabbit does get rich, and he does build more stately

1. Oliver Wendell Holmes, "The Chambered Nautilus," lines 29–35.

mansions, yet he also carries the shell of his past on his back, a spiraling reminder of his complicity in the misery of his family members. Updike even manages to attach Holmes's image of the shell as a "spiral" to
the theme of heredity, as Rabbit marvels, again and again throughout
the novel, of the miracle of "those narrow DNA coils" (86/698).

From these disparate yet related themes Updike constructs the sun-
niest and most successful of the four Rabbit novels. In many respects,
it is Updike's best book. Certainly, it is his most decorated work of fiction, snagging the Pulitzer Prize, the National Book Critics Award, and
the American Book Award for the year following its publication. It also
put him on the cover of *Time* for the second time in his career. (The
magazine apparently offered him a third cover to celebrate the publication of *Rabbit at Rest,* but he declined.) Updike himself agrees that it is
one of his best, calling it the "replete but airy product[ ] of a phase when
such powers as I can claim were exuberantly ripe" (xix). He may write
a better novel, but it seems unlikely.

Perhaps the reason *Rabbit Is Rich* works so well is because its author
had two previous tries at "getting it right." In most novels, the author must
content him/herself with suggesting, in the form of metonymy, a fictional past out of which the narrative "present" grows. In *Rabbit Is Rich,*
the fictional past is as real as its reader's past, which it in many ways parallels. Harry Angstrom, moreover, always a believable and well-round-
ed character, achieves in *Rabbit Is Rich* an almost eerie three-dimen-
sionality that, with an impatient sweep of the author's accomplished
writing hand, makes all arguments against the claims of realistic fiction
seem specious and ineffectual. And whereas *Rabbit, Run* is an early novel sometimes marred by its author's relative inexperience, and *Rabbit Redux* is a cranky, embittered novel that is at times weighed down by its
complex theological and sociological thesis, *Rabbit Is Rich* feels almost
idea-free, an astonishingly realized work of pure fiction that eschews abstract ideas for the palpable touch of felt experience. Updike, meanwhile, has never written better. In this bright book he finally discovers
how best to marry his own urbane lyricism with his hero's middle-class
pragmatism. As a result, the prose is indivisibly double-voiced and mul-
ti-layered. Sentences lurch and twist and turn in ways that defy syntactical decorum and yet at the same time ride as smoothly as Harry's luxury Toyota Corona.

Although life seems to be going smoothly for Harry in *Rabbit Is Rich,* the same thing cannot be said for his beloved nation. Set during the summer, fall, and winter of 1979, the novel traces not only Rabbit's good fortune but also the declining fortunes of Jimmy Carter's inflation-plagued, energy-sapped America. As in the two previous novels, this national situation stands in glaring contrast to the plight of its representative figure. Before addressing the themes outlined above, then, it is necessary first to situate these issues within the contemporary, national context with which they interact.

I. Entropy and the Lost Energy of the Dead

Each Rabbit novel, Updike has explained, needs a "clear background of news, a 'hook' uniting the personal and the national realms" (xvii). In *Run* that "hook" is the disappearance of the Dalai Lama, in *Redux* it is the Apollo moon shot, and in *Rich* it is OPEC's sham "energy crisis" of the late 1970s. Updike sounds this keynote as early as the opening sentence: "Running out of gas, Rabbit Angstrom thinks as he stands behind the summer-dusty windows of the Springer Motors display room watching traffic go by on Route 111, traffic thin somehow and scared compared to what it used to be" (3/623). The date is June 30, 1979, that panicked American summer of gas lines and filling-station shootouts. In the numerous news reports Rabbit listens to throughout the novel, the gas crisis invariably leads, all of which is of especial interest to him, since he now co-owns with Janice his father-in-law's Brewer Toyota dealership.

For his coworker Charlie Stavros—the same Charlie Stavros with whom Janice had her affair ten years ago—the oil crisis is little more than a conspiracy rigged by President Carter and the oil companies (8/627). Many of Rabbit's tony new friends share the same sentiment. For Rabbit, however, the crisis is a metaphor for a general and widespread decline in energy, a kind of national entropy.[2] OPEC's gas shortage, real or not, is for Rabbit merely the next step in the increasing decline of the

2. For a considerably different exploration of Updike's use of entropy and the Second Law of Thermodynamics, see Campbell, *Thorns Spell a Word,* 135–46.

American dream, about which he complained so bitterly in *Rabbit Redux*. It is additional evidence that "the great American ride is ending" (3/623). With inflation at a postwar high, the dollar's power, its energy, keeps diminishing as well. "People are going wild, their dollars are going rotten" (3/623), he thinks early in the book. Later, he imagines the inflationary cycle in entropic terms, with money as a closed system from which its buying power "leaks": "Money is like water in a leaky bucket: no sooner there, it begins to drip" (25/643). Likewise, his own town of Brewer, "once the fourth largest in Pennsylvania," has now slipped to seventh, while its "structures speak of expended energy" (32/649). The city has even quit building schools, due to the "zero growth rate approaching" (34/651). Skylab is falling, the Three-Mile Island nuclear reactor is leaking radioactive neutrons (49/664), and the president of the United States has lately begun suggesting that the country is suffering from "a crisis of confidence." Even Carter is running out of energy, collapsing while "running up some mountain in Maryland" (219/735).

Less obviously but equally as important, the gas crisis becomes in *Rabbit Is Rich* a metaphor for an entropic decline of Harry's fighting spirit. Ironically—though, in Updike's work, not surprisingly—this decline is presented as a product of contentment and success. According to the second law of thermodynamics, the total amount of energy in a closed space will decrease as disorder increases: the hot and cold molecules merge and intermingle, producing a uniform temperature without friction. In the first two novels, Rabbit's energy, his desire to *run*, is presented as a product of his dialectical situation. Biology competes against society, freedom fights against domesticity, and so on. In entropic terms, that dialectical tension is a form of order, which in turn produces energy. For Rabbit, this energy manifests itself as *angst*. In *Rabbit Is Rich*, however, that tension has been diluted. The claims of biology in this middle-aged man have now squared with the claims of society, producing a blending of opposites that Updike's Kierkegaardian vision would repudiate and which the second law of thermodynamics would regard as *disorder* leading to stasis and heat death. Society is no longer Rabbit's enemy because it now rewards him in a way it never did before. As a rich man, he benefits from following the rules. Not even the energy crisis can touch him. As a dealer in compact, gas-efficient automobiles, Rabbit benefits from the petroleum panic. He does not even have to promote his product, as the "cars sell themselves," thanks to the Toyota commercials on television "preying on people's mind" (6/625). On one hand, this prosperity is a blessing, and Harry knows it. "[L]ife is sweet," he is moved to think more than once in this novel. "That's what old people used to say and when he was young he wondered how they could mean it" (6/626). Now he knows. At the same time, such prosperity carries a spiritual price. By making him content, his money has sapped him of his anxious energy. By diffusing his old battle with the confining dictates of the middle-class social order, his wealth has removed his angst. In *Redux* he told Jill, "Fear. That's what makes us poor bastards run" (*Redux* 170/412). Now no longer a "poor bastard," he, like the upper-class Jill, has lost his fear. The news does not grab him anymore, primarily because his wealth insulates him from such turmoil. Stripped of that personal stake and subjective identification, the news has lost its sting. Likewise, the natural world's drying up, its depletion of energy sources, does not fill him with terror at the prospect of his own death, as it might have done years ago, but rather "makes Rabbit feel rich, to contemplate the world's wasting, to know that the earth is mortal too" (12/631). All the things he used to fear—nothingness, confinement, death—comfort him now. He is rarely happier, for instance, than when he tools around Brewer in his compact Toyota.

His chaotic inner life has become more placid as well, its competing demands and desires and ambitions now diffused with "blanks . . . patches of burnt-out gray cells where there used to be lust and keen dreaming and wide-eyed dread; he falls asleep, for instance, at the drop of a hat. He never used to understand the phrase" (13/631). Sated with consumer goods and more money than he can spend, he finds he "wants less," even less sex. He blames this lack of interest on "money, on having enough at last, which has made him satisfied all over" (49/664). It has freed him of his desire, of that restless search for freedom which "he always thought was outward motion." Now he sees freedom as really an "inner dwindling" (97/708), that is, as freedom from desire. This "inner dwindling" is itself a form of entropy, a dissipation of energy within a narrowing space. Indeed, so content is he in his narrow, happy life that he now understands "how men can die willingly, gladly, into eternal release from the hell of having to perform" (91/703). Rabbit's middle-aged sense of contentment contrasts directly with the abiding sense of angst that haunted him in his twenties. Back then, he felt the breath of death in the confinement of his own apartment. Now such confinement seems to him a form of freedom.

Perhaps it is precisely Rabbit's "inner dwindling," his contentment and loss of energy, that has put him on such comfortable terms with the dead. For the dead in Rabbit's life have proliferated abundantly. The list of lost loved ones includes both his parents, Janice's father, Jill, baby Becky, Marty Tothero, and Skeeter, who was killed in a shoot-out with police outside his Messiah Now Freedom Family communal dwelling. Rather than be afraid of their example, however, he feels only gratitude. They make space. It is only through the death of Fred Springer, for instance, that Rabbit is able to take over the Toyota dealership. The dead also, he feels, absolve him, leave him free of responsibility, of the guilt borne from complicity in human misery. With Skeeter alive, Rabbit had learned to feel keenly his shared racial guilt. Now that Skeeter is dead, he merely "feels safer" (32/649).

Many of these passages on the dead access the same language of entropic decline employed in the references to the gas crisis and the inflationary cycle. That is to say, the dead are more "lost energy," their power to move Rabbit leaking from his body like the radioactive neutrons leaking from Three Mile Island. Like the petroleum that is alleged to be running out, the dead live in the ground, in the slowly decaying closed system of mortal Mother Earth. Midway through the novel, Harry takes up jogging (run, Rabbit). In both of the two long stream-of-consciousness passages devoted to Harry's running, Updike makes the point, in one way or another, that Harry is "running over the dead." "The earth is hollow," he reflects one day on the golf course, "the dead roam through caverns beneath its thin green skin" (177/781). Moreover, these dead lovers and family members represent those aspects of Rabbit's past which, he thinks, have also ceased to touch him. For it is not just Skeeter himself who has ceased to move him, but also "that part of him subject to Skeeter's spell" (32/649). The past, regarded here as chronological aspects of the self, dies off, too, in the closed space of the subjective consciousness.

Yet like that petroleum, like those leaking neutrons, the energy of the dead and the influence of the past, though buried, are really just forms of latent energy, whose full manifestation must await the passage of time. In other words, the novel's motif arrangement invites us to draw a parallel between the power of the dead and the production of natural energy. As Updike would very well know, gas is derived from plant and animal deposits buried, without access to oxygen, in sedimentary rocks. After millions of years, partial distillation of this organic matter produces gas and oil. Similarly, the energy from Rabbit's past, the energy of the dead, bubbles up around him long after it has been buried. Interestingly enough, Updike, as if in imitation of his own thesis, leaves this idea buried in *Rabbit Is Rich* only to let it manifest itself in full ten years later in *Rabbit at Rest*. Whereas in *Rich* he draws no direct parallel between natural energy and the buried dead, he does announce the connection overtly in *Rest*. In that novel, the narrator will observe, "It has always vaguely interested [Harry], that sinister mulch of facts our little lives grow out of before joining the mulch themselves, the fragile blown rotting layers of previous deaths, layers that if deep enough and squeezed hard enough make coal as in Philadelphia" (468/1475).

From this subtle conflation of two seemingly unrelated ideas—the irretrievable past and the energy crisis, if you will—Updike develops his succinct hedge against the seemingly unavoidable facts of entropy. According to Updike's formulation, death does not lead to stasis and decline but to even *more* energy, albeit energy that will appear only latently, in some deferred future. The best illustration of this idea in *Rabbit Is Rich* is the character of Annabelle Byer. At the end of *Rabbit, Run,* Ruth is still pregnant with Harry's child. In the opening of *Rabbit Is Rich,* that child, now a twenty-year-old woman, appears at Springer Motors. Or at least Rabbit thinks that is who it is. And she does have Ruth's "browny-red many-colored hair" (14/633). Connecting the woman, Annabelle Byer, with his other dead daughter, he imagines, in their first meeting, "an unwitting swimming of her spirit toward his" (14/633). During a test drive in one of his new Celicas, he compares his secret knowledge of her paternity to "seed that goes into the ground invisible and if it takes hold cannot be stopped, it fulfills the shape it was programmed for, its destiny, sure as our death, and shapely" (23/641). The appearance of Annabelle Byer, as well as his mostly instinctive conviction about her parentage, reawaken in him that part of his inner self subject to Ruth's spell. And when he travels into Galilee to get a glimpse of Ruth, he realizes that the "mysterious branch of his past" which she embodies "has flourished without him" in a place "where lost energy and lost meaning still flow" (113/722). The energy exerted by her may have leaked from his spirit, but it has not disappeared entirely.

II. Money and Sex

In addition to invoking the theme of entropy, Annabelle Byer's appearance also opens up another of the novel's main themes, paternity, and its related theme, ontological guilt. Like almost everything else in the book, these themes are in turn associated with money. We have already noted how Rabbit's new wealth has diluted his interest in sex. The connection between money and sex does not end there, for money has also become a fetish in its own right. By associating sex and money in this way, Updike establishes a metaphoric triangle in which these two coordinate points are joined by the mediating theme of heredity and paternity. The triangle works as follows: Sex gets conflated with money, paternity becomes debt, and debt produces guilt. Which brings us back to Kierkegaard. But that is jumping ahead. Before arriving at the debt/guilt apex, we must first explore the numerous ways in which money, sex, and debt are linked. Only after that groundwork has been established will we be prepared to explore this novel's exploration of infinite guilt, a theme each Rabbit novel takes up in a specific way.

To set up this tidy triangle, Updike first associates money with marriage, or at least with Rabbit's marriage. If Rabbit is rich, it is only because Janice is rich. After the tumultuous events narrated in *Rabbit Redux,* Harry and Janice moved into the Springer's Mt. Judge home, whereupon Fred Springer put Rabbit to work at the car dealership, exactly as he did for a brief period in the late 1950s, when Harry returned from his affair with Ruth. He and Janice now share one-half ownership of the lot, while Bessie Springer sits on the other half. Hence Janice is the source of his wealth, while his fidelity to her is the "price" he pays for his position. Yet he is not unhappy with her, nor with his situation. He not only realizes how indebted he is to her but also freely concedes that her money is the *source* of their fidelity, the bond that holds them together. When she first appears in the novel, the narrator observes, "He is rich because of her inheritance and this mutual knowledge rests adhesively between them like a form of sex, comfortable and sly" (40/ 656).

Yet it is not just the "knowledge" of their shared wealth that functions as a "form of sex": the wealth itself performs the same function. As we saw in our discussion of *Rabbit, Run,* Harry once regarded sex as an arena in which he could feel his "specialness," while Janice's failure to provide that reassurance sent him into the arms of Ruth. Likewise, it was Harry's failure to provide Janice this same type of reassurance that drove her into the redeeming arms of Charlie Stavros. Now, both Rabbit and Janice have found this same validation in their wealth, and their sex life together is correspondingly wrapped up in that wealth. Three times in *Rabbit Is Rich* he and Janice make love, and in at least two of these episodes their lust is directly inspired by news of their rising fortunes. In the last of these three scenes, Harry and Janice absentmindedly drift into lovemaking while discussing the possibility of buying a new house. In fact, his seduction of her accompanies his attempt to convince her to join him in this endeavor: "His hand has crept well up into her nightie; in his wish to have his vision [of the new house] shared, he grips her breasts" (353/941). Likewise, she gets increasingly more aroused as she listens to him lay out the financial details of the purchase (354–56/942–44). Their shared orgasm, finally, corresponds to their agreement to go through with the deal (357/945). Even the one anomaly to this pattern, the first episode, makes overt connections between money and sex, as a tipsy and turned-on Janice comically tries to direct her husband's attention away from a recent issue of *Consumer Reports* (51–55/665–70).

Ultimately, though, it is in the second episode that Updike most spectacularly develops his sex/money theme. On the advice of his friend Webb Murkett, and as a hedge against runaway inflation, Rabbit decides to invest in gold, which has lately been rising in price in response to the bad news from the oil market. Fiscal Alternatives, where he buys the gold, looks to him from the outside like it might be "peddling smut, for its showcase front window is thoroughly masked by long thin blond Venetian blinds, and the lettering on its windows is strikingly discreet" (210/811). While there, he purchases thirty Krugerrands at $377.14 apiece, the full weight of which hangs heavily in his pockets "like a bull's balls" (211/812). He hides them in his bedside drawer where, we are pointedly told, "he used to keep condoms" (212/812). When Janice comes to bed later that night, he arranges himself on the bed, in his underclothes, before displaying his new wealth. He is so excited by his coins and their promise of sex that he begins acting like a child, like a little boy in a tree fort, as he tells Janice, "Don't tell your mother or Nelson or anybody" (216/816). Likewise, his arousal is as quick and eager as it was in his adolescence. As Janice strokes the new coins—a sexual gesture in its own right—he finds himself instantly tumescent, an event so rare in this, his ripe middle age, that he is moved to admit that he "hasn't had a hard-on just blossom in his pants since he can't remember when" (217/817). The money counted and fawned over, Janice and Rabbit then make love amid their new wealth, playing with the coins as might children. Afterwards, when they note with horror that one of the precious coins is missing, Updike makes another sly nod to his entropy theme: if the coins are read as symbols of Rabbit's sexual vitality, then the missing coin suggests a depletion of that energy. On the other hand, they find the missing coin, one hint among many in the novel that entropic depreciation is not the final word.

Judie Newman notes that in this episode Updike dramatizes the extent to which Harry's new station in life is attributable to his wife. Specifically, she cites the moment in which Harry delicately balances the coins on top of Janice's body. Yet Harry's next gesture is even more telling, as he pretends to insert one of the coins into her vagina, "as if to insert it in a slot" (218/818). The message is clear: Janice is his money machine, while the coins serve as substitute semen. Meanwhile, Detweiler detects a mythic subtext in this scene, reading Rabbit as Zeus and Janice as Danaë, who was impregnated by a "shower of gold."[3] Indeed, at the end of the episode, as the two lovers lay spent among the scattered coins, Updike describes them as "Gods bedded among stars" (219/819). And although Detweiler does not make the connection, this reading is particularly resonant in view of the fact that late in the novel, Rabbit and Thelma Harrison will urinate on one another, thus giving whole new meaning to the phrase "shower of gold."

This money/sex axis also brings to a culmination the prostitution

3. Judie Newman, *John Updike,* 71; Detweiler, *John Updike,* 176.

theme that has been slowly developing throughout *Rabbit Angstrom*. We have already seen how Jill regards sex as a transaction, and we have also discussed how this attitude allies her with her *Rabbit, Run* counterpart, Ruth, who was once a prostitute herself. Having resisted both of these women's association with prostitution, Rabbit now seems to have embraced this same fiscal view of sex. "Nothing like the thought of fucking money," he thinks while considering making love to his wife. The irony here is that *Rabbit* has now become the prostitute, for it is he who has sex for money—namely, Janice's money. Newman rightly regards this thread in the novel as a critique of the consumer culture at large.[4] Rabbit's obsession with money, and the way it has replaced his former— and in Updike's terms, relatively healthy—obsession with sex is borne, she suggests, from the media's mass marketing of desire for economic gain, a process Rabbit no longer tries to resist, as he did in *Rabbit Redux*. Now he wants to identify with the mass media images of comfort and self-satisfaction depicted in magazines and broadcast on television. He reads *Consumer Reports* in order to decide what to buy next, and his livelihood is supported by the seductive promotional devices employed in Toyota spots. Whereas he once feared that Ruth's past as a prostitute vitiated the power she had to make him feel special, he now locates that specialness precisely in his economic status. Consequently, he no longer regards sex as an arena in which he can affirm his individuality. Rather, he treats it the same way advertisers do, as one more measure of financial worth.

The character in the novel who most embodies this link between sex and media-determined financial status is Webb Murkett. If Janice is Rabbit's "money machine," Murkett's young wife, Cindy, is the primary object of his desire. He desires her not so much for her beauty and youth as for her symbolic status as an economic signifier. He wants her primarily because Webb has her, and Rabbit wants whatever Webb has. "Harry envies Webb," the narrator reveals when Webb is first introduced, and that is, to say the least, an understatement. Repeatedly Rabbit thinks of Webb as "that lucky stiff." He envies Webb's steady golf swing, he envies Webb's money, and he envies Webb's house: "It would be nice to have a patio, along with a sunken living room like Webb Mur-

4. Newman, *John Updike*, 67.

kett does" (81/693). Cindy is just one more symbol of Webb's wealth, and that is why Rabbit wants her.

But Rabbit is being taken in, for Updike is careful at all times to frame Webb as a symbol of a consumer culture's vision of wealth. At the club, with Webb as both his audience and his model, Rabbit tends to bellow loudly, primarily because he has "watched enough beer commercials on television to know that this is how to act, jolly and loud, on weekends, in the bar, beside the barbecue grill, on beaches and sundecks and mountainsides" (60/674). Newman also points out that the Murketts are once perceived by Harry as looking "framed as for an ad" (172/776). In coveting so intently Webb's outward image of wealth, Rabbit engages in an offshoot of pornography which Tom Wolfe has coined as "pluto-graphy: depicting the acts of the rich."[5] The term "pornography," which translates literally to mean "writing about prostitutes," derives from the Greek *pornographos,* a combination of the root words *porne,* or "prosti-tute," and *graphein,* "to write." Similarly, "plutography" is derived from *ploutos,* the Greek term for wealth. Because Wolfe did not coin the term until 1989, it obviously does not appear anywhere in *Rabbit Is Rich,* let alone *Rabbit Angstrom.* Nevertheless, Updike seems to have had some-thing similar in mind in his own examination of the connections be-tween wealth, imagery, and sex. Whereas Wolfe's conception of pluto-graphy consists of a simple one-for-one substitution of wealth for sex, Updike's unnamed version conflates the three issues in such a way that they are all present simultaneously. Like pornography, plutography has as its primary intention the creation of desire, even sexual desire. Also like pornography, plutography is concerned with the acts of "prosti-tutes," the difference being that the sexual content of the act is back-grounded in favor of pecuniary concerns. The introduction of such a hybrid term is necessary if we are to understand properly the novel's lib-eral use of sexually explicit material. For graphic as *Rabbit Is Rich* might be, little to none of the novel's ostensibly "pornographic" material is free from this "plutographic" association with wealth. When Harry and Jan-ice visit a strip club, for instance, they go to the Gold Cherry. The fe-male models who appear on the front cover of *Consumer Reports,* Rab-bit's new monthly Bible, are also involved in plutography. On one cover,

5. Ibid.; Bonnie Angelo, "Master of His Universe," 92.

a model advertises an article on liquid soap by holding up her hand and displaying a "dab of gooey white face cleaner," an image that makes Rabbit think, "Jism, models are prostitutes" (81/693). But he does not make this reflection pejoratively: rather, he picks up the magazine and reads avidly about new air-conditioners. The woman uses sex to sell consumer status, while Rabbit's desire is piqued at the thought of both. Similarly, Rabbit's desire for Cindy qualifies as "plutographic" in the sense that it is directed less at Cindy *qua* Cindy than at Webb and all he represents, financially, to Rabbit.

The Murketts' desire for one another is similarly "plutographic." Early in the novel, Cindy reveals that she and Webb have purchased a Polaroid SX-70 Land Camera, whose film develops before your eyes. Although they originally bought it "as kind of a novelty," they both admit to being utterly, and inordinately, fascinated by it, so much so that it has acquired a kind of "super*na*tural" significance. "It's magical," she explains to the crowd around her. "Webb gets really turned on [by it]" (59–60/674). Later, Rabbit learns that Cindy was being quite literal. While snooping around in the Murketts' bedroom, Rabbit opens up the bedside drawer and, "remembering the condoms he used to keep in a parallel space" (his gold is there now), finds hidden among the debris a pile of SX-70 color Polaroids of the Murketts having sex. The pictures were apparently taken by the Murketts themselves, during the act. Here Updike levels his most direct indictment against the values of Harry's hero: so preoccupied is Webb with embodying the image of the successful and happy consumer that he transforms even his own sex life into one more manifestation of that image. His relationship with Cindy—his third wife—only validates him if it is captured *as* an image. Sex for the Murketts is therefore plutographic. It is less an act of physical desire for one another than an arena in which the two partners can validate their economic status, a status they register by emulating the images provided by advertisements and so on.

This scene with the Polaroids not only represents an instance in which Updike indicts the Murketts' shallow values but also provides Harry with some crucial insight into the flaws inherent in his hero-worship of Webb. As Newman argues, the images themselves "undercut the mass libidinal fantasy" depicted in mass-marketed pornography such as *Playboy,* where this portion of the novel was originally published.[6] Cindy appears to him as less than ideal, with breasts that "droop more to either side than Harry would have hoped" (306/898) and bare thighs that suggest the unavoidable truth that "[s]he will get fatter. She will turn ugly" (307/899). Webb's age shows through as well. And although the couple appear "golden" in the photographs, the furniture reflected in the bedroom mirror—of course, the narcissistic Murketts keep a mirror by the bed—is described as "dim in blue shadow as if underwater" (308/899). As we have already seen, any description in *Rabbit Angstrom* invoking water in this way suggests death. There are also two missing pictures from what *Consumer Reports* has informed Harry is a ten-picture roll. These photos he finds downstairs in the Murketts' living room. Ostensibly innocent, they, too, suggest an undermining of the Murketts' stylized presentation of economic health and happiness. One shows Webb's five-year-old son standing "*sadly* on the bricks of the patio" (309/901, emphasis added), while the other depicts the three-year-old daughter smiling obediently at her father, who has his arms "lifted to his head as if to scare her with horns" (309/901), horns being the cuckold's signature.

III. Oedipal Tension, Paternal Debt, and Ontological Guilt

Still, the sexual photos turn Harry on, so before returning to the party, he takes a moment to deflate the erection the pictures have inspired. What finally does the trick is the thought of "gloomy Nelson." Nelson does not just present a gloomy picture to Harry: he also makes Harry himself rather gloomy. Nelson tugs at Harry the way debt nags at a money-obsessed man, a fitting analogy in view of the fact that Nelson functions in this sex/money network precisely *as* debt. If coins are semen, then children are the products that semen "buys." And expensive products they are. Hastily "purchased" by Harry and Janice in the heat of their youth, Nelson now appears to Harry like nothing so much as an expensive debt he can only clear through a nonterminal installment plan.

Ronnie Harrison, one of Harry's Flying Eagle buddies, is the most direct spokesperson for this metaphor of children as debt. An insurance

6. Newman, *John Updike*, 73.

man by profession, Ronnie regards not only his own children but also the sons and daughters of his clients simply as financial burdens, or "dependents," in the language of his trade. Although his own children have grown up and left him "feeling out of the woods," he still advises his customers to shoulder huge premiums in case of accident (297/890). Webb's children, various and sundry, are also costing him plenty. In his effort to keep himself decorated with a perpetually young wife, he has put himself in enormous debt, so much so that after three wives and two divorces, he now has a total of seven children and two former lovers on his payroll. "[P]oor Webb," Cindy tells Rabbit. "You know he had five other children by his other wives, and they're both after his money *con*stantly. Neither has married though they're living with men, that's what I call immoral, to keep bleeding him that way" (294/887). Harry even imagines his new daughter-in-law Pru in financial terms, seeing her as "a new branch of his wealth" (289/882).

Of all the offspring mentioned in *Rabbit Is Rich,* however, none goes so far out of his way to raise the value of this hereditary debt as Nelson Angstrom. At every stage of the plot, Nelson costs his father money. In his first appearance in the novel, having just returned mysteriously from Colorado, he is seen digging into Harry's pockets, fishing for car keys, to which Harry says, "Hey . . . what're ya robbing me for?" (79/691). Yet even Rabbit acknowledges the curious fiscal nature of their relationship, for it is not until he hands his son a ten-dollar bill that he feels comfortable asking Nelson about his personal life: "'We ought to talk sometime, Nellie, when you get some rest.' The remark goes with the money, somehow" (79/691). When Nelson gets married, it is Harry, not the bride's parents, who must shell out for the wedding—an expense that includes the catering, hotel rooms for the bride's working-class mother, and a cake that cost "eighty-five American dollars." As Harry sits in the church taking stock of this new expenditure, the narrator observes, "Every time Nelson turns around, it costs his father a bundle" (235/834).

By figuring children as debt, Updike seems to be literalizing one of the central tenets from which Sigmund Freud built his oedipal model. According to Freud, children are in debt to their parents for their very existence, while oedipal resentment results from the recognition of that unpayable debt. In "A Special Type of Choice of Object Made by Men," Freud writes, "When a child hears that he *owes his life* to his parents, or that his mother *gave him life*, his feelings of tenderness unite with impulses which strive at power and independence, and they generate the wish to return this gift to the parents and to repay them with one of equal value. It is as though the boy's defiance were to make him say: 'I want nothing from my father; I will give him back all I have cost him.'"[7] In other words, the competition intrinsic to the oedipal drama is a function of that child's wish to clear that debt. In *Rabbit Is Rich*, the debt gets refashioned in real monetary terms. Rather than try to pay off that debt, the children in *Rabbit Is Rich*—and Nelson in particular—use their debt as a weapon. As is common knowledge, Freud posits as the central conflict of the oedipal drama a feeling of sexual rivalry between father and son. Not surprisingly, Updike treats this sexual rivalry also in monetary terms, yet one more instance in *Rabbit Is Rich* in which sex and money are linked. In this case, the son deliberately increases his debt so as to make his father "pay" for "stealing away" the rival sex object. Money is simply the "currency" through which this rivalry is exchanged.

In the case of Harry and Nelson's oedipal drama, the rival sexual object is not Janice, as one might immediately assume, but Jill, whom Nelson feels Harry "killed." In *Rabbit Redux*, Updike makes several oblique references to the possibility of a sexual relationship between Nelson and Jill.[8] In *Rabbit Is Rich*, he seizes upon this tantalizing possibility as the basis for Nelson's resentment of his father. Regardless of whether he slept with her or not, Nelson continues to think of Jill as his first love, and his subsequent anger at his father for letting her die is further compounded by jealousy. Further supporting this overtly oedipal reading of Nelson and Rabbit's relationship is Nelson's response to the news that Jill has presumably perished in the burning house. In a fit of rage, he turns to his father and shouts, "You fucking asshole, you've let her die. I'll kill you. I'll kill *you*" (*Redux* 320/544). A fourth of the way through *Rabbit Is Rich* Harry recalls this chilling moment (99/710). Of course,

---

7. Sigmund Freud, *The Freud Reader*, 393.
8. At one point Rabbit wonders "[w]hat they do. In that little car. Well, they don't need much space, much contact: young bodies. . . . If she'd offer to give hairy old heavy him a blow job the first night, what wouldn't she do?" (*Redux* 163/406). Later, he confronts her directly: "O.K., what *about* sex, with you and the kid?" (192/430). Rather than offer a denial, however, she evasively answers, "He likes me" (192/431).

Nelson does not kill his father. He does, however, punish his father in other ways. What galls Nelson most is that Harry, far from doing penance for this "murder," seems to have been amply rewarded. All Harry did in the way of punishment was to go back to Janice, settle down at the Toyota dealership, and watch his bank account swell. Seeing that the world did not make Harry pay, Nelson decides to take on the job himself.

The main targets of Nelson's campaign are Harry's beloved cars. The source of Harry's wealth, these cars are what Nelson imagines has replaced him as the focal point of his father's attention. As he tells Rabbit at one point, "All you care about is money and *things*" (119/728). Similarly, early in the novel, he sneers, "Dad's really into cars, isn't he. . . . Like they're magical, now that he sells them" (83/696). Ironically, they seem more magical to Nelson than to Rabbit. The mere thought of the cars sends Nelson into paroxysms of rage, an anger and resentment he takes out on the cars themselves. He begins his reign of terror by smashing the fender of Harry's beloved Toyota Corona. When his father explodes, Nelson remarks, "Dad, it's just a *thing*; you're looking like you lost your best friend" (107/717). Feeling slighted and suffering from "injured merit," Nelson decides to destroy all of his Harry's "best friends" one by one. Although Nelson never overtly announces that this is what he is doing, he does say to Melanie, "I wish I'd smashed up all Dad's cars, the whole fucking inventory" (134/741). And he almost succeeds. Before the book is over, Nelson will wreck no less than five of Harry's cars: in addition to the Corona, he does damage to Janice's Mustang, Ma Springer's Chrysler, and two convertibles he has bought with the lot's money, a '72 Mercury Cougar and a '74 Olds Delta 88 Royale. Some of the wrecks are clearly accidents, while others—the convertibles, for instance—are quite deliberate acts of sabotage. Harry, however, sees them all as deliberate. Upon learning of the scrape on the Mustang, he refutes Janice's insistence that Nelson is "embarrassed about it." "The fuck he is," Rabbit snaps back, "he loves it" (233/832). Harry has a point: Nelson *does* seem to take curious satisfaction in all these smashed cars. In some strange way, he does "love it." At the conclusion of a typically violent episode of *Charlie's Angels,* for instance, Nelson "laughs in empathetic triumph over all those totaled Hollywood cars" (148/754). Harry even takes to calling his son a "car killer" (123/732).

Yet in Updike's either/or world, this notion of oedipal tension works both ways. If children are indebted to their parents for their life, then parents incur a matching *spiritual* debt to their children for the "crime" of passing on the burden of Original Sin. In *Being and Time,* Heidegger cleverly associates "debt" with "guilt" by appealing to "everyday common sense," which, he says, "first takes 'Being-guilty' in the sense of 'owing,' of 'having something due on account.'" Hence, for Heidegger, the ontological condition of 'Being-guilty' is tantamount to "'having debts ['*Schulden haben*']." Updike seems to be playing with similar associations in his analysis of Rabbit's paternal debt to his offspring. In doing so, he reprises a theme he introduced back in *Rabbit, Run.* Prior to baby Becky's drowning, Rabbit is visited by the harrowing conviction that "as a consequence of his sin Janice or the baby will die." Moreover, he imagines that sin as a "black clot embodied in the entrails of the birth" (196–97/169). In chapter 1 we explored how this passage reveals Updike's adherence to the stern Calvinistic idea that Original Sin moves from generation to generation through the reproductive process. In this regard, Updike seems to be taking as his source not only the *New England Primer* and its concise warning, "In Adam's Fall / We sinned all," but also St. Augustine who, in *The City of God,* draws a sharp distinction between Adam's sinless conception from the dust and the sin-laden conception of all subsequent human beings. Augustine writes,

> [T]he descent of man from man is not like the derivation of man from the dust. Dust was the raw material for the making of man; but in the begetting of a human being man is a parent. Hence, although flesh was made out of earth, flesh is not the same as earth, whereas the human parent is the same kind of thing as the human offspring. Therefore the whole human race was in the first man, and it was to pass from him through the woman into his progeny, when the married pair had received the divine sentence of condemnation. And it was not man as first made, but what man became after his sin and punishment, that was thus begotten, as far as concerns the origin of sin and death.[9]

Augustine's formulation is especially pertinent to our present concerns for the way it locates the *father* as the agent through which passes this

9. Heidegger, *Being and Time,* 327; St. Augustine, *City of God,* 512.

"divine sentence of condemnation," which is, simply, death. Although there is no way of telling whether or not he had this specific passage in mind, Updike seems to have seized upon this paternalistic idea as the metaphorical kernel for his own exploration of paternity and Original Sin, or what we have been terming ontological guilt.

Updike first introduces this idea of paternal debt not through the agency of Nelson but rather through Nelson's step-sister, Annabelle Byer, the child Rabbit had with Ruth. Annabelle's first appearance at the lot inspires in Rabbit several telling observations about the miracle of heredity and paternity that feed into the novel's overarching exploration of ontological guilt and Original Sin. In a passage already quoted, Rabbit thinks of his secret knowledge about her paternity as a "seed that goes into the ground invisible and if it takes hold cannot be stopped, it fulfills the shape it was programmed for, its destiny, sure as our death, and shapely" (23/641). This compact image refers not just to the secret itself but to the message that secret portends. His role in the miracle of her existence is in fact the seed, or, more specifically, it was his seed that made her existence possible. With absolutely no help on his part, this seed—*his* seed—fulfills the destiny that was programmed into it, namely, corporeal growth leading inexorably to death. Paternity, then, is tantamount to the transmission of Original Sin, as the seed of life contains within it the eventuality of death. Rabbit's part in transmitting this seed is the debt he owes children. In his regard, we are meant to regard this debt as responsibility. Rabbit is responsible for, that is, "in debt to," his progeny for their own guilt-laden existence. What is more, this debt is both wholly his to accept and entirely outside his control. Ten pages later, he thinks again of his "daughter," imagining her as a physical embodiment of his own sin come back to haunt him: "There is no getting away; our sins, our seed, coil back" (33/650). These thoughts concerning his daughter apply equally to Nelson, and in more than one case, Rabbit conflates the two children. Noting various physical attributes of his own that have passed on to Nelson, Rabbit observes, "Amazing, genes. So precise in all that coiled coding they can pick up a tiny cowlick like that. That girl had Ruth's tilt, exactly: a little forward push of the upper lip and thighs" (79/692). At one point, he even applies these ideas about heredity and sinful destiny to Janice and her mother, thinking by the by, "We carry our heredity concealed for a while and then it pushes through. Out of those narrow DNA coils" (86/698).

Nelson and Annabelle Byer, then, in receiving from Harry the seed of their own deaths, are the walking embodiments of Harry's own sin and guilt. Nelson in particular is peculiarly suited for this role, since he also possesses damaging inside information. More so than any other character in the tetralogy, Nelson has borne witness to all of Harry's worst transgressions, from Ruth to Skeeter to Jill. To Thelma Harrison Rabbit confides, "I think one of the troubles between me and the kid is every time I had a little, you know, slip-up, he was there to see it. That's one of the reasons I don't like to have him around. The little twerp knows it, too" (73/777). In other words, Nelson reminds Rabbit of his mistakes, so much so that the mere sight of him recalls to Rabbit the full scope of his guilt, the same species of guilt Updike feels lies inherent in all human activity, sexual or otherwise. And it is in this light that Nelson fully assumes his role as the novel's embodiment of Rabbit's ontological guilt, that is, the guilt associated with the curse of Original Sin.

Accordingly, each of the incidents involving Nelson's car wrecks is written in the language of atonement and guilt. Viewing the damage on the Corona, for instance, Harry "feels his own side has taken a wound. He feels he is witnessing in evil light a crime in which he has collaborated" (107/717). Harry's personal stake in this mishap extends beyond his fetishizing obsession with his beloved car, what Nelson calls Harry's "best friend." The "crime in which he has collaborated" is in fact his paternity, his bringing into life a guilt-laden son. As a "car killer," Nelson attempts to force Rabbit, literally and figuratively, to "pay" for this crime —the crime of his, Nelson's, existence. And Rabbit realizes this. Not only does he know that Nelson "loves" wrecking the cars, but he also knows that the target of these acts of destruction is him. Reflecting on the scrape on the Mustang, Rabbit groans, "He has my head in a vice and he just keeps turning the screw" (233/832). At the same time, he accepts his metaphoric collaboration in these willful acts of destruction. His guilt, passed down through procreation, now resides in his son. Each time his pocketbook takes a hit, he pays for that guilt.

These themes get further explored in the episode in which Nelson destroys the two convertibles. Symbolically, he buys the convertibles in order to make his father "pay." On the other hand, his doing so inadvertently diminishes Harry's spiritual debt to him, a debt incurred through the passage of hereditary guilt. Perhaps sensing that his plan has backfired on him, Nelson tries to double the debt by climbing into the Delta

'88 and deliberately ramming it into the Mercury. For a brief but significant moment, Harry even imagines that Nelson is going to drive the car into him: "He thinks the boy might now aim to crush him against the door where he is paralyzed but that is not the case" (170/774). Here, more so than in any other episode in the novel, Nelson's willful destruction of the cars gets rendered as a component of his sexual aggression, as Detweiler has suggested.[10] Yet Rabbit does not feel despair or even anger at his son. Rather, the sight of all this crushed metal sends "strange awkward blobs of joy" (170/774) through his throat. What inspires this joy is Rabbit's happy realization of his shared guilt with his son, or, more specifically, the realization that he is finally being made to pay for this guilt. As he observes later in the novel, the reason "we love disaster [is because] it puts us back in touch with guilt and sends us crawling back to God. Without a sense of being in the wrong we're no better than animals" (344/933). Nelson also feels a sort of joy in this disaster, his arising from a similar realization that his resentment at his father is a form of misdirected love. In short, this sweeping attempt to rack up debt has only narrowed the gap between them, evening the debt they owe one another and, in the process, bringing them closer. Telling his Flying Eagle buddies about the incident a week later, Rabbit says, "If the kid'd come out swinging my gut would've been wide open. But sure enough he stumbles out all blubbery and I could take him into my arms. I haven't felt so close to Nelson since he was about two" (170/775). Granted, this is a momentary reprieve in a fierce ongoing battle, yet it is significant nonetheless. In this moment, Updike demonstrates not only the mutual resentment Rabbit and Nelson feel for one another, but also a way out of this angry stalemate.

And there is still more, for Nelson's repeated attempts to make his father pay for his own existence have yet another theological component. In each Rabbit novel, Updike has connected his hero in some way or another with God. In *Rabbit, Run,* he accomplishes this by identifying Rabbit with the Dalai Lama. In the politically minded *Rabbit Redux,* he has Harry represent pre-sixties America, while at the same time he makes America itself a stand-in for Barth's Wholly Other God. In *Rabbit Is Rich,* a novel of paternity and generation, he continues this pat-

10. Detweiler, *John Updike,* 174.

tern by having Nelson, the son, perceive his own father as a madden-
ingly indifferent deity. Rabbit is Nelson's Wholly Other God.

Deliberately or not, Updike prepared the way for this reading as early as *Rabbit Redux*. During the episode in which Harry and Nelson stand
in the street and watch their house burn to the ground—a house that
apparently contains Jill—Updike has Rabbit turn to his son and ask,
"Blame me, huh?" Nelson responds, "Sort of," to which Rabbit adds,
"You don't think it was just bad luck?" (325/548). The narrator continues, "And though the boy barely bothers to shrug Harry understands
his answer: luck and God are both up there and he has not been raised
to believe in anything higher than his father's head. Blame stops for him
in the human world; it has nowhere else to go" (325/548). In *Rabbit Is
Rich*, Updike uses this passage as the springboard for twenty-three-year-
old Nelson's late-1970s attitude toward "luck and God," both of which
stop precisely at his father's head. First, Nelson blames his father for both
Jill's death and his own existence. In so doing he positions his father as
the most convenient symbol for his own wide-ranging resentment at the
adult world writ large, a world in which, as with so many of his peers,
he cannot seem to find his place. He sees the grown-up world as a dis-
tant, unreachable "bubble where the mystery resided that amounted to
power"—in this case, power over his own life, power to act and assume
responsibility. He is constantly haunted by irrational fears associated
with his childhood, such as "that old fear of being in the wrong place,
of life being run by rules nobody would share with him" (331/922). In
his confusion, Nelson rationalizes his fear of growing up by clinging to
the comforting childhood conviction that everything bad that happens
in his life is someone else's fault, particularly his father's. "Everything's
his fault," Nelson declares, "it's his fault I'm so fucked up" (134/742).

So rather than see Jill's death as a product of God's indifference to
human activity, Nelson still insists, even ten years after the event, on
blaming his father. Moreover, the language he uses to level these charges
echoes almost directly Rabbit's language concerning God's culpability
for death through his noninvolvement in human life. Musing on the list
of dead people in his life, Rabbit thinks, "[S]o many more have joined
the dead, undone by diseases for which only God is to blame." Then he
adds, "Think of all the blame God has to shoulder" (73/686). Seventy
pages later, Nelson will repeat this same sentiment, only this time sub-

stituting Rabbit for God: "You think of all the misery he's caused. My little sister dead because of him and then this Jill he let her die" (134/ 741). And although Melanie is careful to object, "Your father's not God," Nelson seems not so sure. At one point he even imagines his father as the grinning "giant" from one of his childhood storybooks. In one of the book's illustrations, the giant gazes at the reader from the far end of a tunnel, at the foreground end of which appear the backs of the hero and heroine's heads. Nelson imagines himself as one of those children: "he Nelson is in a tunnel and his father's face fills the far end where he might get out into the sun" (361/949). Here Updike makes a subtle connection between Nelson's childhood "giant," Rabbit, and God. In *Rabbit, Run,* Updike renders Harry's faith in God as a form of "sun" worship, whereby the sun represents the God of Life. Similarly, in *Rabbit Redux* he makes the barren moon symbolize the God of Nothingness and Death. Both of these ideas in turn inform Nelson's image of his father as the murdering giant who blocks out the life-giving sun. If Harry's "new religion" in *Rabbit, Run* explains death as "lovely life eclipsed by lovely death" (see *Run* 283/242), then Nelson's paternalistic religion explains death as "lovely life eclipsed by Dad."

For all its immaturity, Nelson's entirely familial—or, more specifically, oedipal—conception of the divine order is nevertheless informed by some very Updikean notions of good, evil, and faith. To be sure, Nelson is vibrantly, fascinatingly unlikable, a whirlwind of whining resentment. Even his own wife is moved to remark, "You're a little Napoleon. You're a *twerp,* Nelson" (334/924). Yet like his callous and often hardhearted father, Nelson is not wholly unsympathetic, for as with many of the other antagonist figures in *Rabbit Angstrom,* Updike uses the ostensibly negative aspects of Nelson's character primarily as the springboard for a rich exploration of larger spiritual concerns. Indeed, what is Nelson's obsessive gripe against his father's blithe, self-satisfied indifference to the misery all about him but a benign parody of Rabbit's own faith in Barth's equally blithe, self-satisfied, and indifferent God? And just as Skeeter tried to make Rabbit recognize and embrace the brutal and death-dealing aspect of God, so does Nelson seek to make the world recognize the hard-heartedness that lies at the core of his father. At one point in *Rabbit Redux,* Buchanan says to Harry, "Nasty must be your middle name" (*Redux* 133/380). Revealing this secret middle name eventually becomes one of Nelson's chief obsessions: "Nobody except Nelson in the world seems to realize how nasty Harry C. Angstrom is and the pressure of it sometimes makes Nelson want to scream" (314/906). As he tells Pru, "If I could *just once* make him see himself for the shit he is, I maybe could let it go" (317/908). Nelson also reads into his father's indifference to his misery—and hence Harry's culpability in producing it—a very Updikean message about the essentially God-forgotten world. He also distinguishes himself in this regard from the kids back in college, kids very much like the sixties radicals who so angered Rabbit in their privileged disregard for the essential brutality of earthly existence: "[T]he world was brutal, no father protected you, you were left alone in a way not appreciated by these kids horsing around on jock teams or playing at being radicals or doing the rah-rah thing or their own thing or whatever" (316/907). The world Nelson describes here is, in effect, a domestic model of Updike's free-floating, nominal universe, with its obdurate physical laws and it's Wholly Other God. In both worlds, as Nelson would say, "no father protected you."

One last twist in this complex matrix of oedipal archetypes and Updikean theology demands our attention. Again, we flip the coin and investigate Harry's view of Nelson. Remember, each issue in an Updike novel has two sides. Whereas Nelson sees his father as a frustratingly indifferent deity, Rabbit sees Nelson, finally, as competition. What Rabbit most resents about Nelson is the fact that Nelson is not only a son but also, within the novel's largely oedipal framework, a competitor as well, someone who is seeking to make space for himself by pushing Rabbit out of the way. And Rabbit has cause for alarm, for Nelson has returned home primarily to see if he can secure a job for himself at Rabbit's beloved Toyota dealership. For obvious reasons Rabbit sees this desire on Nelson's part as a subtle, even personal threat. As he explains to Janice, "You can't give him a place without taking a place from someone else" (185/789).

As we saw in the two previous chapters, Updike has argued elsewhere that fallen creatures establish space for themselves "through a willingness to fight."[11] In accordance with this dictum, Updike suggests that Rabbit's sense of being threatened extends all the way to Nelson's mere

11. Updike, *Self-Consciousness*, 130.

existence. Why? Because Nelson's existence marks the limits of his, Rabbit's, existence. For Nelson to thrive, space must be made in the world, and Harry, in his exuberant love of life, is loathe to surrender his space, particularly to his own son, who has the most direct claim on that space. During one of his several internal monologues, Rabbit recalls Janice asking him "why is his heart so hard toward Nelson." His answer clues us into the source of Rabbit's fatherly resentment: "Because Nelson has swallowed up the boy that was and substituted one more pushy man in the world, hairy wrists, big prick" (225–26/825). And that is why, as Rabbit admits in an earlier monologue, "the kid's growing up should seem a threat and a tragedy to him" (138/745). Nelson even recognizes his father's uneasiness about the presence of other vital men, of other competitors. "The trouble with Dad," Nelson thinks, "is he's lived in a harem too long. . . . Any other man around except Charlie who was dying in front of your eyes and those goons he plays golf with, he gets nasty" (314/906). Harry, of course, has a less unflattering take on this issue. Referring only in part to Nelson, he announces to his family, "Take over, young America. Eat me up. But one thing at a time. Jesus. There's tons of time" (122/731).

In a passage midway through the novel that concisely articulates these themes, Rabbit recalls two images from his life that "mark the limits of his comfort in this matter of men descending from men." In the first image a twelve-year-old Rabbit stumbles upon his own father standing pantless in front of his bureau. What persists in Rabbit's memory is the sight of his father's "bare behind, such white buttocks, limp and hairless, mute and helpless flesh that squeezed out shit once a day and otherwise hung there in the world like linen that hadn't been ironed" (212/ 893). The image seems a reminder to Rabbit of his father's delicate mortality. Here was a man like other men, constructed of "mute and helpless flesh" and left to "hang" in the world with no hope of protection. The twelve-year-old son, emerging into his own and slowly shrugging off his childhood sense of oedipal inadequacy, sees his father finally as someone who can be replaced. In the second image, and true to his perennial role as "the man in the middle," Rabbit himself becomes the aging father made of "mute and helpless flesh." In this episode, Rabbit stumbles upon a twelve-year-old Nelson stepping out of the shower. What Rabbit remembers from this image is Nelson's "man-sized prick, heavy and oval, unlike Rabbit's circumcised and perhaps because of this looking brutal, and big. Big" (212/893). Nelson appears to him here not mute and helpless but positively erumpent, a competitor gaining ground. Before this episode, Rabbit perceived Nelson's "occupation of the room down the hall" as if it were merely "the persistence of [his] own childhood in an annex of his brain." After this episode, and after the "stuff with hormones and girls and cars and beers began," he saw Nelson as a threat, as another pushy man in the world. It was at this point in his relationship with Nelson that "Harry wanted out of fatherhood" (212/893). Unfortunately for Rabbit, fatherhood is a job from which you can't resign.

IV. Nelson, Run

Earlier, we examined St. Augustine's famous articulation of how Original Sin gets passed on from father to child. We also noted that Updike would have been struck by the specifically paternalistic slant of Augustine's analysis. What also might have struck Updike about that passage, had he encountered it in his preparations for the composition of *Rabbit Is Rich,* is Augustine's insistence that "the human parent is the same kind of thing as the human offspring," an idea that necessarily works both ways, of course. In *Rabbit Is Rich,* this idea, though obvious at first glance, takes on rich thematic significance. Building on this use of the Calvinistic doctrine of inherited sin, Updike extends its application to include not just "the divine sentence of condemnation" but also specific sins passed on from father to son. For as different as Nelson and Rabbit seem on the surface, they are really very much alike. Late in the novel, Rabbit is moved to observe, "For all that is wrong between them there are moments when his heart and Nelson's might be opposite ends of a single short steel bar, he knows so exactly what the kid is feeling" (387/ 972). The parent really *is* "the same kind of thing" as the offspring— and vice versa. As if to underscore this notion, Updike has Nelson repeat, almost verbatim, many of the same mistakes Rabbit made when he, Rabbit, was roughly Nelson's age. In fact, much of *Rabbit Is Rich* functions as a direct, one-to-one rewriting of *Rabbit, Run,* this time with Nelson at the tumultuous center of things. In setting up this generational parallel, Updike does more than simply provide his colossal, four-part structure with thematic coherency and structural balance. He also transforms this plot device into his most forceful argument against the seemingly insurmountable condition of entropic decline. Although it appears to Rabbit that his past is dead and buried, and that the often reckless energy of his youth has left him completely, in fact it has only passed down from one generation to the next, fully intact and as destructive as ever. Earlier in this chapter, we noted how Rabbit viewed Ruth's farm as a place "where lost energy and lost meaning still flow" (113/722). Significantly, that farm is located in Galilee, an actual town in Pennsylvania named after the place of Christ's growing up. A resurrection is therefore implied. Likewise, Nelson, in his replaying of Rabbit's youthful indiscretions, becomes another source of resurrected energy and meaning, an ambiguously comforting embodiment of continuance and permanence. In Updike's world of mixed blessings, Nelson's helpless re-enactment of Rabbit's youthful mistakes becomes not so much cause for despair as, curiously enough, an occasion for celebration.

For nearly half the length of the novel, Updike cleverly conceals these affinities, perhaps in order to emphasize the differences rather than the similarities between Rabbit and Nelson. His chief device in this subtle sleight-of-hand is Melanie, a young woman whom Nelson inexplicably brings with him from Colorado. For the first 130 pages, Updike remains securely in Rabbit's consciousness, and in this way he is able to leave the nature of Nelson and Melanie's relationship tantalizingly ambiguous. Updike also throws the reader off Nelson's trail by presenting Melanie as something of a stand-in for Jill. For one thing, she is a hippie, of the late-seventies variety. Like Jill, she combines her studied anti-Establishment dreaminess with the kind of polished poise and graciousness borne from a moneyed background. Also like Jill, she favors Indian philosophies and pop mystics like G. I. Gurdjieff: "Melanie was mystical, she ate no meat and felt no fear, the tangled weedy gods of Asia spelled a harmony to her" (148/148). She possesses a "mocking implacable Buddha calm" that infuriates Nelson every bit as much as Jill's lack of self-consciousness infuriated Rabbit, while her attitude toward sexual intercourse echoes Jill's selfless altruism: "Melanie hardly ever tries to come when [she and Nelson] make love, takes it for granted she is serving the baby male and not herself" (134/742). These surface connections are further supported by Melanie's overall psychological profile, for like her counterpart in *Rabbit Redux,* she too suffers from a father-figure complex, having left behind a much older and married lover in Colorado. As she puts it, "I mean, one of the reasons for my coming with you was to clean my head of all this father-figure shit" (132/740).

Based on the evidence provided by these details, then, it would seem that *Rabbit Is Rich* sets itself up as, in part, a reworking of *Rabbit Redux,* with Nelson repeating his father's experience with Jill. Yet Melanie is not really taking up with Nelson, or at least not intensely. Rather, Updike sets up the *Rabbit Redux* parallel through a subplot involving Charlie Stavros. If Charlie functions in *Rabbit Redux* as a stand-in for the freedom-loving, life-giving Rabbit of *Rabbit, Run,* then he functions in *Rabbit Is Rich* as a similar stand-in for Rabbit's reactionary incarnation in *Rabbit Redux.* Ten years after his experiment with free love and leftist politics, Charlie has become a conservative. During one of his and Rabbit's newsy conversations, he ends up sounding exactly like the Vietnam-obsessed Rabbit of 1969. He refers to the Irish as "dumb Micks," and laments that the whole "country is sad, everybody can push us around" (270/865). Charlie further repeats Rabbit's 1969 experience by taking up with Melanie, as Rabbit did with Jill. He even takes Melanie to Valley Forge (158/763), which is where Jill went right before she invited Skeeter into Rabbit's home (*Redux* 199–200/441).

If Melanie is Charlie Stavros's "Jill," then what does she represent for Nelson? In a sense, she is Nelson's "Ruth," for it is her he runs to when he feels too keenly the tightening net of impending domesticity. Also like Ruth, Melanie does not offer a placid safe haven. Rather, she both accepts Nelson for who he is and sees right through his selfishness. The latter insight makes her something of a threat to him. He sees Melanie as "smiling out at him from within that bubble where the mystery resided that amounted to power"—the bubble, it will be remembered, that he associates with the grown-up world (149/755). And despite her gracious decision to accompany him back to Pennsylvania as he tries to secure a spot for himself at his father's lot, she blithely refuses to take Nelson's side in his ongoing battle with Harry. Nelson shies away from her challenges the same way he avoids facing up to the fact that, ultimately, Harry is not the cause of all his troubles. He shies away primarily because, as he puts it in the narrator's third person transcription of his thoughts, "Against the Melanies of the world he will always come up tongue-tied" (151/757).

In the end, then, Melanie is the main component of an elaborate narrative trick on Updike's part, for the more suitable stand-in for Jill is actually Nelson's bride-to-be, Pru. As Newman cogently notes, Updike has carefully constructed the text so that many of Nelson's references to Pru prior to her actual appearance in the novel seem to be references to Jill. Specifically, Newman cites a scene in which Nelson looks past Melanie to an unnamed, "more shallow-breasted other, abandoned" (131/739). Because the novel has thus far made no direct reference to Nelson's pregnant girlfriend, the reader can only assume that his "abandoned" other is Jill.[12] Whereas Melanie, like Ruth, was physically ample, Pru, like Jill, is a "slender slouching shape" with a "look about her of wry, slightly twisted resignation" (182/786). Pru is also older than Nelson. To Rabbit's observant eye, this slight difference in age makes Nelson "look years younger than when Melanie was about, a nervous toughness melted all away" (183/786). Melanie forces on Nelson the full awareness of his immaturity and his reluctance to grow up. Pru, on the other hand, returns Nelson to the comforting security of his boyhood, when the object of his most urgent affections was another slender cloud of positive reinforcement.

But Jill is not Pru's only correlative, for she is also informed by Updike with qualities that ally her with two of Rabbit's other women, Ruth and Janice. Like Ruth, Pru is working class, "casually tough," with a past considerably more tumultuous than Nelson's. She also makes Nelson feel special in the same way that Ruth did for Rabbit: "His tales [of growing up] seemed pale in comparison. Pru made him feel better about himself" (315/907). His first sexual encounter with Pru further connects her with Ruth. Nelson recalls her taking him to her apartment "assuming without making any big deal of it that fucking was what they were both after" (316/907), while her easy orgasm gave him "intense gratitude" in such a way that he quickly found himself "locked in, too precious to let go of, ever" (316–17/908). In becoming pregnant, however, she splits with Ruth and becomes, in a sense, Janice, for her re-

12. Newman, *John Updike*, 130.

sponse to the news is not to take her child and run from Nelson but rather to demand that Nelson assume his responsibility as a father. Nelson keeps this last detail from his father because, according to Janice, "he was afraid [Harry would] be mad. Or laugh at him." But Rabbit denies this, immediately noting the parallels between himself and Janice: "Why would I laugh at him? The same thing happened to me" (184/ 788). There is only one difference between Rabbit and Nelson in this regard: this time it is Nelson, not the pregnant soon-to-be wife, who has the money. "A-*ha*," Rabbit says when he learns of her working-class background. "Blue collar. She's not marrying Nelson, she's marrying Springer Motors." "Just like you did," Janice serenely responds (188/ 791). Accordingly, Rabbit imagines he sees a bit of his own mother in Pru, "awkward and bony, with big hands, but less plain" (187/790).

All these compressed and simultaneous echoes of Rabbit's women converge in a brilliant, powerful scene, told from Nelson's erratic point of view, in which Nelson and Pru nearly reenact Rabbit and Janice's horrific drowning incident with Becky. The scene, which involves a party at the apartment of someone named Slim, a gay friend of Nelson who will later figure prominently in *Rabbit at Rest*, is surreally presented as if it were taking place underwater, dead Becky's element, the element of death. Updike seems to have borrowed his technique from Marcel Proust, for the scene reads like a brilliant homage, or perhaps even parody, of Proust's famous "water goddesses" scene of the Guermantes at the Paris Opéra.[13] The apartment overlooks Weiser Square, the same commercial enclave that, in *Rabbit, Run*, housed the Chinese restaurant at which Harry met Ruth, and, in *Rabbit Redux*, skirted the street that featured Jimbo's, the bar where Rabbit met Jill. As the scene begins, Nelson is found sitting on the floor, stoned and drunk, staring up at the holes in the apartment's pegboard ceilings. This image recalls that crucial moment in *Rabbit Redux* in which an equally stoned Skeeter stares up at Rabbit's ceiling and sees holes there signifying the holes punctured in the nothingness through which "new somethingness comes pouring in from exactly nowhere" (*Redux* 261/494). That "somethingness" is tantamount to chaos and death, which, in Skeeter's apocalyptic vision, is "God's holy face." Accordingly, Nelson, amid the general entropic chaos

13. See Marcel Proust, *The Guermantes Way,* 35–55. In particular, note 35–36.

of the party, imagines the pegboard holes in the apartment ceiling are "trying to tell him something, an area of them seems sharp and vivid and aggressive" (321/912). This impression fades and gets taken up by another vision in which Nelson imagines that "a jellyfish of intensity is moving transparently across the ceiling" (322/913). The jellyfish signals the reader to the presence of the angel of death. Other water images include a room packed with plastic pink flamingos and an "aquarium without fish in it but full of Barbie dolls and polyplike plastic things [Nelson] thinks are called French ticklers" (335/925). The floating Barbie dolls and French ticklers compose a ghoulish tableau symbolizing, perhaps, his dead sister, drowned in a bathtub partly as a result of his father's reckless sexuality.

Midway through the scene Nelson meets Annabelle Byer, Ruth's nineteen-year-old daughter and the same woman who visited Rabbit at the lot in the novel's opening scene. Although the facts surrounding her paternity are left ambiguous, there is a very good chance that she is Nelson's step-sister, in which case she also becomes, in this scene, the physical embodiment of his dead sister, Becky. She possesses Rabbit's "tipped up nose" and small ears, and Ruth's "gingery hair" and welcoming bulk. Nelson is drawn to her the same way Rabbit was drawn to Ruth. At one point he even thinks about saying, *"You're not fat, you're just nice"* (328/918), an almost direct transposition of Rabbit's line to Ruth: "You're not fat. You're right in proportion" (*Run* 68/60). Fittingly, the two young people—neither of whom, it should be pointed out, know of their probable connection to one another—discuss their respective fathers. She claims her father—Ruth's aged husband after her affair with Rabbit—is dead, while Nelson simply says of Harry, "Oh . . . my father's a prick." Yet his saying this line does not demonize his father but rather lends Harry's imagined face "a mournful helplessness" (330/920). This insight into what Updike feels is the obdurate truth about Harry's metaphysical condition becomes charged with significance in view of the fact that the ghost of dead Becky hovers so urgently overhead, a jellyfish traveling across the ceiling. In response to this outburst, Annabelle tells Nelson, "You shouldn't say that," which line makes Nelson "feel guilty and scolded. Her own father dead. She makes him feel he's killed his" (330/920). As yet another carrier of Rabbit's transmitted guilt, Annabelle forces on Nelson an awareness of his own guilty burden. His oedipal threat from *Rabbit Redux* returns to him as a charge, as evidence of his own oedipal debt.

From this ghost of his dead sister, Nelson turns his attention to the physical embodiment of that debt, his child. During his conversation with Annabelle, Pru is seen dancing with drunken, stoned abandon in the middle of the apartment living room. Having been made aware by Annabelle of his own complicity in his father's transmission of guilt, he stands up and "becomes" the Rabbit of *Rabbit, Run*. Like Janice in the opening scene of that novel, Pru is both tipsy and pregnant, the combination of which fills Nelson with every bit as much impotent and unjustified fury as it filled Harry twenty years ago: "She is unsteady, pulled out of the music, and this further angers him, his wife getting tipsy. Defective equipment breaking down on purpose just to show him up" (331/921). This is, of course, Nelson's characteristic response to all his own anxieties—that the world is conspiring against him, purposely. Pru throws this insight right back at him: "You expect your mother and poor old grandmother to take care of you no matter what you do. You're horrid about your father when all he wants is to love you, to have a halfway normal son" (334/924). Though they stay at the party for a little while longer, Pru returns to him "dead pale, a ghost with the lipstick on her face like movie blood and worn in the center where her lips meet" (335–36/925). The death-and-water imagery multiplies as Nelson imagines that "[t]hings are being dyed blue by something in his head" (336/925). And as they leave, he is visited again by a vision of the "jellyfish of intensity" (337/926).

That "jellyfish" asserts its purpose on the landing outside the upstairs apartment. As Pru pushes past him impatiently her hip brushes Nelson's. Nelson cannot remember—and so the reader does not know for sure—if he "gives her a bit of hip back" (337/927). In any case, Pru falls, hitting the ground "like one of those plastic floating bath toys suddenly accidentally stepped on" (338/928). The image of the bath toys connects Becky's drowning in the tub with the floating Barbies in the aquarium. Updike's deliberately ambiguous handling of Nelson's complicity in this accident also connects the incident to Rabbit's equally ambiguous involvement in Becky's death. Like father like son.

But this baby does not die, the news of which fills Pru with profound gratitude and a sense of her own guilt. The only damage is to Pru's broken thigh. In the scene at the hospital that follows—a scene which echoes the hospital scene in *Rabbit, Run,* during which Rabbit and Janice reconcile for the first time—Pru makes overt identifications between herself and Janice, another tipsy baby-killer. She tells Janice she believes the broken thigh is a form of divine punishment: "I honestly believe . . . it's God telling me this is the price He asks for my not losing the baby. . . . [W]hen I felt my feet weren't under me and I knew there wasn't anything for me to do but fall down those horrible stairs, the thoughts that ran through my head. You must know" (342/931). In this passage Pru declares that the accident has inspired a "leap of faith." It has presented her with an awareness of not only her own helplessness in the face of accident and death but also the need for a divine safety net, the same insight Rabbit gleaned from the death of his own baby. In singling out Janice in this way, moreover, Pru provides Rabbit with an oddly unsettling sense of his own faith-induced absolution: "He feels rebuked, since the official family version is that the baby's dying at Janice's hands was all his fault. Yet now the truth seems to declare he was just a bystander" (343/932). Note that Rabbit does not feel absolved but "rebuked." He apparently needs to recognize his complicity in Becky's death, for such awareness keeps him "in touch with guilt" and sends him "crawling back to God" (334/933).

Nelson, however, does not heed the message imparted by this near disaster. He is still in the early stages of his own Rabbit-like search for that allusive freedom, for a way out of his punishing dread. Rabbit recognizes this when he snaps at Nelson, "[T]he crazy way you're going, zigzagging around and all those drugs, you'll be lucky to get to my time of life " (351/939). The phrase "zigzagging around" represents a subtle reprise of Rabbit's characteristic image from his own twenties. Nelson does, however, feel a nagging sense of his shared responsibility for Pru's fall, and tells Rabbit as much, admitting that he "can't remember" if he pushed her or not. When Rabbit asks why he would ever do such a thing, Nelson replies, "Because I'm as crazy as you are." Rabbit not only takes this admission in stride, but also recognizes the underlying truth behind it, that is, the truth of their shared angst-ridden condition. "We're not crazy," he assures Nelson, "either of us. Just frustrated sometimes." The narrator then notes that this "seems information the kid is grateful for" (380/966).

Eventually, these frustrations—Nelson's angst, in other words—provoke some very Rabbit-like zigzagging behavior on his part, for just before his child is born—and while Harry and Janice are vacationing in the Caribbean—Nelson, much like his father before him, runs. The circumstances surrounding his desertion correspond exactly to Harry's run of 1959. As Janice tells it, "He and Pru had a fight Saturday night, he wanted to go into Brewer for a party with that Slim person and Pru said she was too pregnant and couldn't face those stairs again and he went by himself. . . . And he didn't come back" (424–25/1005). Rabbit's response to this news is not anger, and not even despair at seeing his own mistakes being repeated by his son. Rather, as the narrator observes, he feels "vindicated. And relieved, actually" (425/1005). He is vindicated, perhaps, because this escapade validates his assessment of Nelson as "a rat." His relief, on the other hand, is more complex. Although Updike does not elaborate on this second emotion, it seems clear that Rabbit sees himself as finally absolved of responsibility for Nelson's "problems," whatever they were. He recognizes Nelson's desertion as arising out of emotions and conflicts he himself experienced, and occasionally still experiences, and which cannot be attributed solely to good or bad parenting. As such, Harry is released from responsibility: Nelson is on his own adult journey, and will have to make his way as Harry did, by trial and error, without a father to blame and without a participatory God to consult.

Rabbit's sense of relief, of being released of parental responsibilities and paternal debts, is first hinted at in two previous scenes. In the first episode, Rabbit reflects on his own situation twenty years ago—young, full of energy, and trapped into an unexpected marriage—and tells Nelson, "I just don't like to see you caught. . . . You're too much me" (208/809). Although Nelson responds, "I'm not you! I'm not caught!" Rabbit remains unconvinced and offers Nelson a way out: "They've got you and you didn't even squeak. . . . All I'm trying to say is, as far as I'm concerned you don't have to go through with it. If you want out of it, I'll help you" (208/809). But Nelson does not take advantage of the offer. During Nelson's wedding, this urge to provide an escape route returns to Rabbit so intensely that he breaks down into tears (244/842). He sheds the tears in recognition of Nelson's own helplessness in withstanding the future that awaits him, what Harry terms "that daily doom" of marriage. He sheds the tears in recognition of his, Harry's, own help-lessness to protect Nelson from what he has undertaken. And he sheds the tears in recognition of the inevitable adult griefs that await Harry's sole seed, now no longer his son and responsibility but the carrier of responsibility himself.

By the time the wedding is done and over with, however, Rabbit has returned to form. Thinking about Nelson on his honeymoon, for in-stance, his first response is to worry that Nelson will "burn the cottage down frying his brain and his genes with pot." But then he remembers "it's not [his] funeral." His feelings of grief and helplessness for his lost son quickly transform into relief: he no longer has to worry about the kid. As the narrator observes, "Now that Nelson is married it's like a door has been shut in his mind, a debt has been finally paid" (259/856). The rest of that debt gets paid when Nelson deserts his wife. In a sense, by repeating Rabbit's mistakes, Nelson has taken over responsibility for them. Perhaps Rabbit sees that giving Nelson some of his own space in the world is not such a terrifying thing after all, for it also means that Nelson must take on many of the burdens Rabbit no longer wants to carry. This insight ties into Rabbit's earlier recognition of "how men can die willingly, gladly, into eternal release from the hell of having to per-form" (91/703). With the shedding of those tears, Rabbit makes his first gesture toward leaving responsibility for the world to the next genera-tion. In doing so, he seems to recognize that such a transference does not represent a loss of energy on his part but rather an exchange of en-ergies. That knowledge, too, is a relief, for it suggests the possibility of continuity, an idea made concrete by the arrival, on the last page of the novel, of his granddaughter, Judy. Before arriving there, however, we must follow Rabbit on one more leg of his journey toward an under-standing and an appreciation of his own entropic decline, and his own dissolution into the nothingness that awaits him.

V. Filthy Lucre and the Tunnel of Death

Unlike in the two previous Rabbit novels, God seems to have been pushed to the margins of *Rabbit Is Rich*. There is no Eccles to challenge Rabbit in his Kierkegaardian faith, nor is there a powerful Skeeter-like figure to overturn all of Rabbit's most cherished assumptions about white justice and the God-sanctioned American dream. There is only Harry and his whining son, the latter of whom has more faith in the veracity of the "Amityville Horror" phenomenon of the late seventies than he does in Harry's subjective, Wholly Other God (161/766). Comparatively speaking, the Harry of *Rabbit Is Rich* is relatively God-free. His prosperity partly accounts for his new attitude: in the same way that "having enough money" has finally taken his mind off sex, so has it vitiated his interest in that unseen world beyond death. Another factor is his past relationship with God and that unseen world, a relationship which has been traumatic, to say the least. Immediately after the discussion about the Amityville Horror, he thinks, "He doesn't want to think about the invisible anyway; every time in his life he's made a move toward it somebody has gotten killed" (162/767). In the meantime, between himself and God there has arisen a "stony truce" (140/767), though one borne of what Harry imagines to be the kind of mutual respect "due from one well-off gentleman to another." All that remains of their old intense relationship is a sort of metaphysical "calling card left in the pit of the stomach, a bit of lead as true as a plumb bob pulling Harry down toward all those leaden dead in the hollow earth below" (231/830).

In part because of statements like these, the critics have by and large taken Rabbit at his word and assumed that theology does not play a major role in the overall thematic theater of *Rabbit Is Rich*. Generally assumed to be the economic section of the tetralogy, the novel is primarily treated as a critique of consumerism, in which money has become Rabbit's "new God." Detweiler's assessment is fairly representative of the critical consensus. According to him, "Consumerism is in fact the main topic of this novel, in conjunction with sex, just as *A Month of Sundays* links sex and religion and *The Coup* blends sex and politics. It is fitting," he adds, "that *Consumer Reports* has become Rabbit's Bible."[14] Yet although it is certainly true that religion is not a central concern of *Rabbit Is Rich*, the metaphysical realm still occupies a large role in the novel. Updike uses this third installment of his tetralogy to explore even further the ramifications of the divinely sanctioned nothing to which

14. Detweiler, *John Updike*, 175.

Ruth and Skeeter introduced Rabbit in the two previous sections. This nothing assumes in *Rabbit Is Rich* an even more central place in Harry's overall religious vision than it has previously. Far from being an anomaly in the tetralogy's four-part structure, the novel in fact constitutes a crucial step in Harry's confrontation with the shadowside of creation.

The first place to begin exploring this unique take on Barth's divine "No" is the novel's lone minister figure, the Reverend Archie Campbell, whom Rabbit refers to derisively as "Soupy." The nickname not only derives from Campbell's Soup but also seems to serve as an oblique reference to what the Angstroms assume to be Campbell's homosexuality. Though not many readers have made the connection, Reverend Campbell is a reincarnation of Reverend Eccles from *Rabbit, Run.* Like Eccles, he is a liberal, largely earthbound Protestant clergyman informed by a tolerant, lax, and primarily bourgeois value system. Also like Eccles, he does not attempt to serve as an exemplar of faith, or a "burning" witness of the unseen world, as the Barthian Kruppenbach advised in *Rabbit, Run.* Rather, he performs the rites and duties of the church the way Harry performs the duties of an automobile salesman. In a prenuptial meeting at the Angstrom's house intended to square away the wedding arrangements, he displays absolutely no concern about Nelson's profession of atheism. Rather, he lets himself be "brought around" to performing the proposed shotgun wedding, since, in his view, his job basically involves the pronunciation of sacred words. His is a service industry, primarily. With regard to Nelson's wedding, Rabbit notes that Campbell simply "has what they want, a church wedding, a service acceptable in the eyes of the Grace Stuhls of the world," Grace Stuhl being a gossipy crony of Ma Springer (200/802). The now successful Rabbit even admires in Campbell this solid sense of vocational pride. "Laugh at ministers all you want," Rabbit thinks during the wedding ceremony, "they have the words we need to hear, the ones the dead have spoken" (243/841). Of course, this view squares with Rabbit's new "stony silence" with God, as well as with his sense of religion simply as something that makes his mother-in-law "feel better."

As a reprise of the blandly ineffectual Eccles, Campbell would seem to serve as little more than a barometer of Rabbit's new attitude. By gauging Rabbit's acceptance of this reincarnation of his old theological antagonist, we can chart his gradual transformation from youthful mystic to complacent bourgeois. Yet Campbell's purpose in the novel is considerably more complex than that, and the key to his significance is nothing less than his homosexuality. Perhaps one reason the book's past readers have generally downplayed Campbell's centrality is because, by and large, they have not explored how the Reverend's homosexuality figures into the novel's overall symbolic terrain. Such downplaying is understandable considering how apparently insignificant his homosexuality is to the novel's plot. With the publication of *Rabbit Angstrom,* however, this assessment should change. For what these same readers had no way of knowing is that Campbell's homosexuality represents yet another link to Reverend Eccles. They had no way of knowing this because a scene announcing Eccles's own homosexuality was cut from the original edition of *Rabbit Redux.* Granted, at one point in *Rabbit, Run,* Harry speculates briefly that "Eccles is known as a fag" (129/111), yet nothing comes of this observation in the novel that contains it, so readers have understandably let the remark go without much comment. And because hardly any mention at all is made of Eccles in the 1971 text of *Rabbit Redux,* he has occasioned little critical attention outside considerations of *Rabbit, Run.* In the version of *Rabbit Redux* that appears in *Rabbit Angstrom,* however, the cut scene has been restored. In his introduction, Updike only passingly comments on his rationale for the restoration, saying simply that the Reverend's "'outing' seemed to deserve a place in the full report" (xxiii). As we shall see, the real reason for reinserting the cut scene relates to its importance in explaining the role of Eccles's 1970s counterpart, Archie Campbell. So illuminating is Eccles's own "outing" that one can almost imagine Updike, during the composition of *Rabbit Is Rich,* wishing he had not cut the scene.

In the now restored episode,[15] Eccles turns up on the same bus Harry rides home from work. Dressed in a pink shirt, he sits down beside Harry "with a stagey sigh" (436). During their brief conversation, Eccles reveals that he has not only lost his wife but has also quit the ministry, both events attributed to what he vaguely refers to as his "indis-

---

15. See *Rabbit Angstrom,* 436–40. The corresponding spot in *Rabbit Redux* from which the scene was excised appears on page 199 of the original 1971 Knopf edition. It would have followed the paragraph ending with *"Amen"* (Updike's italics).

cretions." Now he works variously as a camp counselor and a P.R. agent for a theater troupe. Although his homosexuality is never commented upon directly, the attentive Rabbit senses something different about the new Eccles, particularly the "hungry way" he says, "I can be my own *man*." In the former minister's eyes "there is something new, a hardened yet startled something" (437). To Rabbit's way of thinking, Eccles has somehow "become burlier, more himself" (438). One thing that has brought him out is the sixties in general, his advocacy of which seems to have been the main purpose of the scene. "I think a very exciting thing is happening in Western consciousness," he tells Rabbit. "[A]t long last, we're coming out of Plato's cave" (439). Before leaving Rabbit, moreover, he proclaims, "I think these are *mar*velous times to be alive in, and I'd *love* to share my good news with you at your leisure" (440). Eccles seems to feel at home in the sixties because the tenor of the times has given him not only the courage to "become burlier, more himself," but also widespread validation for his own faithless, earth-bound do-goodism. After freely admitting to Rabbit that he probably never really believed in what he preached, he goes on to characterize his belief system, both then and now, in terms that pit him squarely within the countercultural ethos of free love: "I believed . . . in certain kinds of human interrelation. I still do. If people want to call what happens in certain relationships Christ, I raise no objection. But it's not the word *I* choose anymore" (438). Examined in isolation, the scene neither adds to nor detracts from the overriding message of *Rabbit Redux*. Although Eccles's embracing of the sixties lends credence to Rabbit's rejection of the same, the novel does not need this scene in order to make its point.

On the other hand, its restoration within the scope of the "full report" makes a fairly strong impact. If nothing else, it calls more attention to Campbell's homosexuality. As we have seen, when an element from a previous Rabbit novel reappears in its successor, that element generally returns in a dialectically opposite manner. So seems to be the case with this issue of homosexual ministers. Whereas in *Rabbit Redux* Eccles's homosexuality is presented negatively as part of the novel's widespread critique of the 1960s, in *Rabbit Is Rich* that homosexuality returns in a positive light. In addition to his admiration for Campbell's professional poise, Rabbit in a way also envies the minister's gayness, as we find in the following passage: "Campbell taps out the bowl of his pipe with a finicky calm that conveys to Harry the advantages to being queer: the world is just a gag to this guy. He walks on water; the mud of women, of making babies never dirties his shoes. You got to take off your hat: nothing touches him. That's real religion" (202/803). Rarely does Harry give even the slightest bit of credence to conventional notions of theologically sanctioned morality. As the narrator of *Rabbit at Rest* directly affirms, "Rabbit never had much use for old-fashioned ethics" (400/1413). His attitude toward the Reverend's sexuality is no exception. Rather than view Campbell's homosexuality as a sin, for instance, he sees it as a means toward the avoidance of sin. Clearly, the "mud" of "making babies" refers to the procreative guilt passed down through the generations, with which this novel is so intimately concerned, and so Campbell's nonprocreative sexuality bears for Rabbit a sort of benign innocence free of the Augustinian, lapserian taint of seminal contamination. In this sense, the gay Campbell is the perfect minister, an outsider to the heterosexual world of guilt-making activity and hence a suitable messenger of the otherwise unattainable sinless path. In this way, Campbell becomes, in this passionate novel about the paternal transmission of Original Sin, a curious and unexpected hero of sorts.

The above passage also contains a subtle pun that directs us to an additional, and considerably more significant, feature of Campbell's homosexuality. When Rabbit reflects that "nothing touches him," Updike intends the first word of the clause to serve as both an indefinite pronoun and a noun. In other words, the "nothing" does in fact touch this serenely innocent man of the cloth. Here, too, Campbell's homosexuality is a factor, for in *Rabbit Is Rich*, that "nothing" is intricately and consistently associated with, of all things, the anal cavity. As many previous critics have (sometimes squeamishly) noted, *Rabbit Is Rich* is strangely preoccupied with anal activity. Judie Newman writes, "Rarely in a novel, with the possible exceptions of *Tender is the Night* and *Portnoy's Complaint*, have so many major events taken place in the bathroom." She goes on to assert that the "scatological emphasis is relentless," citing for evidence both the repeated use of the word "shit" and "Harry's fascination with homosexual practices."[16] No mere gesture of

16. Newman, *John Updike*, 62.

provocation on Updike's part, this "scatological emphasis" serves as part of yet another complex metaphorical network linking money with feces, the anus with the void, and the void with the divine nothing hinted at by Skeeter in the previous installment. It is this "nothing" that touches Campbell, and it is this same "nothing" that is beginning to get a handle on Harry. What is most surprising is that both Harry and Updike view this set of circumstances as not such a bad thing after all.

Before we can understand how this is so, however, we must first untangle the interwoven threads of this symbolic web. The first thread involves, not unexpectedly, money. As Newman and others have already noted, Updike utilizes freely in *Rabbit Is Rich* the numerous conflations between money and excrement that have been articulated by such psychoanalytic writers as Sigmund Freud.[17] Nelson is the first character in the novel to make these connections overt, for it is he who tells his father, "People don't *care* that much about money anymore, it's all shit anyway. Money is shit" (169/773). Inadvertently or not, Nelson's remark recalls the basic argument of, among other texts, Freud's brief monograph, "Character and Anal Eroticism." In this provocative essay, Freud speculates about the possible ways in which orderliness, parsimoniousness, and obstinacy might be attributed to a preoccupation with anal sexuality. He suggests that people who bear these three linked character traits might have belonged as infants "to that class who refuse to empty their bowels when they are put on the pot because they derive a subsidiary pleasure from defecating." As a result of this early reluctance, these people develop a "sexual constitution in which the erotegenicity of the anal zone is exceptionally strong." Even more important, they sublimate their infantile preoccupation with anal retention through the development of the three character traits listed above. Freud is especially intriguing on the associations he detects between excrement retention and the hoarding of money. First, he notes the idiomatic use of the terms "filthy and dirty" to denote excessive wealth ("filthy rich"). Second, he calls attention to the myriad ways—in myths and fairy tales, for instance—in which money is connected to dirt. One of the numerous examples he cites is the ancient Babylonian doctrine that associates gold with the "'faeces of Hell' (Mammon = *ilu manman*)." From

17. See, for instance, Newman, 62–63.

these examples, he concludes that it is "possible that the contrast between the most precious substance known to man and the most worthless, which they reject as waste matter ('refuse'), has led to this specific identification of gold with faeces."[18]

It is likely that Updike has this text in mind when he has Nelson make his exasperated charge at his father. What's more, Harry appears to be the novel's most obvious anal retentive. In previous chapters we have already explored Rabbit's stubbornness and his love of order, while in this chapter we have seen how his new wealth has bred a tinge of avarice. Newman also notes in this regard Harry's obsession with "waste," an issue we addressed earlier in our discussion of entropy.[19] Indeed, Harry's interest in sodomy and the anal cavity does not end in his affirmation of Campbell's sexuality. Rather, he finds scatological references nearly everywhere he looks. There is, for example, his poignant memory of his own father's "bare behind" (212/813). There is also his preoccupation with the contents of Webb Murkett's medicine cabinet, in which Rabbit unearths a box of Preparation H. This discovery leads him to recall the recent news that "Carter of course has hemorrhoids, that grim overmotivated type who wants to do everything on schedule ready or not, pushing, pushing" (284/879). As should not be surprising by now, several times in the novel, and in wholly unrelated sections, Harry finds himself identifying with Carter (see, for instance, 176/780 and 219/819). Noting his friend Ronnie Harrison's bald head, meanwhile, he is moved to think, "There's a bald look, go for it. Blank and pink and curved, like an ass. Everybody loves an ass" (287/881). This reflection moves him to consider the plight of homosexuals: "Amazing things they try to put up—fists, light bulbs" (287/881). At the same time, and as Newman has already shown us, the novel repeatedly follows Rabbit into the bathroom—four times, to be specific, twice at the Murketts (283–86/877–80 and 302–4/894–96), and twice more in the Caribbean with Thelma Harrison (411–12/994–95 and 421–22/1004).

Updike is quite clear about the fact that he wants his readers to associate Rabbit's anal fixation with his obsession with money. For starters, Nelson has made this abundantly obvious. Even more significant is the

18. Freud, *Freud Reader*, 294, 297.
19. Newman, *John Updike*, 62–63.

scene involving the thirty Krugerrands, bought, it will be remembered, from a place that, from its outward appearance, "might be peddling smut" (210/811). The coins he buys, the narrator tells us, come packaged "in cunning plastic cylinders of fifteen each, with round blue- tinted lids that suggested dollhouse seats; indeed, bits of what seemed toilet paper were stuffed into the hole of this lid to make the fit tight and to conceal even a glimmer of the sacred metal" (211/811). The image, economical and resonate after Updike's fashion, expertly conjoins money, feces, avarice, and orderliness. Note, for instance, how the toilet paper both secures a "tight fit" and "conceals" the "sacred metal." The gold coins later reappear as a metaphor for urine, another suitable figure for waste and bodily refuse. As Rabbit pees into the Murketts' toilet, he imagines himself filling the bowl "with gold," the bubbles of his urine multiplying "like coins" (302/895). Updike sustains this "filthy lucre" metaphor in the Krugerrand episode's spectacular denouement, related some 150 pages later. On the advice, once again, of Webb Murkett, Rabbit and Janice exchange this gold for 888 silver coins. While counting the coins, he and Janice "titter" with excitement, yet this giddiness is not just sexual. Rather, Harry interprets the "titters" as remnants of infantile anal fixation: "Handling such a palpable luxury of profiles and slogans and eagles makes Janice titter, and Harry knows what she means: playing in the mud. The muchness" (368/955). Here, Updike expertly ushers into play his intricate triad of money, dirt, and shit, all at the same time. As if to make these echoes crystal clear, he later has Rabbit survey his spilled coins and think, "It's all dirt anyway" (375/961).

What is the significance of all of this? As he did with his adaptation of the oedipal model, Updike subtly refashions the archetypal money/shit motif in theological terms. This twist is made apparent at the end of the episode involving the silver. After the coins have been counted and stored in a bag, Janice and Rabbit find that they cannot fit the bulky mass into their safety deposit box. In accordance with the novel's parallel thematizing of money and sex, Rabbit considers making love to Janice while in the vault. Consequently, their comical attempt to shove the resisting bags of silver has a broadly sexual component. For instance, the bag's flaccid resistance to their efforts suggests, obviously enough, impotency: "The thick cloth of the bag, the tendency of the loose coins to bunch into a sphere, the long slender shape of the gray tin box frustrate them as side by side they tug and push, surgeons at a hopeless task" (374/960). Yet to this sex/money image Updike adds an intriguing coda. Back in the vault with his now full safety deposit box of silver coins, Rabbit reconsiders his earlier fantasy of making love to Janice amid all that money. The vault now seems forbidding to him, with "its terraced edges gleaming" and its floor of cold, "waxy white." And as he shoves the heavy container back into its allotted cubicle, he thinks not of sex, but of death: "She lets him slide his long box into the empty rectangle. R.I.P." (374/960). That this "empty rectangle" is meant to be seen as a figure for the anus rather than the vagina is made clear when Harry turns to the bank teller and apologizes, "Sorry we loaded it with so much crap" (374/960).

Here, then, Updike adds a third component to his "filthy lucre" theme, that of the anal cavity as a symbol for the grave. This image is prepared for through the novel's extensive use of a "tunnel," or chute, motif, which is itself connected to the theme of death. The "tunnel" most often appears during Rabbit's several "runs," these distinguished from their *Rabbit, Run* counterparts by their association not so much with angst as with a concern for health. The year is, after all, 1979, when the fitness boom was just crashing down on America. Although Rabbit's running obviously ties into the entropy theme in its attempt to stave off his creeping lack of energy, it also resonates with that theme's related issue, the persistent pressure exerted by the buried dead. Each time he goes running, for instance, he contemplates the dead, who "stare upwards" at him as he imagines himself "treading on them all," with this audience of buried loved ones "cheering him on" (141/748). It is significant, then, that in the middle of one of these jogging excursions the narrator describes Rabbit entering "a tunnel" under which the dead pine needles form "a carpet" (141/748). The tunnel is not just a passageway to death, however, for earlier in the novel Rabbit thinks of the years of Annabelle Byer's existence as a "bloody tunnel of growing and living, of staying alive" (34/651). This latter tunnel image is in turn amended to a reverie concerning the "secret message carried by genes," a message Rabbit has elsewhere conceived as pushing through "those narrow DNA coils" (86/699). From these coordinate points we can begin to map the meaning behind the tunnel motif: it is a symbol for the passage of life, the "bloody tunnel of growing and living," at one end of which lies sinful conception and at the other end of which lies the void that awaits us beyond death. Updike informs us about this concluding destination in a golf-playing sequence that directly echoes Rabbit's metaphysically enhanced golf game, twenty years earlier, with Reverend Eccles. On a day much concerned with anxiety and athletic grace, and one characterized by a nagging "feeling he should be somewhere else," Rabbit imagines "the fairways as chutes to nowhere" (178/782).

In sum, the "tunnels" or "chutes" that appear and reappear in *Rabbit Is Rich* serve not only as unsettling refashioning of Bunyan's Road of Life but also as telescoped figures for the novel's complex linking of themes such as Original Sin, heredity, and death. By introducing this motif in the golf-playing sequence, Updike also connects this novel's exploration of immortality to that of *Rabbit, Run*. In that earlier novel, Harry perceived the game as a window into that "unseen world" whose existence he senses so keenly. The "something behind all this" that Rabbit once imagined was calling out to him made its most forceful appearance on the golf course, via a perfect swing that inspired Rabbit to shout, "That's *it!*" (134/116). Now that the unseen world is revealed to be "nowhere," this latter golf-playing episode, coupled with its employment of the tunnel motif, also functions as a continuation of the divine "No" explored in *Rabbit Redux*.

Indeed, in this third installment of the Angstrom saga, the "something" beyond the quotidian real has become a "nothing," while the God who sanctions that unseen world has become, for Rabbit, exclusively the "nobody" who hovered over his home before the fire that took Jill's life. Nobody, or perhaps No-body, is the Creator who produced the world from nothing and whom Skeeter imagined as Chaos personified. For Rabbit, this God is the same "gentleman" who has withdrawn from his life, leaving only a "calling card" like a "pit in the stomach," and it is this same Nobody who absorbs the dead into the void that is His domain. That Rabbit's Wholly Other God has in fact become "Nobody" is made clear in a brief, deceptively quotidian exchange between Janice and Harry concerning their role in creating Nelson's problems. First, Rabbit speculates, "You sometimes wonder . . . how badly you yourself fucked up a kid like that," to which Janice sensibly remarks, "We did what we could" (312/904). Then she adds, "We're not God." "Nobody is," Rabbit responds. His comeback—with which, significantly, Updike ends the chapter—works as both an offhand response to Janice's clichéd homily and a subtle announcement of this novel's conception of the Creator. In other words, Rabbit and Janice are not God. Nobody is God.

So although the book is principally a recapitulation of *Rabbit, Run,* *Rabbit Is Rich* also functions, thematically, as a continuation of the dark, dialectic vision spelled out in *Rabbit Redux.* In both cases, the void being posited is associated with the kingdom of death, and yet at the same time Updike is careful to insist that this kingdom is also God's kingdom. Where *Rabbit Is Rich* differs from its bitter, unsettling predecessor is in its almost buoyant attitude. Once again, an element from a past Rabbit novel has reappeared in its successor in an entirely new light. The nothing Rabbit encounters in his ripe middle age is not Skeeter's violent "world of hurt" but rather an almost comforting void similar to the inner dwindling that Rabbit now associates with freedom. All the links of Updike's rich symbolic chain are now almost in place. Money is linked to excrement, while the vault holding that "filthy lucre" is figured as a tomb. That tomb is in turn linked to the anal cavity as well as to the tunnel images that serve as this novel's governing leitmotif. By direct association, then, the anal cavity becomes yet another tunnel, for both the tunnel and the anal cavity lead to a void associated with death. The tunnel leads "nowhere," yet that nowhere, that nothing, is still governed by Updike's Wholly Other God, here figured as Nobody.

What's more, this kingdom of entropic death, this nowhere with its resident deity, Nobody, also has a spokesperson who is, in almost every way, Skeeter's polar opposite. That spokesperson is Archie Campbell, the soothing, professional minister in touch with the nothing. Once again, it is Nelson whom Updike utilizes as his unexpected mouthpiece. One night after returning from one of Rev. Campbell's prenuptial counseling sessions, Nelson caustically relates to his parents the substance of Campbell's teachings: "He keeps talking about the church being the be-riide of Ke-rist. I kept wanting to ask him, Whose little bride are you?" (213/814). Then, in one of the novel's most spectacularly provocative moments of bold blasphemy, Nelson supplies the unexpected answer. "I mean, it's ob*scene,*" he whines. "What does He do, fuck the church up the ass?" (213/814). Although Nelson is making a not very funny joke here, the joke nevertheless feeds into Updike's overriding theological speculations. In order to advance his Barthian message, Updike essentially takes the homoerotic underpinnings of John Donne's "Batter My Heart Three-Personed God, For You" and treats them literally. In Campbell's "real religion," the religion of Nobody and His soothing empty Nowhere, the church is indeed a homosexual bride. Consequently, the consummation of this bride with its Christ is tantamount to a sort of divine sodomy, a conjoining that leads not to new life but to the empty void of nowhere, Nobody's kingly realm.

All of this oblique and indirect material serves as background for Rabbit's climactic, life-affirming act of sodomy with Thelma Harrison, a strikingly graphic episode (graphic even for Updike) that has left many past readers slightly bewildered. To be sure, regarded simply on its own, the scene is slightly bewildering (though it is no less effective because of that). It appears to be included primarily as part of what Updike describes elsewhere as the tetralogy's charting of Rabbit's increasingly baroque sexual life. He writes, "In each novel—this much was a conscious decision—[Rabbit's] sexual experience is deepened, his lifelong journey into the bodies of women is advanced. Fellatio, buggery—the sexual specifics are important, for they mark the stages of a kind of somatic pilgrimage that, smile though we will, is consciously logged by most men and perhaps by more women than admit it."[20] What Updike does not say here—because he is in no way obliged to—is that this "somatic pilgrimage" is also, time and again, a metaphor for Rabbit's pilgrimage toward that unseen world, the world beyond life. He begins, in *Rabbit, Run,* expecting to find that something through intercourse with Ruth. Instead, he is tricked by Nature, who "leads you up like a mother and as soon as she gets her little price leaves you with nothing" (*Run* 86/75). By *Rabbit Is Rich,* Harry is experienced enough in sexual matters to expect that nothing. As such, he is finally ready to embrace it. Buggery makes that embrace possible.

The episode with Thelma is preceded by Rabbit's airplane ride to the Caribbean. Aloft, Harry can see, as he never could on land, how insignificant humans must look to God/Nobody. Earlier in the novel, while counting his silver coins, he has a strange premonition of this insight: "now he can imagine how through God's eyes he and Janice might

20. Updike, "A 'Special Message' for the Franklin Library's First Edition Society Printing of *Rabbit at Rest* (1990)," 870.

look below: two ants trying to make it up the sides of a bathroom basin" (371/958). The "bathroom basin" is a particularly nice touch. As if in ironic response to Nelson's conception of his father as God, Rabbit experiences another moment of God-like insight as he looks down from the plane window and sees "how easily the great shining shoulder of the ocean could shrug and immerse and erase all traces of men" (389/974). Immediately after making this observation, Rabbit feels the plane lift in altitude until "no white caps can be detected" and "immensity becomes nothingness" (389/974). Fittingly, the plane at this point becomes for Harry another tunnel leading to nowhere. With its "droning without and its party mutter and tinkle within," it seems, all at once, "all of the world there is." Rather than feel terror at this confinement, however, Rabbit experiences, of all things, God's presence: "God, having shrunk in Harry's middle years to the size of a raisin lost under the car seat, is suddenly great again, everywhere like a radiant wind. Free: the dead and the living alike have been left five miles below in the haze that has annulled the earth like breath on a mirror" (390/975). The God who "is suddenly great again" is clearly Nobody, in whose realm death and life are both annulled, as is the earth and all its guilt-making activity. The plane ride becomes for Rabbit a precursor to that final journey into the "eternal release of having to perform," and it fills him not with fear and loathing but with a joy "that makes his heart pound."

More to the point, the plane ride is also a precursor to his tryst with Thelma Harrison, Ronnie's wife. Rabbit ends up with her through some typical late-seventies spouse-swapping. At first, he is disappointed to be assigned Thelma, for he has coveted Cindy Murkett all that summer. Rabbit even regards the swapping arrangements in financial terms, noting how Webb, more so than any of the other husbands involved, "has the treasure to barter" (407/990). His ending up with Thelma is a redeeming accident, then, for it forces him to accept his new sexual partner wholly on human, rather than financial, terms, something he has not done for some time now, even within the scope of his own marriage. His superficial mass-marketed fantasies about youth, money, and sexuality are first punctured by Thelma's unexpected allure, an allure he was unable to detect in the throes of his Murkett worship, for when she emerges from the bathroom he finds himself surprisingly stirred by her nakedness. Thelma continues to surprise him by her proclamations of love, of which Harry had been completely unaware. What she loves about him are precisely those qualities that Updike affirms about his hard-hearted hero—his selfishness, his faith in himself and others, his mystical ability to remind others of their specialness. "You're so grateful to be anywhere," she purrs, "you think that tacky club and that hideous house of Cindy's are heaven. It's wonderful. You're so glad to be alive" (418/1001). In making these confessions, Thelma, too, reminds Harry of *his* specialness. Thelma, it turns out, is another of Updike's life-givers.

This is particularly poignant considering Thelma is dying from lupus. Accordingly, their love-making is not regenerative in the conventionally biological sense. For one thing, Thelma is menstruating. For another, they never perform heterosexual intercourse, opting instead for sodomy and masturbation. Late in the evening, they even micturate on one another. Thelma's movements are also surrounded by images of death, particularly in the way she "advances timidly, as if wading into water" (414/997). Ultimately, Thelma's close proximity to death makes her the third of Rabbit's three mistresses of the nothing, the first two being Ruth and Jill. Yet of all these women, Thelma is the most redeeming. Not only is she the one mistress who sees Rabbit for what he is and loves him as such, but she is also the only one who embraces death in the way Updike advises as early as *Rabbit, Run,* where death and life are regarded as equally beautiful spheres that merely eclipse one another in repeated succession.

It is this acceptance of death, of the awaiting nothing, that she brings to Rabbit through their act of sodomy. Updike's description of Harry's entry is both memorably graphic and thematically important. "It seems it won't go, but suddenly it does. The medicinal odor of displaced Vaseline reaches his nostrils. The grip is tight at the base but beyond, where a cunt is all velvety suction and caress, there is no sensation: a void, a pure black box, a casket of perfect nothingness. He is in that void, past her tight ring of muscle" (417/1000). Here, finally, Harry experiences the "perfect nothingness" that will await him after death, a void figured as a "pure black box, a casket." This box is markedly different from the "velvety suction and caress" of the female vagina, with its deceptive promise of "something" and its consolation prize of "nothing." The "nothing" here is no consolation prize: it is the prize itself.

And an oddly redeeming prize it is, for after this encounter with the void hinted at by Thelma's "pure black box," Harry relocates, for the first time since the early part of *Rabbit, Run*, that elusive old spark from his days as a basketball hero: "He dares confide in Thelma, because she has let him fuck her up the ass in proof of love, his sense of miracle at being himself, himself instead of somebody else, and his old inkling, now fading in the energy crunch, that there was something that wanted him to find it, that he was here on earth on a kind of assignment" (419/1001). With this overt quotation from *Rabbit, Run* ("there was something that wanted him to find it"), Updike places this scene squarely within the context of the tetralogy's ongoing examination of the interrelatedness of the Divine Something and the Divine Nothing. Ruth first introduces him to that nothing in *Rabbit, Run*. In *Rabbit Redux*, Skeeter continues this "education" by forcing Rabbit to acknowledge the fact that this nothing, and its association with death, is not only an integral part of God's creation but might also be "God's holy face." Thelma takes Rabbit even further into the nothing by showing him its curiously redeeming capacity. Indeed, as this passage and its *Run*-era echoes testify, Rabbit and Thelma's act of sodomy functions as an "answer" to Rabbit's ultimately disappointing sexual experience with Ruth. In that earlier episode, Rabbit sleeps with Ruth hoping to access the "something" that "wants him to find it." Instead, he comes to learn that, in sex, "Nature leads you up like a mother and as soon as she gets her little price leaves you with nothing" (*Run* 86/75). The Rabbit who meets up with Thelma is the benefactor of Ruth's and Skeeter's lessons, and as such, he is better prepared to understand the nothing with which Nature leaves us. Thelma also demonstrates to Rabbit that this "pure black box" is almost indistinguishable from the "something" that Rabbit has been searching for his entire adult life. Having been introduced to this insight, Rabbit finds that he has regained that "old inkling" about the "something," and he has done so through Thelma's wholly selfless gift of the "nothingness" within her, a nothingness we all possess and whose messenger is no less than Reverend Campbell. While languishing in that void, Harry is in Campbell's domain. This is what Updike means by "fucking the church up the ass."

The sodomy episode also recalls *Rabbit, Run* in the way it links sexual redemption with athletic prowess. Indeed, so redeeming is his encounter with Thelma's "underside" that, the next day, he finds that his golf game is "mysteriously good, his swing emptied of impurities" (423/ 1005). As should be obvious by now, a good golf game in Updike is a sure sign of grace.

VI. More Stately Mansions

So resoundingly upbeat and apparently conclusive is Rabbit's Caribbean encounter with the nothing that it would seem to mark the end of the Angstrom saga. This perception is corroborated by the novel's codalike detailing of Rabbit and Janice's happy move into their own home, complete with a sunken living room, just like Webb Murkett's. Because of these redeeming elements in the novel's denouement—so different from the deadly accidents beclouding the conclusions of the two previous novels—most of the critical work on *Rabbit Is Rich* has understandably treated the text as the obvious culmination of the Rabbit series. Unlike its predecessors, *Rabbit Is Rich* seems to wrap up nicely, with all its threads tied neatly into a bow. In fact, however, the novel ends with its successor clearly in mind. The most obvious nod to a sequel is Nelson's sudden abandonment of his wife. The second most obvious nod is the birth of Pru and Nelson's child.

The baby, a girl, is christened Judy, another "J" name that links her to Rebecca June and Jill, Rabbit's two other "dead" daughters. In this novel of energy lost and found, Judy arrives on the last page as the long-awaited daughter Rabbit keeps looking for but can never keep. The language Updike uses to describe her echoes exactly the same language he used some twenty years ago to describe Rabbit's infant daughter, Becky: "Oblong cocooned little visitor, the baby shows her profile blandly . . . the tiny stitchless seam of the closed eyelid aslant, lips bubbled forward beneath the whorled nose as if in delicate disdain, she knows she's good. You can feel in the curve of the cranium she's feminine, that shows from the first day" (467/1045). Compare this passage with its sister passage from *Rabbit, Run:* "In the suggestion of pressure behind the tranquil lid and in the tilt of the protruding upper lip he reads a delightful hint of disdain. She knows she's good. What he never expected, he can feel she's feminine, feels something both delicate and enduring in the arc of the long pink cranium, furred bands with black licked swatches" (*Run* 218/

187). The echoes are so precise as to demand comparison. Yet they also serve as a harbinger of more to come. Though Rabbit has finally been returned the daughter he once lost, that daughter still must go through the "bloody tunnel of growing" that will mar this goodness. Rabbit's sense of a new beginning is fraught with more growing, more fighting to stay alive, just as his introduction to the void that awaits him is haunted by that actual, fateful journey into the void itself. In its numerous direct references to *Rabbit, Run, Rabbit Is Rich* both serves as a long-deferred resolution of that book and an opening to one more final chapter, a fourth installment that will provide a similarly deferred resolution to *Rabbit Redux,* if not to the Angstrom saga as a whole.

Four

Rabbit at Rest
Repetition and Recapitulation

The thing that hath been, it is that which shall be: and
that which is done is that which shall be done: and there
is nothing new under the sun.—Ecclesiastes 1:9

Like its partner volumes, *Rabbit at Rest,* the final installment of John
Updike's Rabbit tetralogy, can be read entirely on its own. Whatever
background the reader needs to know Updike's narrator supplies in the
form of flashbacks, subjective recollections, and, in several instances,
some rather clumsy, almost soap-opera-like expository dialogue, wherein characters remind one another of things about which they really need
no reminding. Nevertheless, such a reading, while adequate for all practical purposes, is ultimately incomplete. What such a reading fails to acknowledge is the novel's masterful orchestration of echoes and allusions
from the previous books. Updike has constructed the novel almost entirely from motifs borrowed from the other three volumes, motifs which
appear and reappear in unexpected juxtaposition with the contemporary
milieu that functions as this novel's structural frame. The most ideal
reading is the purview only of what Updike terms the book's "ideal reader," that is, the "fellow-American who had read and remembered the previous novels about Rabbit Angstrom" (ix). As someone who has followed
Harry Angstrom through three former decades, this ideal reader will be
able to appreciate the repetitions from those previous installments.

The previous novels reappear in *Rabbit at Rest* not just in the form of echoes and allusions but also in the way the novel as a whole is structured. Updike notes that the book, "like *Rabbit, Run,* . . . is in three parts" (xx). This is true enough, as a brief glance at the table of contents will show. But this tripartite structure also invokes the trilogy of novels that lies in the historical and formal background. As a matter of fact, *Rabbit at Rest* in effect replays that trilogy in *reverse.* Near the end of *Rabbit Is Rich,* Harry finally makes it to the tropics, where he experiences a moment of transcendent awareness through the agency of Thelma Harrison. Accordingly, *Rabbit at Rest* begins where that novel left off, not in the Caribbean, but in Florida, which is close enough. The Florida section parallels *Rabbit Is Rich* in numerous other ways as well. Nelson comes to visit once again, and once again he comes harboring a secret about which Harry is the last to know. Harry's granddaughter, Judy, accompanies him on a Sunfish sailing vessel, a scene which in turn replays the episode in *Rabbit Is Rich* in which Harry goes sailing with Cindy Murkett. And a golfing scene with his new friends from his Florida condominium complex directly replays the extended golfing sequences from *Rabbit Is Rich.* Similarly, the middle section of the novel, entitled "PA," encapsulates *Rabbit Redux* in equally interesting ways. Harry and Janice now live in Penn Park, just around the corner from their old sixties home in the neighboring Penn Villas. Meanwhile, the thirty-three-year-old Nelson is revealed to be addicted to cocaine, which not only recalls Rabbit's own drug experiments from *Rabbit Redux* (during which Rabbit himself was roughly Nelson's current age) but also results in a midnight family crisis that functions as Nelson's "answer" to Harry's letting the house burn down twenty years prior. Finally, the novel's final section, "MI" (for "myocardial infarction"), ends with Rabbit finally completing the solo escape to the "white sun of the south" with which *Rabbit Angstrom* began. In both instances, as Updike puts it, he "flees from domestic predicaments" (xx). Finally, with Rabbit's death, the completed work comes full circle, for *Rabbit at Rest* and, by extension, *Rabbit Angstrom* concludes exactly where *Rabbit, Run* and *Rabbit Angstrom* began: on a basketball court.

The novel also performs one additional structural goal for Updike. As suggested in the previous chapter, *Rabbit at Rest* functions within the

four-part design of the completed tetralogy as the dialectical companion piece to *Rabbit Is Rich*. For example, *Rabbit at Rest* echoes its predecessor's three-word title. It is also the second novel of Harry's "rich"
phase, forming a tidy parallel to the two working-class books from the
first two decades. And in its careful and extended exploration of Rabbit
and Nelson's ongoing oedipal drama, it reprises the basic dramatic conflict of *Rabbit Is Rich*. Structurally, then, these two final novels serve as
the linked counterpart to *Rabbit, Run* and *Rabbit Redux*, the two paired
novels from the tetralogy's first half. The final work is therefore constructed of four individual sections that further subdivide into two larger blocks of two novels apiece.

Updike writes in his introduction to *Rabbit Angstrom*, "So many
themes convene in *Rabbit at Rest* that the hero could be said to sink under the burden of the accumulated past" (xxii–xxiii). The same might
be said of this final novel of Updike's crowning achievement. *Rabbit at
Rest* is perhaps too long: at least one hundred pages of this "accumulated detail" could have been cut from the text without compromising the
book's vital content and thematic import. In his 1990 review of the novel, Peter Prescott was moved to assert, "Like Rabbit, this novel would
have profited from losing weight."[1] This assessment will strike the reader as particularly apt if the novel is read simply as the final five hundred
pages of the single fifteen-hundred-page work. The final eighty pages
are especially taxing on the reader's patience, devoted as they are to tran-
scribing in painstaking detail Rabbit's fluid internal monologue during
his final week of earthly existence.

Fortunately, several things redeem the novel's apparent excesses. First
and foremost is Updike's extraordinary agility at capturing not only the
external reality of Rabbit's (and our) world, but also the rhythm and
flow of Rabbit's subjective life, which, in the end, is the tetralogy's final
energizing force. Second is the tetralogy's status as "a kind of running
report on the state of [Updike's] hero and his nation" (ix). Whereas all
this detail can sometimes seem overwhelming to readers who have lived
among the brand names and news events and pop songs with which Updike has stuffed this valedictory novel, the same might not be said for
future readers, who, twenty or thirty years from now, can turn to these

1. Peter Prescott, Review of *Rabbit at Rest*, by John Updike, 66.

books for a fully realized immersion in what will then be a hopelessly, irredeemably vanished world.

I. Airplanes and Death

Thematically, *Rabbit at Rest* picks up exactly where *Rabbit Is Rich* left off. As we saw in chapter 3, the latter novel concluded on a positive note, with Rabbit finally embracing the nothing that, in one form or another, has threatened his faith in the transcendent reality underlying the nominal world. We also saw how Updike used *Rabbit Is Rich* to establish an inextricable link between God's divine something and the nothing usually associated with death. During the plane ride to the Caribbean, for instance, God's infinite realm is revealed to be, at the same time, a void. The nothing from which he created the heavens and the earth, as described in the first verse of the Judeo-Christian Scriptures, becomes for Updike God's ultimate home. Here Updike effects his own negative twist on the Platonic doctrine of the soul's prenatal existence. In Plato's *Phaedo,* Socrates compares living and dying to waking and sleeping, then attempts to prove that the "souls of the dead must of necessity exist somewhere, whence we assume they are born again."[2] That "somewhere," usually figured as some sort of metaphysical heaven, becomes in Updike's vision the void from which God created the world. It is the same void from which we are created and to which we will go after our deaths. And ruling over this void, this divine black hole of nonexistence, is Updike's God of Death, Nobody, the same God whom Skeeter encountered in Vietnam and whom Rabbit accessed through the "pure black box" of Thelma's redemptive anus.

Rabbit Is Rich ended with Harry accepting Nobody's eventual claim on his life. *Rabbit at Rest* begins with Nobody coming to stake that claim. In the novel's splendid opening sentence, Nobody abandons his perch in the immense nothingness and descends, like an angel of death, into Harry's consciousness: "Standing amid the tan, excited post-Christmas crowd at the Southwest Florida Regional Airport, Rabbit Angstrom has a funny sudden feeling that what he has come to meet, what's float-

2. Plato, *Phaedo,* 475.

ing in unseen about to land, is not his son Nelson and daughter-in-law Pru and their two children but something more ominous and intimately his: his own death, shaped vaguely like an airplane" (3/1051). This sentence is meant to correspond to the equally effective opener of *Rabbit Is Rich,* which began, "Running out of gas." That sentence not only established the oil crisis and entropy as themes, but also, thanks to that first word, sent the reader back to *Rich's* parallel volume in the series, *Rabbit, Run.* Likewise, the opening sentence of *Rabbit at Rest* flips the coin from "Running" to "Standing." These two opening words link their respective novels the same way the opening word of *Rabbit, Run,* "Boys," links up with the opening word of *Rabbit Redux,* "Men." At the same time, the word "Standing" also establishes the theme of thanatos as this novel's parallel to *Rich's* exploration of entropy. Rabbit's run is soon to be over.

This sentence reveals two more issues vital to *Rabbit at Rest.* First, it announces the resumption of the various paternal and familial issues raised in *Rich.* Note that it is not only Rabbit's death that is descending from the immense nothingness but also his son Nelson and his grandchildren, Roy and Judy. In *Rabbit Redux,* Nelson declared that someday he would "kill" his father. *Rabbit Is Rich* transforms this vow into the central component of Nelson's and Rabbit's father/son conflict, which is formulated along oedipal lines. In chapter 3 we explored how Nelson does in fact seek to kill Rabbit, if not literally then figuratively through his attempt somehow to displace his father. For Nelson wants not only Harry's position as the head of Springer Motors but also his place in the adult world. Accordingly, Harry views "the kid's growing up" as "a threat and a tragedy" (*Rich* 138/745), for the older Nelson gets, the closer Harry comes to the death he would resist so fervently. In this regard, it is fair to say that Nelson's airborne arrival in Florida does herald Harry's death, an idea which is reinforced by the accompanying arrival of two more competitors for Harry's space, his grandchildren Judy and Roy. Although *Rabbit at Rest* will amply reprise all of these issues for the benefit of the first-time reader, the novel's opening sentence sounds these themes in such a way that long-time readers of the Angstrom saga will be clued in right from the beginning.

The other issue raised by the novel's opening is the connection between airplanes and death. Indeed, Rabbit's death is shaped "vaguely like an airplane." It was in an airplane bound for the Caribbean that Rabbit encountered the "immense nothingness" of God. Accordingly, that same nothingness is evoked by this second airplane ten years later, an airplane holding, it is crucial to add, his son and enemy. As we have seen, each Rabbit novel features a then-recent news event that functions, in Updike's words, as a "'hook' uniting the personal and national realms" (xvii). *Rabbit at Rest* is no exception. This novel's hook is the December 1988 explosion over Lockerbie, Scotland, of Pan Am Flight 103, with the year-old disaster of the space shuttle *Challenger* also making a few crucial appearances. Here, as in so many other aspects, the novel recalls *Rabbit Redux,* whose central hook was another famous airborne event, the 1969 Apollo moon shot. These news-item hooks function in the Rabbit novels as metaphors for Rabbit's changing fortunes: in *Rabbit, Run,* Dalai Lama's disappearance echoed Rabbit's spiritual quest for freedom; in *Rabbit Redux,* the Apollo mission provided a flashy backdrop to Rabbit's free-floating adventure with those two spaced-out aliens, Skeeter and Jill; and in *Rabbit Is Rich,* the OPEC oil crisis functioned as an ironic gloss on Harry's growing fortunes and middle-aged loss of energy. Similarly, the Pan Am and Challenger disasters serve as metaphors for Rabbit's own impending disaster. Both events establish in the reader's imagination the terrifying vision of helpless bodies falling through Nobody's immense nothingness on their way to violent and unthinkable deaths.

In Updike's adept hands, airplanes also become catch-all symbols for the novel's primary issues. We have already seen how the inaugural sentence calls into play the themes of death and paternity. Similarly, in the opening scene at the Florida Regional Airport, Updike manages to introduce a whole host of additional themes that will be sounded throughout the rest of the novel. He does this primarily through a carefully orchestrated arrangement of tropes from the previous Rabbit novels. In one compacted passage, he has Harry think of the long, low hallways leading out to the arrival gates as "crypts," or those "futuristic spaces like those square tunnels in [science-fiction] movies that a trick of the camera accelerates into spacewarp to show we're going from one star to the next" (4/1052). The science fiction movie Rabbit seems to have in mind here is *2001: A Space Odyssey,* for immediately after making this observation he thinks, *"2001,* will he still be alive?" This brief passage, apparently insignificant, in fact links two separate images from two previous Rabbit novels. Updike evokes *Rabbit Redux* with the reference to *2001*, a 1969 film that Rabbit, Janice, and Nelson go to see early in that novel, and which in turn serves as a pop-culture correlative to both Harry's and the nation's outer-space orbits. Similarly, the "square tunnels" in the above passage recall the "tunnel" imagery from *Rabbit Is Rich*. In their new setting, however, these two previously used images take on new meaning. Although *2001* still retains its *Redux* association with sterile technology, it now achieves additional significance as a symbol of icy celestial abandonment. And whereas in *Rabbit Is Rich* the "tunnel" imagery linked up with anal cavities and subterranean graves, here these tunnels are shown to lead to the airless atmosphere of outer space.

These subtle yet suggestive hints open the way for a scene rich in allegorical significance. By way of foreshadowing, for instance, Updike depicts the airport itself as a sort of waiting-room to heaven, an air-conditioned limbo whose only doorway leads out to death. The Muzak which bathes the cool, air-conditioned atmosphere Rabbit thinks of as "music that's used to being ignored, a kind of carpet in the air, to cover up the silence that might remind you of death" (4/1052). The windows looking out to the runway also provide, Rabbit wryly thinks, a perfect view for a plane crash: "The fireball, the fuselage doing a slow skidding swirl, shedding its wings" (8/1055). When Janice loses track of Rabbit and asks where he's been, he says, "Nowhere" (11/1058), though in fact he has simply been standing in front of this window thinking of plane crashes and death. For Rabbit, this airport is a launching pad to nowhere: it is a place where we are "just numbers on the computer, one more or less, who cares? A blip on the screen, then no blip on the screen" (10/1057). When he gets lost in the airport with his granddaughter Judy, he does, in a sense, disappear from the screen: he becomes for his anxious family a blip who is there one minute and then not. As he and Judy wind their way through the cryptlike hallways, Rabbit realizes that he is essentially alone, that there is "nobody he knows, strangers as total as if he has descended into hell" (19/1065). Updike's language here is typically pun-laden and suggestive. Amid this hellish passageway to the immense nothingness that wants to claim him, Rabbit "knows" that "nobody" is present. Later he imagines himself lost amid "this gray airport's bustling limbo" and surrounded by "Ghostly empty shapes, people he doesn't know" (19/1066). Meanwhile, throughout the episode he clings to the sensation that his death has arrived via airplane, and that it has "its claw around his heart: little prongs like those that hold fast a diamond solitaire" (8/1055).

This opening, death-obsessed scene in the airport serves as an overture of sorts to a novel whose every page offers variations on the theme of thanatos. It also establishes the novel's central figure for Harry's own death, the midair explosion of Pan Am Flight 103. Rabbit first thinks of the disaster while looking at those empty runways. He imagines himself on that plane, "being lulled by the big Rolls Royce engines," a coziness that is interrupted by "a roar and giant ripping noise and scattered screams" (8/1055). The "cozy world" of the airborne plane parallels Harry's own "cozy" world, both of which hang suspended above a nothingness. And it is into that nothingness that he imagines himself falling when the plane rips open, "nothing under you but black space and your chest squeezed by the terrible unbreathable cold, that cold you can scarcely believe is there but that you can sometimes actually feel still packed into the suitcases . . . with the merciless chill of death from outer space still in them" (8–9/1055–56). Whereas the Nowhere of God/Nobody seemed in *Rabbit Is Rich* a somewhat comforting realm, a place where Rabbit could be released from "the eternal hell of having to perform," here, as it edges closer and closer to him, it becomes a place of "terrible unbreathable cold," poisoned by "the merciless chill of death from outer space." The barren moonscape of *Rabbit Redux* has returned, yet it is not to be found in a sterile, technological-driven America so much as in Harry's subjectivity, the home of his Kierkegaardian God, a God who, after all these years, has come for Harry in the death-dealing guise of Nobody, the same Nobody who hovered over Janice as Becky plunged to her death and who hovered over Rabbit just before Jill died by fire.

The Pan Am jet symbolizes not only Harry's cozy world but also Harry himself: he is that plane hovering over nothingness, and the bomb that will rip him open is nothing less than his own fat-corroded heart, around which death has closed its hoary claws. During the course of one of the novel's two extended golfing sequences, we learn that one of Harry's Florida golfing buddies, Bernie Dreschel, underwent a quadruple

bypass three years earlier. Bernie's description of his operating-table ordeal functions as the link between the Pan Am flight and Rabbit's own
impending heart attack. Like that exploding jet, Bernie's chest was
"cracked open like a coconut," though the correlations between his
surgery and the plane disaster do not end there. As Bernie explains,
"They *freeze* you, so your blood flow is down to almost nothing. I was
like locked into a black coffin. No. It's like I *was* the coffin" (63/1105).
He then relates how the ghostly, post-op voice of his anesthetist saying
"Ber-nie, Ber-nie" seemed at the time like "the voice of God" speaking
to him from the other side. Thirty pages later, Rabbit conflates in his
imagination the two episodes, Bernie's surgery and the Pan Am explosion: "all those conscious bodies suddenly with nothing all around
them, freezing, *Ber-nie, Ber-nie,* and Lockerbie a faint spatter of stars
below, everything upside-down and void of mercy and meaning" (91/
1132). As we saw in chapter 1, Updike's Wholly Other God is a non-
interfering deity who respects entirely the implacable conditions of the
material universe. As Updike wrote in *Roger's Version,* "all the prayers and
ardent wishing in the world can't budge a blob of cancer, or the AIDS
virus, or the bars of a prison, or the latch of a refrigerator a child accidentally locked himself into."[3] That is what Rabbit means when he
thinks of that "upside-down" world of death as "without mercy and
meaning": in that instance, we become matter and must therefore obey
the laws of matter. If the physical universe demands that we fall from
the heavens and die, God will not interfere, for His creation, which is
separate from him, must be left to obey its own rules in accordance with
the dictates of free will. The same rule applies to people with cancer,
AIDS, or faulty hearts that require quadruple bypass surgery.

From exploding Pan Am jets and Boeing-manufactured angels of
doom, Updike derives a related symbolic conflation of birds with death.
Like those planes that fly over Rabbit's head to announce Nobody's presence, birds appear throughout *Rabbit at Rest* to warn Rabbit of his impending demise. Outside his Florida condominium, a noisy brown bird
sustains a constant cry of foreboding. Harry initially imagines the chirping to be the product of a "cockatoo or toucan at least," but in fact the
bird is the same species of nondescript fowl that "flicker all around in

3. Updike, *Roger's Version,* 170.

Pennsylvania" (46/1090). This latter insight leads him to identify himself with this bird, "a migrant down here just like him. A snowbird" (46/1090). This same bird—or, at any rate, one exactly like it—reappears outside his hospital window following his first heart attack. The mere sound of the bird's constant chirping makes his chest "echo with a twinge" (173/1206). Similarly, outside Thelma's house he encounters a sick robin flopping about in the yard. Reflecting on why the robin is sick, Rabbit reasons that "all these animals around us have their diseases too, their histories of plague" (207/1238). This bird could refer to Thelma, who is dying of lupus, or to Rabbit, who is also dying in ways he does not altogether comprehend. Actually, Rabbit seems the better candidate, as the robin casts on him "a beady eye" (207/1238). And as Rabbit watches it helplessly hobble about, he is moved to think, "Robin, hop," a sly play on the title of the tetralogy's first volume.

Birds also feature prominently in one of Rabbit's most chilling premonitions of his impending death. This moment occurs while escorting his grandchildren through a typically gaudy Florida tourist trap called Jungle Gardens, which features, among other attractions, exotic birds of every variety. By gorging himself on fatty foods and salty snacks, Rabbit essentially eats himself to death. Accordingly, while at Jungle Gardens, he mistakes the parrot food for his favorite snack item, peanuts, his fifty-five-year intake of which has contributed most significantly to his clogged arteries. Judy, on the other hand, thinks the little pellets look like "rabbit turds." Once again, Updike here deftly calls back into play a motif from a previous Rabbit book, in this case *Rabbit Is Rich,* that disturbing novel of money, feces, and death. In eating the parrot food, Rabbit symbolically eats his own shit. According to the complex chain of references Updike set into motion in the previous novel, Rabbit is also eating his own death. Rather than simply experience embarrassment at this mishap, however, Harry undergoes a brief moment of total and paralyzing metaphysical panic. In what is surely one of the more painfully funny moments in the entire tetralogy, the narrator observes: "He is suffused with a curious sensation; he feels faintly numb and sick but beyond that, beyond the warm volume enclosed by his skin, the air is swept by a universal devaluation: for one flash he sees his life as a silly thing it will be a relief to discard" (104/1143). The following day Harry nearly gets his wish, for it is on that day that he has his first heart attack, while on the Sunfish with Judy. Sprawled helplessly on the beach, he recalls this moment of "universal devaluation" and, perhaps seeing it for the strange form of prophecy that it was, tells his frightened granddaughter, "It must have been that birdfood I ate" (142/1178).

II. Water and Death

Based on all this evidence supporting the novel's conflation of airplanes, birds, and dying, it might appear that Updike has compromised the thematic integrity of the completed magnum opus. Up until *Rabbit at Rest*, he has generally depicted water, not the sky, as the tetralogy's chief element of death, a symbolic association originating in the death by drowning of the Angstrom's infant daughter. The sky, however, crucial though it is to the novel's exploration of mortality, supplements rather than supplants water as death's element. The use of the sky as a symbol for the void merely grows out of and completes a set of symbolic associations that has been firmly in place as early as *Rabbit Redux*, with its preoccupation with outer space and the lifeless moon. Updike adds these *Redux*-era ideas to the airplane imagery established in *Rabbit Is Rich* and thus links into one strand two apparently unrelated symbolic chains. At the same time, he continues to develop the water/death motif that has been growing, link by link, ever since the tetralogy's first volume. The above reference to Rabbit's first heart attack on a Sunfish sailboat gives evidence to that. Perhaps most important, Updike combines the sky imagery with the tetralogy's well-developed water motif in order to create a holistic vision of life and death that sits at the heart of *Rabbit at Rest*'s culminating strategy.

The bulk of the novel's water imagery can be found primarily in the Florida sections. In fact, the entire state of Florida becomes yet another "element of death," and not entirely because of its close proximity to the Atlantic Ocean and the Gulf of Mexico. Updike makes resourceful symbolic use of the state's profile as a retirement haven for the country's growing mass of senior citizens. It is, Rabbit thinks at one point, "death's favorite state" (162/1196). All along the flat, desolate freeways he encounters an endless line of "sunstruck clinics" comprising one of the chief industries of "this state dedicated to the old" (4/1051–52). Along the Tamiami Trail—the "most steadily depressing" road Rabbit has ever driven on—liquor stores and gas stations compete with "low pale buildings" that "cater especially to illness and age," while on telephone wires, "instead of the sparrows and starlings you see in Pennsylvania, lone hawks and buzzards sit" (29/1075). Updike's Florida is a vast wasteland of the aging and dying, where everything has a false, flimsy quality to it, as if in anticipation of a rapid citizen turnover. Rabbit's Florida golfing partners are a markedly different breed from the rambunctious crowd at the Flying Eagle, for in Florida, Rabbit reflects, "people are so cautious, as if on two beers they might fall down and break a hip. The whole state is brittle" (70/1112). His Florida friendships are so "thin" and "provisional" perhaps because "people might at any minute buy another condominium and move to it, or else up and die" (73/1115). Late in the novel, Rabbit even reads a news item that reveals the curious statistic that "Florida has more deaths by lightning than any other state" (469/1477). Harry sums it up best when, gazing at the brittle, dried bark of a palm tree, he thinks, "There's a lot of death in Florida, if you look" (59/1102).

Parallel with its aging citizenry, as well as its vengeful, lightning-throwing god, Florida also evokes death through its association with the sea. As is only fitting, Rabbit, with his lifelong fear of water, finds the ocean the least appealing attraction the state has to offer. For him, Florida is simply a place where he can play golf in the winter. Still, he cannot entirely escape the presence of water, Florida's chief commodity, for it permeates everything about the state—its seasonal economy, its look, its national image. In keeping with the spirit of the place, Janice has their condominium kitchen done up in aqua, that watery color, with "creatures and flowers of seashells" added for adornment. Gazing at this decor makes Rabbit "feel panicky, shortens his breath," for, as the narrator directly tells us, "Being underwater is one of his nightmares" (54/1097).

Although Harry hates the water primarily because it reminds him of his daughter's death, he also views the element as a metaphor for all the subterranean, decay-ridden aspects of physical existence he would just as soon ignore. That is why he also dislikes anything even associated with the water—fish, seashells, algae, and so on—for all of it carries the same distasteful associations. Explaining why he hates seashells, the narrator explains, "Whenever [Rabbit] sees them he can't help thinking of the blobby hungry sluggy creatures who inhabit them, with hearts and mouths and anuses and feelers and feeble eyes, underneath the sea, a murky cold world halfway to death. He really can't stand the thought of underwater, the things haunting it, eating each other, drilling through shells, sucking each other's stringy guts out" (105/1144). As we saw in chapter 3, Updike first introduces the seashell motif in *Rabbit Is Rich,* where shells symbolize the accreted past, just as they do in Oliver Wendell Holmes's "The Chambered Nautilus," the novel's epigrammatic poem.[4] In *Rabbit at Rest,* those shells symbolize something slightly different. Here, it is not the shells qua shells that he hates so much. It is the thought of the creatures that once inhabited them that he finds so repellent. To see a seashell is to see all that remains of a creature now dead, a soft-bodied creature that, without its covering husk, is little more than a moiling mound of organs ("hearts and mouths and anuses and feelers and feeble eyes"). The organs are particularly repugnant to him, or at least the thought of them is. As he enters the first stages of his seniority, and finds himself surrounded by the fragile dying bodies of his aging friends, Rabbit has begun to reject all thoughts of the physical body, a vessel he once thought of as a portal to the something but which has now been revealed to be a "soft machine" helpless in the face of decay and death. What's more, the organs comprising that soft machine appear in his imagination exactly like those grotesque sea creatures bereft of their shells. As the narrator explains at one point, "His insides are like the sea to him, dark and wet and full of things he doesn't want to think about" (113/1152). Being underwater is for Rabbit not unlike being "under the skin": in both instances, the real as well as the imaginary, he recoils from the idea of floating aimlessly amid all that decay, all that helpless, organic physicality.

Still, for the sake of his grandchildren, Rabbit does consent to brave the dreaded element at least once, arranging on his own initiative to take Judy out on a Sunfish sailboat. As Updike pointedly explains in his introduction to *Rabbit Angstrom,* Rabbit's "adventure on the Sunfish with Judy rehearses once more the primal trauma of *Rabbit, Run,* this time

---

4. For more on the use of Holmes's poem in *Rabbit Is Rich,* see the introductory sections of chapter 3.

successfully, with the baby saved by the self-sacrificial parent" (xxii). Up-dike writes "once more" because this scene also has a fairly direct pre-cursor that also "rehearses . . . the primal trauma of *Rabbit, Run*"—that is, the episode in *Rabbit Is Rich* in which Rabbit ventures out on a Sun-fish with Cindy Murkett (*Rich* 402–5/986–89). It is, as even the nar-rator admits, an "inglorious episode" whose only instance of "trauma" comes when the Sunfish tips, sending Harry and Cindy into the water. Although Harry panics for a brief moment— *"Air* he thinks wildly" (405/988)—his life vest quickly saves him from meeting his dead daughter's fate. In the episode's companion piece from *Rabbit at Rest*, he is not so lucky.

Yet despite the fact that Rabbit experiences a heart attack while on the Sunfish, Updike insists on describing the event as a "success." Why? Because, as he suggests, the episode also functions as a redemptive coun-terpart to Becky's drowning in *Rabbit, Run*. Obviously, a reading such as this requires us to view Judy as Becky's reincarnation. The previous quotation from the introduction to *Rabbit Angstrom* treats this inter-pretation as a given. Yet only readers of the entire tetralogy could be ex-pected to make this connection between the two little girls, as Becky's presence in *Rabbit at Rest* is fleeting and largely insignificant. More im-portant, the textual evidence for this conflation of Judy and Becky is contained not in *Rabbit at Rest* but, as we saw in the previous chapter, in *Rabbit Is Rich*—on the final page of that novel, in fact. In that book, Updike depicts Rabbit's first encounter with his new granddaughter as a reprise of his first glimpse of Becky. He does this by repeating much of the same language he used in *Rabbit, Run* (*Run* 218/187 and *Rich* 467/1045).[5] By the time of *Rabbit at Rest* Judy is ten years old, which means Updike no longer has the opportunity to equate her with Becky, who died less than a month after her birth. The only way for first-time readers of *Rabbit at Rest* to make the Judy-as-Becky connection is to make note of Nelson's not untypical reaction to Rabbit's plan to take Judy sailing. Rather than be grateful to his father, Nelson whines, "I don't know. . . . How safe *are* those things?" (110/1149). The reason given for Nelson's uneasiness is actually provided more than fifty pages

---

5. To view the two complete passages side by side, see the final paragraph of chapter 3.

earlier, during a scene in which Rabbit throws out the idea of taking Judy golfing, an idea Nelson similarly shoots down. The narrator explains, "The boy's been trying ever since that business with Jill twenty years ago to protect women from his father. His son is the only person in the world who sees him as dangerous" (49/1093). Only longtime readers of the Angstrom story will be able to make the jump from Jill to Becky and hence from Becky to Judy, yet that is precisely the jump Updike wants his reader to make.

The sailing scene itself is vividly and memorably realized. Interwoven through the wealth of concrete physical detail are suggestive metaphors that clue longtime Rabbit aficionados into the episode's larger significance. Updike's chief metaphor in this regard is the name of the sailing vessel Rabbit and Judy take out on the water: a Sunfish. Though the brand name of an actual product, the word conveniently joins the novel's two parallel realms of death, the sky ("Sun-") and water ("-fish"). To understand the significance of this conjoining of apparent opposites, one needs to go all the way back to *Rabbit, Run,* specifically to Rabbit's dream of the sun and the moon (see *Run* 283/242). In the dream, the weaker moon covers the stronger sun, which action Rabbit interprets as an "explanation of death: lovely life eclipsed by lovely death" (*Run* 283/242).[6] What is particularly telling about the dream is the way it joins life and death, both of them deemed "lovely," into one holistic vision. The "Sunfish" sailing vessel effects a similar conjoining, linking the life-giving "sun" with death-dealing water ("fish").

The action of the episode also conflates life and death into one inextricable whole. Although Harry's heart has been signaling to him from as early as the opening sentence, and although this scene represents the first instance in which that heart makes its motives known, Harry experiences no morbid foreboding before setting sail. Rather, he "feels tall" and fully possessed of "his old animal recklessness" (126/1164). These life-affirming sensations are perhaps inspired by the natural elements "pour[ing] out all around him—water and sand and air and sun's fire, substances lavished in giant amounts yet still far from filling the limitless space" (126/1163). Note that both the "sun's fire," associated in

6. Throughout *Rabbit at Rest,* Harry experiences numerous variations on this same dream. See particularly 46/1090 and 500/1505.

Rabbit's dream with life, and "water and sand," generally suggestive of death, fill a single, undivided "limitless space." Similarly, out in the water he is struck by the "immensity of his perspectives" (128/1166). The water and the air, merged in this beach setting into one vast, immense horizon, provide Harry with a vision of infinity—an infinity that promises both a spiritual immortality and an eternally silent death. Though grateful for this vision of the fate that awaits him, Harry nevertheless realizes that such a limitless realm is no place for the living. This realization is provided to him by yet another prophetic bird, this one a "bent-winged tern" who "hangs motionless against the wind and cocks its head to eye them as if to ask what they are doing so far out of their element" (129–30/1166). Their element, the tern warns, is back on land: the sky and the sea belong to God.

Even the most ostensibly life-affirming moment in the entire sequence—Harry's "saving" his granddaughter from drowning—is undercut by the equally powerful presence of death. Actually, Judy comes nowhere near drowning. Like Rabbit ten years earlier, she is wearing a life vest that keeps her safely afloat. What's more, Updike provides ample evidence that Judy is only pretending to drown. For one thing, she has told Rabbit that she won a prize in her fourth-grade class for "staying underwater longest" (55/1099). For another, Pru is inclined to discredit Rabbit's story that Judy was trapped underwater, as she asks Nelson, "Aren't the sails awfully small? You know what a good swimmer she is. Do you possibly think . . . [t]hat she was just pretending, hiding from your father as a sort of game, and then it got out of hand?" (161/1196). Finally, Judy herself tells Rabbit she only "teased" him by "hiding under the sail" (264/1290). Yet while at sea, Rabbit, perhaps mindful of his wife's horrifying experience thirty years earlier, feels convinced he has lost her, and fights frantically through the water trying to save her from Becky's fate. In saving her, moreover, he feels that he is fighting the water, which is tantamount in his mind to fighting death. When the Sunfish first capsizes he feels his head being enclosed by "a murderous dense cold element" (131/168). And as he floats back to shore, out of breath and out of shape, he imagines "the water . . . hates him yet wants him" (135/1172). And it almost "gets" him, for while flailing around looking for Judy, he experiences his first heart attack. Significantly, the infarction grips him at the exact moment he finds Judy. In fact, he confuses his heart attack with his happiness at finally saving a daughter: "Joy that Judy lives crowds his heart, a gladness that tightens and rhythmically hurts, like a hand squeezing a ball for exercise" (133/1170). Clearly, this is the moment of his heart attack, and yet it is also, simultaneously, the affirmative, redemptive moment Updike waxes so lyrically about in his introduction.

In this case, fortunately, lovely life has eclipsed lovely death, for Rabbit survives this first brush with mortality. And although he originally confuses his heart attack with joy, he quickly begins to understand what has just happened to him. As the pain spreads though his arms and legs, he recalls once telling "someone, a prying clergyman, *somewhere behind all this there's something that wants me to find it.*" Then the narrator adds, "Whatever it is, *it* has found him, and is working him over" (136/1172). The prying clergyman, obviously, is Eccles, while the something is whatever lies in that water, whatever it is that "hates him yet wants him." What wants him is death, or Nobody, yet that Nobody is here revealed to be the same something he has been looking for all his life. The creator God and the destroyer God are really the same God. "Love and death," he thinks to himself a month later, in an entirely different context, "they can't be pried apart anymore" (203/1234).

III. The Rabbit Angstrom Show

Try though he might, Rabbit also cannot pry himself apart from his ailing, fat-corroded heart. Death gets its claws around it on page one and refuses to let go until its owner, having just made his final victorious basket, is left splayed out, alone, on a basketball court in the African American district of Deleon, Florida. But pry himself apart from his heart is precisely what Rabbit wishes he could do. Throughout the novel, Updike depicts the heart as having a will of its own, as being separate somehow from Rabbit himself. He employs this descriptive device not only to chart Rabbit's steady acceptance of his own death but also to open up a general, wide-ranging exploration of the emotional disassociations of modern life. These "disassociations" are the product primarily of a culture addicted to televised and filmic entertainment. Nearly all the main characters in *Rabbit at Rest* seek to identify themselves with the army of fictional characters that march at them from video and motion-picture screens. In so doing, they often feel as if their messy, intractable lives pale in comparison to the glittering and stylized world depicted in movies and television sitcoms. In the younger characters, Judy in particular, this rage for identification often leads them to confuse the fictional landscape of the mass media with the quotidian terrain of the real world.

Rabbit, too, suffers from a form of disassociation, yet his is not so much the product of the mass media as it is of his own impending mortality. Specifically, Rabbit insists upon a radical disconnection between his physical, corporeal body and his "essential self," the latter of which he feels qualifies him as a "God-made one-of-a-kind with an immortal soul breathed in" and a "vehicle of grace" (237/1265). He refuses to accept the idea that his ailing body will take his cherished subjectivity with it when it dies. In accordance with Updike's ongoing strategy of uniting the "personal and national realms," the novel suggests a fascinating connection between Rabbit's body/soul disruption and the general culture's confusion of the real and the hyperreal. As we shall see, it is precisely through the plot device of Rabbit's heart attack that Updike manages to make this connection.

In our discussion of the novel's water/death motif, we touched upon the issue of Rabbit's late-blooming repugnance toward his own physical body. There, we saw how Rabbit tends to view his "insides" as like the sea, "dark and wet and full of things he doesn't want to think about" (113/1152). This idea in turn assumes a central and pivotal role in the passages devoted to Rabbit's heart troubles. Certainly, his heart is one of the chief things he doesn't want to think about, and so, to assuage his anxiety about his condition, he regards it variously as an "enemy" or as a "child inside him" that is "playing with matches" (91/1131). He fluctuates between taking responsibility for this desperate, dying organ and feeling like its hapless victim. Sometimes it seems to him like "a tiny creature, a baby, pleading inside him for attention, for rescue" (473/1480). At other times it seems like "a sinister intruder, a traitor muttering in code, an alien parasite nothing will expel" (473/1480). In both instances, it is something separate, a resident inside that part of him that is "God-made" and "one-of-a-kind." Of course, this conviction about the irreconcilability of the body and the soul dates back to *Rabbit, Run:*

it is, in fact, that novel's central site of tension. Conversely, in *Rabbit at Rest* he depicts this irreconcilation as an act of will, or perhaps even an act of cowardice.

Rabbit's squeamish attitude toward his heart troubles contrasts tellingly with that of Charlie Stavros, who, from his first appearance in *Rabbit Redux,* has been suffering from a dangerous murmur. Updike brings Stavros back for a brief scene that functions as direct reprise of an episode in *Rabbit Is Rich* in which he and Harry eat lunch at the then-fashionable Crêpe House (see *Rich* 87–91/699–703). In the new scene, he and Rabbit eat at the same restaurant—now renamed Salad Binge—where Rabbit, despite his doctor's strict orders to avoid fats, orders the Macadamia and Bacon Salad. And a beer. As he tells Charlie about his heart troubles, and particularly about his reluctance to undergo multiple bypass open-heart surgery, he learns to his surprise that Charlie has already had the same operation. A level-headed pragmatist to the end, Stavros blithely explains that his aortic and mitral valves have been replaced with pig heart valves. Moreover, he dismisses the actual operation as little more than a minor discomfort. Like Bernie Dreschel, Stavros, too, was "frozen," yet rather than regard this experience as some sort of metaphorical precursor to death, as Bernie did, Charlie simply thinks of the whole ordeal as a "piece of cake" (237/1265). "You're knocked out cold," he tells Rabbit, with exasperation one feels. "What's wrong with running your blood through a machine. What else you think you are?" (237/1265). Although Rabbit does not answer Stavros, the narrator records his silent response, the gist of which we have already alluded to. The full passage reads as follows: "A God-made one-of-a-kind with an immortal soul breathed in. A vehicle of grace. A battlefield of good and evil. An apprentice angel" (237/1265). As if in response to Rabbit's unvoiced reflections, Stavros adds, "You're just a soft machine," a line that reads like a direct refutation of Rabbit's own Christian idealism.

This brief exchange sets up a typically Updikean dialectic, whereby we are asked to choose between two irreconcilable alternatives. Either we are "God-made one-of-a-kinds," or we are "soft machines." To embrace the former idea is to ignore the obvious fact that we are basically animals like any other. To embrace the latter is to surrender that instinctive sense of supreme importance dictated to us by our egos. The apparent incompatibility of these two interpretations of our corporeal existence constitutes what Updike has elsewhere described as one of the chief mysteries of life: "The mystery that more puzzled me as a child was the incarnation of my ego—that omnivorous and somehow preëxistent 'I'—in a speck so specifically situated amid the billions of history. Why was I I? The arbitrariness of it astounded me; in comparison, nothing was too marvelous."[7] In this instance, one could say that Charlie is the voice of "arbitrariness," while Rabbit stands up for the claims of "that omnivorous and somehow preëxistent 'I.'" Yet what "puzzled" Updike as a child, and what seems to puzzle him still, is the coexistence of these two mutually exclusive notions. Midway through *Rabbit at Rest*, Updike even paraphrases the above passage, which was written way back in 1962. Although he shifts the locale from Shillington to the fictional Brewer, he otherwise keeps the basic sentiment more or less intact. Lying in his hospital bed, Harry tries to "view his life as a brick of sorts . . . just one life in rows and walls and blocks of lives" (293–94/ 1316–1317). Although this view gives him a "faint far-off communal thrill"—borne from the sense that we are each an insignificant component of a larger structure, which idea can assuage some of the anxiety one feels at being the sole caretaker of one's life—Rabbit ultimately rejects it in favor of "his original and continuing impression that Brewer and all the world beyond are just frills on himself, like the lace around a plump satin valentine, himself the heart of the universe, like the Dalai Lama" (294/1317). We're back to *Rabbit, Run* and the Dalai Lama. And just as *Rabbit, Run* explored the tension that arises between the claims of biology and society, instinct and law, so does *Rabbit at Rest* examine the clash between spirituality and physicality.

No scene better dramatizes this clash than the one devoted to Rabbit's angioplasty. The operation requires the doctor to insert a catheter into the top of Rabbit's leg, threading it up through his torso until it enters his heart. Although Rabbit prefers this relatively mild procedure to the bypass surgery, he nevertheless finds the mere thought of it "repugnant." It is simply the lesser of two evils, in his view, a much more palatable alternative than, as he characterizes the bypass, "being frozen half to death and sawed open and your blood run through some complicat-

7. Updike, "Dogwood," 182.

ed machine while they sew a slippery warm piece of your leg vein to the surface of your trembling poor cowering heart" (269/1294). Here, again, Rabbit thinks of the ailing organ as a volitional creature in its own right, "trembling" and "cowering" from the surgeon's scalpel. This conviction grows as he watches a video of the actual procedure. What he sees is not a miracle of medical science but rather an *invasion* of a sacred place: "cold narrow scalpels attack the shapeless bloody blob as it lies there in your chest like a live thing in a hot puddle, a cauldron of tangled juicy stew, convulsing, shuddering with a periodic sob, trying to dodge the knives, undressed of the sanitary pod God or whoever never meant human hands to touch" (269/1295). The heart is not just a "live thing in a hot puddle," but rather something capable of emotion, as it "convulses" and "sobs." Most important, the exposed organ appears to him as the victim of an act of sacrilege. In Rabbit's view, human hands were no more meant to see the inside of the living body than he was meant to leave his "element" and venture into the limitless horizon offered by the open sea. The internal body is as forbidden and sacred a place as the sea, both realms ruled over by "God or whoever." But what most amazes Rabbit about the video is the news that, during the part of the surgery in which the blood is pumped through a machine, the heart "lies there dead in its soupy puddle." For Rabbit, this also is a kind of sacrilege, unimaginable to someone who thinks of himself as a "God-made one-of-a-kind with an immortal soul breathed in." As he puts it, "You, the natural you, are technically dead" (270/1295).

Of course, the patient does *not* die, both Bernie and Charlie being living examples of this fact. During the procedure the machine keeps the patient alive as successfully as does a living, convulsing, sobbing heart, all of which gives credence to Charlie's view that we, too, are little more than "soft machines." Despite the evidence before his eyes, Rabbit resists this conclusion: "Harry has trouble believing how his life is tied to all this mechanics—that the *me* that talks inside him all the time scuttles like a water-striding bug above this pond of body fluids and their slippery conduits. How could the flame of him ever have ignited out of such wet straw?" (270/1295). The "me" to which Harry here refers is, of course, one and the same with Updike's "omnivorous and somehow preëxistent 'I.'" Like the heart, it, too, is figured as a separate thing, that is, as a "water-striding bug," with the difference being that Harry is *reluctant* to accept this idea. Whereas he eagerly imagines his organs in their "pond of body fluids" as independent entities, he cannot abide by the idea that his "me" is yet one more component of his corporeal body, yet another cog in the soft machine. Rather, that "me," that essential self, is the "flame" without which there is no Harry "Rabbit" Angstrom. Or, as Rabbit thinks elsewhere, "That little electric twitch: without it we're so much rotting meat" (447/1456).[8]

Once again identifying himself with the Dalai Lama, Rabbit compares the existence of that "flame" with the crown of godhood lavished on the Tibetan leader. Midway through the novel, for instance, Rabbit recalls a recent news item in which it is reported that the Dalai Lama has asked to resign his position, a request his followers reject out-of-hand. As the narrator observes, the "Dalai Lama can no more resign godhood than Harry can resign selfhood" (294/1317). So how could it possibly be true that his "immortal soul" is really no more than another mechanical device, replaceable by a machine and as interchangeable as a kidney or a pancreas? It is no accident, for instance, that the video makes him think of "those horrible old Frankenstein movies with Boris Karloff" (269/1295).

The Frankenstein motif gets further explored during the angioplasty procedure itself. His modern-minded doctor arranges for Rabbit to view the operation as it is happening on a video monitor. To his horror, Harry watches himself get transformed into "jerking bright lines" and "vital signs" in what he sardonically refers to as "the Rabbit Angstrom Show," complete "with a fluctuating audience" consisting of his two doctors, the circulating nurse, and "some others never named to him" assuming the roles of "lime-green extras" (271/1296). Amid all this technology and sterile expertise, Rabbit finds himself unable even to pray. He feels there is "too much crowding in, of the actual material

8. From *Self-Consciousness:* "Those who scoff at the Christian hope of an afterlife have on their side not only a mass of biological evidence knitting the self-conscious mind to the perishing body but a certain moral superiority as well: isn't it terribly, well, *selfish,* and grotesquely egocentric, to hope for more than our animal walk in the sun, from eager blind infancy through the productive and procreative years into a senescence that, by the laws of biological instinct as well as by the premeditated precepts of stoic virtue, will submit to eternal sleep gratefully? Where, indeed, in the vast spaces disclosed by modern astronomy, would our disembodied spirit go, and once there, what would it do?" (214).

world. No old wispy biblical God dare interfere" (272/1297). His sacred, inviolate insides have been sacrilegiously opened into the "actual material world" in such a way that the sacred has now become itself godless and material. Despite his stubborn denials, his body has become exactly what Stavros said it was: a soft machine, as free of the redemptive qualities of spiritual grace as a slab of meat. Not only does God decline to interfere in this high-tech procedure, but he does not even seem present. For instance, Rabbit notes that modern hospitals no longer employ nuns and rabbis (272/1297). And it is precisely because of its "godlessness" that Rabbit regards the procedure not as life-preserving but as death-dealing. By being turned into a soft machine in this way, he has been made to face up to the possibility that he is not, in fact, God-made and one-of-a-kind. The "mechanically precise dark ghost" of the catheter that enters his leg strikes him as "the worm of death." Likewise, as the tube rises higher and higher through his body, he begins to feel as if he is being raped into submission, into accepting Stavros's materialist view of human life: "Godless technology is fucking the pulsing wet tubes we inherited from the squid, the boneless sea-cunt" (274/1298). Even his voice during the procedure "sounds high in his ears, as if out of a woman's throat" (274/1299). Later in the novel, he will characterize the whole experience of watching his operation on television as "insulting" (475/1482).

For all this language of rape and invasion, he still retains some sense of that God-made part of himself. Although he recognizes the fact that "godless technology" is keeping him alive, he also feels that his cherished "me" remains untouched by this exposure of his insides to the "actual material world." "Still here," he tells his doctor at one point, and so he is. Likewise, the images he watches on the screen—images not only of the inside of his body but of the *inside of his heart* as well—seem as "remote from his body as the records of his sins that the angels are keeping" (274/1299). If "godless technology" is the new religion, then that religion is not entirely unlike Rabbit's own Barthian Christianity, both of them presided over by a remote and indifferent deity who does not compromise our "precious creaturely freedom."

Ultimately, what allows Harry to maintain a distinction between the "video images" provided by the "Rabbit Angstrom Show" and his subjective existence are his deep-seated religious convictions. By clinging to his belief in a spiritually sanctioned, supremely sacred subjectivity, he separates himself from the surface images provided by technology, images that Kierkegaard would regard as "aesthetic" tools of disavowal. The screen may suggest he is a soft machine, but Rabbit knows otherwise. Conversely, the absence of those convictions prevents many of the other characters from achieving the same distinction. Here is where Updike draws curious connections between the current mass media and Harry's own convictions about the soul/body split. For his surgeons, the images provided on the video screen—the "Rabbit Angstrom Show"—represent all of Rabbit that there is to know. His left anterior injuries are nothing special—"By far the most common site of lesions," Dr. Breit matter-of-factly tells Harry—nor are they evidence of anything more than mechanical malfunctioning that can be corrected. These views in turn become the cornerstone of the novel's critique not only of technology but of the popular media culture as well. The first clue to this thematic link is Harry's sardonic description of the video component of his procedure as the Rabbit Angstrom Show. Yet the doctors also treat Harry's condition like a television program, and they do so without irony. Dr. Raymond, for instance, speaks of Harry's operative progress as if he were endorsing a product on television: "'Whaddya mean?' Dr. Raymond responds—'looking *great*,' like those voices on television that argue about the virtues of Miller Lite" (275/1299). In the late seventies, Harry was the one trying to model his life according to the dictates of the commercial mass media, this owing primarily to his sudden and unexpected brush with wealth. Now, on the other hand, he has not only settled into that wealth but has abandoned his worship of the Webb Murketts of the world. His new heroes are the wise, stoic Jewish men with whom he plays golf in Florida. Whereas he once coveted Webb Murkett's house and young wife, he now treasures his Jewish friends' "perspective: it seems more manly than his, sadder and wiser and less shaky. Their long history has put all that suffering in its pocket and strides on" (57–58/1101). In contrast, everyone else is now the way Harry used to be—shallow, image-conscious, and trapped by the need to identify themselves with the shallow fictional depictions of life presented in films and television.

Janice is the most obvious example of this cultural development. In *Rabbit Redux,* she took over Harry's abdicated role from *Rabbit, Run* as adulterer and freedom-seeker. Likewise, in *Rabbit at Rest* she becomes a resurrected version of the money- and image-obsessed Harry of *Rabbit Is Rich*. Untouched by and unconcerned with current geopolitical developments, she only follows the tawdry personal lives of movie stars and sitcom sirens in the Lifestyles section of the *Fort Myers News Press*. When she and Harry take the grandchildren to go see Melanie Griffith in *Working Girl*, Janice finds a model she all at once wants to emulate. "*I* want to get a job, too," she tells Harry. "The movie we saw this afternoon, all these women working in New York skyscrapers, made me so *jealous*"(113/1151). The announcement annoys Rabbit, and only in part because, as a white male of his generation and demographic background, he is uneasy with the idea of working women in general. What chiefly bothers him is Janice's phony, staged projections, her sense of herself as one more actor in a glitzy drama: "Janice didn't use to dramatize herself. Ever since her mother died and they bought this condo, she has been building up an irritating confidence, an assumption that the world is her stage and her performance is going pretty well" (113/1151). She does in fact get a job, not in a New York skyscraper but as a realtor in Mt. Judge. Her first project is to sell, against Harry's objections, the Angstrom's Penn Park home. She also identifies with *thirtysomething* ("realistic domestic drama") and with the scandal-ridden stories of infighting on the set of the *Today* show.[9] "[R]eally nothing's private anymore," she thinks, "the scandalmongers never rest" (310/1331). Yet it is not just the scandal mongers that have robbed us of our privacy. It is the proliferation of television in general. By identifying herself with the characters on television, Janice reduces her own sacred selfhood to another image, which action parallels Harry's vision of life as a brick on the wall, whereby we each become just "one life in rows and walls and blocks of lives."

---

9. There is an interesting postmodern moment regarding *Rabbit at Rest*. In one of the episodes from the final season of *thirtysomething*, a copy of *Rabbit at Rest* is placed, as a prop, on the bedside table of the program's principle characters, the ever-whining Hope and Michael. Had the fictional characters in the program actually read the book they are alleged to be reading, they would have seen that they were in fact merely characters in a television program which the fictional characters in the novel watch pretty regularly.

The other characters in the novel suffer from a similar inability to separate the reality of their lives from the lives of television characters. Judy, for instance, is a chronic channel surfer, a typical American child of today who, like others of her generation, is unable to keep her attention focused on anything for longer than ten minutes. Her inner life is bereft of anything more solid than commercials and sitcoms, as is evidenced by the touching scene out on the Sunfish in which she soothes Rabbit's aching heart by singing to him snatches of commercial jingles, the only songs other than nursery rhymes that she knows by heart. "It is like switching channels back and forth," Rabbit reflects (140/1176). Throughout the novel, Rabbit reduces himself to watching television with his granddaughter, as she flicks back and forth from rerun to rerun. At one point she begins telling a story about a kid at school whose basic thread Rabbit suspects she actually lifted from the tube: "Her talk is a little like her excited channel-flipping and it occurs to Harry that she is making it up or confusing her own classroom with classroom shows she has seen on television" (333/1352). Even Rabbit occasionally gets in on the act, gorging himself on family sitcoms like *Cosby* and *Roseanne,* the former of which he is a big fan. ("The door is on the right in *Cosby* and on the left on *Roseanne,"* he correctly notes [468/1476]). He is not even above dramatizing himself like Janice. When Janice presents to him the idea of selling their house, he objects in strident terms that outweigh how he actually feels. More than anything else, the narrator explains, Harry enjoys "the sound of his voice, indignant like one of those perpetually outraged fathers on a TV sitcom" (397/1410).

Ultimately, however, Rabbit alone in the novel is able to keep his individuality intact in the face of all this televised sameness, and he is successful for the same reason he succeeds in resisting his doctors' attempt to turn him into a soft machine. Once he begins to accept the fact that his time is running out, he eschews his addiction to sitcoms and "finds that facts, not fantasies are what he wants" (295/1317). The movies and sitcoms suddenly seem thin and pale, while the sports broadcasts seem like a waste of time, "stories told people with time to kill, while he has time left only for truth." Accordingly, he watches nature programs and documentaries, which depict existence not as idealized and easily resolved, but as messy and violent, as "struggle and death." Without a sense of that truth, the sitcoms make him "restless." Very late in the novel, he experiences a significant revelation about those TV families that solidly delineates the difference between Rabbit's attitude toward mass commercial entertainment and that of the other characters in the novel: "TV families and your own are hard to tell apart, except yours isn't interrupted every six minutes by commercials and theirs don't get bogged down into nothingness, a state where nothing happens, no skit, no zany visitors, no outbursts on the laugh track, nothing at all but boredom and a lost feeling" (468/1476). *Theirs don't get bogged down into nothingness.* What neither the doctors nor Janice, Judy et al. seem to recognize is that televised versions of life absolutely and unequivocally *lie* about the boredom and spiritual emptiness that sits at the center of human existence. On television, that boredom and emptiness, symbols both of the nothingness that awaits, get shoved aside in favor of nonstop activity, quick resolution, and new beginnings. Television serves the same purpose as the Muzak Rabbit hears in the airport early in the novel, that is, "to cover up a silence that might remind you of death" (4/1052). Janice, on the other hand, largely accepts what she sees on television. As she says of *Unsolved Mysteries,* a program Rabbit hates, "They couldn't put the show on television if there weren't some truth to it and that Robert Stack seems ever so sensible" (309/1330). But the "mysteries" offered up for our consideration on such programs are no different from the "Amityville Horror" business that had so enthralled Nelson ten years before. These films and programs are just more Hollywood entertainment masquerading as "real life." As such, they further blur the boundary between actual existence and make-believe. What Rabbit said of Nelson ten years ago on the occasion of the Amityville Horror conversation holds true even more in the cable-TV, remote-control world of *Rabbit at Rest:* "Spineless generation, no grit, nothing solid to tell a fact from a spook with, Satanism, pot, drugs, vegetarianism. Pathetic. Everything handed to them on a platter, think life's one big TV, full of ghosts" (*Rich* 161/766). In Rabbit's view, on the other hand, life is what happens inside that vast cathedral of subjectivity, where his "*me*. . . talks inside him all the time." There lies his God-sanctioned specialness, his selfhood, which, like the Dalai Lama's godhood, no doctor or television program can touch.

IV. Nelson Redux

Of all the characters in the novel, none is so frazzled and affected by the mass media's fantasy of instant gratification and effortless success as Nelson. Ten years after commencing his campaign to destroy his father's automobile empire, Nelson is as dissatisfied and ill-equipped to deal with the responsibilities and anxieties of adulthood as he ever was. In fact, he is in worse shape than before. In *Rabbit Is Rich*, Harry's heart would skip with rage at the mere thought of Nelson "drinking and eating up the world, and out of sheer spite at that" (357/945). In the late-eighties world of *Rabbit at Rest*—a world of yuppies, greed, and conspicuous consumption—Nelson's propensity for selfish whining and profligate expenditure meets widespread support from the culture at large. In the same way that Updike portrayed the sixties world of *Rabbit Redux* as having caught up with the mystic-minded, freedom-loving Rabbit of the 1950s, so does he suggest that the famously self-absorbed eighties have merely caught up with Nelson Angstrom's 1970s fantasy of unlimited cash-flow and wounded emotional development. "[I]f there's anything you can count on Americans to be these last ten years," Janice thinks to herself one afternoon, "it's selfish" (310/1331).

Significantly, she has this thought on her way over to Nelson's house on the same morning in which Nelson is scheduled to enter a drug rehabilitation clinic to help with his cocaine habit, a habit that has resulted in his throwing Harry's Toyota dealership into irreparable bankruptcy. As a metaphor for the national leveraged spending spree of the Ronald Reagan era, Nelson's cocaine habit is hard to beat. Yet this plot development also serves two additional purposes within the continuing structural design of *Rabbit Angstrom*. First, it continues the story, begun in *Rabbit Is Rich*, of Nelson's attempt to make Harry pay for what Nelson regards as his father's numerous paternal sins. Second, it functions as an analogue to Harry's involvement in *Rabbit Redux* with the sixties drug subculture, a tentative act of experimentation that resulted in the burning down of Harry's house, just as Nelson's parallel experiments result in the destruction of the Toyota lot. In these myriad ways, *Rabbit at Rest* manages to provide a sort of deferred resolution to the 1960s installment of the Angstrom saga, making this final book of the tetralogy, among other things, a sort of "Nelson Redux."

In the first section of the novel, Updike conceals Nelson's addiction the same way he concealed for awhile Nelson's impending fatherhood in *Rabbit Is Rich.* The addiction, in fact, serves as this novel's correlative to Pru's pregnancy. As in the previous novel, Harry is the last person in the family to know Nelson's secret, and because the reader is limited to Harry's center-of-consciousness for much of this early section, we, too, are implicated in Updike's narrative strategy. Even readers who have followed Rabbit and Nelson through three previous books will not initially see anything out of the ordinary in their conflicted dealings with one another. Rabbit is still made uneasy by Nelson's presence, and he still looks upon his son as a hostile competitor, out to take away his coveted place in the world. The Nelson who appears in the early sections of *Rabbit at Rest* appears more or less like the same character who wreaked havoc in *Rabbit Is Rich.* He just seems a bit more sinister. Throughout *Rabbit Is Rich,* Harry maintained to Janice that Nelson was a "rat" (424/ 1006). Now, as if in fulfillment of a prophecy, and in keeping with the fashion of the times, Nelson actually sports along the back of his neck a stringy tail that Harry immediately terms a "rat's tail" (15/1059). Nelson even wears a matching "mouse-colored" mustache (24/1070). Although these details, the mustache in particular, serve as symbolic clues to Nelson's predicament, they are not out of sync with what readers have come to expect from him. Nor should readers be surprised to learn that Nelson, to his father's dissatisfaction, has expensive taste in clothes, and that he still holds to the view that money is "shit" and easy to come by. As he puts it in a passage that reprises the sex/money motif from the last novel, "People don't make money an hour at a time anymore; you just get yourself in the right position and it *comes*" (39/1084). What is new about Nelson is his "exhausted" look, which even Harry notes with some alarm. Moreover, Nelson's characteristic nervousness has manifestly increased. Harry notes, for instance, that Nelson compulsively shapes the ash of his cigarette "into a perfect cone" before stabbing it out, and that his "hands shake more than a young man's should" (36/ 1081). Although this sort of nervous behavior might be revealing to a drug therapist, or even to someone of Nelson's own generation, to Harry it signals nothing specific.

Once Harry and, by extension, the reader finally learn the significance of all these clues, the denouement of Nelson's own part in the

Angstrom story falls easily into place. In fact, the cocaine addiction happily localizes for Updike a whole host of issues that have hovered around Nelson for at least two novels. First and foremost, it provides Updike with a way to dramatize the repercussions attendant upon Nelson's specific brand of angst. Whereas his father's anxiety is the product of a Kierkegaardian blend of fear and trembling, Nelson's angst lacks any sort of spiritual element. As a result, it admits of no relief. Harry manages his dread through stoic acceptance and faith. Nelson, on the other hand, can only seek temporary relief from what is, essentially, an ontological condition. In terms that directly apply to Rabbit's wayward son, Bernie Dreschel explains to Harry cocaine's appeal to Nelson's "spineless" and faithless generation. "What they see in it," Bernie theorizes, "is instant happiness" (58/1101). Nelson employs similar language in explaining his drug use to his mother: "It's hard to describe. You know that expression about drunks, 'feeling no pain'? After a hit, I feel no pain. I guess that means I feel pain the rest of the time. Everything goes from black and white to color. Everything is more intense, and more hopeful. You see the world the way it was meant to be. You feel more *powerful"* (148/ 1183).[10] For "pain" above, read "anxiety." Just as Bernie suggested, cocaine gives Nelson "instant happiness," actually a temporary relief from anxiety. His pervasive, constant fear of nothing is momentarily replaced by an illusion of "hope" and sustained happiness, which is the way he thinks the world "was meant to be." This childish belief in a safe and trouble-free world has been dogging him all his adult life. His chief complaint about his father is that Harry has neglected to provide for him such a world. Without Harry's hard-nosed appreciation for the essential unhappiness of human life, Nelson can only seek artificial ways to create the happy and frictionless world he thinks has been denied him. Cocaine is his solution. "It's right for me," he explains. "It makes me feel *right,* in a way nothing else does" (154/1188).

Another issue Updike is able to explore via cocaine is Nelson's ongoing attempt to exact in real monetary terms his oedipal debt to his father. In *Rabbit Is Rich,* Nelson literalizes that debt by systematically wrecking an entire fleet of Harry's cars. Automobiles, in fact, become

10. The final lines in this passage—"You feel more *powerful"*—represents an addition to the original published version.

the novel's chief symbols for Harry's and Nelson's sexual rivalry. In effect treating his father's beloved cars as surrogates for the various women the two men have competed for through the years—Janice and Jill, for instance—Nelson destroys each one as a way to make his father pay for stealing these women away.[11] In *Rabbit at Rest,* Updike resumes this narrative thread by weaving it into the issue of Nelson's cocaine addiction. Even before Harry learns the full details of Nelson's drug problems, he recognizes something amiss in the financial reports coming in from the car dealership. Used sales seem to be down. The reason the numbers are small is because Nelson has been selling used cars off the books and pocketing the money in order to finance his narcotic use. By the time Harry moves in to try to salvage the lot, Nelson has succeeded in robbing the company of nearly two hundred thousand dollars. The sum is large enough to sink the company for good. Nelson has succeeded, finally, in making his father repay the sexual debt Nelson feels he is owed, for in bringing down the company, Nelson also brings down his father.

Rabbit knows it, too. When he first learns the full extent of Nelson's recklessness, he feels himself go "cold with the premonition that this debt will swallow him" (361/1377). Before the novel is over, that debt, and Nelson as well, will succeed in doing just that, as the debt Nelson accrues hastens Harry's death. First, the debt frees Harry of all responsibility, or, to put the case less positively, it robs Harry of anything to live for. Second, it releases Harry from his own spiritual debt to Nelson, a debt which, in chapter 3, was figured in terms of transmitted Original Sin. Harry is in debt to Nelson for passing on the stain of sin, while Nelson is oedipally in debt to Harry simply for his existence. Nelson's destruction of the Toyota dealership, then, represents something of a Pyrrhic victory for him. Although he has finally succeeded in making his father pay for all the misery he thinks Harry has caused him, he has also inadvertently freed Harry of all spiritual debts. The realization of this is a mild relief to Harry, so much so that he takes solace in the idea that, thanks to Nelson's screw-up, he "is off the hook for once" (299/1322).

Nelson absolves his father of guilt and responsibility in one addi-

---

11. For a more detailed discussion of this issue and its significance in *Rabbit Is Rich,* see chapter 3, section III.

tional way as well. More than just a physical embodiment of Rabbit's own transmitted guilt, Nelson also represents the only living eyewitness to Rabbit's most egregious sins. After all, Nelson is the only surviving character in the Rabbit story who was present during the tumultuous events of 1969, a fact which bothers Rabbit immensely. As he tells Thelma Harrison in *Rabbit Is Rich*, "I think one of the troubles between me and the kid is every time I had a little, you know, slip-up, he was there to see it. That's one of the reasons I don't like having him around" (73/777). Rabbit cannot forget those little slip-ups so long as Nelson is still around as their living reminder. Yet on the night that Nelson flies into a rage over some lost cocaine and begins hitting his wife and children in the process, Rabbit no longer has to bear this burden, as Nelson abdicates his role as his father's moral superior and objective conscience.

Indeed, the whole scene reads like a rewriting of the episode in *Rabbit Redux* in which Harry is roused from his evening with Peggy Fosnacht with the news that his house is burning down. In the new scene, of course, the midnight phone call comes not from Skeeter but from Pru, yet otherwise the scene shares with its parallel episode in *Rabbit Redux* the same mood of deep-evening calm shattered by the threat of chaos. On the drive over to Nelson and Pru's house, Rabbit replays a train of thought he first entertained on his nighttime drive, twenty years ago, to his burning house in Penn Villas. In *Rabbit Redux,* Harry looks out his car window and thinks, "The universe is unsleeping, neither ants nor stars sleep, to die will be to be forever wide awake" (*Redux* 317/541). The corresponding passage from *Rabbit at Rest* reads as follows: "Stars do not sleep, but above the housetops and tree crowns shine in a cold arching sprinkle. Why do we sleep? What do we rejoin?" (256/1273). Significantly, Harry's and Janice's drive from Penn Park, through West Brewer, and out to Joseph Street exactly reverses the direction of Nelson's and Harry's parallel drive twenty years ago, which took them from West Brewer and back to Penn Villas: in the tetralogy's detailed topography, Rabbit crisscrosses his own path. At the site of this new domestic disaster, moreover, Rabbit thinks, "In crises there is something in our instincts which whittles, which tries to reduce the unignorable event back to the ignorable normal" (253/1280). The passage functions as yet another echo of a similar passage in *Rabbit Redux,* in which Harry looks at his burning house and notes within him "an engine murmuring

Undo, undo, which wants to take [Jill and Skeeter] back to this afternoon . . . and have it all unhappen" (*Redux* 325 / 548). Finally, as Rabbit studies Nelson's erratic behavior during this "intervention," he notes in Nelson's eyes little "sparks like that time outside the burning house at 26 Vista Crescent" (254 / 1281). These echoes point to Updike's formalistic intentions: the newer scene is meant to be an answer to the former.

Crisis or not, what Harry encounters at Nelson's house is nothing short of vindication. After twenty years of feeling Nelson's resentment about Jill's death, and after thirty years of shouldering Nelson's disappointment at not having a perfect, sinless father, Rabbit finally gets to witness Nelson slip up in front of his children. Nelson's chief gripe with his father is that, in standing aside to let Becky drown in the bathtub and Jill burn in the Penn Villas house, Harry effectively got away with murder. Perhaps mindful of these charges, Rabbit throws the same charge back at his son when he accuses Janice, "[Y]ou keep letting Nelson get away with murder" (249 / 1276). Rabbit is released.

Yet this narrative of debt repayment only completes something that was first inaugurated back in *Rabbit Is Rich.* Although the destruction of the lot completes the narrative, it is only icing on the cake for Rabbit. Indeed, as we saw in chapter 3, he began washing his hands of responsibility for Nelson the moment Nelson got married. As the narrator explained in *Rabbit Is Rich,* "Now that Nelson is married it's like a door has been shut in [Rabbit's] mind, a debt has finally been paid" (259 / 856). So why does Updike sustain a narrative that was partially resolved ten years ago? He does so in order to include Janice among the targets of Nelson's reign of destruction. Here, again, *Rabbit at Rest* parallels *Rabbit Redux* in the way it situates Janice as a sort of belated reincarnation of her husband. Just as Janice repeats Harry's *Run*-era adultery in *Rabbit Redux,* so does she relive in *Rabbit at Rest* Harry's *Rich*-era battle with Nelson. Whereas in the previous novel she functioned as Nelson's protector, here she becomes another of his enemies. The only person he affected by wrecking cars was Harry. By destroying the lot, he also hits Janice where it hurts her most. After all, it is she, not Harry, who principally owns the dealership, having had it willed to her from her father. As Rabbit himself observes three pages into the novel, "Janice is rich" (5 / 1053). Also, in agreeing to seek professional help for his addiction, Nelson tries to place the blame for his condition on her, just as he blamed Harry for all his miseries in *Rabbit Is Rich.* In that novel, he was wont to whine, "Everything's his fault, it's his fault I'm so fucked up" (134/742). Now he amends that diagnosis of his troubles to include his mother: "What about what you did to me, all that mess around when Becky died so I never had a sister, and then that time you ran away with your oily Greek and crazy Dad brought in Jill and then Skeeter into the house and they tried to make me take dope when I was just a little kid?" (315/1336). Now the finger of blame points all the way back to Janice. Jill died not just because Harry let her but because Janice left the family, thus opening a space for Jill and Skeeter to move in. According to Nelson's reasoning, he would not be addicted to cocaine now if Janice had simply stayed with Harry back in the sixties. Nelson also levels at her the same charge of greed that he once leveled at his father. In *Rabbit Is Rich,* for instance, Nelson tells Harry, "All you care about is money and *things*" (119/728). Now Nelson shoots a similar accusation at Janice: "You care more about the dumb lot than you care about me" (315/1336).

Janice's response to these accusations resembles Harry's reaction ten years ago. On the one hand, she wonders if Nelson doesn't have a point. "Abandoning a twelve-year-old like that," she cries to Harry, "I'm the one should have been put in jail, what *was* I thinking?" (322/1342). Like Harry, she detects a curious spiritual truth inherent in Nelson's accusations. She, too, is to blame for Nelson's misery, for it was she who, in giving him birth, saddled him with St. Augustine's "divine sentence of condemnation." That is why she feels that she, not he, should be going to "jail." Looking at her son, she realizes that, "[w]ith all her maternal effort she's brought destruction into the world" (313/1334).

Interestingly enough, Nelson might actually have a case against his parents. At times, Updike suggests the source of Nelson's problem might in part lie in Harry's and Janice's coddling. They have secured for him both a job and rent-free living, as Nelson and his family live in the old Springer home on Joseph Street. In fact, Pru traces Nelson's childishness directly to his parents' failure to let him assume more responsibility. As she tells Harry, "By continuing to accept the blame he's willing to assign you, you and Janice continue to infantilize him" (125/1163). Perhaps too long after the fact, Janice arrives at the same conclusion as Pru, eventually rejecting Nelson's version of events. As if recalling Nelson's tendency in *Rabbit Is Rich* to perceive his father as a stand-in for Updike's aloof, Wholly Other God, she tells Nelson, "You know, Nelson, when you're little you think your parents are God but now you're old enough to face the fact that they're not. . . . You're of an age now to take responsibility for your own life" (316/1337). With this statement, Janice washes her hands of culpability for Nelson's troubles exactly as her husband did, ten years ago, in *Rabbit Is Rich.*

Although Harry and Janice try to absolve themselves of responsibility for Nelson, the world is less ready to let them off the hook. At the beginning of this section it was suggested that Nelson's losing the Toyota dealership as a result of his cocaine addiction might be read as a metaphor for the conspicuous consumption that overtook the country during the 1980s. Such a reading is made possible primarily by the tetralogy's strategy of marrying the national with the personal. Although Harry is usually employed as the connecting link between the private and the political, there is no reason to think that Updike cannot use the other characters in the drama to make similar linkages. Such seems to be the case with Nelson and his cocaine habit. His drug use not only feeds into his abiding sense of anxiety but also reflects his tendency to consume selfishly, without regard to consequences. Harry has consistently viewed Nelson as a black hole of consumption, or a voracious id that takes and takes and puts nothing back. "You want, you want," he sourly tells Nelson in *Rabbit Is Rich* (345/934). In *Rabbit at Rest,* on the night the Angstroms learn that Nelson's cocaine habit has gotten out of control, he nearly repeats this line verbatim, not to Nelson but to Janice: "He wants, he wants" (245/1272). So when Nelson's unchecked appetite for drugs results in the loss of the Toyota dealership to its Japanese creditors, this propensity for profligate consumption logically becomes a metaphor for America's gradual loss of its manufacturing empire to Japanese business interests.

This reading is made manifest during the scene in which a representative from the Toyota home office, Mr. Shimada, pays a visit to Springer Motors to inform Harry that the dealership is to return to corporate ownership. Mr. Shimada prefaces his bad news by relating to Harry an allegorical reading of America's gradual fall from its position as an economic powerhouse. After the war, he begins, the Japanese viewed America as "big brother," and in their role as "little brother" to this political and economic powerhouse, they humbly tried to follow General Douglas MacArthur's advice to "rebuild burned cities" and "learn democratic ways." This effort resulted in successful multinational corporations such as Toyota. But when Mr. Shimada shifts gears in his story and starts explaining to Harry why America began losing its edge in the postwar global economy, his characterization of Harry's beloved country begins sounding suspiciously like a characterization of Harry's troubled, prodigal son: "But in recent times big brother act rike rittle brother, always cry and comprain. Want many favors in trade, saying Japanese unfair competition. Why unfair? Make something, cheaper even with duty and transportation costs, people rike, people buy. American way in old times. But in new times America make nothing, just do mergers, do acquisitions, rower taxes, raise national debt. Nothing comes out, all goes in—foreign goods, foreign capital. America take everything, give nothing. Rike big brack hole" (390/1404). Mr. Shimada's list of sins reads like an exact replica of Harry's own grievances about Nelson: always complaining, raising debt, producing nothing, etc. America, in Mr. Shimada's view, has become a nation of whiners, a country that has forgotten how to "make money an hour at a time." All it knows is the easy, short-term thrill of mergers and acquisitions, in which a few lucky people get themselves "in the right position" so that, as Nelson would say, the money just *"comes."* Mr. Shimada's America also evokes Nelson in its function as a "big brack hole." The black hole of debt that Shimada obliquely prophecies will swallow America parallels Nelson's own void of debt, which is poised to swallow Harry, Updike's representative character for the America that was displaced by the technology and unrest of the sixties.

Mr. Shimada's diagnosis of America is not limited to economic matters only. In the course of his conversation with Harry, he becomes one of Updike's unlikely mouthpieces as he proposes a psychological explanation for America's widespread malaise. Moreover, by locating the source of this malaise in the nation's younger generation, he provides additional evidence supporting our reading of Nelson as a representative for the new America coming into existence. "Young people most interesting," he begins. "Not scared of starving as through most human history. Not scared of atom bomb as until recently. But scared of something—not happy" (391/1405). Although he does not mention angst specifically, clearly Updike intends us to read Mr. Shimada's statement along Kierkegaardian lines. The diagnosis is in fact founded on the Kierkegaardian principles of dialectical tension and ontological anxiety. After favorably noting America's love of freedom, he qualifies this advocacy with a warning. Unchecked freedom, he suggests, leads inevitably to disorder. "Skateboarders want freedom to use beach boardwalks and knock down poor old people," he explains. "[D]ogs must have important freedom to shit everywhere" (392/1406). What is missing in the American cry for freedom is a counterbalancing doctrine of restraint. To explain what he means, he cites the Japanese terms *"giri* and *ninjo, "* which refer to the competing needs of the outer world and inner being, respectively. We are back, in other words, to the central point of tension of *Rabbit, Run.* America has failed to keep *"giri* and *ninjo"* in proper balance, the result of which has been "too much disorder. Too much dogshit" (392/1406). Yet young people are not the only targets of Mr. Shimada's critique, for in leveling these charges he clearly means to include the likes of Harry as well, father to feckless young Americans like Nelson Angstrom. "Who is father and mother of such son?" he asks Harry, after Harry tries to distance himself from Nelson's mistakes. "Where are they? In Florida, enjoying sunshine and tennis, while young boys prays games with autos" (393/1406). Parents, Mr. Shimada suggests, are the *giri* to their children's *ninjo,* the Super Ego to their offsprings' Id. And on that note, he informs Harry that Toyota is revoking Springer Motors' franchise charter.

Still, all is not lost with regard to Nelson. As indicated on the inside flap of the original 1971 edition of *Rabbit Angstrom's* second installment, the definition of *redux* is "led back; specif., *Med.,* indicating return to health after disease." If *Rabbit at Rest* is to be read in part as a sort of "Nelson Redux," then Nelson, too, is due for a "return to health after disease." He receives this cure at the hands of Narcotics Anonymous. After six weeks in a rehabilitation center, Nelson returns to the Angstrom nest as a sort of prodigal son, worldly-wise, repentant, and eager to make amends. Rather than view this development with satisfaction, however, Harry grows resentful. Part of his resentment stems from his anger at the sight of Nelson "getting away with murder," which is the same thing Nelson always felt about Harry. More important, Rabbit is suspicious of Nelson's newfound serenity, the product of the quasi-

Kierkegaardian religious faith woven into the Alcoholics Anonymous Twelve-Step program. In AA and its offshoot programs, the first of the famous twelve steps requires participants to accept their "despair," which is described specifically as helplessness in the face of addictions. This helplessness in turn requires the AA participant to admit dependence on a "higher power." This higher power is not a specifically Judeo-Christian God, however, but, as Nelson puts it, "God as we understand Him" (403/1415). Such a God is sublimely subjective, accepted by faith and clung to out of despair. But Rabbit cannot accept Nelson's new faith, similar though it is to his own. Of the new Nelson, Rabbit says, "He's full of AA bullshit" (408/1420). Part of what is missing from Nelson's faith, he feels, is doubt. Listening to Nelson describe his religious awakening, Harry "has to fight the temptation to argue," primarily because "[e]verything sounds so definite and pat" (403/1415). Nelson does not strike him as a creature of fear and trembling but as a "minister, a slightly sleek and portly representative of some no-name sect" (401/1414). Nelson has become Reverend Eccles. Like Eccles, Nelson proposes a "pat and definite" faith of temporal good works that lacks the element of scandal written into Kierkegaard's otherwise similar subjective religiosity—that is, the scandal of Christ's birth and resurrection. In Kierkegaardian thought, Christ is the agent of doubt and hence faith. Nelson's AA religion, on the other hand, requires little more than belief in "God as we understand Him."

Rabbit also hates all this "talking through" and "processing" Nelson and his therapists tend to do. As far as he is concerned, such tactics strip people not only of their God-made individuality but of their existential freedom as well. "Processing," he thinks, "cheapens the world's facts; it reduces decisions that were the best people could do at the time to dream moves, to reflexes that have been 'processed' in a million previous cases like so much shredded wheat" (348/1366). Like technology and the media, the modern pop psychology that sits at the heart of Nelson's twelve-step religion turns people into soft machines whose actions represent only what the (malfunctioning) mechanism requires. Repair the mechanism, fix the machine. Reducing our decisions to archetypal "dream moves," moreover, puts them in the same category as those insipid plots on the television sitcoms Rabbit and the members of his family watch with such absorption. Via "processing," events get stripped of their contingency and specificity until they correspond to some preset pattern, the solution to which has already been determined. Such solutions are always, in Updike's view, "universal" and therefore "esthetic." As Rabbit remarked back in *Rabbit, Run,* "Everybody who tells you how to act has whisky on their breath" (29/26). In light of all these objections, Rabbit concludes that Nelson has not changed all that much. He has simply bought into another televised ghost, not much different from the Amityville Horror business he believed in ten years ago.

Finally, Harry rejects Nelson's new religion because he cannot help but view it as a con designed to let the boy off the hook. In fact, Pru even calls Nelson a "monster con-artist" (320/1340). Accordingly, late in the novel, Harry even begins equating Nelson with Jim Bakker, the PTL Club televangelist who was found guilty of robbing his devoted followers of millions of dollars. With relish Rabbit listens on the radio to a Bakker news update detailing Bakker's alleged emotional breakdown while in prison. Bakker's accuser, Jessica Hahn, is then reported to have said, "I'm not a doctor but I do know about Jim Bakker. I believe Jim Bakker is a master manipulator. I believe this is a sympathy stunt just like it is every time Tammy gets on TV and starts crying and saying how abused they are" (439/1449). Nelson's twelve-step faith, in Harry's opinion, is also a "sympathy stunt," a parallel whine to his characteristic complaint that everything that happens is somebody else's fault. As Rabbit tells Pru, "Just because he got over crack he doesn't have to turn into Billy Graham," silently adding, "Or Jim Bakker" (446/1455).

V. Rabbit's Last Run

By divesting his hero of not just a livelihood but, in Nelson, a formidable enemy as well, Updike prepares the way for Rabbit's death. Other factors also contribute. Simultaneously with the loss of the Toyota franchise, Janice acquires her real estate license, providing her with a new career and a new lease on life. While Harry is in the hospital, moreover, she gets her first glimpse of widowhood, and, to her surprise, she does not entirely dislike what she sees. "With Harry gone," the narrator explains, "she can eat Campbell's chicken noodle soup out of the can if she wants . . . and not have to worry about giving [Harry] a low-fat low-sodium meal that he complains to her is tasteless." Then the narrator adds, "Maybe being a widow won't be so very bad is the thought she keeps trying not to think" (309/1331). With this passage, Updike also removes Janice from Harry's list of responsibilities. Before letting Rabbit make his final drive south to the "something that wants him to find it," however, Updike opens even wider Rabbit's path toward death. This path is widened through Rabbit's interactions with four more principal characters, only one of whom is a family member.

The first of these characters is Lyle, the gay friend of Nelson who, in *Rabbit Is Rich,* worked at Fiscal Alternatives and who, in this novel, serves as Nelson's partner in crime at Springer Motors. It was at Lyle's party ten years ago that Pru fell down the fire-escape steps and nearly killed her baby, and it was also Lyle who provided the sacks in which the Angstroms lugged their silver from Fiscal Alternatives to the safety deposit box Harry imagined as his own coffin (see *Rich* 368/955). In *Rabbit at Rest,* Lyle returns to serve as the bookkeeper at Springer Motors, helping Nelson carry out the used-car scheme that eventually brings down the company. Whereas gayness in *Rabbit Is Rich* is portrayed positively, in keeping with the novel's generally upbeat attitude toward the nothing, in *Rabbit at Rest* homosexuality has acquired a more ominous quality, as has the nothing homosexuality invokes. Lyle has AIDS. As one of the new employees at Springer Motors points out, Lyle's current illness has probably been lying dormant in him for ten years (213/1243). This means that Lyle, like Harry, has been marked for an early death as long ago as 1979, the year chronicled in *Rabbit Is Rich.*

In his dealings with Lyle, Harry still evidences a curious approval of the sex lives of homosexual men, noting, once again, "the peculiar charm queers have, a boyish lightness, a rising above all that female muck, where life breeds" (220/1249). This line almost repeats verbatim Rabbit's assessment, in *Rabbit Is Rich,* of Nelson's homosexual wedding minister, Archie Campbell. "[T]he world is just a gag to this guy," Rabbit observed ten years ago. "He walks on water; the mud of women, of making babies, never dirties his shoes. You got to take off your hat: nothing touches him" (*Rich* 202/803). In the AIDS world of *Rabbit at Rest,* on the other hand, Rabbit is forced to concede, "Being queer isn't all roses" (219/1248). At the same time, the dying Lyle still maintains a peculiar charm for Harry, as Harry realizes that nothing *still* touches him. As Lyle says, "One good thing about [dying] . . . is you become harder to frighten. By minor things" (218/1248). Later, as he lies in his hospital bed after his angioplasty, Rabbit begins "to know how Lyle felt" (281/1305). And when lawyers approach Lyle about taking legal proceedings against him for his part in the Springer Motors debacle, Rabbit envies and admires Lyle's blithe dismissal of such threats as ineffectual in view of his condition. "I had to laugh," Harry says, adding, "Dying has its advantages" (383/1397).

Lyle is not the only character in *Rabbit at Rest* who provides Rabbit with insight into some of the advantages of dying, for Thelma Harrison also dies, her lupus finally staking its claim on her life. At her funeral, the minister speaks of her as a "model housewife, mother, churchgoer, sufferer." The narrator then adds, in a palimpsest of his own and Rabbit's voice, that the "description describes no one, it is like a dress with no one in it" (373/1388). The minister has, in effect, reduced Thelma's brave, laudatory life into a cliché. Through this eulogy, she has become a brick in a row, a cut-out version of an archetypal figure identifiable by fans of television family sitcoms or by therapy participants interested in disclosing easily diagnosable "conditions." Yet the minister's eulogy also provides Harry with a strange hope. On one hand, Harry realizes that the clichéd version of Thelma being presented to the attendees at her funeral is really all that remains after death—the archetype and nothing more. On the other hand, Harry can take solace in the knowledge that the part of Thelma not being addressed by the minister—that is, the God-made part, with its breathed-in soul—has in fact gone with Thelma into the nothing.

Thelma's death also puts Harry back into contact with her husband, Ronnie Harrison, whom Rabbit thinks of as his "old nemesis" (377/1392). Through his interactions with Ronnie, Rabbit finally reconciles himself to his dying body, from which he has tried to keep a distance throughout *Rabbit at Rest*. For a non–family member, Harrison has played a fairly big role in the Angstrom family drama, as he alone appears prominently in three of the four books. In every book he is portrayed as crass and obnoxious, an adult version of a "dirty-mouthed plug-ugly" locker-room clown who, Rabbit distastefully remembers, was always playing grab-ass and making obscene jokes. Having known

Ronnie since kindergarten, Rabbit nevertheless thinks of him as "just about his least favorite person in the world" (304/1326). One of the reasons Harry hates Ronnie is because he feels that Harrison has been "shadowing" him "with fleshly mockery, a reminder of everything sweaty and effortful Rabbit hoped squeamishly to avoid" (305/1327). In another, yet related, passage, Rabbit thinks of Ronnie as "always there, like the smelly underside of his own body, like the Jockey underpants that get dirty every day" (378/1393). Ronnie, then, is the physical embodiment of Rabbit's corporeal body, that imperfect, time-bound soft machine that undermines his sense of himself as a "God-made one-of-a-kind with an immortal soul breathed in." Perhaps his hatred of Ronnie inspires him to continue his ten-year affair with Thelma. In any case, after Thelma's death, Rabbit finds himself unexpectedly inviting Ronnie to play golf, this despite the fact that, with Thelma gone, Rabbit is effectively free of any link to Harrison whatsoever. Their game ends in a draw, yet Rabbit realizes that he can no more disregard Ronnie than he can divorce himself from his own body. As their final match winds to a close, Harry acknowledges that, all his life, Harrison has been "a presence he couldn't avoid, an aspect of himself he didn't want to face but now does. That clublike cock, those slimy jokes, the blue eyes looking up his ass, what the hell, we're all just human, bodies with brains at one end and the rest just plumbing" (410/1422). Indeed, alone in Florida just before his death, Rabbit finds that his heart, far from being an "invading enemy," has become "his companion. He listens to it, tries to decipher its messages" (470/1478). At the cusp of his own death, Rabbit finally reconciles the monstrous individuality of his spiritual identity with the soft machine that encases it. Only after this reconciliation is Rabbit ready for rest.

The last character from *Rabbit at Rest* who prepares Harry for his final run is Nelson's wife, Pru, with whom Rabbit, one wild windy night, ill-advisedly makes love. Ostensibly, Pru hastens his desperate drive to Florida by revealing the details of their tryst to Nelson and Janice. Harry flees to avoid the heat. As the narrator puts it, "He could have gone over that night and faced the music but how much music is a man supposed to face?" (470/1478). More important, his sexual encounter with Pru functions as a symbolic return to the womb, itself one of Updike's numerous metaphors for death. After his first heart attack, Harry recalls its "blissful aspect: his sense . . . of being in the hands of others, of being the blind, pained, focal point of a world of concern and expertise, at some depth was coming back home, after a life of ill-advised journeying" (163/1197). During his four-day drive to Florida, moreover, he "sleeps as in his mother's womb, another temporary haven" (457/1465). His near-incestuous encounter with Pru ties into this motif in the way it uses the incest element to suggest a return, though dying, to the Edenic world of childhood. For one thing, in both this novel and its predecessor, Pru is consistently presented as a reincarnation of Harry's mother. She has his mother's hands, for instance (14/1061). Also, the sight of her nakedness reminds him of "lovely pear trees in blossom," an image of rebirth that made him feel, at the time, like the world was "all his . . . a piece of paradise blundered upon, incredible" (346/1364). Finally, he later thinks of the actual lovemaking itself as a kind of culmination of his life. As he remembers it, their sex took place upon a bed that released "Ma Springer's musty old-lady scent," which smell in turn released a whole "interwoven residue of family fortunes." "All those family traces," he thinks, "descended to this, this coupling by thunder and lightning" (361/1377).

The return-to-the-womb motif also governs the structure of this final section of *Rabbit Angstrom*. The tetralogy concludes, in a sense, back in its own womb. Indeed, Rabbit's solo drive to Florida directly replays the solo drive south with which the tetralogy famously began. Again, Updike clues us into his methodology by repeating phrases from the corresponding episode. In both novels, Rabbit makes his decision to flee suddenly, as if in response to a revelation. Accordingly, Updike describes this moment of revelation with the exact same sentence: "His acts take on decisive haste" (*Run* 22/21 and *Rest* 435/1445). Both episodes feature extended transcriptions of the radio broadcasts Rabbit listens to en route, complete with the relevant news broadcasts. Even Rabbit's sinister encounter thirty years ago with the drunk gas station attendant—the same attendant who told him, "The only way to get somewhere, you know, is to figure out where you're going before you go there" (*Run* 28/26)—gets replayed, only positively so. In *Rabbit at Rest*, this strange prophetic character gets replaced by a warmhearted trucker, who gives Harry, now finally sure where he is going, precise directions to Florida.

Yet this second drive south does not merely repeat its corresponding episode from *Rabbit, Run;* it reverses it exactly. That is to say, this trip ends where the other one began—on a basketball court. The passage describing Rabbit's first encounter with the playground on which he will die also recalls the opening of *Rabbit, Run* almost word for word. *Rabbit, Run* begins: "Boys are playing basketball around a telephone pole with a backboard bolted to it. Legs, shouts. The scrape and snap of Keds on loose alley pebbles seems to catapult their voices into the moist March air above the wires" (*Run* 3/5). The corresponding passage from *Rabbit at Rest* reads as follows: "A small pack of black boys are scrimmaging around one basket. Legs, shouts. Puffs of dust rise from their striving, stop-and-starting feet" (486/1493). This instance of syntactical repetition returns *Rabbit Angstrom* to its womb, so to speak, a stylistic gesture that serves as a formal analogue to Rabbit's own return to the nothing from whence he came.

Fittingly, Harry experiences his final, fatal heart attack on the basketball court, the one place where, as a young man, he felt sure of his specialness. That specialness is now available to him only through his voluntary death, for it is the one thing that cannot be appropriated by the esthetic leveling of the mass media, of "processing" therapists, or of doctors and their godless technology. Basketball also used to provide Harry with evidence of the unseen world, of that something that wanted him to find it. In *Rabbit, Run,* for instance, Updike makes numerous connections between the round rose window in the church outside Ruth's apartment and "the high perfect hole" of the basketball net, with its "pretty skirt of net." Through both round holes flow evidence of the unseen world. Beginning with *Rabbit Redux,* however, Updike has steadily transformed that hole motif to include the nothing. In Skeeter's view, for instance, holes are openings through which also flows evidence of the nothing, Updike's metaphor for God/Nobody's kingdom of death (see *Redux* 261/494). Now the something and the nothing are joined into an unbreakable unit. As in Rabbit's dream of "lovely life eclipsed by lovely death," this final basketball episode of the completed tetralogy gathers together a whole host of dialectically related motifs from the preceding novels and compresses them into a single, unified, tension-filled (w)hole.

All of these motifs and symbols converge in the book's penultimate scene, during which Rabbit plays his final basketball game with a black teenager whom Rabbit terms, because of a sports-shoe insignia on his shirt, "Tiger." The boy serves as a messenger of death, evoking perhaps William Blake's "Tiger of Wrath," the same way Updike's God/Nobody recalls Blake's Nobodaddy. In any case, the boy certainly recalls that other tiger of wrath from Harry's life, Skeeter. As such, he bears on his shoulders the whole weight of Updike's complex analysis of blackness, guilt and death, as spelled out in *Rabbit Redux*. With all this preceding material firmly in play, the game between the white Rabbit and the black Tiger serves as the final emblem in *Rabbit Angstrom* of Updike's unified, dialectical vision. The episode joins white and black, life and death, earth and sky, and sky and water. For instance, the narrator explains that the "nature" of the game is "to mix [Rabbit] with earth and sky" (504/1509). He mixes with the earth via contact with, among other things, the "pink-tan glaring dust" raised by his and Tiger's feet. And he mixes with the sky every time he "looks up to follow his shot or the other's." After his heart attack, moreover, as he lies alone on the empty basketball court, he looks up at the sky—across which flies a tell-tale airplane (506/1511)—and hears, in the distance, ambulance sirens, which some of neighboring residents mistake for a hurricane alert announcing the arrival of Hugo. In other words, the heavens have become, symbolically, a teeming ocean, and vice versa. The sky God of life and the water God of death have merged in this final moment of Harry's conscious existence, just as they did in Harry's dream of thirty years ago, in which death is shown as "lovely death eclipsing lovely life." After 1516 pages, four novels, and three decades' worth of sustained creativity, Rabbit is, finally, at rest.

Conclusion

Inside America

[Rabbit] had thought, he had read, that from shore to shore all America was the same. He wonders, Is it just these people I'm outside, or is it all America?

— Rabbit, Run

In his introduction to *Rabbit Angstrom,* Updike prepares Rabbit's way by evoking, first, "The United States," and, second, "such masterpieces as *Moby-Dick* and *Huckleberry Finn*"—all within the first two sentences. Clearly, the author has high hopes for this single-volume edition of his career-long project. These hopes are well founded, I feel, for the simple reason that the omnibus edition of the tetralogy allows readers to experience his thirty-year project as the single, sustained achievement that it is. The Rabbit books are really one book. What's more, they constitute Updike's best book, the one book that will unquestionably outlive him. Like his other fecund contemporaries—John Barth, Philip Roth, Joyce Carol Oates—Updike has perhaps published too much. With more than forty book titles already to his name—the whole corpus comprising, thanks to the indulgence of Alfred A. Knopf, a tidy uniform edition—he runs the risk of writing himself into oblivion. The reader of the future, surveying Updike's sagging shelf of books, will understandably wonder which one of the forty (and counting) volumes will provide, in distilled form, the essence of Updike. *Rabbit Angstrom* is that book.

Yet why the Rabbit novels in particular? Why not, say, *Couples,* or *Pigeon Feathers?* Updike himself has described those "last, fragmentary stories in *Pigeon Feathers*"—by which he means the book's two concluding pieces, "The Blessed Man of Boston, My Grandmother's Thimble, and Fanning Island" and "Packed Dirt, Churchgoing, A Dying Cat, A Traded Car"—as his "best."[1] Two stories, however, do not a posthumous reputation make. Posterity demands novels—big novels, preferably, with enough formalistic complexity and novelistic detail to sustain prolonged study. No single one of Updike's novels provides enough of those two ingredients to base a reputation on, though *Couples, The Coup,* and *In The Beauty of the Lilies* come close. The four Rabbit novels, on the other hand, provide formalistic complexity and novelistic detail in abundance. And as time telescopes into nonexistence the ten-year gaps between the publication of each installment, the single-minded coherency of all that complexity and detail will emerge even more fully than it does for the work's contemporary readers.

Related to this idea of coherence and complexity is the tetralogy's abundantly rich thematic significance. As this study has tried to demonstrate, the Rabbit novels, in addition to being intensely realistic documents of contemporary American existence, are also conduits for Updike's holistic ethical and religious vision. Nearly everything Updike has to say to the world he manages to say, in one way or another, in the Rabbit novels. Although he admits in his introduction that, "[a]fter a tetralogy, almost everything is still left to say" (xxi), the fact remains that the Rabbit novels reveal in rich detail the full spectrum of Updike's views on Christianity, sexuality, postwar America, money, science, technology, racism, immortality, death, birth, divorce, adultery, gender, class, and so on. In 1968, in the midst of his *Paris Review* interview with Charles Thomas Samuels, Updike ventured to list his principal concerns as a writer: "Domestic fierceness within the middle class, sex and death as riddles for the thinking animal, social existence as sacrifice, unexpected pleasures and rewards, corruption as a kind of evolution—these are some of my themes."[2] Although this laundry list was composed before there was even a sequel to *Rabbit, Run,* it nevertheless reads like a

---

1. Updike, *Self-Consciousness,* 97.
2. Updike, "Art of Fiction," 45.

direct transcription of the primary issues at work in the tetralogy. Even those texts from Updike's oeuvre in which he gives direct and unmediated voice to these views—the memoir *Self-Consciousness,* for instance, or the four books of collected critical writing—often read like afterthoughts to the Rabbit novels. One of the reasons this study features so many citations from Updike's essays and interviews is because the correlations between these nonfiction texts and the Rabbit novels are so direct. What is perhaps most astonishing in this regard is the fact that Updike has managed to weave into this lengthy account of a high-school-educated car salesman a fully coherent theological and moral vision adapted from the writings of, among others, Søren Kierkegaard and Karl Barth. Nearly everything of significance about Updike's artistic and ethical vision can be found in this massive volume.

This is not to say that Updike should be read solely as a "novelist of ideas." In the same Samuels interview, he goes on to assert, "My work is mediation, not pontification . . . I think of my books not as sermons or directives in a war of ideas but as objects, with different shapes and textures and the mysteriousness of anything that exists."[3] Certainly the Rabbit novels are not sermons, for their overriding mood is less pontification than ambiguity. Moreover, the chief rhetorical stance of the four novels is ironic, wherein moral dilemmas are presented as paradoxes admitting of no easy solution. As Updike asserts in his introduction, "Rather than arrive at a verdict or a directive, I sought to present sides of an unresolvable tension intrinsic to being human. Readers who expect novelists to reward and punish and satirize their characters from a superior standpoint will be disappointed" (xiii). That insistence upon the "unresolvable tension intrinsic to being human" is not only the most important component of the theological vision articulated in the Rabbit novels but also the very heart of what is meant by "Updikean."

"Mastered irony" also lies at the core of Updike's vision of America. For, in the end, the postwar United States, in all its sprawling excess and success, is *Rabbit Angstrom*'s great, vast subject. As suggested above, Updike makes this point abundantly clear in the opening paragraph of his introduction to the new volume. "The United States," he begins, "democratic and various though it is, is not an easy country for a fiction-

3. Ibid.

writer to enter: the slot between the fantastic and the drab seems too narrow" (ix). It is at this point in the essay that he summons the ghosts of *Moby-Dick* and *Huckleberry Finn*. The fiction writers responsible for these two thunderheads of American literature, Updike implies, somehow managed to find a suitable "slot between the fantastic and the drab," and they did so by taking an "outsiderish literary stance." *Rabbit Angstrom,* and the character who provides the work with its name, serve as Updike's slot into the drab and fantastic. He goes on to say, "[M]y impression is that the character of Harry 'Rabbit' Angstrom was for me a way in—a ticket to all the America around me. What I saw through Rabbit's eyes was more worth telling than what I saw through my own, though the difference was slight; his life, less defended and logocentric than my own, went places mine could not. As a phantom of my imagination, he was always, as the saying goes, *there* for me, willing to generate imagery and motion. He kept alive my native sense of wonder and hazard" (ix). With this passage—placed in such close proximity to that invocation of Huckleberry Finn and Ishmael—Updike boldly asks us to see Rabbit *as* an emblem of "all the America around [him]." Which is to say, all America *period.*

Updike's America is, ostensibly, white and middle-class. It is also predominantly male. As a northeastern Lutheran, he aligns himself—voluntarily, it is important to add—with the Puritan New England tradition. Aggressively Protestant in his thinking, Updike portrays his American citizens as set in direct interaction not so much with society as with God. His characters—Rabbit in particular—are less in conflict with the cultural order than with their own subjective impulses. His is a traditionally democratic America in which the individual in isolation assumes primary importance. Alexis de Tocqueville's famous analysis of this particularly individualistic strain in American thinking corresponds nicely with Updike's novelistic depiction of the same. In *Democracy in America,* Tocqueville argues that citizens in a democracy do not generally see themselves as interacting with a cultural order and its inherited habits, as do citizens in aristocratic societies. Rather, he writes, "They form the habit of thinking of themselves in isolation and imagine that their whole destiny is in their own hands. . . . Each man is forever thrown back on himself alone, and there is danger that he may be shut up in the solitude of his own heart." Tocqueville's nineteenth-century diagnosis of the American spirit still applies to Updike's characters. They, too, are shut up "in the solitude of [their] own heart[s]"—perhaps none more so than Harry Angstrom. As one of Harry's doctors tells him late in *Rabbit At Rest,* "Get interested in something outside yourself, and your heart will stop talking to you" (476/1483). Yet it is this very notion of solipsistic self-regard that constitutes the lifeblood of Updike's conception of the American spirit. And that is why Harry "Rabbit" Angstrom, one of the most solipsistic characters in his oeuvre, serves as Updike's representative American. If almost everyone in democratic America is primarily engaged in contemplation of him/herself—as both Tocqueville and Updike concede—then the true American hero is the average citizen, in isolation, shut up in the solitude of his/her own heart. This, for Updike, is the essence of the democratic hero, as opposed to the traditional hero of aristocratic societies. As he said in 1966, "The idea of a hero is aristocratic. As aristocracies have faded, so have heroes. You care about Oedipus and Hamlet because they were noble and you were a groundling. Now either nobody is a hero or everyone is. I vote for everyone."[4] The individual in contemplation of himself: that is the heart of Updike's American ideal.

It is wrong, then, to look to *Rabbit Angstrom* for a comprehensive, sociological account of American society. One can, however, find there a comprehensive account of one American's life, primarily his internal life. America is only entered, Updike explains in his introduction, *through* Rabbit. As a historical account of the second half of the American Century, *Rabbit Angstrom* does not take the reader into the smoke-filled rooms and foreign battlefields where history is generally thought to be made. The history that happens in *Rabbit Angstrom* occurs off-stage, as background. Rabbit's interaction with American history is limited to his television watching and newspaper reading. Although the work addresses many of the most important American historical events of the last forty years—Vietnam, the moon shot, and the late-seventies hostage crisis, to name but three—it never lets these events become anything more than embroidery on the complex fabric of Harry's internal life. If *Rabbit Angstrom* is, as Updike suggests, a ticket to "the America all around

4. Alexis de Tocqueville, *Democracy in America,* 508; Updike, "Nice Novelist," 10.

[us]," it enters that America only from the inside of a single character.

At the same time, by virtue of his individuality and isolation, Rabbit is, paradoxically, representative. His is a specimen life that is like other lives in America in its singleness and self-absorption. It is on this paradox that Updike establishes Rabbit as a symbol for the nation as a whole. As almost every reviewer of *Rabbit At Rest* conceded, Updike seems to ask his readers to see Harry's dying condition in that novel as a metaphor for America's atrophied status in the world at large. Harry is fat and bloated, surfeited with consumer goods and dying from too much junk food. His heart, one of his doctors explains, is "tired and stiff and full of crud. It's a typical American heart, for his age and economic status, et cetera" (166/200). His son's reckless drug addiction destroys his father's business and places it in the hands of the more efficient Japanese. Rabbit even assumes the role of Uncle Sam in his granddaughter's grade-school Fourth of July parade. It would be a mistake, however, to treat these hints too literally—that is, to treat Harry simply as a symbol, and to regard *Rabbit Angstrom* primarily as an allegory for "what's wrong with America." Although Updike invites us to make these connections between Harry's and America's fate, the connections, too, are mere embroidery. As Hermione Lee pointed out in her 1990 review of *Rabbit At Rest,* "[Rabbit] is the emblem of the obnoxious age, but he is also outside it, minded by it, alienated by it. A lonely Rabbit" (35). In other words, Harry is both an emblem and a check against emblematization. He is *both* representative and individuated. He exists at a point of unresolved tension between the claims of the culture at large and the needs of the inner self. Or, to employ Mr. Shimada's terminology, he functions as a figure of both *giri* and *ninjo,* the outer world and the inner being. And it is the existence of this tension, ultimately, that makes Rabbit Updike's representative American, much more so than Rabbit's junk food habit or his careless handling of his business interests. Perhaps Updike puts the case most succinctly when he writes in his introduction that Rabbit "is the New World's new man, armored against eventualities in little but his selfhood" (xxi).

Rabbit Angstrom, then, paints a two-sided, ambiguous vision of America. It is both critical and celebratory, historical and ahistorical, objective in scope and subjective in intention. That is why the book consistently disappoints those critics who try to extract from it a unified, coherent critique of America. That critique, though present, is undercut by Updike's unsentimental interest in Harry's individuality, just as that individuality is counterbalanced by Updike's use of Harry as an unflattering representative of America. Jan Clausen dismisses this twofold approach as Updike's attempt to "have [his] critique and eat [his] patriotism too" (51). Presumably, Clausen wants her critique served up cold. She unambiguously sees the "American state" as "parlous," and so demands that Updike's fictional rendering of that state arrive at the same unambiguous conclusion. By remaining ambiguous about America—and about Harry, as well—Updike, in her view, turns what could have been "an authentically critical fiction" into "what might best be termed a legitimating critique" (51). Similarly, Gary Wills asserts that Updike began his tetralogy "with the aim of saying some hard true things about what is wrong with America. By succumbing to his own stylistic solipsism, Updike ends up exemplifying what is wrong."[5]

Yet both of these critics only end up faulting Updike for *not* doing what he never set out to do in the first place. They want his book, as he puts it, to "arrive at a verdict and a directive," when in fact Updike's primary concern is to "present sides of an unresolvable tension." His attitude toward his country and his hero is likewise tension-filled and unresolved, poised between critique and patriotism, between cultural analysis and psychology. In his articulation of Harry's solipsism, Updike does, as Wills accuses, "exemplify what is wrong," yet exemplification, not critique, is precisely what he is after. His artistic agenda is marked by what he calls in his introduction the "religious faith that a useful truth will be imprinted by a perfect artistic submission" to the "quotidian details" (xiii). For instance, Mary O'Connell, in her recent book *Updike and the Patriarchal Dilemma: Masculinity in the Rabbit Novels,* honors Updike's credo as she examines the function of gender in the tetralogy. Rather than simply dismiss Updike as a sexist male novelist—not an uncommon charge among Updike's critics—O'Connell finds that, upon close examination, the books both exemplify and critique, often at the same time. "When I examined the texts closely," she writes in her Preface, "I found a great deal of evidence demonstrating patterns of psychological and physical abuse. But, unexpectedly, I also accumulated ev-

---

5. Jan Clausen, "Native Fathers," 51; Wills, "Long-Distance Runner," 14.

idence, including structural evidence, suggesting that Updike was not just portraying Rabbit as a stereotypical male; he was scrutinizing masculine gender identity." Significantly, O'Connell arrives at her even-handed reading only after examining the *structure* of the novels. And this structure, which she also sees as dialectical, renders any decisive statement about, say, gender roles as inconclusive until it is placed within the either/or design of the overall work.[6]

Hence, Updike's faith in a "perfect artistic submission" is deeply intertwined with his method of mastered irony. The final truth imprinted by the book is the truth of ambiguity, whereby dialectical disunities are left unreconciled. Both sides speak in *Rabbit Angstrom,* the patriot as well as the critic. Which side of the fence Updike finally sits on is left deliberately undetermined. Updike is not convinced, as is Clausen, that the American state is unequivocally "parlous," nor is he convinced that it is invincible and without fault. If the book is read as a celebration of America, it is, as Updike would say, a "yes-but" celebration. If the book is read as a critique, that critique is a "no-but" critique. Irony balances at the apex of the "yes" and the "no" in that it allows both sides a say, deferring onto the reader any conclusive judgment. "Irony irritates," Milan Kundera writes in *The Art of Novel.* "Not because it mocks or attacks but because it denies us our certainties by unmasking the world as an ambiguity." That ambiguous world, Kundera adds, is the world of the novel, as the novel is, "by definition, the ironic art."[7] And Updike the social critic always takes a backseat to Updike the novelist.

His work "irritates" some critics for this very reason. In fact, it is this same "irritating" quality that Updike alludes to when he says—as he was quoted as saying in the first chapter of this essay—"There's a yes-but quality to my writing that evades entirely pleasing anybody. It seems to me that critics get increasingly querulous and impatient for madder music and stronger wine."[8] For many readers, his work does not "mock" or "attack" *enough.* But to mock and attack requires the kind of ethical and moral certitude that Updike so strongly eschews. The satirist not only

6. Mary O'Connell, *Updike and the Patriarchal Dilemma: Masculinity in the Rabbit Novels,* x.

7. Milan Kundera, *The Art of the Novel,* 134.

8. Updike, "Nice Novelist," 16.

knows his enemy but is confident in his superiority over that enemy. The ironist, on the other hand, submits to the complex reality of the enemy with as much attention as he submits to the complex reality of his compatriot. Such a submission to complexity and ambiguity is the intoxicating ingredient of John Updike's particular brand of wine. And *Rabbit Angstrom* is John Updike's most intoxicating achievement.

Bibliography

Angelo, Bonnie. "Master of His Universe." *Time* (February 13, 1989): 92.

Augustine. *The City of God.* Trans. Henry Bettenson. London: Penguin Classics, 1984.

Barth, Karl. *Dogmatics in Outline.* Trans. G. T. Thomson. New York: Harper and Row, 1959.

————. *The Word of God and the Word of Man.* Trans. Douglas Horton. New York: Harper Torchbooks, 1957.

Barthes, Roland. *Writing Degree Zero and Elements of Semiology.* Trans. Annette Lavers and Colin Smith. London: Jonathan Cape, 1967.

Bloom, Harold. "Introduction." In *John Updike: Modern Critical Views,* ed. Harold Bloom. New York: Chelsea House, 1987.

Campbell, Jeff. *Updike's Novels: Thorns Spell a Word.* Wichita Falls, Texas: Midwestern State University Press, 1987.

Chernyshevsky, Nikolai. *What Is to Be Done?* Trans. N. Dole and S. S. Skidelsky. Ann Arbor, Mich.: Ardis, 1986.

Clausen, Jan. "Native Fathers." *Kenyon Review* 14 (spring 1992): 44–55.

Crews, Frederick. "Mr. Updike's Planet." In Crews, *The Critics Bear It Away: American Fiction and the Academy.* New York: Random House, 1992.

Denby, David. "A Life of Sundays." Review of *Self-Consciousness,* by John Updike. *New Republic* (May 22, 1989): 29–33.

"Desperate Weakling." Review of *Rabbit, Run,* by John Updike. *Time* (November 7, 1960): 108.

Detweiler, Robert. *John Updike.* Boston: Twayne Publishers, 1984.

Diem, Hermann. *Kierkegaard: An Introduction.* Trans. David Green. Richmond, Va.: John Knox Press, 1966.

Dostoevsky, Fyodor. *Notes from Underground and The Grand Inquisitor.* Trans. Ralph E. Matlaw. New York: Dutton, 1960.

Freud, Sigmund. *The Freud Reader.* Trans. Peter Gray. New York: W. W. Norton and Company, 1989.

Galloway, David. *The Absurd Hero in American Fiction.* Austin: University of Texas Press, 1970.

Gilman, Richard. "A Distinguished Image of Precarious Life." Review of *Rabbit, Run,* by John Updike. *Commonweal* (October 28, 1960): 128–29.

Greiner, Donald. *Adultery in the American Novel: Updike, James, and Hawthorne.* Columbia: University of South Carolina Press, 1985.

Heidegger, Martin. *Being and Time.* Trans. John Macquarrie and Edward Robinson. San Francisco: Harper Collins, 1962.

———. "What Is Metaphysics?" In *Basic Writings,* ed. David Farrel Krell. San Francisco: Harper Collins, 1993.

Hick, John. *Evil and the God of Love.* Rev. ed. San Francisco: Harper and Row, 1977.

Hicks, Granville. "A Little Good in Evil." Review of *Rabbit, Run,* by John Updike. *Saturday Review* (November 5, 1960): 28.

Horton, Andrew. "Ken Kesey, John Updike and the Lone Ranger." *Journal of Popular Culture* 8 (winter 1974): 570–76.

Hunt, George W. *John Updike and the Three Great Secret Things: Sex, Religion, and Art.* Grand Rapids, Mich.: William B. Eerdmans Publishing, 1980.

Jackson, Edward M. "Rabbit is Racist." *College Language Association* 28 (June 1985): 444–51.

Kierkegaard, Søren. *The Concept of Anxiety.* Ed. and trans. Reidar Thomte and Albert Anderson. Princeton, N.J.: Princeton University Press, 1980.

———. *The Concept of Irony, with Constant Reference to Socrates.* Trans. Lee M. Chapel. New York: Harper and Row, 1965.

———. *The Concluding Unscientific Postcript to the "Philosophical Fragments."* Ed. and trans. Howard V. Hong and Edna H. Hong. Princeton, N.J.: Princeton University Press, 1992.

———. *Either/Or.* Vol. 2. Trans. Walter Lowrie. Princeton, N.J.: Princeton University Press, 1972.

———. *Fear and Trembling/Repetition.* Ed. and trans. Howard V. Hong and Edna H. Hong. Princeton, N.J.: University of Princeton Press, 1983.

Kundera, Milan. *The Art of the Novel.* Trans. Linda Asher. New York: Harper and Row, 1988.

———. *Testaments Betrayed.* Trans. Linda Asher. New York: Harper Collins Publishers, 1995.

Lee, Hermione. "The Trouble with Harry." Review of *Rabbit at Rest,* by John Updike. *New Republic* (December 24, 1990): 34–37.

Locke, Richard. Review of *Rabbit Redux,* by John Updike. *New York Times Book Review,* November 4, 1971, 1–24.

Mann, Thomas. "Preface: Dostoevsky—In Moderation." *The Short Novels of Dostoevsky.* New York: Dial Press, 1945.

Markle, Joyce B. *Fighters and Lovers: Theme in the Novels of John Updike.* New York: New York University Press, 1973.

Menand, Louis. "Rabbit Is Dead." Review of *Rabbit at Rest,* by John Updike. *Esquire* (November 1990): 96.

Murdoch, Iris. *The Sovereignty of Good.* New York: Schocken Books, 1970.

Neary, John. *Something and Nothingness: The Fiction of John Updike and John Fowles.* Carbondale: Southern Illinois University Press, 1992.

Newman, Judie. *John Updike.* London: MacMillan Publishers, Ltd., 1988.

O'Connell, Mary. *Updike and the Patriarchal Dilemma: Masculinity in the Rabbit Novels.* Carbondale: Southern Illinois University Press, 1996.

Plath, James, ed. *Conversations with John Updike.* Jackson: University Press of Mississippi, 1994.

Plato. *Phaedo. Great Dialogues of Plato.* Trans. W. H. D. Rouse. Ed. Eric H. Warmington and Philip G. Rouse. New York: Mentor Books, 1956.

Prescott, Peter. Review of *Rabbit at Rest,* by John Updike. *Newsweek* (October 1, 1990): 66.

Proust, Marcel. *Remembrance of Things Past.* Vol. 2. Trans. C. K. Scott Moncrieff and Terence Kilmartin. New York: Vintage Books, 1982.

Raines, Craig. "Introduction." In *Ulysses,* by James Joyce. London: David Campbell Publishers, Ltd., 1992.

Ristoff, Dilvo I. *Updike's America: The Presence of Contemporary History in John Updike's Rabbit Trilogy.* New York: Peter Lang, 1988.

Schiff, James A. *John Updike Revisited.* New York: Twayne Publishers, 1998.

Spanos, William V. "Heidegger, Kierkegaard, and the Hermeneutic Circle: Towards a Postmodern Theory of Interpretation and Disclosure." In *Heidegger and the Question of Literature,* ed. William V. Spanos. Bloomington: Indiana University Press, 1976.

―――. *Repetitions.* Baton Rouge: Louisiana State University Press, 1987.

Staples, Brent. "Why So Hard on Rabbit?" *New York Times,* November 5, 1990.

Tillich, Paul. *Systematic Theology.* Vol. 1. Chicago: University of Chicago Press, 1951.

Tocqueville, Alexis de. *Democracy in America.* Trans. George Lawrence. Ed. J. P. Mayer. New York: Harper and Row, 1969.

Updike, John. "The Art of Fiction XLIII: John Updike." In James Plath, ed., *Conversations with John Updike,* 22–45. Jackson: University Press of Mississippi, 1994.

―――. *Assorted Prose.* New York: Alfred A. Knopf, 1965.

―――. "A Book That Changed Me." In Updike, *Odd Jobs,* 843–44. New York: Alfred A. Knopf, 1991.

―――. *Buchanan Dying.* New York: Alfred A. Knopf, 1974.

―――. "Can a Nice Novelist Finish First?" In James Plath, ed., *Conversations with John Updike,* 9–17. Jackson: University Press of Mississippi, 1994.

―――. "The Dogwood Tree: A Boyhood." In Updike, *Picked-Up Pieces,* 151–87. New York: Alfred A. Knopf, 1976.

―――. "Elusive Evil." *New Yorker* (July 22, 1996): 62–70.

―――. "Faith in Search of Understanding." In Updike, *Assorted Prose,* 273–82. New York: Alfred A. Knopf, 1965.

―――. "Forty Years of Middle America with John Updike." In James Plath, ed., *Conversations with John Updike,* 221–28. Jackson: University Press of Mississippi, 1994.

―――. *Hugging the Shore.* New York: Alfred A. Knopf, 1983.

―――. "Interview with John Updike." In James Plath, ed., *Conversa-*

tions with John Updike, 74–83. Jackson: University Press of Mississippi, 1994.

———. "Introduction to 'The Seducer's Diary,' a chapter of *Either/ Or.*" In Updike, *More Matter,* 139–44. New York: Alfred A. Knopf, 1999.

———. "Introduction to *Soundings in Satanism.*" In Updike, *Picked-Up Pieces,* 87–91. New York: Alfred A. Knopf, 1976.

———. "John Updike Talks about the Shapes and Subjects of His Fiction." In James Plath, ed., *Conversations with John Updike,* 46–54. Jackson: University Press of Mississippi, 1994.

———. "Lifeguard." In Updike, *Pigeon Feathers,* 211–20. New York: Alfred A. Knopf, 1962.

———. "Midpoint." In *Collected Poems, 1953–1993,* 64–101. New York: Alfred A. Knopf, 1993.

———. *A Month of Sundays.* New York: Alfred A. Knopf, 1975.

———. *More Matter.* New York: Alfred A. Knopf, 1999.

———. *Odd Jobs.* New York: Alfred A. Knopf, 1991.

———. "One Big Interview." In Updike, *Picked-Up Pieces,* 493–518. New York: Alfred A. Knopf, 1976.

———. *Picked-Up Pieces.* New York: Alfred A. Knopf, 1976.

———. *Rabbit Angstrom.* New York: Everyman's Library, 1995.

———. *Rabbit At Rest.* New York: Alfred A. Knopf, 1990.

———. *Rabbit Is Rich.* New York: Alfred A. Knopf, 1981.

———. *Rabbit Redux.* New York: Alfred A. Knopf, 1971.

———. *Rabbit, Run.* New York: Alfred A. Knopf, 1960.

———. "Religion and Literature." In Updike, *More Matter,* 50–62. New York: Alfred A. Knopf, 1999.

———. *Roger's Version.* New York: Alfred A. Knopf, 1986.

———. *Self-Consciousness.* New York: Alfred A. Knopf, 1989.

———. "A 'Special Message' for the Franklin Library's First Edition Society Printing of *Rabbit At Rest* (1990)." In Updike, *Odd Jobs,* 869–72. New York: Alfred A. Knopf, 1991.

———. "A 'Special Message' to Purchasers of the Franklin Library Limited Edition, in 1981, of *Rabbit Redux.*" In Updike, *Hugging the Shore,* 858–59. New York: Alfred A. Knopf, 1983.

———. "A 'Special Message' to Purchasers of the Franklin Library Limited Edition, in 1977, of *Rabbit, Run.*" In Updike, *Hugging the Shore,* 849–51. New York: Alfred A. Knopf, 1983.

———. "Thoughts of Faith Infuse Updike's Novels." In James Plath, ed., *Conversations with John Updike,* 248–59. Jackson: University Press of Mississippi, 1994.

———. "Updike Redux." In James Plath, ed., *Conversations with John Updike,* 59–66. Jackson: University Press of Mississippi, 1994.

Uphaus, Suzanne Henning. *John Updike.* Hong Kong: Macmillan Publishers Ltd., 1988.

Vargo, Edward P. *Rainstorms and Fire: Ritual in the Novels of John Updike.* Port Washington, N.Y.: Kennikat Press, 1973.

"View From the Catacombs." *Time* (April 26, 1968): 66–68.

Vigilante, Richard. "The Observer Observed." Review of *Self-Consciousness,* by John Updike. *National Review* (May 19, 1989): 51–54.

Wills, Gary. "Long-Distance Runner." Review of *Rabbit at Rest,* by John Updike. *New York Review of Books,* October 25, 1990, 11–14.

Wood, Ralph C. *The Comedy of Redemption: Christian Faith and the Comic Vision of Four American Novelists.* South Bend, Ind.: University of Notre Dame Press, 1988.

Index